WAYBACK

WAYBACK

a novel

sam batterman

VMI Publishers • Sisters, Oregon

Published by
VMI Publishers
Sisters, Oregon
www.vmipubishers.com

ISBN 10: 1-933204-87-7
ISBN 13: 978-1-933204-87-1

Library of Congress: 2009926131

Printed in the USA

Cover design by Joe Bailen

This is a work of fiction. Characters, corporations, institutions, and organizations in this novel are either the product of the author's imagination or, if real, used fictitiously without any intent to describe their actual conduct.

Visit the Author's Web Site at
www.sambatterman.com

For my family—
my wonderful wife, Susan, and my glorious children,
Samantha and Parker.
Thank you for your unconditional love, the joy you bring to my life,
and for supporting me in achieving my dreams.

To my Father of Lights,
who loved me, gave his Son for me,
and knew me before the foundation of the world.

There is something fascinating about science. One gets such wholesale returns of conjecture out of such a trifling investment of fact.

MARK TWAIN

But of that day and hour knoweth no man, no, not the angels of heaven, but my Father only. But as the days of [Noah] *were,* so shall also the coming of the Son of man be. For as in the days that were before the flood they were eating and drinking, marrying and giving in marriage, until the day that [Noah] entered into the ark, And knew not until the flood came, and took them all away; so shall also the coming of the Son of man be. Then shall two be in the field; the one shall be taken, and the other left. Two *women shall* be grinding at the mill; the one shall be taken, and the other left.

Watch therefore: for ye know not what hour your Lord doth come.

JESUS CHRIST
MATTHEW 24:36-42, KJV

Prologue

The Bell

february 1945

he amber glow from the cigarette lighter lit up Hans Voss's sharp, Aryan facial features. He snapped the silver lid shut and exhaled a plume of silvery-blue smoke into the still night air. The spruce trees climbed high into the starry sky, concealing the concrete blockhouses and heavy equipment parked around the secret complex. In the distance, the faint but constant pounding of Allied bombs falling on Voss's homeland could be heard, like the heartbeat of a giant coming ever closer. Intermittent flashes of light danced on the horizon, marking the end of a manufacturing plant, a church, a neighborhood the coming end of the Third Reich.

The gravel pebbles crunched under his leather boots, and the slight clinking sound of the medals awarded him by the Luftwaffe elite announced his approach to a concrete reinforced guardhouse. A drop gate with a red and white alternating pattern barred his entrance to the complex, and a young German soldier stood guard in front of the barrier.

Young—too young, thought Voss.

The young guard's blond-and-black German shepherd strained on its thick leather leash, snarling at the approaching airman. The guard, struggling with a fur-covered razor blade, clicked on his flashlight and shone it on Voss, blinding him for an instant. The glint of light across Voss's Iron Cross medal snapped the young soldier to attention. He clicked the heels of his boots together, and his right arm shot out in a familiar salute. "Heil Hitler," he said with fervor.

Voss returned the salute robotically. His fervor had died a long time ago.

As the soldier examined Voss's credentials, the Luftwaffe ace took a last long drag on his cigarette and dropped it onto the concrete ramp leading to a deeply fortified complex, hidden in the bowels of the mountains of Bad Ischl, a small village fifteen miles from Ebensee, Austria. The young soldier returned Voss's credentials and saluted the airman again before raising the gate. Voss extinguished the burning cigarette with the heel of his leather boot and walked up the ramp to the massive hangar opening.

As he crossed the bunker-like threshold, his mind filled with the images of two other Luftwaffe pilots—close friends—both of whom had crossed this same threshold in the last month and disappeared. Their families were told that they were killed in combat, and there were no bodies for a funeral. The truth, Voss knew, was much more complicated. He hoped, and secretly prayed, that this test would be successful.

Voss was met at the top of the ramp by an SS liaison. A dangerous man whose entire role in life was to ensure that the secrets of the Reich stayed just that: secrets.

"Are you ready to make history, my friend?" asked the SS officer. Voss put on his best poker face and simply nodded.

The officer led him through a narrow entryway that opened into a circular expanse—the main hangar. Ultra-clean, white cement floors reflected the ominous shape at the center of the hangar. A saucer-like craft with smooth, polished aluminum skin shimmered under the high intensity lights that hung from the ceiling. Only a single symbol, a black swastika on a red background, adorned the craft. If not for the rivets that wrapped the craft in a grid of recognizably man-made construction technique, the vehicle might have been mistaken for something from outer space.

The Bell, as the craft was known, was the crown jewel of Hitler's super weapons program, virtually unknown to anyone outside of a small group of the Führer's trusted inner circle. Those products of the program that had made it to production had frightened the enemy and instilled horror in them. The V1 "buzz bombs" and V2 rockets rained terror and death into British cities after launching from their protected bases in Peenemünde. But this vehicle rendered all the earlier advances obsolete.

The SS officer led Voss across the hangar floor toward a medical lab in an adjoining chamber. A large, cube-shaped auxiliary power unit hummed ominously beside the Bell. Placards adorned the wall with warnings about high voltage. Cables and power lines lined the walls of the hangar. Voss glanced upward at a strange, mysterious spike shape directly above the Bell, which extended from the ceiling. The door to the medical lab opened, and three technicians moved out of their way, revealing a hospital bed in the center of the room. Cabinets containing all manner of medical examination devices were in full supply. Voss tried to focus his attention on other things as the three medical technicians took his blood pressure, listened to his heart, and performed a test on his reflexes.

On the wall of the medical lab, a framed photograph of the Führer leered at Voss and the toiling technicians. The SS officer stared affectionately at the photo, as if he was mentally rehearsing his acceptance speech for whatever award the mighty Führer would lavish on him for keeping the Bell secret from the Allies.

Voss carefully concealed his disgust of their über-leader. Every time he saw the photograph he thought about how that madman was destroying everything his countrymen had worked and sacrificed for. It was clear to Voss that Germany would carry the emotional baggage of Hitler's insane conquest for a century.

It will shock the world, he thought. *When the truth of what is happening in the concentration camps reaches the west—it will change everything.*

Voss thought of the technicians swarming around him, men who only a year before had been prisoners at Mauthausen Concentration Camp. Heinrich Himmler had personally collected the best Polish and Jewish scientists, engineers, and mathematicians who were scheduled for termination and placed them under the chief scientist of the Bad Ischl weapons complex.

It has a certain sick irony, Voss thought. *The very people Hitler considers inferior are the people who can break through existing scientific and technologic barriers to create a weapon with the potential to bring victory to the desperate Third Reich.*

The technicians helped Voss don a thick canvas flight suit with a heavy, zippered front and a flight helmet with a glass faceplate. The helmet was fitted with a sophisticated airtight latch, and an oxygen hose provided him with breathable air from a small green cylinder.

The door of the medical lab swung open, and a blond scientist in his mid-forties walked in.

Viktor Schauberger was the chief scientist in the complex, and the strange, shiny aircraft in the hangar was his life's work. Reichsführer Heinrich Himmler had personally shepherded Schauberger and his work for more than ten years, providing funds and resources that most scientists could only dream about.

Voss acknowledged him and shook his hand, and he was mentally transported back to the place where he had first met Schauberger. As the chief scientist exchanged platitudes with Voss, the test pilot thought of that night one year ago. Adolf Hitler had invited SS officers and the Luftwaffe elite to the Wolf's Lair, the Führer's private mountain retreat. Voss replayed the scene. The colors, the tones, the sounds of a more optimistic time filled his mind.

Tall, snow-white curtains hung beside the granite blocks of the castle wall, waving slightly in the cool mountain air. The smell of pork tenderloin, potatoes, schnitzel, and other German foods wafted through the air. Champagne glasses clinked, and the buzz of the German social and military elite trading stories and gossip filled the air, barely audible over the pompous music of Wagner.

Toward the end of the opulent evening, Heinrich Himmler had briefed a select group of Luftwaffe and SS about a top-secret mission—a mission so secret that there was no written expression of it. It was at this meeting that Voss, the most famous German test pilot in the Luftwaffe, had learned of the Bell and its remarkable capability.

"Herr Voss?" asked Schauberger.

Voss's mind snapped back to reality. The beautiful castle surroundings melted away, and the sterile medical lab came into focus.

"Are you ready?" asked the chief scientist.

Voss nodded once, and he slid his heavy metal-soled boots to the floor one by one and struggled to stand up in the thick canvas flight suit. Sweat dripped down his forehead and began to pool inside the helmet around his neckline as he followed Schauberger to the Bell. The chief scientist opened

the hatch leading to the cockpit and held the small door open for Voss. A
kind smile graced Schauberger's face. Voss returned the smile and shook
the brilliant engineer's hand.

Voss knew that Schauberger would die with the other scientists. The
SS officer would see to that. The work on the Bell was so secret, so revolutionary, that Hitler and Himmler would never allow it to be seen by the
Allies. Regardless of Voss's success or failure, Schauberger's fate would be
the same as that of the Jewish and Polish scientists toiling alongside him
in the underground complex.

Voss stepped into the cockpit and clicked the thick canvas straps into
their buckles. Schauberger helped him cinch the straps tight and patted his
shoulder. An order rang out from a loudspeaker, and the other scientists
and engineers finished their final check of the aircraft and dutifully filed out
of the test tunnel. Schauberger sealed the hatch, and the countdown was
underway.

A radio crackled to life in the craft, and Voss could hear Schauberger
barking orders to the engineers at various status and system stations.
Schauberger began to move through a memorized checklist.

"Start the torsion field." A loud hum sounded throughout the underground complex.

Outside, the mountains surrounding the secret complex seemed to
flicker, like a hundred lightning bugs, as the power in the humble homes
around Bad Ischl fluctuated and failed.

"Set destination coordinates!" yelled Schauberger over the increasing
whine of the engines.

"Coordinates are set!" shouted an engineer.

"Power now at 50 percent!" yelled out a scientist watching a meter at
his station.

"Increase power to 90 percent!" shouted Schauberger. The tension and
excitement in his voice were still discernible over the whine of the engines
that were reaching deafening levels.

Inside the test tunnel, a blue arc of energy spiked out of the top of the
Bell and connected to a large, spike-shaped electrode suspended twenty
feet above the craft.

As the energy level increased, the blue arc began to split into separate parts—first two arcs, then four, then sixteen, and on and on until the blue arc morphed into an enormous tornado of blue-green energy, swirling menacingly above the Bell. Voss stared out of his viewport in awe, wondering if he would survive this test. He felt helpless. This was not like testing a new airplane with a jet engine instead of a propeller. It was beyond that—otherworldly.

"Power at 90 percent!" yelled the scientist monitoring the energy output of the arcing beam. The needle inside the meter buried itself to the right of the measurement ring as the torsion field's power reached maximum levels. The torsion field was now drawing all the electrical power available in the lower part of Austria.

Schauberger gave the final command.

"Open the bridge!"

An engineer threw a switch, and the undulating tornado of energy swirling above the Bell seemed to hesitate for a second as though it was endued with intelligence. Then it swirled to the floor of the test tunnel, swallowing the Bell whole.

An ear-piercing burst of radio feedback filled the cockpit of the Bell, and suddenly it was silenced.

A blinding sphere of light and torsion energy filled the entire chamber and instantly disappeared. A burst of sparks flashed from an overloaded telemetry station, and the lights went out in the control room—leaving the scientists and engineers wondering if they had succeeded.

A fiery glow surrounded the Bell as it traveled through the swirling light, and then everything stopped in utter silence.

It was profoundly dark. Inside the aircraft, Voss reached for his flashlight and flicked it on. Tremendous pressure pulled down on him.

The vehicle must be positioned upside down, he thought.

He released the buckle that secured him to the seat and immediately fell against the instrument panel, cracking his glass faceplate on a sharp metal corner of the instrument panel. A rapid whooshing noise filled his ears as the oxygen in his helmet vented into the cabin. He pulled his helmet off, gasping for the air that was fast becoming the scarcest element inside the Bell.

The transfer of the craft had created condensation that covered its interior, and Voss was almost afraid to touch anything for fear of creating a short in the still-powered relays, capacitors, and vacuum tubes that lined the walls of the cockpit. The water beads on the inside of the viewport obscured his view of the outside. He wiped the viewport clean with a handkerchief and pointed the flashlight out through the small window. Its light reflected instantly from a porous, rough surface.

His breathing stopped for a moment as he recognized the object outside of the thick glass portal. Voss saw veins of rock and ore, tendrils of colorful minerals, and glittery specks of quartz that meandered through a gray and beige background. He quickly checked the starboard side of the craft—the same. More granite veins.

Voss was dizzy and sweating profusely as he realized that he was buried alive—encased in a block of granite.

He closed his eyes, trying to control the terror growing in his mind. His hands and legs shook convulsively as he began to lose control of his motor functions. He was growing weak, and the dizziness increased to the point of nausea as the objects inside the Bell seemed to spin all around him.

He saw himself as a young boy, diving off the dock into an ice-cold lake in Germany. His wedding, his beautiful wife, his parents—the memories accelerated now. University, war college, marches in Berlin, seeing his baby girl for the first time—placing a small white flower of edelweiss in his wife's hair just before leaving for this mission. His brain, struggling to assemble the images with so little oxygen, could no longer function, and the colorful images of Hans Voss's life dissolved into a soup of gray.

Later, the faint glow from his flashlight went out as the batteries died, just as its owner had many hours before.

Arrival

present day

White smoke curled up beneath the massive tires of the C-5 Galaxy aircraft as the transport landed at China Lake Naval Station near the Mojave Desert of California. China Lake was like an acknowledged version of Area 51, a place for the Navy to test both classified and declassified ordnance in a safe and secretive environment.

The C-5 taxied toward a gray hangar just east of the main runway and began to shut down its four powerful engines. The whining of the engines faded out against the sounds of other jets arriving and taking off. The August heat rolled off the runway and the metal surfaces of the aircraft, creating a blurring smear effect of mirages where man-made structures and desert environment swirled into one.

Admiral Nathan Turner appeared at the doorway of the transport, adjusted his mirrored sunglasses, and with a noticeable limp, stepped down the stairs to the burning asphalt runway. The scorching 134-degree heat wrapped itself around him like a fiery blanket as he gazed at the distant Sierra Nevada mountain range to the west of the base.

Turner had been in the Navy his entire adult life, educated at the U.S. Naval Academy in Annapolis. He began his service aboard the infamously mysterious USS *Liberty*. As a cryptologist aboard the spy ship, in the wrong place at the wrong time, he had been injured when the Israeli army mistook the *Liberty* for an Egyptian warship during the Six-Day War in 1967. Most of the people in the belly of the antennae-covered spy ship had been killed when an Israeli torpedo slammed into its side, killing thirty-eight sailors and injuring twice that number.

As Admiral Turner walked slowly into the hangar, another officer, dressed in navy with a chest full of striped bars and shiny medals, saluted. "Admiral Turner, I'm here to escort you to the facility," he said. Turner returned the salute, and his steel-blue eyes evaluated the captain standing before him. Captain Richard Loren was something of a legend in the Navy SEAL community, having performed numerous black operations for the United States during the Cold War, including one in the first Gulf War that had directly involved Turner.

"Rich, it's great to see you again," Turner said, shaking Loren's hand. "So, our friends have come through with something, huh?"

"Yes, sir," replied Loren.

"You can brief me in the car on the way to the facility."

As the admiral finished speaking, an immaculate black limousine pulled up to the hangar doors.

"You gotta love the Navy—always on time," said Turner with a wink.

The limo pulled away from the hangar and headed through a number of guard stations on its way to Highway 178 and the thirty-mile ride to Trona, California, a small city tucked away in a shallow canyon between China Lake and the entrance to the Mojave Desert.

"So, tell me, Rich, how long have you been involved with the facility?"

"I'm coming up on five years. At first it was simply a consulting gig, nothing too unusual—just military oversight and feedback—and then, they made a breakthrough." Loren paused for a moment. "I mean, *the* breakthrough. Sir, I am quite sure they've made a discovery of enormous strategic concern—bigger than stealth, bigger than nuclear weapons—it renders them all obsolete. At the very same time, the issues with managing it could ignite world wars on every continent."

"That's what the people in Washington seem to think too," said Turner, lighting up a cigarette. The smoke curled and swirled through the interior of the limo. Loren pressed his window button to provide some ventilation. Loren was in perfect physical condition—running five miles every morning and working out with weights kept him fit—but it wasn't his place to remind the admiral of the Surgeon General's conclusion on cigarettes.

"It's a nasty habit," said Turner, acknowledging Loren's need for oxygen, "but it keeps me from losing my mind in this business." Turner looked out the tinted windows. The desert was a lonely place—only the limo and a few other travelers dotted the highway. There was nothing but desert and rocky outcrops as far as the eye could see. Occasionally a scraggly Joshua tree, guarding a cluster of scrub brush with its green, bayonet-like leaves, would make an appearance across the bleak landscape. Turner turned away from the desolate view out the window and back to the captain.

"So, this breakthrough happened six months ago, right?" asked Turner.

"Correct. The initial expedition was very simple, but it proved that Two Roads could perform the task repeatedly on demand. The next few expeditions brought back artifacts, and I must say, sir, that these artifacts alone could change vast volumes of accepted thought about both ancient and western civilizations."

"Tell me a little about Mr. Stevens—is he as eccentric as the press paints him?"

"Absolutely not," replied Loren. "Stevens is, without a doubt, the brightest, most energetic leader I have ever met—especially for a civilian. All that money doesn't seem to make him feel superior; in fact, he gives enormous amounts of it away on a regular basis. He does guard his privacy well, which leaves little for the press to feed upon. Most of what you read about him is a fabrication. I've watched him up close for almost five years—he's an impressive man."

"Married?" asked Turner.

"Yes, to the same woman, Meredith, for fifteen years; but no kids. She handles many of the charitable giving initiatives of the Stevens Foundation."

"She doesn't seem annoyed that he works all the way out here?" asked Turner.

"He regularly returns to his home in Silicon Valley, but he also has a mountain retreat in the Sierra Nevadas, where they meet," explained Loren.

Admiral Turner took a last drag on his cigarette and pitched the butt out the window. "It must be nice to be rich," he mused. Loren agreed.

The limo arrived at the small town of Trona and took a recently asphalted road east into an area of rocky canyons. The road ended at a

gateway with a security checkpoint. A red sign with white letters was
mounted on the guardhouse.

Property of TRC and the Department of Energy
Warning. Restricted Area.
Use of Deadly Force is Authorized

"My kind of place," said the admiral with a smile.

Loren explained. "The high security went up after the first few expeditions. As soon as the device proved successful, Stevens contacted a number of people in the State Department and Intelligence and showed them
its potential. From that moment, this place was locked down."

"A patriot, huh?" asked Turner, stretching his bum leg.

"It would seem," replied Loren.

The limo continued past the guardhouse to another security checkpoint that seemed to run into the face of the mountain—a road that went
nowhere. "I'll have to get out for this one," said Loren, opening the door
and stepping out of the car. The guard at the gate examined his credentials
and then asked the captain to place his hand in a rectangular box, mounted
about three feet from the ground on a steel pole. The device scanned the
biometric measurements of his hand and queried the personnel database.
A green light on top of the box illuminated, and Loren got back into the
car.

"And if the light had been red?" asked the admiral.

"You don't want to know," Loren replied.

The rock face in front of them opened like a giant vault, its camouflage
blending in seamlessly with the canyons that encircled the guardhouse.
There was no indication to the outside world of what was being worked
on in the laboratories and buildings hidden inside the bowels of the mountain.

The Facility

The limousine pulled through the massive vault-like door and proceeded down a long, ventilated road deep into the mountain. A small multi-level parking garage presented itself, and the driver pulled up to the main entrance. Turner and Loren got out and approached the lobby entrance. Two large, frosted-glass doors, electronically sensing their approach, quietly slid open.

The lobby was spartan but stylish, with white marble floors and dark granite walls displaying embossed letters: *Two Roads Corporation.*

The attractive receptionist behind a large, brushed-steel divider welcomed them. "Welcome back, Captain. Mr. Stevens is expecting you," she said with a smile.

"Thank you, Sally—good to see you again." The captain and the admiral walked down a granite hallway to an opening at the end. The space opened up into an enormous wing—the place had the feel of a museum with large and small exhibits, some quickly recognizable, some not so.

In the center of the exhibition stood a tall, slim man in his late thirties. Dark-brown hair turned almost pure white just above his ears. His face had a handsome, hawk-like appearance.

"Mr. Stevens, I presume," said the admiral, extending his hand. Neil Stevens gave the admiral's hand a welcoming, solid shake. "Welcome, Admiral. I trust the drive out wasn't too hot or too long."

"Not at all—I had good company," said Turner, gesturing to Captain Rich Loren.

"Captain Loren has been a fantastic resource for us. We're fortunate to have him helping us." Stevens shook the captain's hand and turned back to Admiral Turner.

"Welcome to Two Roads Corporation, Admiral. As you may know, I started this think tank about ten years ago. This private research firm has some of the brightest scientists in the nation. More than three hundred PhDs work here in all kinds of disciplines—basic science research, physics, astrophysics, energy, climatology, optics, computational chemistry, computer science, and mathematics. We've published more than five hundred academic papers—many of them the leading papers in their respective fields." Stevens paused for a moment. "But I don't imagine you've flown over four hours to hear about something you could read on our Web site," he said with a smile.

"Six months ago we made a breakthrough in three fields simultaneously—energy, physics, and mathematics. The results from this singularity are the items on display in this room." Stevens waved his hand broadly toward the various exhibits on the floor. "Now, I could take you directly to the briefing room and explain how we made this breakthrough, but before we do that, I'd like you to take a look around at these exhibits."

Stevens faced his visitors with a sly, almost knowing look. "I'll give you ten minutes, and at the end of that time, please meet me at the briefing room over there at that end of the room."

"That sounds good to me," said Admiral Turner.

Stevens' leather loafers clacked on the Brazilian cherrywood floor that spanned the exhibit hall as he walked to the briefing room, checking his e-mail on his cell phone.

Both Admiral Turner and Captain Loren walked over to the first exhibit. A glass slide connected to the wall by four steel rods contained a small, white piece of paper that read:

```
LIVERPOOL
11 APRIL 1912
METEOROLOGICAL BUREAU...
ICEBERGS PROBABLE...
REDUCED SPEED ADVISABLE.
```

A plaque below the paper stated, "Taken from the desk of Captain Smith at midnight on April 12, 1912, two days before the *Titanic* sank. This item was added to the collection in May 2007."

"Three months ago…but that paper is almost one hundred years old—and it's in mint condition," said Turner.

"That's because it's only existed for three months, and it's spent most of that time here," said Captain Loren.

Turner looked at Loren with a confused expression.

"Trippy, isn't it?" asked Loren.

The second exhibit was a few meters away. This time, an enlarged photograph was mounted on the wall with a gold frame and black matte surrounding it. The photograph was in color, but the subject matter didn't seem to go with the vibrant, high-tech color of the modern film. All the known photos of the subject had always been in black and white.

The picture was of a sharpshooter dressed in everyday clothes, with a rifle pulled close to his face and the muzzle pointing out of a half-open window. The shooter was surrounded by cardboard boxes.

Below the picture, a plaque read, "Lee Harvey Oswald at the moment of the final and fatal shot fired at President John F. Kennedy. Sixth floor of the Texas School Book Depository on November 22, 1963, at exactly 12:30:16 P.M. Added to the collection in April 2007."

"Absolutely amazing!" Turner said, touching the photograph—he almost felt like he was in Dealey Plaza witnessing the tragic assassination. He allowed himself a wry grin, thinking about all the controversial theories that surrounded this one historic event. "Well, I guess that puts the conspiracy theorists in the corner."

"I think a lot of those conspiracy nuts will have to start dating again," said Loren with a chuckle.

The two men moved on to the next exhibit, a wooden ship of war. It had the look of a replica, like a rebuilt ship of antiquity. Its wooden planks were smoothly fitted into a long hull about 120 feet long. The strangely shaped bow sloped away from the top of the boat toward what would be the water line and ended in a long ramming pole. Two menacing eyes glared at the visitors, one on either side of the bow.

A steel pole held a sign that read: "This warship is one of more than 170

Athenian triremes that were deployed in the Battle of Aegospotami, the last of the naval battles of the Peloponnesian War in 404 BC. According to historical records, the entire Athenian navy, of which this ship was a part, was completely destroyed. This item was added to the collection in July 2007."

Another sign next to the warship held a color panoramic photograph of the armada of triremes under the command of Conon, the famous Athenian general.

"Think of it, Admiral," said Loren. "A photograph, not of a recreation of the battle, but of the actual event—more than two thousand years before the camera was even invented."

The admiral was quiet, trying to grasp the reality of the situation in which he found himself. "The implications of only these two items are staggering. One thing's for sure: we don't have enough security around this place."

Both the captain and the admiral heard footsteps echoing off the wall and turned to find a confident but quiet Neil Stevens behind them. "I can assure you, Admiral, the security you have witnessed is only a tenth of what is really in use to keep us secure. Perhaps most importantly, no one in the real world knows what goes on here. Keeping this facility secret is our biggest security device."

"How'd you do this?" asked Admiral Turner, trying to suppress his amazement.

"I'll show you." Stevens gestured toward the conference room. "You can continue your tour of these exhibits during the break in about an hour."

An enormous round table with inlaid wood designs was centered in the perfectly round room. Track lighting in the ceiling illuminated the deep leather seats surrounding the table. Dark plasma display panels with some sort of screen saver played on all the walls, with the exception of the entrance. The panels seemed to be showing a darkly colored visualization of turbulent clouds. Periodically, the title "Two Roads Corporation" would fade in for a few moments and then disappear in a dissolve.

Another gentleman joined the group. He was wearing jeans and a black T-shirt. As he got closer, Turner recognized the man as Cameron Locke, the world-famous physicist. Locke held degrees in mathematics, physics, and computer science from MIT and Stanford. He had recently received the Fields Medal for some brilliant work in complex dynamics, a branch of mathematics that dealt with uncertainty.

"Admiral Turner, may I introduce you to Dr. Cameron Locke, our head of research."

"It's a real pleasure to meet you," Turner said as he shook Locke's hand.

The men took a place around the table as an assistant brought each of them a bottle of water. A digital photograph of a crushed aircraft embedded in the side of a strip-mined mountain flashed onto the plasma screen behind Stevens as he began to brief the two officers.

"In 1992, right after the Cold War ended, a number of miners in western Canada found an object embedded in rock strata that had been carbon-dated to more than one hundred thousand years ago. This object was from Nazi Germany—specifically, from the advanced weapons project the SS ran until the end of the war. Some weapons became operational from this group, like the V1 and V2 rockets that rained down on Britain, and some of these weapons were so revolutionary, so far ahead of their time, that virtually no one has heard of them."

Stevens paused for a moment to take a sip of water while the history lesson sank in with the visitors.

"The object that we found was called 'the Bell' by the Nazi scientists. In the last few weeks of the war in Europe, Allied bomber crews reported seeing glowing, saucer-like shapes that would rise up through the flak and chase the bomber formations with speed and agility that no one had ever witnessed before."

Turner interjected, "You're speaking of the Foo-Fighters."

"Yes, Admiral, the Allied bomber crews nicknamed these objects Foo-Fighters," Stevens replied. "Not one of these mysterious objects was recovered after the war, at least not by American or British forces."

He paced around the wooden table. "However, as the war was ending, the United States conducted a secret mission by the name of Operation Paperclip. This mission was to collect and round up as much German technology and as many of the scientists and engineers that had worked on these secret projects as possible. Many of the scientists who were captured said they had worked on a high-energy program codenamed Chrona. For a very long while, there were rumors that the Nazis had been working to master anti-gravity, and this helped to fuel the idea of Foo-Fighters and flying saucer craft. In retrospect, the Foo-Fighter Project, as we refer to it now, was a smaller part of the overall Chrona program."

Stevens stopped pacing abruptly. "Gentlemen," he said, "the Nazi scientists were working on a time machine."

Turner's mouth dropped open.

"NATO resources recovered the Bell from Canada, and the intelligence community from Britain, Canada, Australia, and the United States began to unwind some of the mysteries of this strange project. It took Two Roads Corporation, with some additional help from the intelligence community, about ten years to crack the code. Dr. Locke was instrumental in figuring out the math and developing the methods we use to stabilize the wormhole, and I think I'd like for him to continue this presentation to explain how such a device can work." Stevens sank down into a plush leather chair.

Locke stood up and walked toward the plasma screen directly across from the admiral. He touched the surface of the panel with his index finger, and a small visualization for feedback formed. It was as if a stone had been dropped into a lake, and as the ripples cascaded across the surface of the panel, an enormous computer desktop appeared with open documents and diagrams. Locke walked over to a specific diagram and tapped the document twice with his index finger, and it jumped to the top of all the other documents stacked on the virtual desktop. He quickly moved his hands over the stacked virtual documents and shifted them to another stack, as if he were handling real papers. Once he located the presentation he was looking for, Locke tapped twice on the plasma screen, and the document filled all of the screens of the conference room, wrapping the small team in a blanket of information. A strange, slowly spinning geometrical shape filled the plasma display before the two visitors.

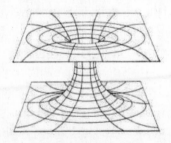

"The Nazis discovered how to create a high-energy field that we call a torsion field," Locke said. "Field theory predicts that if you can generate a torsion field with enough energy, then you can bend time and space around the generator. The more energy, or torsion, you can create, the more space and time you can perturb."

"What do you mean by 'perturb'?" asked Turner.

"Sorry about that; it's a technical math term. I mean offset, or bend," said Locke with a smile. Locke ripped a blank page from his legal pad and held it up the way a magician might present a trick to an audience.

Neil Stevens interrupted Locke with a snide remark and a smile. "I install a multi-million-dollar, state-of-the-art presentation system, and my head of research uses a ripped piece of paper to make a point to important visitors. Does anyone else have a problem with this?"

Cameron ignored Stevens' good-natured jab with a smirk. He continued.

"Einstein stated that time and space were like a giant grid extending infinitely in all directions, but that gravity was like a force pulling down on certain points—creating a shape that we sometimes call a rubber sheet. If you think of our solar system as a rubber sheet, then the sun is like a basketball in the center of a sheet that's being held tightly by four corners. The sheet bends beneath and around the basketball, representing the sun's gravity, and then pulls back out around the equator of the basketball. The mass, or in this case, the weight of the sun, makes the sheet somewhat conical or curved, which makes objects nearby tend to gravitate or move toward the sun—objects such as Mercury, Venus, Earth, Mars—all the planets are affected by the immense gravity of the sun. You follow so far?"

Both Captain Loren and Admiral Turner nodded.

Locke continued. "So, there's another concept that's called an Einstein-Rosen Bridge. Just like the grid showing the distance of the planets from each other—you can think of time in the same way." Locke held the paper up and said, "Time extends across this paper. Think of the bottom as the past and the top of the paper as the present." He folded the paper so that the bottom was in contact with the top. Instead of folding the paper in half, he left it simply loose and curving around. "The Einstein-Rosen Bridge allows time and space to fold up against another point of space-time. It's this initial framework that the Nazis discovered how to manipulate."

"So, the Bell object that was found in Canada was part of this program, and the Nazis succeeded in sending this object back into the past?" asked Turner.

"Yes, we think so," Stevens answered. "It's difficult to ascertain what point they went back to, but the equations they were using were wrong, and the power supply they used was not strong enough to control the bridge between the two time periods."

"Both of the craft we have recovered had dead pilots inside," Locke said.

"Both?" inquired Turner.

"Yes. In 1998 we found another craft near Los Alamos, New Mexico, during a seismic reading."

"Los Alamos?" Turner questioned.

"Yes," Stevens answered. "From some of the items in the Bell, we could see that the Nazis seemed to know that the Manhattan Project was being managed and explored there. Most people in Intelligence believe there was some leak that made it to the German High Command. We think that Germany was going to try to steal the design of the atomic bomb, sabotage the project, or even use it against an American city, like Washington."

"That's outrageous! I've never heard of such a thing. Who knows about this at the Pentagon?" asked Turner.

"Some higher-ups do, but very few people know about this Nazi project, and even fewer know about the finding at Los Alamos. Imagine the hysteria of knowing that the existence of your entire country or civilization could be erased or changed at any moment."

"And that's only the half of it," said Locke. "There was at least one more flight of the Nazi Bell that was destined for the year 1900 BC—that's before Christ, not 1900 AD. This information was only recently declassified to a few Intelligence officials. The Soviet Union documented that a Nazi scientist was captured by the Red Army and tortured to death to get to this information."

"Why in the world would the Nazis go that far back?" Turner asked with a confused look.

"Well, it was the last days of the war—desperation was setting in. Now, this is speculation on my part, but the only chronicled event that's within a five-year time frame of 1900 BC is the birth of Isaac," Locke said.

"Isaac…as in Isaac, the son of Abraham?" said Turner, recognition setting in.

"Yes, one of the fathers of the Jewish race," replied Locke. "Apparently they were planning to stop the Jewish race from ever existing by killing the top of the family tree."

"It sounds like a movie—like *Terminator* in biblical times," Turner said.

"Now you start to realize how this technology can be weaponized in the wrong hands," said Stevens.

Turner frowned, grappling with the effects of information overload combined with the implications of this incredible discovery. "So, you're saying—and the evidence in the next room bears proof—that you've succeeded in creating an Einstein-Rosen Bridge and have even been able to bring objects back from the past?"

"Yes, that's correct. We've sent back ten expeditions, and nine have succeeded," replied Stevens.

"What do you mean by expeditions, and what happened in the case of the expedition that did not succeed?" Turner asked.

"When we had succeeded in sending small objects around the lab and making them appear in the past intact, we decided to go back in time to key points and document our capability to send humans to a specific point and return them safely," stated Stevens. "All of the items we brought back had to be part of collections that would have been destroyed anyway. That's why the trireme and the telegraph notice received by the *Titanic* were selected. The trireme is our most recent addition, and it represents our ability to return a large object intact."

Turner held his head in his hands as if he were having a migraine. "OK, so you've proven that you can transport humans and objects, like cameras, back in time to collect information or objects and bring them back successfully…and the lost expedition?"

A pained expression filled Neil Stevens' face. It was clear to both Turner and Loren that this subject was not a simple matter.

"In one of our early missions, the second one to be exact, we sent a small squad of soldiers and a historian to the year 100,000 BC, just outside of what we would now call Kansas City. We picked this time frame because we thought there would be no people in North America—or at least nothing with organization, like a government, town, or city. There would be nothing to corrupt the timeline in case we came into contact. It was considered the safest of all the planned missions," said Stevens.

"So what happened to them?" asked Turner.

Stevens spoke softly and clearly with his voice almost trembling. "When they began to leave this time period, they were incinerated—they vaporized."

Turner had lost men under his command before, and while this was a civilian standing before him, he recognized the tone: personal responsibility and guilt. His hands came up from his side, and he placed his elbows on the beautiful wood table and rubbed his temples. "Was there a problem with the machine?" he asked.

Locke spoke up. "There's only one reason we've been able to arrive at, based on the equations. If there's not a rational destination point, then all matter in the transfer is obliterated—like hitting an invisible wall."

Turner's eyes widened with understanding. "You're saying that either the Kansas City location or the date was not valid and that the machine could not deliver its payload, so everyone and everything in the transfer was destroyed."

"Or both. That's correct," said Locke.

"Well, the earth is over 4 billion years old," Turner said, turning toward Locke. "It must have been the location."

"That's what we thought…originally," Locke said, his words trailing off.

Stevens explained, "Since that incident, we have begun to send inanimate objects back through time just to test that their transmission through time is valid. We decided to send back wood that would be indistinguishable in any time period from a processing perspective."

Cameron Locke jumped in. "What Neil means is that we didn't send back cubes of wood or ingots of steel. A culture that saw something like that might start to research these items sooner than we know they did and alter history in an unknown way."

"OK, and what was the result?" asked Turner.

"The experiment was to send these objects back to the same Kansas City point but alter the timeline by hundred-year increments," Stevens said.

"We attempted to send back more than nine hundred objects—each payload was incinerated," Locke said.

"So that means...what?" asked Turner.

"It means what it meant originally—that the Kansas City location or the timeline, or both, did not exist," said Locke. "We have attempted to send those objects to points other than Kansas City, even locations in Antarctica and the Pacific Ocean. We thought the ocean would be there by then for sure. We were so sure of it," Locke said, looking at Stevens.

"Nothing?" asked Turner.

"Nope. Nothing. Everything we tried to send disintegrated."

"So what's your professional opinion?" asked Turner.

"It means that one of the following is true, since we can successfully send and retrieve humans and objects after 404 BC to the present. It means that somewhere between that point and the ancient past, either the equations break down or are different, or the energy source we have is not sufficient—for which we have no evidence—or time and matter did not exist until somewhere around seven thousand to ten thousand years ago."

Stevens spoke up. "If indeed the third possibility is true, then the scientific community will be turned on its ear in a single day—the truth will relegate theories in everything from astrophysics to anthropology to the dustbin of history."

"Show me this machine," Turner said.

3

The Machine

Neil Stevens led the group to the hallway elevator, inserting his personal cardkey and PIN to allow entry. Admiral Nathan Turner's head was starting to spin with everything he had witnessed in the last hour—TRC's written briefings to Naval Intelligence were clearly not as revealing as they could have been. Once inside the elevator, Stevens pressed one of six buttons on the console.

Welcome to Two Roads Corporation

Lobby
Offices & Laboratories
Data Center
Platform Bay/Operations Center
Power Plant
Living Quarters

"We'll start with the power plant first and then work our way up," Stevens said.

"How many people work directly on the time machine project?" asked Turner.

"About one hundred people are needed operationally, and as you will see, seventy of those people are needed for power services. The remainder are split pretty evenly between the data center and manning the operations center for the Platform."

"Platform?" asked Turner.

"We call the machine 'the Platform,'" Locke said. "It's where we transfer out and also bring back objects."

The elevator stopped, and the doors slid open. They were greeted by two armed guards who stood in front of a biometric recognition station. Stevens flipped open his credentials for one of the guards to review. Stepping to the recognition station, Stevens placed his head on a small shelf shaped like the chinstrap of a football helmet. The machine scanned Stevens' retina, and a moment later the lock on the thick steel door clicked and the door yawned open.

"Welcome, Dr. Stevens," said the recognition machine's robotic voice.

"This room monitors any radiation that might be on personnel either entering or exiting the power plant floor," Stevens said.

He handed everyone a pair of headphones with a microphone wand that protruded from the set. "It's going to be pretty noisy, so we can use these headphones to save your hearing and also take your questions while we're in here."

In Turner's ear, a calm robotic voice spoke. "Audio check. Check successful."

The airlock opened, and the group stepped onto a metal catwalk that extended the length of the power plant bay. On either side of the catwalk, powerful turbines hummed. "This room generates enough energy to supply New York City with electricity for a week on the hottest day of the year. It takes all of this energy to open and close the wormhole," Stevens said.

The room was wall-to-wall with ultra-clean concrete. Yellow and red paint marked special points on the floor, and a large crane hook hung suspended from the ceiling on a massive hoist. The place was bustling with operations people, all wearing hard hats and steel-toed boots. It reminded Turner of a nuclear power station.

Stevens pointed to a number of diesel generators directly behind them. "These provide power to the rest of the building, and we have enough fuel to operate them autonomously for up to one year."

"The turbines are nuclear, I assume?" asked Turner.

"Yes," Stevens answered with a mischievous smile. "We're the largest private reactor in the world. Our relationship with the Energy Department helps us keep this hush-hush."

"If the turbines are nuclear, how do you power them out here in the desert?" Turner asked.

"We've tapped an aquifer that underlies this entire region, and we use some geothermal energy as well," answered Stevens.

"We believe that the Nazis were not able to generate a stable field, and that resulted in their craft and pilots being embedded in rock strata—the wormhole was vibrating too much on delivery," Locke said.

"OK, let's go up to the data center and see what keeps us from making those same mistakes," Stevens said, leading everyone back to the airlock and then to the elevator.

As the elevator traveled up to the data center, Turner turned to Locke and asked, "Does it require the same amount of energy to bring back a person or a boat, or does mass present a difference?"

"Good question," said Locke. "The energy is used exclusively to manipulate the mouth of the wormhole—you could bring back a pebble or the Empire State Building. You get the transfer for free. Everything goes into manipulating the wormhole."

Turner let out a low whistle. With his clearance, he had seen many incredible technical breakthroughs, but nothing like this.

"I told you it was trippy," said Captain Loren with a smile.

Everyone in the elevator burst into laughter, and Turner shook his head slowly. Hearing a highly regarded Navy captain using a drug-culture reference to describe a scientific breakthrough was disturbing, inappropriate, and accurate.

The elevator arrived at the data center, and once again the group was put through a security check. Upon entering the data center, Turner saw row after row of six-foot tall black computers with brushed-aluminum accents. Each node of the supercomputer was about as big as a refrigerator. Turner did a quick calculation by the rows in the room—there must have been about sixty of these units, all tied together in an arch that connected the top of each row of processing units.

Neil Stevens walked through a few of the rows of high-powered computers and turned to face the visitors, raising his arms above his head and resting them on a sturdy black plastic arch overhead that connected the rows of powerful machines together.

"This is a Cray X1 Supercomputer. If this supercomputer was disclosed to the public, it would be one of the top ten systems in the world from a speed perspective. In total, it contains over 23,000 processors, connected in a 3D torus topology. That's what these arches are all about." He patted the hard black plastic. "This system can process over 100 trillion operations per second, and we need every one of them to keep the wormhole reliable."

Locke put his hand out to the side, with his palm facing the admiral and the captain. "You can feel a definite breeze moving past this equipment. The amount of heat this room generates is mind-boggling. The chillers—oops, sorry; that's what we call them internally—the refrigeration systems to keep these boxes from melting down could powder a Vail ski run with artificial snow in about ten minutes."

Over against the far wall, a strange object took up the entire wall, top to bottom. Stevens noticed Turner's interest.

It was a pure black, rectangular shape with shoe box shaped panels arranged in a grid, top to bottom and left to right. A waterfall of clear liquid was pouring from the top across the front of the grid and collecting in a pond at the bottom. The entire enormous sculpture was encased in clear Plexiglas that kept the liquid from splashing out and recycled the fluid from the pond at the bottom of the chassis back across the delicate electronics.

"That's the drive farm, the storage system for recording the telemetry of the wormhole and the payloads going through it. There are over ten petabytes of storage in those hard drives. That's ten thousand terabytes—or one hundred thousand gigabytes, which you might be more familiar with," Stevens said.

"What's with the waterfall?" asked Turner.

"That's fluoroinert—it's not water. The electronics of the hard drive are actually immersed in this liquid, which runs across them and takes the heat away when they're operating at top speed. It's the only way to keep the system cool without it melting into a gigantic mess."

"It takes two solid weeks for this system to complete the wormhole calculations before any expedition can transfer," Locke said. "During operations, we use the data to model and control the wormhole—all the telemetry from the model is thrown into this storage system." He gestured to the waterfall of coolant behind him.

"What exactly do you mean by 'model'?" asked Turner.

Locke replied, "Well, you've seen on public television how scientists are trying to model tornados and storms in order to understand how they work, right?"

"Sure," said Turner.

"This is the same concept, except our model is an exact duplicate of the physical phenomenon we are unleashing by opening a wormhole. There are no good instruments for recording the real thing—too much is happening too quickly, so we model it precisely using this system and record it over there."

"Let's go see the Platform," said Stevens.

Within a few minutes, and after numerous security checks, the group was standing on the floor of what Neil Stevens called the Platform. It was a large, enclosed concrete room, about three hundred feet long by two hundred feet wide. The operations center was separated from the main Platform floor by a thick concrete wall with a three-foot-high portal of bulletproof glass. A crisscross of steel trusses rose around and above the center of the floor. A giant yellow steel hook was suspended from a stout cable that hung from the steel hoist, which was used to move laterally across the expanse of the room and position large equipment. Junction boxes and regulators jutted out from the walls at regular intervals, and an occasional white placard with a red lightning bolt and the words WARNING: HIGH VOLTAGE decorated the thick, reinforced concrete wall.

A low humming noise from the overhead blue halogen lamps could be heard at all times. The Platform floor was elevated on a thick steel frame above the concrete main floor. Its top was a translucent surface arranged in a grid of opaque blue glass panels. Overhead, a circular port extended ten feet down from the ceiling, with network cabling and conduits that wrapped themselves around the Platform in a serpentine pattern. It seemed as though every cable and vent that meandered around the room ended up connecting to the circular port in one way or another.

Stevens pointed to the vent-like shape. "We call this the portal. It becomes the mouth of the wormhole when the Platform is operational. Everything in this room is transferred through the wormhole that is generated just in front of this device."

"You're telling me that huge boat in the collection came through that ten-foot hole?" Turner asked, pointing to the ceiling.

"No," said Locke. "The wormhole envelopes the entire floor—the space and time are transferred, but the object remains intact. Don't think of it as an air shaft where air flows through to get to a destination. Think of it more like the transporter on *Star Trek,* and you'll have fewer headaches."

Turner laughed at his inability to think in more than three dimensions at once. "Oh, I'm glad we cleared that up!"

Stevens led the group to the operations center, separated from the large cavern containing the Platform by a thick concrete wall with a large glass window. The view looked out on the steel trusses and the blue glass floor where transfers to other time periods occurred.

The ops room was furnished in a typical Mission Control-like layout. Various stations were manned by men and women in casual attire, and huge computer displays filled the walls.

As the visitors followed Stevens and Locke into the darkened room, a beautiful young woman who was sitting at a workstation stood up and smiled. "Welcome to the ops center. I'm Alicia King."

Locke hustled past Stevens to introduce his colleague. "Miss King is our team leader and is responsible for all operations during an expedition. We are fortunate to have her on the team." Alicia King blushed a bit and shook the two men's hands.

"Once a team is sent, can you communicate with them in any way?" asked Turner.

"Not verbally, but periodically we can open a small wormhole and transfer information from one point to another—kind of like instant messaging with stone tablets," Stevens said, putting his hand on Alicia's shoulder. "In fact, Miss King is doing some groundbreaking work with carrier waves to try to resolve this, but for now we have the team meet at a certain place at a certain time, and we transfer everyone and everything back."

"The throat of the wormhole causes some strange effects on the difference between the two timelines. It distorts the differences so that time seems to go on as normal for the destination team, but very fast for the team managing the return here at TRC," added Locke.

"Like a time zone?" Turner asked.

"Not really—more like a year on Earth versus a year on another planet. Every trip is a little different, and we had to use some funky math to figure out how to calculate the difference. Generally, for every hour we experience, it's something like three to five hours for the away team," explained Locke.

Turner noticed a station called News and Records and asked, "What is that station used for?"

Locke answered. "Before we hit that one, let's talk a bit about how we protect ourselves from changes on the timeline. One of the reasons we built this facility into a mountain is that all of our floors are enclosed in a giant electric cage. You could best think of it as a gigantic Faraday cage. When a wormhole is opened, the entire cage is energized. That protects the facility from any change to the timeline. It's an isolated bubble in time during the transfer."

Turner scratched his head. "So this facility is time-neutral during a transfer cycle? For what reason?"

Stevens replied, "Here's a good example that's also terrifying. Let's say some knucklehead goes back in time with a nuclear device and blows up the Mojave Desert five minutes ago. Blam-o! Not one of us exists."

Turner crossed his arms over his chest and stared directly at Stevens. Locke and Stevens exchanged a glance as if they had been over this before.

"Look, I can see that description worries you…" said Stevens.

"You're not even close, Mr. Stevens," said Turner. "When you talk like that you are entering the world of national security, not just some neat science experiment in the desert with your private money."

Stevens nodded at the comment. "Fair enough."

Locke spoke up in an attempt to break the tension. "The Faraday cage protects us by cocooning the entire building in its own torsion field with reference to our timeline. In short, we can undo anything that another person does in time."

Stevens jumped in as well to soothe Turner's concerns. "The News and Records station is like our own personal Internet search engine. We harvest every major news channel on the planet and record it here; every past news story, digital or analog, as well as most history books, have been archived in our database. After a mission, we run a comparison of the new timeline against the old and look for contradictions. So far there have been none. If we find a contradiction, we can go back to where the timeline skews and resolve whatever happened."

Turner sighed deeply in contemplation. "Neil, you and your team have built some amazing technology—it's as big an advance as I've ever seen, heard, or even *thought* of. As a member of the military and homeland security community, I thank you for getting us involved."

Stevens acknowledged the admiral's comment with a kind smile, relieved that the relationship between them had returned to a more civil tone. "There is one more thing I'd like to talk with you about before you head back to China Lake."

4

Plans

B ack in the conference room, Admiral Nathan Turner sat down in his leather seat, mulling over all the things he had heard and witnessed in the past few hours. He looked down the hallway toward the exhibit area and saw the bow of the trireme jutting out like an exclamation point to his confused thoughts.

Neil Stevens touched the plasma screen that curved behind him, and the rippling action that emanated from his touch revealed a timeline that stretched across all the screens.

"Admiral," Stevens said, "we want to mount an expedition to the year 2300 BC."

"What happened then?" Turner asked, taking a sip from an exceptionally hot cup of coffee.

"The Flood, the Deluge, Noah's Ark," Stevens replied.

Turner nearly sprayed the inlaid wooden table with a varnish of Hazelnut Supreme. "You must be joking—Noah's Ark is a myth!" Turner exclaimed.

"Yes," Cameron Locke said, raising an ironic eyebrow and crossing his arms as if to mock the admiral's showing in the ops center, "and one hour ago you thought the earth was 4 billion years old."

Turner scowled at Locke. He didn't like the man's condescending tone of voice, but inside, Turner knew that Locke was right.

Neil Stevens positioned himself between TRC's volatile head of research and the admiral and softened his voice, but he looked the man straight in the face earnestly. "Admiral, every culture has its own reference to the Flood. The ancient Sumerians referred to it in the Epic of Gilgamesh. The Aztecs, the Chinese—all cultures have some sort of reference to this event."

Turner cleared his throat and took another sip of coffee. He needed this organization as much as Neil Stevens needed him. The technology that he had been shown had implications for the country, and he didn't need to make enemies, at least not this early. He smiled up at Stevens.

"If indeed the earth is about seven thousand years old, and this expedition to Noah's Ark succeeds, it will change thinking in all quarters of the world. This expedition, if we go forward, must be kept absolutely top secret until we can ascertain what it is that we find there. The results could ignite an ideological war."

"Agreed," said Stevens.

"Why the Flood and Noah's Ark? Why not just go back to the beginning and cut through all of this? Let's just go back seven thousand years and chronicle what the earth looked like then," said Loren.

"It might not be that simple," said Locke. "We can decipher the Flood timeline from genealogical information, but it isn't clear that the Garden of Eden..."

"Good question," interrupted Stevens, raising a hand to quiet the science lead. "And assuming we survive this expedition, we will likely go back to the beginning—but understanding what happened at the point of the Flood will be critical to understanding why carbon and argon dating methods and ice-core drillings have all been so inaccurate in establishing a reliable timeline. The fossil record, upon which most dating methods in archeology and paleontology are based, is also in jeopardy. Everything we take for granted in the scientific community—the erosion of the Grand Canyon over millions of years, red-shift from stars—it may all be wrong. The Flood, if it occurred, is the epicenter for why our world looks like it does today."

Turner nodded. "I agree that this seems like a good strategy: divide and conquer the timeline to discover some of these mysteries. I do have one big question, though—if you go back in time to 2300 BC, and it's a scientific expedition, won't you have to take scientific instruments with you?"

"Yes, sir, we will—we won't be able to prove our findings without the measurements in that time," Stevens said.

"And if the equipment is discovered by man of that age, would it not alter our timeline?" Turner asked.

"Yes, it would," Stevens answered, "which is why we have two fail-safes for all the equipment going back."

"Please explain," said Turner.

"First of all, all each piece of equipment has a small charge that will destroy the instrument if the identity of the person using it cannot be authenticated. There is a small fingerprint sensor attached to all our equipment, and the digital identities of everyone on the team are stored in a flash card. So if Zorg, the caveman, picks up the seismometer, the device will destroy itself. The charge won't be large enough to hurt the human, though."

"Sounds like a good plan—and the second fail-safe?" asked Turner.

"The Flood itself," replied Stevens.

Turner cocked his head in confusion.

"The record of the Flood is that everyone and everything dies—with the exception of the eight people in the Ark."

Turner leaned forward in the plush leather chair. "Stevens, you're taking a huge professional risk with this line of reasoning. There are scores of scientists out there that would question your sanity based on your last sentence. I can't believe you are actually assuming that the Flood really happened."

Stevens stood his ground confidently. "Admiral, if everything we know about prehistory is wrong, as proven by the loss of our expedition and our ongoing experiments to establish the timeline—well, I'm willing to go on a little faith."

Turner pushed back from the table and sighed. It was hard for him to disagree with that.

"Admiral, I would like the permission of the government to pursue this expedition, and I want Captain Loren with me," Stevens said.

"I need to talk to a few people in Washington in order to grant that, but yes, assuming there is support for this mission—and assuming that Captain Loren is in agreement—we will support you in any way we can," Turner said.

"We'll need to get some experts in a number of fields," said Locke, clicking them off audibly. "Paleontology, language and linguistics, geology, and some experts in the timeline so we can make the proper calculations."

Turner extended his hand with a smile. Both Neil Stevens and Cameron Locke shook hands with the admiral and the captain and walked them to the lobby. "Go ahead and start building your team. Begin the calculations; I'll get you the support you need in Washington."

Now it was time for the real work to begin.

5

The Team

Base Camp, Eli Village, Turkey

T he icy high winds beat upon the thick yellow-and-black nylon of Troy Scott's shelter as he crawled out of the tent and stood up to face the sun that was coming up over the mountain. He took a deep breath of the brisk morning air and let his gaze follow the mountain's line to its summit, more than 5,100 meters high—Mount Ararat, the legendary final resting place of Noah's Ark.

Troy Scott was a self-made adventurer—a classic adrenaline junkie, with a litany of dangerous sports that read like a suicide note for the average person. Skydiving, base jumping, scuba diving, mountain climbing, rappelling—he did them all, sometimes at the same time. With the hundred million dollars he had made in his sale of Terra-Imaging, a dot-com venture he had founded in the late 1990s, he had the resources and the time to do whatever he wanted to do. But he wasn't just a rich person who got a high from jumping out of a perfectly good airplane—Scott was a well-known and outspoken Christian. His adventures and funded expeditions revolved around the discovery of archaeological items that would buttress the Judeo-Christian scriptures in some way.

Scott was pulled away from his mountain-gazing by a weather report breaking on his digital scanner. He squinted in the sunlight as he read the high-resolution display: "Dying winds; clear and sunny skies for the next thirty-six hours." Scott smiled; he had a busy day ahead of him—five hours of hiking to get to Green Camp at 3,200 meters and begin the acclimatization process in preparation for the summit. Scott had been to Ararat two other times, and both excursions had ended in poor weather and bad visibility. He was hoping for perfect weather this time.

Scott went back into his shelter to layer up and performed a final check of his equipment. The guides were already starting to gather the expedition members for an early start.

As he zippered his backpack, he heard the unmistakable thumping of whirling helicopter blades disturbing the morning air. The shelter began to vibrate with the rotor wash coming from the helicopter as it landed on a gravel helipad about two hundred feet away.

Scott stepped out of his shelter to see a blue Sikorsky S-76 helicopter with a large white emblem on the side—a Y-shaped logo that said "Two Roads Corporation." Scott recognized it immediately as belonging to his friend, Neil Stevens. The whine of the helicopter's turbine changed pitch as the engine shut down, and the translucent, whirling disc slowed into four distinct red-and-white blades.

Scott ran to the side of the helicopter as the door popped open and Cameron Locke, the lead scientist for TRC, stepped out.

"Cameron, it's great to see you again! What in the world are you doing here?" asked Scott.

"Troy, I tried to call your cell phone, but apparently there's no coverage here for the Sherpa and sheep," Locke said, smiling like a high-school prankster. "I hope I'm not catching you at a bad time."

Troy glanced down at his climbing gear. Pitons were dangling from his belt and from his thick nylon weather shell and expensive climbing boots. Every inch of him was suited for conquering the mountain that loomed over them.

"Not at all. What can I do for you?"

"Listen, Troy, I don't have a lot of time here," Cameron Locke said.

"Likewise," said Troy, gesturing to the crowd of climbers assembling around the burros and guides five hundred feet away. The burros brayed as the mountain guides piled more and more equipment on their backs. The lead Sherpa whistled at Troy and waved for him to give the order to head for the summit.

Cameron placed a hand on Troy's shoulder, pulling his attention back from the expedition.

"Troy, we've made a massive breakthrough at TRC—the one that Neil has spent years chasing. We need your expertise."

"Cameron, you guys have more money than Peru—you can buy any expert you want. I'm interested, I really am, but the expedition is leaving in just a few minutes, and this might be the trip when I finally get to see the Ark. The expedition will be going near the Ahora Gorge—it's the chance of a lifetime."

"Troy, do you trust me?" asked Cameron.

"Of course," replied Troy.

Cameron stared intently into Troy's face. "Troy, we want you to lead a more important, more relevant, expedition to the Ark."

Troy Scott looked at Cameron with wonderment, his face at first blank, and then a giant smile filled his face. "You did it, didn't you? You cracked the code!"

"Troy, this is the expedition you were born for—forget the ruins up there in the ice. You can see how they really built it, what it looked like, and what the civilization was like that perished because they were not on it when the Flood came."

Troy didn't even deliberate; he threw his backpack into the back of the chopper and left his tent and other equipment behind. Within seconds, the loud helicopter hovered, spun on its axis, and headed back in the direction it had come from just minutes before.

The Ahora Gorge expedition members looked at each other quizzically as the helicopter carrying the person who had funded the expedition and spent six months negotiating with three different governments abandoned them without explanation and disappeared over the horizon.

Cornell University, Ithaca, New York

Fernanda Vegas rifled through the papers on her desk and sighed in frustration. Her frazzled graduate assistant moved out of her way as she looked in overstuffed folders and dog-eared books for her lecture notes; she was late for class, again. Vegas, an athletic, deeply tanned woman in her late twenties, had recently completed her doctorate in the anthropology of prehistoric civilizations. Since her childhood in Brazil she had been fascinated by the study of ancient peoples and what they were able to achieve.

Specifically, Vegas was hunting for commonalities between the cultures of the Sumerians, Egyptians, Aztecs, and even cultures in Cambodia.

Fernanda Vegas was well-liked by her students, who considered her one of the best professors from whom to take courses. She worked hard to make history come alive for her students in ways that other instructors could only dream about. The academic community also respected her—she was known to have an open mind and work well with teams of other researchers.

Just as she was preparing to head for her anthropology class, she heard metal taps clacking on the tile floor in the department hallway. The casualness of the university—tennis shoes and jeans—seemed violated by this militarized sound. It was like hearing a typewriter in an office amid the age of word processing.

She looked up from her hunt to find an impeccably dressed naval officer looking down at her from her office doorway.

"Dr. Fernanda Vegas?" asked the officer.

"Yes, I am—how can I help you?" she replied, looking out of the corner of her eye around the room, still searching for the missing notes.

"My name is Captain Richard Loren, U.S. Navy. Could we have a word privately?"

Fernanda looked at her watch—five minutes after ten. She gestured to her graduate assistant and said, "Dave, do your best to get through chapter six, and start the review for the test."

The grad assistant nodded and left the room to tend to the restless students.

Fernanda offered the visitor a seat and closed the door to her office for some privacy.

"Now, Captain Loren, what would the Navy need with a professor of anthropology?"

Loren took off his hat and placed it on Fernanda's beautiful wooden desk as he sat down. "Dr. Vegas, I'm currently assigned to a joint military-civilian project that has need of your unique skills and knowledge."

"What kind of project?" asked Fernanda.

"The kind that changes the world, to put it bluntly," said the captain. "Everything I'm about to tell you is classified."

Fernanda nodded. "I understand," she said, leaning forward in her chair and giving the naval officer her full attention. The missing lecture notes were now a casualty of war as Loren's mysterious project pushed its way front and center.

"The U.S. Intelligence Community and a privately held think tank called Two Roads Corporation are mounting a trip—and by 'trip' I mean an expedition, and I think you will probably want to be on this journey. We could certainly use your expertise. You are known in the academic community for your passion for discovering commonality between cultures, as well as for your basically unspoken feeling that all ancient civilizations seem to be connected in ideas, mythology, religion, and even in their knowledge of science."

Fernanda nodded, acknowledging his simplistic yet accurate description of her life's work. "Where is the trip heading?" she asked.

"Mesopotamia," he replied.

"I've already spent three summers working in that area of the world," said Fernanda, waving her hand and learning back in her chair.

The captain qualified his earlier answer. "Mesopotamia...about 2300 years before the birth of Christ." The words cut the quiet of the room like a knife.

Fernanda stared at the captain in stunned silence.

"I can't say anything more here," the captain said, standing up from his chair. He put an airline ticket jacket on her desk. "If you want to know more, be on this flight at 7 P.M. tonight."

Captain Loren shook the doctor's hand and left the office. Fernanda sat in her office, staring at the ticket on her desk long after the taps from the captain's shiny shoes clacking on the tile floor had faded from her hearing.

National Security Agency, Fort Meade, Maryland

Pam Shaffer sat in the darkness of the NSOC—the National Security Operations Center of the National Security Agency—evaluating the information that was streaming across her conjoined sixty-inch computer display. Pam had worked for the NSA for fifteen years, since the end of the Cold War. Recruited directly from Stanford's mathematics program as a graduate student, she was put to work breaking codes and ciphers collected from America's enemies.

Pam had risen quickly through the cryptanalytic department ranks and was considered a double threat by her management—her grounding in mathematics allowed her to pick up language and linguistics very easily. She was fluent in German, Hebrew, French, Russian, and Chinese, and had recently mastered Arabic. She had also done work in ancient languages, and she counted many exotic, long-dead languages among her fluencies. She had a fondness for Egyptian hieroglyphs, and she had recently published some papers on Sumerian and archaic cuneiform alphabets that had received national attention.

Her eight-hour shift in the NSOC would end in a few minutes, and she had a date for dinner—a rare event in Pam's life. Pam was strikingly beautiful, slender with long blond hair and symmetrical facial features, but her job kept her from having a normal relationship with any man she dated. The NSA was so secret an agency that people who worked there referred to it as "No Such Agency." It was the most secret and most highly funded of all the spy organizations in the U.S. Intelligence Community.

NSA was a giant ear for the community—the eavesdropper on enemies and friends alike—and any electronic or analog transmission of information could be caught in the thick electronic web with which the NSA surrounded the planet. Within this most secret of all agencies, the NSOC was considered the inner sanctum of American secrets. NSOC's mission was to take raw intelligence collected from around the world that was deemed super-critical in nature and move it to points of the government that could use it immediately. Sometimes this information was mundane and watchful, like stopping drug shipments, and sometimes it was heroic—stopping terrorist attacks as large as or larger than September 11 before they became front-page news. Pam had personally been involved in stopping three large 9-11 type attacks, plots that never came to fruition because of her efforts and those of many others at the agency. It was hard to listen to the media worldwide describe the NSA as the American version of George Orwell's Big Brother, all the time knowing what good the NSA was doing. This was the world of Pam Shaffer, and she loved it.

She triaged her e-mail inbox while waiting for her shift to end, separating messages that pertained directly to her and required action from messages that were just informative. At the top of the list a message appeared with a red exclamation point, indicating high priority.

From: Admiral Nathan Turner, National Security Council
Miss Shaffer:
Your presence is requested for a high-priority meeting with the admiral at 1700 hours in the admiral's office, Operations Building A, Mahogany Row.
Due to the sensitive nature of this meeting, no other details can be described in this e-mail.
Admiral Nathan Turner
NSC/Group A
National Security Agency
Fort Meade, Maryland

Short, yet cryptic, thought Pam. She had met the admiral only twice before, and only on exceptionally delicate matters of national security. She picked up the gray phone, an outside, unencrypted line, and happily canceled her dinner date. Her replacement arrived early, and after a short debrief of what was occurring in NSOC, Pam jumped out of her seat to be at the admiral's office on time.

Pam walked briskly down the polished marble floor of the corridor connecting NSOC with the Operations Building, a massive black building that most people associated with the NSA as they drove down the busy Baltimore-Washington Parkway. Mahogany Row, as it was called, referred to the administration offices of the NSA, and the entire corridor was made of wood, paneled with paintings of current and previous directors of the super-secret agency, some of whom Pam had heard of and many of whom had served in relative obscurity. They were "Top Secret Famous," as people at the agency described it.

Pam informed the administrative assistant of her arrival, and to her surprise she was ushered into the admiral's office immediately. Two men were in the room, one behind the enormous wooden desk in the middle of the office, and she instantly recognized Admiral Nathan Turner.

The admiral rose to his feet, recognizing a woman's entry in an old-fashioned habit he still performed. "Miss Shaffer, thank you for coming so promptly—things can get a little hectic in NSOC, and I know how hard it can be to break away at the end of a shift."

"Thank you, Admiral. How can I be of assistance?" Pam asked. She was in the presence of one of the highest-ranked people at the NSA, and she wanted to know why.

"Miss Shaffer, I want you to meet Dr. Cameron Locke of Two Roads Corporation."

Pam extended her hand. "Dr. Locke, I've read many of your papers on dynamics."

"It's a pleasure to meet you, Miss Shaffer," replied Cameron, returning the handshake with a smile. "I'm very impressed that with all of your responsibilities you still make time to stay up-to-date with contemporary mathematics journals."

"Please, have a seat." Admiral Turner sat back down behind the imposing desk. "We have a special need for you, Miss Shaffer. Specifically, your ability to pick up dialects and languages so rapidly, as well as your cryptanalytic abilities, will be in demand on this mission."

"What mission, sir?" asked Pam.

Cameron adjusted his glasses and half-stood, half-sat against the admiral's desk. "Pam, we need you to be our linguist on perhaps the most audacious expedition in all of history."

"What sort of expedition?"

Cameron exchanged glances with the admiral. "Well, you can certainly tell she's an analyst…more questions than answers," Cameron said with a chuckle.

Admiral Turner looked at Pam with a serious expression. "Miss Shaffer, Dr. Locke works for a private research firm called Two Roads Corporation. In conjunction with the U.S. government, TRC has discovered how to successfully transfer people and items from the present to the past and vice versa."

The admiral studied Pam's face for any reaction, but it was devoid of any expression. She remained quiet for a moment before she asked, with an even, almost monotonous tone, "You're telling me that a non-government entity can travel to any point in history on demand?"

Cameron laughed at her button-down, national-security-first reaction.

"We're sending an expedition back in time to the year 2300 BC, and we want you on that team, Pam," Cameron said.

Pam's jaw dropped open—her surprise was obvious as unbridled excitement replaced her guarded and carefully concealed reactions. "What happened in 2300?" she asked.

"The Flood," Cameron replied.

"You mean *the* Flood—Noah's Flood? I'm sorry for my skepticism," Pam said, struggling to regain her professional composure. "I'm sure you have good evidence for believing that the Flood actually happened."

The admiral handed her an airline ticket. "Miss Shaffer, I'm not asking you to believe this straight out—there is a place for skepticism, and your opinion is very valuable to me. Your flight leaves at 2200 hours from BWI—just enough time for you to go home and pack."

Shaking both men's hands, Pam turned and hustled down the corridor toward the entrance.

The admiral faced Cameron and said, "Well, those were the easy ones—now for the last member."

Supai Canyon, Grand Canyon, Arizona

Dr. James Spruce swung his hammer into the sunset colors of the canyon wall while suspended three hundred feet from the top of the canyon. This was his last day at Supai Canyon, an offshoot of the Grand Canyon Gorge, and he was determined to make every minute count.

Spruce was a professor of geology and paleontology at the University of California at Berkeley. He was known for having a short temper and zero patience with people who did not agree with him. Still, he was considered one of the top minds in his field of study—a fact he relished.

Spruce was known to lash out verbally at youngsters new to the world of geology and paleontology, criticizing their upbringing and beliefs. He especially enjoyed mocking young Christians who happened to blunder into his class. His thoughts on religion were quite simple: religion was based on faith and mythology, while science was based on fact. In his lifetime, he was convinced, science would wipe away the need for religion and the search for the spiritual. In Dr. Spruce's world there was no place for both science and religion. They were like matter and antimatter—together they tended to annihilate one another.

Spruce reached into the tool bag hanging on his belt and felt around to retrieve a wire brush. Slowly and carefully, he brushed the sepia-toned limestone and aggregate that he had just exposed with his rock hammer. Spruce pushed back on the rock under his feet and moved slowly around the sheer cliff face, evaluating the rocks and strata. He rubbed his hand across his once-red beard, now almost completely white, as he contemplated where to continue his research.

The air was still, and he could hear the low roar of Mooney Falls and an occasional shriek from the ravens circling high in the azure sky.

Above Spruce's head, a miniature waterfall of red and orange sand coursed down the canyon wall, followed by a thousand-pound test line braided with purple and green strands of Kevlar. The unmistakable sound of a person rappelling ripped through the air, and Spruce looked up to find another climber descending rapidly to his position.

Neil Stevens had not rappelled down a canyon wall in five years, but he still remembered the basics. Braking the rope that was coursing through the bracket on his harness, he stopped exactly even with Spruce.

"Dr. Spruce, I presume," he said with a smile.

"Who in the world are you?" asked a startled Spruce.

"My name is Neil Stevens." With that he extended his glove for a handshake three hundred feet above the ground.

The name connected in Spruce's mind. He had read a dozen articles about Stevens, his fortune, and some of the crazy ventures he was now pouring his money into.

"Oh, yeah, OK. Neil Stevens—rich, eccentric guy. I've read about you. I'm Jim Spruce." He took Neil's hand and gave it a firm shake.

Neil looked behind him at the multicolored, layered sandstone that seemed to levitate out of the canyon below them.

"Magnificent, isn't it?" Spruce said, pointing at the layered wall across from them. "It took that river down there about 100 million years to carve this gorge out. All of these colors got laid down as the river was cutting that portion of the canyon."

"That little river down there?" said Stevens with a smile and a laugh. "I don't think so."

Spruce scowled and continued his examination of the cliff wall, ignoring the pest on the rope next to him. "Your *professional* opinion?" he grunted.

"How would you like a chance to prove your ideas about how this canyon might have been formed?" Neil asked him.

Spruce stopped his work for a moment and raised both arms to his side. "What do you think I'm doing out here on the end of a rope, ordering a pizza?" Spruce asked.

Neil reached into his shirt pocket, pulled out a small manila envelope, and handed it across the short chasm between them.

"Inside that envelope is an airline ticket to the greatest geological discovery of all time."

With that, Stevens released the brake on his rope and continued his descent down the wall. Spruce watched him reach the bottom and walk to a large outcrop of rock. A helicopter flew in from the opposite side of the canyon, landed on the outcrop, and collected Neil. Within two minutes, the echoing sounds of helicopter blades in the air over the Grand Canyon had subsided.

6

Citation Flight

The white, aluminum skin of the sleek Cessna Citation 10 sliced through the warm air currents coursing over the western coast of Europe. The corporate jet's mirrored finish reflected the brilliant blue hues of the Atlantic Ocean as its powerful twin turbine engines accelerated to six hundred miles per hour on its climb to a 45,000-foot cruising altitude. A large Y-shaped corporate logo, just above the call number, graced the tail of the aircraft.

TRC's corporate jet was state-of-the-art and designed to be both comfortable and productive in its job of transporting the think tank employees around the world. Inside the fuselage, a combination of plush leather seats, sofas, and work surfaces made from burled walnut were arranged on the Berber high-traffic carpet.

The jet had refueled in Lisbon, having flown directly from an airport in Turkey, where the helicopter that extracted Cameron and Troy from the Ahora Gorge expedition had landed. With a 3,400-nautical-mile range, the aircraft could now head to Boston where it would refuel again before completing the final leg of the trip to Trona, California.

The fifteen-hour trip from Turkey to California was exhausting, but TRC's jet had a number of amenities to reduce the stress and pain that riding on a commercial airline would inflict on a traveler.

No question about it, thought Troy with a smile; *This is the way to travel.*

He stretched out on the blond leather sofa and looked at the various papers fanned out across the floor. Diagrams and specifications of equipment, backgrounds on the proposed expedition members, and large-format color LandSat maps tiled the Berber carpet.

A work table nearby held a massive, curved computer display that was ninety inches wide. Digital documents, e-mail messages, and an open mathematics program were all taking liberal space on the screen, and there was still room left over for a game of solitaire to fit comfortably. Cameron Locke sat in front of the display, studying a series of differential equations for another project at the TRC research labs.

"Hey, Cameron, can I ask you a personal question?" Troy said, sitting up from the leather sofa.

"Why not? We still have about nine hours of travel time left. We won't have any personal secrets left after this trip," replied Cameron with a wry grin.

"What are your feelings about this expedition?" asked Troy, tossing the photographs and papers he had been reading into a pile. "I guess what I mean is, this is a very different mission than going back to the *Titanic* for a weather report or to the Peloponnesian War for an ancient warship."

Cameron arched his back and stretched his arms, contemplating Troy's question for a moment before replying.

"I've known for quite a few months that most of what science and history take for granted is probably wrong. After the second expedition team died and we conducted our experiments to establish a timeline, as each payload was incinerated it was like an exclamation point on the end of what I've suspected for a long time—science is headed for a big 'crunch.'" Cameron made quote marks in the air with his fingers.

"What do you mean by crunch?" asked Troy.

"A few years back, I was at a scientific conference on string theory, during which an intellectual food fight almost broke out—each group declaring that it was on the side of truth. That had a huge impact on me. Truth and falsehood are supposed to be provable, or else things tend toward the world of faith and philosophy. For decades, scientists have looked at faith and science as separate worlds, but increasingly, science is becoming more and more faith-like," said Cameron.

"Why is that?" queried Troy.

"It's a lot of things, but in the case of string theory, it's all based on math and elegant equations that cannot be proven. No instruments can be built to check for the ten or eleven dimensions the theory says must exist, and the 'strings' themselves will take many years to even detect, if they do indeed exist. The equations are beautiful and seem to solve a lot of problems to help unify the standard model and the world of quantum mechanics. There's just one problem—it can't be proven empirically yet. Another issue is that string theory makes few if no predictions, even if they're wrong predictions."

"Why do people keep pouring resources into it if it cannot be proven or disproven?" asked Troy.

"Well, right now it's the only game in town," Cameron explained. "The problem is that science, and especially cosmology, has worked itself into a back alley that is increasingly looking like a dead end. When someone finally does make a breakthrough that takes the subject of cosmology in a different direction, it will wreck a lot of careers and departments that have been working on string theory since 1984."

"Is that a bad thing?" asked Troy.

"Nope, that's science. Science is punctuated by breakthroughs that take the scientific community in completely different directions. The same will be true here. While at TRC, I've seen a lot of things—worked on a lot of things—that have me revisiting my basic thoughts about belief and science and how they can be harmonious instead of always at odds with one another." Cameron paused.

"Working for Neil Stevens and being the Science Leader at TRC is probably seen as contradictory by your colleagues in academia," said Troy. "How do you balance it?"

"Are you kidding me?" asked Cameron with a chuckle. "If it wasn't for the fact that almost every year we publish papers that lead to huge break-throughs and valuable patents, the rest of the scientific world would completely ignore TRC. It's always a struggle. I have to be incredibly vigilant to approach the academic world with the right vocabulary and terminology that won't set off fire alarms."

Cameron tapped his fingers nervously on the wooden desk. It was as if he had mentally rehearsed this conversation a hundred times.

"After Neil Stevens' conversion to Christianity and his proclamation that science—for him—was about discovering *how* God did something and *why* it works the way it does, as opposed to striving to falsify the concept of God, I started to think about things in that regard."

Cameron put his hands to his side and stared back at the equations that seemed to beckon for his attention, lines of worry marking his face. "I have to be very careful about how I approach this subject. It's not just my career or TRC's reputation that's at risk. It's all the people who work there. Their careers and their reputations are also on the line. It's like nitroglycerin." Cameron slapped his hands together. "Too much motion and bam! It's all over. I love my job, but sometimes I wish I was like you, Troy."

"Like me? Why would you say something like that?"

"It's hard for me, you know?" Cameron stated with exasperation. "I mean, I'm the head of one of the most prestigious science labs in the country. If I start talking about God and creation, will I still be able to attract the best minds in cosmology and biology? They've been trained their entire academic careers to think about complexity and mechanism of action outside of a divine designer. Will even one of my published papers ever be taken seriously?"

"I can see your point," said Troy empathetically.

Cameron continued, "Even if I embrace the same conversion, will I have to live two lives—one as a Christian and one as a well-known physicist? It would be career suicide for me."

The conversation apparently done, Cameron swiveled his chair to refocus his attention on the differential equations arranged on the impressive computer display. Equations that were cryptic to 99 percent of the human population brought Cameron solace and distracted him from his real concern: how to unify the concepts of God and modern science.

Troy gazed out of the thick cabin windows at the cloud cover thousands of feet below the plane and thought about Cameron's dilemma. A few minutes later, he fell asleep.

The vibration and mechanical whirring sounds of the landing gear jolted Troy from his slumber. A voice came over the audio system of the cabin. "Ten minutes until we land, Dr. Locke," said the pilot, lining up with the runway. A distant black rectangle punctuated with dashes of white paint appeared amid an immense open desert.

7

The Destination Debate

The team members had now been arriving over the course of five hours, and each of them was personally welcomed by Neil Stevens and escorted to the living quarters on the bottom floor of the complex. Fernanda Vegas had arrived first, followed by Pam Shaffer. James Spruce arrived just before dawn.

Cameron Locke and Troy Scott were still inbound on the TRC private jet. They were due to land at a local airstrip in a few minutes.

Neil was in the conference room early, going over his notes and reviewing maps and diagrams on the massive, multi-panel display that encircled the room. The plan was to convene at 9 A.M. It wasn't every day you asked a team of people to go back in time almost four thousand years, and Neil was mentally bracing himself for what promised to be a challenging morning.

A large LandSat map with differing hues of magenta and cyan loomed on the screen, and Neil Stevens studied the convergence of four different ancient rivers. He took a sip of coffee to help him wake up and found it needed a warm-up; he headed for the kitchenette near the exhibit room.

Fernanda Vegas had awakened early and taken the elevator to the visitor's lobby. As the doors of the elevator slid open, she found Neil Stevens walking across the marble floor to a small kitchen.

"Good morning, Fernanda," Neil said, extending his hand.

"Morning, Neil. This is quite a facility; I thought I could get a chance to look around a little before the meeting started."

"This is the only floor that's accessible without the proper credentials, but we'll get that resolved later this morning. Can I get you a cup of coffee?" asked Neil.

"That would be wonderful, thank you. Now what's this all about?" asked Fernanda, looking at the exhibits across the expanse.

"Tell you what…I'll get your coffee ready and bring it out to you. Why don't you go take a look at that boat over there?" Neil turned and walked into the kitchen.

Fernanda headed toward the trireme and read the information panel.

As Neil came out of the kitchen, he saw Fernanda inside the rope barrier, running her hands across the hull. She stopped at the bow and studied the painted eyes that looked out menacingly toward long-dead enemies.

"How in the world did you get this?" she asked in amazement.

"We'll go over that in a few minutes; I think the others are starting to arrive."

"I could spend six months just studying the construction of this warship," Vegas said, gazing at the ancient ship before her and running her hand across the smooth planking of its hull.

"You haven't seen anything yet," said Neil with a smile.

Just then, the elevator bell dinged and Cameron Locke and Troy Scott walked out, followed by Pam Shaffer, James Spruce, and Captain Richard Loren.

"Cameron, Troy, how was the flight?" asked Neil.

"Long and tiring, and I smell like an animal," said Cameron.

Neil gave Troy a bear hug. "Thank you for agreeing to come," he said to Troy. "Gang, there's coffee in the conference room and some bagels and pastries—please forgive the abbreviated breakfast; we have a lot of work ahead of us this morning."

He led the crowd to the conference room and adjusted the light levels. Everyone took a seat around the large, circular table.

The lights darkened, and Neil began the briefing.

"Ladies and gentleman, welcome to Two Roads Corporation. In the next few minutes you will learn things that very few people on the planet know. I must stress that everything you will be shown while here at Two

Roads is considered classified. Each of you was selected because of your expertise in a specific field of study."

By way of introduction, Stevens enumerated the names and positions of those seated around the table. "Fernanda Vegas, anthropology. Pam Shaffer, linguistics and language. James Spruce, geology and paleontology. Captain Rich Loren is a Navy SEAL and in charge of security and protection. Troy Scott and myself will be leading the expedition."

Neil leaned forward against the table. "In one week, this team will go back in time to the year 2300 BC." The attention of the team keyed up a notch.

Before anyone could ask the obvious question, Stevens continued the briefing. "Six months ago, TRC and the Department of Energy succeeded in manipulating time and space using something called a torsion field. This device allows us to manipulate a wormhole and position people and objects in any time period and at any place on earth. The objects that some of you saw in the exhibit area were brought through the wormhole." Stevens looked at Fernanda Vegas. She acknowledged the explanation of the massive boat in the other room with a nod.

"Ten expeditions have gone back through the machine to all parts of time—nine of which were successful. We have proof of these expeditions in the museum that you just walked by—the Peloponnesian War, the maiden voyage of the *Titanic*, Diamond Head on the morning of the attack on Pearl Harbor, the JFK assassination, Roswell in 1947, and others. Not everything has gone perfectly, though. We had one expedition that attempted to transfer to the year 100,000 BC, and everyone on that team was killed during the transfer process. We have since discovered that the timeline seems to end around seven thousand years ago."

"That's preposterous!" exclaimed James Spruce.

"That was exactly what we thought," interjected Cameron Locke. "But we've proven it many times over."

Stevens raised his hands to quell the debate before it erupted. "There will be time for debate later; for now, let's press forward. We selected 2300 BC because of the general agreement across many cultures and legends that a major cataclysm occurred at about that time. In addition, because the ancient history premise of millions of years seems not to apply anymore, we have used other sources for a reference as to where to specify our destination point."

"Like what, the Bible?" snorted Spruce.

"Precisely," said Stevens.

Jim Spruce banged his hands on the wooden table. "This is ridiculous! It's an insult to everything that science and history has chronicled in this century."

Stevens didn't flinch. He was confident and secure in his research and the work of the people in TRC.

Fernanda Vegas spoke up. "Jim, virtually every culture on the planet has some reference to the flood that is described in Genesis. Both the Koran and Torah refer to it, and while most anthropologists take issue with the idea of a universal flood, the idea of a localized flood in the plains of Mesopotamia is not debated."

Spruce folded his arms across his chest and sulked; clearly he was disturbed by the direction this conversation was headed.

"I'd like Troy Scott, our expedition leader, to talk a little bit about our selected destination point," said Stevens, taking a seat near Fernanda Vegas.

As Troy stood up, Spruce let out a snicker. "What's your degree in? Sunday school?"

"Business," replied the multimillionaire as he stepped up to the Land-Sat map spread across the high-resolution plasma panels. Troy was tense, but only Neil Stevens sensed it. A hundred million dollars could buy a lot of things, but patience with arrogant geologists was not one of them.

Troy pointed to an incredibly detailed map on the screen. "This is a collage of high-definition images and LIDAR taken in the last week over Baghdad, Iraq. You'll see that we have adjusted the imagery and removed modern cities and roads, and we've enhanced the rivers and deltas in the region. The Euphrates and Tigris split apart here, and there is evidence of some ancient rivers that used to cross the region vertically. According to legend and ancient sources, ancient civilizations were gathered between the Tigris, which was called the Hiddekel then, and the Euphrates River. Notice how each of these ancient rivers seems to originate at a head up here in modern Turkey, along with the Tigris and Euphrates, and empty here at what is now the Persian Gulf."

Troy stepped back to the table and picked up a leather-bound book that everyone recognized. "Now let me read you something from the Bible—Genesis 2:10–14: 'And a river went out of Eden to water the garden; and from thence it was parted, and became into four heads. The name of the first is Pison: that is it which compasseth the whole land of Havilah, where there is gold; and the gold of that land is good: there is bdellium and the onyx stone. And the name of the second river is Gihon: the same is it that compasseth the whole land of Ethiopia. And the name of the third river is Hiddekel: that is it which goeth toward the east of Assyria. And the fourth river is Euphrates.'"

Troy circled a point just a few miles south of the mouth of the Euphrates River. "Here's the destination region for the expedition," he said. A yellow annotation that looked like a highlighter followed his touch and left a circled area as he pulled his finger from the display.

"Now we need to decide on the specific point within that circle," he explained. "Our destination point needs to be isolated from any civilization. We can walk to our observation points. We'll want to stay clear of the delta area of these two rivers. There is bound to be civilization there."

"What tells you that? A magic eight ball?" snickered Spruce.

"Two things—first, most agriculture-based societies would need good irrigation, and the rivers would provide ample water and rich soil."

"You're assuming that everyone has a farm like Kansas did in the 1950s, and that these ancient people are not just berry-picking and foraging for survival," Spruce said.

"And the other reason," Scott continued, trying to ignore Spruce's verbal attack, "would be that people of this time period will likely have an aversion to this part of the region." Troy pointed at a confluence of the two major rivers on the map.

"And why is that?" asked Spruce, leaning back in his chair.

Scott pointed to the map, a little southeast of the destination point. "Because the Garden of Eden is probably here and is a guarded point."

"You must be joking!" exploded Spruce. "Why don't you just plan your expedition by reading comic books and rolling chicken bones across the table?" He looked at Neil Stevens with disgust.

Troy Scott gave Neil Stevens an exasperated look that communicated a clear message: *Help me!*

Stevens, deft in dealing with prima donnas, had anticipated Jim Spruce's reaction, and in a strange way, his heart went out to the man. Like Spruce, he had at one time accepted everything that the academic community claimed without a second thought. His mind spun with a dozen approaches of how to disarm the situation. He had to be careful not to insult Jim or make him look foolish, but he needed to open Spruce's mind to the possibility that everything he knew—everything he had been taught and had taught to others—might not be true.

"Jim, how old do you think the earth is?" Stevens asked.

"Most scientists agree that the earth is around 4.5 billion years old," Spruce said, folding his muscular arms across his chest.

"So, around one hundred thousand years ago, there would be a stable landmass in North America?" inquired Stevens, setting the trap.

Spruce spat out, "Absolutely! No question about it."

"Roll the video," said Stevens to Cameron Locke.

Cameron strolled up to the display panel and opened a file folder containing numerous videos. He moved his hand across the enlarged window until he found a video titled "Expedition2." He tapped on the icon representing the file, and a media player fired up.

Stevens spoke quickly as the video loaded into the media player floating on the plasma screen. "This is the second expedition we sent; the destination was the flatlands of Kansas—near modern-day Kansas City in 100,000 BC. This is Dr. John Jespers, professor of geology at CalTech. I think you knew him, Jim."

"Yes," replied Spruce. Jespers had disappeared in a classified expedition, and no one really knew what had happened to him.

The video had been taken from a stationary camera mounted above the Platform, facing out from the operations room.

The expedition team of six people was standing on a shiny blue glass platform. An operations person could be heard going through a checklist similar to those done before a space shuttle launch.

Among many other voices on the audio track, an operations person clearly said, "Open the Einstein-Rosen Bridge."

Suddenly, the Platform area was filled with light, and a greenish-blue vortex swirled around the top of the room, its mouth growing in radius by several feet. It swept down over the expedition team. The volume of the operations people increased as they stated that their readings and instruments seemed to be blank. The screen flashed with red light, and where six human beings had stood just moments before were now burning piles of ash.

The media player finished the video, and the room was dark for a moment before the lights came up.

"So what's that prove?" asked Spruce, standing up and pointing at the video. "The machine could have malfunctioned, or your equations could be wrong."

"Jim, in a few days you can discover for yourself what the truth is, but I'd like you to dial the sarcasm back a bit—if you're wrong, it might help you save face a little," Stevens said.

Spruce dropped into his leather seat and folded his arms in silence. A few members of the team shook their heads in disgust at Spruce's reaction. It was clear that some, at least, were willing to give the expedition a chance.

Fernanda Vegas tried to ease the conversation in a new direction. "Troy, what are your thoughts on where that garden might be located?"

Troy Scott smiled appreciatively and responded, "We hoped you could help us a little here—we have some descriptions we would love to get a comment on."

Vegas approached the digital map. "Well, you said the four rivers describe a position near Eden where the Tigris—the modern name for the Hiddekel—the Euphrates, the Pison, and the Gihon come together, right?"

"Correct," said Stevens and Scott in unison.

Jim looked over at Pam, who was seated next to him, and stage-whispered, "I love this Bible story—especially when they use a flannel-graph to tell it. By the way, what's the snack today? Graham crackers and punch?"

Pam rolled her eyes and moved her chair as far away from Jim as she could.

Fernanda continued. "OK, so the Tigris and Euphrates most likely remain in many ways how they looked back then—with a few exceptions.

We know that both Ur and Erido, some of the oldest, if not *the* oldest cities in the world, were positioned just a few miles south of the Euphrates, right here on the confluence of the Euphrates and the Persian Gulf."

Scott perused the map with a confused expression. "But the Persian Gulf is way over here," he said, pointing to a spot on the digital map.

Jim Spruce jumped in and surprised everyone with an attempt to be civil. "But back then there was likely more water on the planet—not deeper water, just more shallow water—and perhaps not as much polar ice. So the Persian Gulf would have been closer to the mouth of both the Tigris and Euphrates rivers, here."

"In fact, ancient Sumerian texts refer to Ur as a seaport, supporting Jim's point," Fernanda said. She turned to the map once more.

"Now, let's tackle this other river, the Gihon. The Bible's 'land of Ethiopia' may not refer to the modern country of Ethiopia; it may refer to the Kashshites, who were said to occupy the eastern plains of Mesopotamia, here. Today we refer to this as western Iran."

Pam saw an opportunity to contribute to the conversation. "I don't know if this helps, but the word 'compasseth' in Hebrew can mean to revolve or wind around."

Troy stepped over to the display and placed his hands about three inches apart on the surface of the screen, then moved his hands apart. The digital map immediately zoomed out and allowed more territory to be seen on the massive display.

"Here," said Fernanda, tapping on the digital display with her index finger, "is a river called the Karun, located in Iran. The terrain of the Zagros Mountains makes the river zig and zag all over the place—just as Pam described. Its course is more than 500 miles long, but if you measure it in a straight line, it's only 175 miles. That certainly passes the test for revolving and winding around!"

"I would have to agree with that assessment," said Troy, clearly impressed with Fernanda's take-no-prisoners logic and reasoning prowess.

"OK, so that's three rivers. The last one is called Pison," Fernanda said, barely able to contain her excitement. "Now the verses say that the Pison River 'compasseth,' or surrounds, the land of Havilah, and that there is gold in that country."

Fernanda grabbed a bottle of water from a nearby table and took a sip, then stood back from the digital map, studying it intently. "Well, Arabia is definitely Havilah; we have evidence of that from many different ancient texts. But modern-day Saudi Arabia has no river that runs from the western mountains of Arabia to the head of the Persian Gulf."

Neil smiled. He admired Fernanda's knowledge of the region and her ability to knit a team of arrogant experts together. Her reputation had preceded her, putting her high on the short list for the expedition, but seeing her up close and personal, he realized that she truly was something special.

Jim again jumped in to help complete the puzzle. "There have been reports that an ancient river ran parallel to the Wadi al-Batin here, which is basically a dry riverbed."

Fernanda smiled at him. "Thanks, Jim—great work!"

He continued on as if he didn't need an anthropologist's permission to talk about his specialty. "The Wadi al-Batin disappears under these sand dunes here, but comes back up over here, where the satellite image shows some fossilized river channels, and it seems to run directly to Mahd adh Dhahab." Jim traced the path with his finger on the digital monitor. "You might know it better as King Solomon's Mines."

"It's said that King Solomon's Mines generated at least thirty tons of gold, and there's plenty of evidence that it was being mined way before Solomon showed up," Fernanda added. "Also, bdellium is gum resin from balsam plants. The most likely place for balsam to have grown in that area of the world at that time is southern Arabia. Perhaps the Pison River was used for transporting and trading that gum resin."

Pam jumped in. "You know, there's a curious word that's used in the verse. From the moment I heard you read it, I've been thinking about the translations around the phrase 'went out.'"

"What do you mean?" asked Fernanda.

"Well, 'went out' means that the river starts in Eden, and then outside the Garden it forms into its various branches—the rivers we've been talking about for the last hour. 'Went out' may not be speaking so much of direction as describing how it merges together. So I'm thinking that the rivers may actually all merge inside the Garden—a spring, directly within the vicinity of the Garden itself. The Garden has a spring that forms the head of the rivers, which split up and head out of the area. Sometimes 'X' really does mark the spot."

"It's going to be hard to figure that one out until we get there," Neil said.

"You're probably right, Neil. Sorry for the diversion," said Pam.

"Not at all, Pam. *All* of this is important."

Fernanda squinted at the map. "OK, so the rivers have been located, and we assume that the Persian Gulf extended up here near Ur, so my best guess is that the Garden would be here, north of modern-day Basra."

"We know that civilizations crop up between the Garden and Ur— there are numerous mounds all through the region that used to be cities and settlements. The hard part is guessing whether they were there before or after the, um, the event," Jim added.

Troy smiled mischievously and worked desperately to keep from laughing out loud. "And by 'event,' would you mean the Flood?"

Everyone in the room looked at Jim and smiled.

Jim waved his hand dismissively and grunted something in response, then went to refill his coffee cup.

Tying Up Loose Ends

(T) he team woke up excited about the day's activities. Some last-minute debates remained to be settled, and some final decisions to be fed back into the computer model to complete the destination point. The night before the expedition consisted of a nice steak dinner and some lively banter between Jim Spruce and virtually everyone else on the team. Everyone could feel it—the team was beginning to bond.

Once again Neil Stevens made it to the conference room early, and he fondly remembered the great discussions that had occurred the previous day. He was proud of the way the team had put aside professional and ideological rivalry and worked together to determine the approximate location of the Garden of Eden. The decisions that loomed before them this day revolved around what they could expect when they transferred back to the Antediluvian Age.

Stevens heard voices in the hallway and watched as the entire team walked in, laughing and joking with each other. He knew he had picked a great team, and it gave him supreme confidence in what they would achieve on the expedition.

As the team of tired but excited scientists and adventurers sat around the table in leather seats nursing their morning coffees, Neil displayed the map from the previous day, now highlighted with a translucent green area labeled "Garden of Eden" just north of the Persian Gulf.

Cameron Locke, seated at the end of the table, spoke. "The computers were chewing on the timeline last night, and the best estimate, based on the biblical genealogy and a collection of ancient texts, is that we should transfer into the timeline at 2348 BC. That should be before the Flood. Construction on the Ark will certainly be underway, and may even be complete."

A stylized timeline filled the display, with the destination point marked with a glowing red triangle.

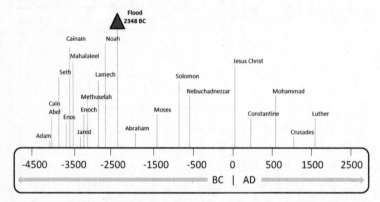

Neil took over. "Before we decide on the actual physical spot for transfer, let's talk a little about what we can expect from the environment and the civilization there. Oh, and one more thing," said Neil, looking at the men around the room. "Guys, stop shaving, now. It's very doubtful that the people of this time will have seen a clean-shaven man who's not some sort of leader or king."

"Done," said Jim Spruce, rubbing his hands across his ten-year-old white beard.

"Fernanda, I think your area of expertise will help us the most here, but speculation from everyone is obviously invited," said Neil.

Fernanda responded, "Well, in looking at the timeline, we have almost no surviving text or history to help us—the Sumerian civilization is still hundreds of years away. In fact, most academics consider Noah and the Ark a myth. So we really are speculating here. If you look at the timeline, though, you can see that almost two thousand years have elapsed between the point of creation and the Flood." Fernanda blushed a bit as she glanced at James Spruce. The wholesale embracing of the creation myth was dangerous territory for a young rising star at Cornell. "I was just quickly reading the first few chapters of Genesis last night. There are references to agriculture, cattle and husbandry, music in the form of harps and organs, and even limited metallurgy, with brass and iron mentioned explicitly."

Jim Spruce spoke up, his voice reluctant. "If you're right about the Ark, the technology of the period must have been pretty good, perhaps even astounding." Everyone in the room raised their eyebrows and looked at him, momentarily silent.

Fernanda breathed an internal sigh of relief. Jim had broken the mental logjam that prohibited a passionate discussion of the possibility that this Antediluvian world had indeed existed.

"Well, at least it would have been better than people typically consider for the time of Noah," Jim continued. "I mean, an old geezer with three sons builds a boat that's about the size of a modern nuclear submarine out of wood. That indicates design, measurement, and basic manufacturing. They had to have some consistency in producing something like nails or brackets to hold the hull of the boat together."

"That's a great point," said Pam. "Think about this—how much has technology changed just in the last one hundred years? And we're talking about nearly twenty of those time periods stacked up—after creation, I mean."

Fernanda tried to corral the conversation. "OK, so we have agriculture and cities and seaports and smelting and music, which indicates some basic mathematics."

"Cities?" asked Captain Loren. "How many people do you think live in these cities?"

Fernanda grabbed a Bible from a stack of reference books lying nearby. "This will blow all of your minds; I know it blew mine," she said. "Most of the people alive at this time are living to be about nine hundred years old." Jim spilled coffee on himself, but the others ignored him as they focused their attention on Fernanda's briefing.

Fernanda laid the Bible open with Genesis 4-6 cascading across its crisp pages. "That's according to the Bible," she said.

Cameron Locke jumped into the conversation. "There's a mathematical formula that can be used to simulate a biological population, so let's run some numbers." He fired up a copy of Mathematica, a computer program that did for numbers what word processors did for words, and clicked on the formula.

"Let's see. To crunch the numbers for a population total for two thousand years, we'll need a couple of things—the length of a typical generation and the number of kids per family."

The hard drive of the laptop whirred, and within a few seconds a graph appeared on Cameron's screen.

"Whoa!" Cameron hurriedly connected his laptop to a loose video cable and sent the results of the program's run to the huge projector powering the plasma panels, causing the graph to wrap itself around the walls of the room. A graph with exponential notation on its y-axis and generations on its x-axis appeared, with projection lines representing predicted population totals at each generation.

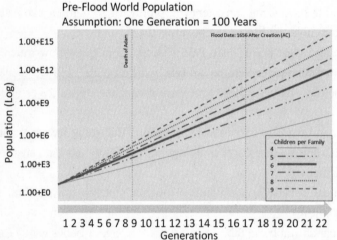

Pre-Flood World Population
Assumption: One Generation = 100 Years

"If we say that one generation lasts a hundred years, as some of the verses in Genesis indicate, and that people had four to nine kids in the eight hundred to nine hundred years that they lived, then we're dealing with a population of billions of people in a very short time. Certainly the total could be three billion, and possibly as high as nine billion—far larger than the population of today."

Jim stood and paced in the back of the room, making the others nervous. "Well, there may have been a lot of people, but not all of them lived super-long lives. Just imagine what the flu or the common cold did to those populations. I mean, we carry around all kinds of diseases in our bodies, and we've developed antibodies and resistance to many things that probably killed millions of these people regularly. Disease would have been like a nuclear bomb to these populations."

Cameron agreed. "You're probably right, Jim. This means we must be very careful with our contact with these ancient people. The Conquistadors almost wiped out South America because the natives there had no antibodies to combat the virulent diseases that the Spanish brought with them from Europe."

"So," Fernanda cut in, "I think the major point to take away here is that we won't be seeing cavemen. We'll be seeing millions and millions of people living in cities with iron implements and agriculture."

"Sounds like Pittsburgh!" said Jim. The entire room exploded in laughter.

"Imagine the way they could transfer knowledge," said Pam. "We archive our knowledge on the Internet and in books, but for hundreds of years these people could ask the person who originated the thoughts and developed them. Imagine having a question about calculus and being able to ask Sir Isaac Newton about it—or asking Abraham Lincoln what Gettysburg looked like when he gave his famous speech."

Fernanda agreed. "The amount of institutionalized knowledge would be astounding, and they would need to pass this down to each generation. So when Noah and his family got on that Ark and the rest of the population died in the Flood, we really lost almost every bit of knowledge that had accumulated to that point in time. It's really a shame that Noah and his sons had to spend 120 years building a boat—they probably didn't have much time to talk to the remarkable people around them."

Troy Scott sat up a bit straighter in his chair. "I think we might be forgetting one big thing."

"What's that?" asked Pam.

"Violence. The Bible speaks of tremendous violence occurring on the earth at that time. If you think about it, we have at least two different factions in play here—generations of people descended from Cain, who took up settlements east of Eden, and generations who came from Seth, of which Noah is one. While these people were advanced and probably very knowledgeable, they were destroyed by God for a reason."

"Hey, we live in a violent world now—you could be killed in any major American city just by looking at someone wrong," Spruce said dismissively.

Troy ignored Jim's comment. "We can assume that these cities are full of murderers, bandits, and worse. So what are we planning to do about protection for ourselves?"

"Well, the basic rule will be trying not to make contact with anyone in this time period. But that's probably easier said than done," said Stevens.

"And failing that?" asked Scott.

"Captain Rich Loren is a former SEAL, and we'll have two other Special Operations men with us on the expedition—specifically called upon to provide security for the team," Stevens replied. "So now the conversation should turn to location of the transfer."

Troy Scott had been thinking about this question for quite a while. "I'd like to make a suggestion, and we can refine it after that."

"Go ahead, Troy," Neil said.

"I recommend that we transfer to a point about forty miles northeast of Ur, closer to the Garden and near the southern side of the Tigris. It's close enough to all the points we need to access, and we could get to those points in a few days if necessary. My guess is that the Ark is near Ur—possibly near the harbor or seaport—and not east of Eden, where Cain's descendants will be."

Fernanda liked the choice. "All the archaeological mounds, with the exception of Amara, are south of that point and seem to build up through the Euphrates—it's as if the people avoided the area around the Garden."

"Maybe it'll be as easy as showing up and saying, 'Dude, where's the boat?'" laughed Cameron.

"I doubt if the word 'dude' was in use in any vocabulary at that time in history," Pam said dryly.

"Can someone get me some more coffee, and Pam a sense of humor?" asked Jim Spruce.

"From a security perspective, it would be optimal if we could transfer in at night. It would give us a few hours to get some reconnaissance done before morning light," said Captain Loren.

Jim pointed at Captain Loren and said, "I like his idea."

Neil clapped his hands together, startling Pam, and said, "I think we've done enough for today. I want you each to enjoy the evening and relax a little bit. It's likely to be the last normal sleep we will experience for a few days. But before we go down to the living quarters, I have a medical assistant who is going to embed a tracking device into each team member's arm. It won't hurt—much—but if we get separated, the radio beacon it emits can be triangulated by some tracking equipment that we're bringing along. Hopefully we won't need it, but we should take every precaution."

"Can it be removed once we get back?" asked Pam, rubbing her forearm as if the miniature device had already been implanted.

"Absolutely," replied Neil.

The team rolled up their sleeves, and each took a turn with the medical assistant implanting the tracking device. They spent the last few hours relaxing and enjoying each other's company. Everyone had bonded quite well, and Neil was proud of how each person, especially Jim Spruce, had jettisoned pride and arrogance to become part of a unified group, ready to embark on an expedition of unknown outcome.

9

The Encrypted Message

nside a shadowy maintenance corridor, water pipes and cable conduits wound around one another, crawling along the wall like enormous boa constrictors. A continuous drip of water droplets could be heard in the background against the humming of the halogen lights.

The door to the corridor opened suddenly and closed just as fast. The man who had entered kept his hand on the door handle and matched his muscle strength to that of the door's pneumatic arm, guaranteeing a quiet closure. Sweating, he wiped his brow and pulled a small device from his lab coat. His hands were shaking as he nervously typed a message on his BlackBerry.

TRANSFER SET FOR 4A
PREPARE FOR ENTRY AROUND 6A

He pressed a few buttons on the miniature keyboard, and the message encrypted itself into an unreadable scramble of characters.

He pressed "Send," firing the message wirelessly into the electronic ether, and put the small device back into his pocket. He closed his eyes tightly, willing his heart rate down—breathing deeply—deliberately. He reopened the steel door, glancing up and down the corridor.

The hall was empty.

He jogged down the hall and into the bustle of the operations center to prepare for the big day.

10

Zero Hour

T he team had dressed in dark camouflage garb and was busy getting the cargo bins, filled with scientific instruments and other survival gear, up onto the Platform area. Each team member had written a final will and letters to loved ones, just in case the expedition ran into problems. Every contingency had been considered, but based on the destination, which very well could have been Mars, such preparation seemed like a prudent idea.

Cameron was talking with Neil in hushed tones in a corner of the room. The physicist would remain behind, while Neil would help Troy Scott lead the expedition. Fernanda Vegas, Pam Shaffer, and Jim Spruce talked among themselves and went over a map of the region.

Captain Rich Loren finished a last-minute briefing for the two Special Operations soldiers who had flown in the day before on a Blackhawk helicopter. Captain Loren and the soldiers approached the team.

"Team, I'd like you to meet Commander Christopher Belkins and Lieutenant Roger Calmont." Each team member smiled, nodded, and expressed thanks for their service, and some shook hands with their new colleagues. "These two men have seen action in the war on terror and have run black operations missions that will remain classified for the rest of our lives. They will help provide protection, as well as consulting on the expedition from a security perspective," Loren said.

Neil Stevens stood on the Platform and looked down at the team. Each member showed nervous tics, and the excitement in the room was palpable—like the entire team was wound up like a mighty spring, ready to explode.

"Ladies and gentlemen, I thank you all for pulling together as a team. I feel that we are fully prepared and are passionate to see this ancient civilization, of which there is no secular record. Should this expedition be declassified in the future, each of you will be remembered and revered just as the explorers of the past are now. Each of you represents a new generation of explorer—the Christopher Columbus and Lewis and Clark of the 21st century. Godspeed, team."

"Hopefully we've gotten the directions right better than Columbus did on his first voyage," Spruce said.

Neil Stevens yelled over to the operations room, "Cameron, let's light this candle."

Stevens took his place on the Platform, and each team member climbed up the steel steps from the concrete floor and assumed his or her position on the shining blue glass Platform. A number of camouflaged cargo bins, about six feet across and three feet wide, were stacked in the center of the team's formation. The two Special Operations soldiers wore night-vision goggles on their heads and carried automatic weapons fitted with silencers. Captain Loren stood at the back of the team, facing the rear.

Loren adjusted his night-vision goggles and said, "Remember, gang, we're going to be arriving around four A.M. We should have about an hour before the sun begins to rise, but be alert for any early birds."

In the operations center, everything was a beehive of activity. Large plasma screens displayed the map of Mesopotamia and the landing zone marked with a red rectangle. Various screens displayed numeric and graphic representations of energy levels and latency readings on the hard-drive farm.

Cameron spoke into his microphone: "Initializing transport."

Red and orange strobe lights began to revolve and illuminate the Platform bay.

Fernanda felt her heart rate increase.

Above the team, the vortex vent began to hum.

"Destination point is locked; waiting for elevation sample," said an engineer.

"Bring the power to 25 percent," said Cameron.

The whine of the turbines in the power plant increased. Needles on the power meters in the operations center began to move to the right of their measurement bands.

"Power is approaching 25 percent. All systems reading normal," called out an engineer.

Cameron looked at the monitor in front of him, adjusting a few exotic parameters on the wormhole calculations to steady the transfer as much as possible.

"Bring the power up to 80 percent slowly."

The entire Platform bay was now whining with the sound of the generated power coursing through the vortex ten feet above the team.

"Power the Faraday cage," Cameron said.

"The cage has integrity!" called out an engineer.

"Open the bridge," Cameron commanded.

A blue, cloud-like formation burst from the vortex and began rotating and undulating above the team. Yellow and orange spark tracers shot out of the center of the portal and swirled down among the team members until they seemed to lose gravitation and be caught up into the inverted, swirling tornado of blue-green energy.

Pam's fear and excitement were so high that she was confused about which was the greater feeling. She closed her eyes and braced herself for transport.

A red digital clock on the wall above the operations center window counted down.

10…

"Alicia, go head and take the power to 100 percent," Cameron shouted.

Alicia King nodded and began orchestrating the work of bringing the turbines to full power and collecting all the essential telemetry from the Platform.

9...

Alicia typed rapidly on her workstation. A swirling simulation danced on her monitor—a near-perfect mathematical model of the energy phenomenon now revolving above the team on the Platform. "Dr. Locke, we have acquisition of the target point. Elevation data is now available."

8...

"Lock the elevation data into the formula," said Cameron.

7...

"Prepare the bridge for transfer!" Cameron yelled above the scream of the turbines.

6...

Jim Spruce started to feel a strange sensation in his inner ear, and small star-like bright spots began to dance in front of his eyes. A gray tunnel formed, and his peripheral vision began to lose its acuity. Leaning against a cargo bin, he wobbled on his feet, struggling to keep his balance. Jim looked at his other teammates. Fernanda, Pam, Neil, even the SEALs were having the same symptoms. He closed his eyes and tried to overcome his feeling of nausea.

5...

"Last check on measurements—approaching point of no return," cried Cameron.

The engineer overseeing the overall performance of the transfer responded. "Good to go—green across the board!"

3...

"Engage bridge!" came the final order from Cameron.

A storm of light coursed through the Platform bay, and for a moment time appeared to stand still, and the noise of the swirling energy seemed to stop.

2...

Everything felt as if it were happening in slow motion.

1...

The raging storm of light and sound vibrated uncontrollably as it swirled violently down over the stacked cargo containers and illuminated the human explorers. The light seemed to bend as it passed between the team members. As the swirling mass of energy hit the Platform floor, a burst of white light fired from the center of the bay, and the energy mass completely disappeared. The sounds of the roar reverberated in the bay for a moment, and then came total silence.

"Transfer complete," said Alicia, out of breath.

11

The Grove

The team was caught in a mighty burst of white light, and their knees buckled. The next moment they were all lying on soft, wet ground that felt like grass. The SEALs and Captain Loren flipped their night-vision goggles down and surveyed the ground around them. The grainy green images revealed some small animals, but nothing human. The odor of rich loam and fragrant tropical flowers overpowered the team members' sense of smell. Hundreds of yards ahead, the jagged black shapes of palm leaves and a canopy of trees seemed to block out the endless expanse of stars, slightly obscured in a veil of mist.

"Clear left. Clear right," said the two SEALs in the front of the group.

"Clear on our six," Loren said quietly.

Jim Spruce opened the first cargo box noiselessly and pulled out a tripod with a black box mounted on top. He turned on the sensor and adjusted the mast atop the tripod so that it was about six feet tall. A laser, imperceptible to the human eye, scanned the terrain in a 360-degree survey. Jim looked at the readout on a small display that bathed his hard features in LCD light.

"Good," he said, "no major edifices within a mile of us. It looks like we're in the middle of a field with a small group of hills about two hundred yards west of us. There's a grove of trees directly south—maybe three hundred yards."

As Jim folded the legs of the tripod and stowed the laser, he let out a loud "Whoa!"

"What is it?" asked Neil. Jim was staring up at space, the moon fixed in his gaze.

"The moon is so different! It's so clean-looking. In our time it's pock-marked with craters."

Neil looked up and examined the silver, luminous orb. Indeed, the moon lacked the familiar distinct craters and graying—it was like a giant, flawless mirror reflecting the sunlight back to the earth.

"Let's get these cargo bins out of the field and head for that grove," Neil Stevens said, looking at Captain Loren for approval.

Loren nodded.

"Lieutenant Calmont?"

"Yes, sir?"

"Take the lead and get out ahead of us about one hundred yards—check out that grove."

"I'm on it!" The SEAL slowly moved out ahead of the team and disappeared into the dark, ancient landscape around him.

Captain Loren and Jim Spruce picked up one of the cargo bins and began walking toward the grove. Pam and Fernanda swung their heavy packs over their shoulders and followed Loren and Spruce through the wet, knee-high vegetation. Troy Scott and Commander Belkins carried away the final cargo bin.

The air was thick and hot—much more so than Troy Scott had assumed it would be. The atmosphere felt like Amazon territory.

Troy looked at the other teammates, who were beginning to shed their outer garments. The humidity had made their clothes instantly cling to their skin.

Pam pulled her black sweatshirt off and stuffed it into her backpack. "Man, it's hot here! I feel like I'm walking in a plastic trash bag."

"Yeah, but it's a *dry* heat," replied Troy with a smirk. The heat was anything but dry.

Fernanda nodded. She had been to the area around the Euphrates for three summers in a row. It had always been arid. The climate here was like a rain forest—*Very strange*, she thought.

Lieutenant Calmont moved stealthily forward, always alert and constantly checking left and right across the meadow. As he passed into the grove, the ankle-length grass became thicker and higher, with broad-leafed plants replacing the thin slivers of grass that carpeted the meadow. He crouched down in the thick undergrowth and listened quietly. Nothing— this would be a safe place to set up camp.

Lieutenant Calmont spoke quietly into his microphone.

"KEYHOLE, this is SPEAR, over."

"This is KEYHOLE; what is your location? Over," Commander Belkins answered back.

"I've reached the grove; no sign of any inhabitants. Over."

"Good work, SPEAR; we are two hundred yards behind you. Meet you at the center of the grove," the commander radioed.

Calmont pressed the microphone button and replied, "I'll secure the perimeter."

The team reached the perimeter of the grove. Banana trees and palms populated its outskirts. As the team made their way forward, the lush vegetation closed behind them, obscuring the path to the interior of the forest.

The grove was about five hundred feet long and three hundred feet wide. Because it would offer shelter from the sun and conceal the cargo bins, it was a perfect place to hide the team's equipment—just the location from which the group could plan its next steps for the expedition.

Commander Belkins pulled out a machete and cleared a disc-shaped space in the center of the grove, about thirty feet across. The encircling plants lucky enough to escape Belkins' blade were tall enough to conceal the team's cargo.

"This seems ideal," Stevens said, surveying the area.

Commander Belkins addressed Calmont. "Lieutenant, let's get some proximity sensors up; I want to have plenty of warning if we run into any 'fun' here."

The lieutenant nodded and headed for the cargo bins.

Troy Scott gazed at the sky. Pink and orange streaks had begun to tint the hazy atmosphere, and the black canvas of night was giving way to the violet hues that preceded sunrise.

"The sun will be up within the hour," Troy announced.

"Let's get some readings of the atmosphere," Spruce suggested.

While Jim wrestled with the instruments in one of the cargo bins, the two SEALs worked on building a network of wireless sensors that would inform the group of anyone passing nearby. Each sensor was cube-shaped, two inches per side, and had Velcro straps for mounting the device to any conceivable surface.

Jim pulled out a gray instrument pack and powered it up. The instrument paused during boot up, and a message appeared across the screen:

BOOT UP IN PROGRESS
SYSTEM INITIATING
PLEASE AUTHENTICATE YOURSELF TO THE INSTRUMENT

Spruce pressed his thumb into the hooded thumbprint reader attached to the side of the instrument pack.

AUTHENTICATION SUCCESSFUL

The display on the screen cleared, and a number of readouts appeared. The instrument had a long, plastic tube about one inch wide protruding from the top. Jim pressed a button on the front of the box, and a sucking sound like that made by a large syringe plunger could be heard. Within moments, a table of percentages appeared, listing the elements detected in the atmosphere around them.

Element	Current Sample	Normal
Nitrogen	70.0%	77.0%
Oxygen	22.9%	21.0%
Water Vapor	3.8%	0.5%
Argon	1.0%	1.0%
Carbon Dioxide	2.1%	0.3%
Other	0.2%	0.2%

"Hmm," said Spruce, "that's pretty interesting."

"What?" said Troy, struggling with a cargo bin.

"There's quite a bit more oxygen here than in our time period, and the water vapor percentage is way up, but the nitrogen level is down."

Troy, still wrestling with the cargo, nodded in agreement with Spruce's water vapor assessment. Everyone on the team was struggling to adjust to the rain forest-like humidity.

"Barometric pressure is way, way up, too. It's like a hyperbaric chamber," Spruce said.

"Well, the increase in oxygen makes some sense. Look at all this vegetation pumping it up," said Fernanda.

"This oxygen increase is probably a contributing factor to the human longevity that Fernanda was describing back at TRC. Here, our blood is probably highly oxygenated, meaning we can do more, lift more, and have better stamina," said Jim.

The sky was becoming a deeper pink and orange with the imminent sunrise. Pam had moved to the edge of the grove to watch the sun peek over the horizon. As the beams of sunlight lit up the ancient landscape, Pam let out a gasp—"Guyyys!" she called out. The others stopped what they were working on and hurried to the edge of the grove.

As the team members reached the edge of the dense vegetation, they found themselves peering out over a plain that sloped downhill and ended in an inlet, and the reason for Pam's gasp became apparent.

Nestled along the side of the inlet, and reflected in the water, was a herd of dinosaurs!

They were blue-gray and numbered about thirty. The tops of their heads had a curved shape—a prominent bony structure extended from the backs of their heads. The dinosaurs were enormous and looked too heavy to be bipedal. Nevertheless, they rose on their hind feet and snapped low-hanging branches from trees overhanging the inlet.

"Parasaurolophus!" said Jim Spruce, getting a closer look at the magnificent beasts through a pair of binoculars.

The dinosaurs began to bellow into the morning air—like a host of trumpets. The noise disturbed other nearby animals, and the field suddenly came alive with birds, insects, and other smaller creatures. The dawn seemed to activate the entire plain between the stunned spectators and the herd of dinosaurs in the inlet. Thousands of winged insects danced in the sunlight, their translucent wings creating a glittering effect across the long blades of grass and flowers carpeting the field.

A deafening, horn-like honk pulled the team's attention from the inlet to the rain forest along their right side. A long, thick neck reached through the top of the canopy, trying to get a better look at the expedition members.

"That's a brachiosaur," Jim said numbly, turning to Troy and Neil, who were grinning from ear to ear. "How is this possible?" he wondered aloud. "They've been extinct for over 60 million years."

"I guess we weren't even close with our initial thoughts about the environment in this time period," Troy said.

"You have a gift for understatement," replied Jim.

12

Aaron

As the group admired the surroundings from the shady glade, Captain Loren began to open one of the cargo bins.

"Let's see what else is out there before it gets much lighter," he said.

A collection of lightweight aluminum, carbon-fiber, and electronic components began to take the recognizable shape of a miniature helicopter as Captain Loren assembled the parts, deftly fitting each component in its intended position. Finished, the craft measured about eight feet in length and was about four feet tall. It had a carbon-fiber cowl to protect its complex machinery and delicate electronics. A large camera that swiveled on a motorized carriage hung under the nose of the vehicle. Aluminum skids extended below the body of the craft, designed to keep it free of the long grass in the glade.

"What in the world is that?" asked Fernanda.

"Guys, meet AARON," Loren said like a proud parent.

Troy ran his hand across the smooth, carbon-fiber rotor blade. "What does 'AARON' stand for?"

"Autonomous Airborne Reconnaissance vehicle," the captain replied.

"Sorry we asked," said Spruce. "Can it make us some omelets?"

Loren ignored the wisecracking geologist. "AARON is outfitted with a high-resolution digital camcorder that's mounted on a gimbaled, rotating carriage, so we can point it at anything we want."

"Um, isn't that thing going to make a huge racket?" asked Pam.

"You'd think it would be noisy, but it isn't," said Loren, pressing a button on an electronics bay between the aluminum skids and revealing a sophisticated array of fuel cells and multicolored wires. "It flies on hydrogen fuel cells, so it's electric-powered and much quieter than something this size would be if it used an internal combustion engine."

"What's its maximum flight time?" asked Spruce.

"About six hours. We can refresh the batteries if needed."

Pam and Jim examined a stack of additional blue fuel cells stacked neatly in a nearby cargo bin while Loren fired up a laptop. The laptop booted quickly, and Loren moved a metal joystick that caused the camera to pitch its lens up and down, startling Pam.

"Let's go fly!" said Loren with a mischievous grin.

"What area do you want to check out first?" asked Loren as Troy helped him move the helicopter to a clearing between the grove and the inlet.

"Let's check out the northeast—toward where we think the Garden would be."

The group stepped back as Loren pressed a few keys on the laptop.

"Contact!"

The electric motor began to emit a high-pitched whine. It was quieter than Pam had thought it would be. The ten-foot-long black carbon-fiber blade began to rotate, slowly at first, and quickly turned into a translucent black whirl. The rotor wash made the vegetation nearby bend away from the downward air flow.

Loren clicked on the hover icon, and the helicopter rose into the air. Its tail boom rotated around the lateral axis of the helicopter indecisively until the tail rotor came up to speed and began to counteract the torque of the main rotor. The helicopter continued to rise into the air until it was about one hundred feet above the steamy canopy of foliage.

The dinosaurs beside the inlet saw the spinning contraption and bolted in the opposite direction, jostling and mashing against each other in their hurry to flee from this strange, shiny bird.

A map of the region appeared on Loren's laptop, and he clicked a waypoint onto it. The nose of the helicopter dipped slightly forward before the craft sped away.

The team crowded around Loren's laptop, watching the video feed from the camera mounted below the helicopter's nose.

"Can you get it to fly a little higher?" Troy asked. Loren made a few adjustments on the laptop and watched the numbers on the altimeter rise to four hundred feet.

"Wow," said Spruce, "the terrain is pretty flat. I was expecting something more, but these are just hills. Maybe the tallest is three hundred feet. We should be able to see something pretty soon."

The helicopter continued its track above the tree line. The vehicle's internal computer made a million calculations per second to correct pitch, yaw, and torque, allowing Captain Loren to devote his attention to the camera and onboard instrument packs and leave the tedious job of flying to the helicopter's sophisticated flight computer.

About fifteen minutes into the flight, Loren saw something very different on the monitor: it was hard-edged, not soft and ill-defined like the top of the tree canopy.

"Hello!" said Troy.

Loren clicked on a few features of the user interface and brought the helicopter to hover above the tree line.

The image on the screen looked like a line of black X's. Loren moved the camera left and right to pan across the terrain.

"What's that?" asked Neil.

"It's definitely man-made, whatever it is," Loren said. "It's a regular repeating pattern." Loren pressed a few more icons on the screen and turned on the pattern recognition package. "We can drop out the vegetation and focus on the shapes themselves with this filter." The entire screen turned black with distinct white edges, forming large crisscrossed barriers every thirty feet.

"How far away is that?" asked Neil.

Loren studied the map intently. "Maybe ninety minutes—it's about two-and-a-half miles."

"It's a fence—it's gotta be a fence!" said Troy.

Loren nodded. "I think you're right, Troy. Those beams have sharpened points on the top, like giant spikes, and they're positioned in the form of an X like an international symbol for *No*."

Spruce examined the image closely. "Those things must be thirty feet high."

"Can you follow the perimeter?" asked Neil.

"Sure," said Loren. He pressed a few keys on the laptop, and the helicopter began to fly sideways along the perimeter of the fence, keeping the camera focused on the enormous segments that comprised the man-made barrier.

"Can you turn off the filter, Rich?" asked Jim.

"Sure thing." A click of the mouse returned the image of lush vegetation with a corral of diagonal fence posts standing in front of the rain forest beyond it, like a sentinel guarding a post.

"What are they protecting, and why is there a fence in the middle of a rain forest?" asked Pam.

Beyond the fence the camera could make out more trees, just more of the same.

Neil and Troy glanced quickly at one another, recognition forming on their faces. Suddenly, Neil jumped up and clapped his hands together, startling the group.

"It's the Garden!"

13

The Arabian Shield

As Captain Loren piloted AARON away from the Garden perimeter, Troy Scott's attention turned to Jim Spruce, who was struggling with a large piece of equipment. Troy ran over and helped Jim pull the bulky skid-like object out of the cargo bin.

"Man, that's heavy. What do you have in here? A dead geologist?" asked Troy with a smile.

Jim returned a courtesy smile. "This will tell us what we're standing on—it's a seismometer." He opened a gray instrument pack and ran his thumb across the hood to authenticate himself to the device. "I've been dying to perform this test ever since we had the discussion about the four rivers running out of Eden." Jim typed into his laptop keyboard as Neil, Troy and Pam crowded around him.

"What experiment is that?" asked Fernanda stowing her pack and approaching the group huddled around Jim's display.

"In modern times, the Persian Gulf sits atop something called the Arabian Shield, a six-mile-thick stratum of sedimentary rock. Now, the way we were talking in the conference room, I got the impression that the rivers emerged out of the ground—like an underground spring."

"So?" said Fernanda.

"So, there are two options here. One, the entire Garden sinks into the ground and disappears during the Flood, which will be unlikely if this instrument returns a six-mile-deep barrier underneath us that matches what we have in modern times; or two, the entire Garden is swept off the top of the Arabian Shield."

Jim clicked an icon on the screen, and the device made a humming sound.

"Here comes the return," he said. The screen lit up with a series of green waves across a numeric axis. Jim turned some dials on the seismometer and adjusted the sensitivity of the band.

"It looks like the Arabian Shield is already here. Sedimentary rock exists before the Flood," Jim said, tapping on the screen. "That very likely means there's petroleum in some form in those layers of rock—but more to the point, at least some stratification of the rock formations might have been a function of the earth's creation. It doesn't all happen during the Flood."

"You know," Fernanda said, "since we arrived, I've been blown away by the amount of vegetation here. With all the dinosaurs and the difference in the atmosphere, it feels like we're millions of years back, but that's not right—we're only about four thousand years back."

"What's your point?" asked Jim.

"My point is that in modern times this is desert—and we know it's going to be desert for sure in about one thousand years from this time period."

Neil took a look around at the glade and the lush plain heading toward the inlet. "Gang, I think we're standing in the middle of the future oil fields that power all the modern countries of the world in our time period."

"So, if all this stuff is swept away and doesn't collapse into the ground, and this is future organic material that gets compressed into oil and other types of petroleum, then how does it get so deeply into the earth?" asked Pam.

Jim looked at Pam and at the same time beyond her into the massive vegetation that spread without hesitation into the distance. "That, my dear, is the question of the ages."

Jim began to stow the laptop, the cables, and the other equipment he had used to power the seismometer. "This can't be the only explanation… there are other ways this could happen," he mumbled as he wrapped the cables up and powered down the instruments.

His thoughts were churning now, evaluating a dozen other possibilities all at the same time—looking for anything that didn't include a divine designer. Ancient geology was similar to what he had seen in the twentieth century, and the experiment with the Arabian Shield had buttressed his point of view. Still, the landscape around him was so different from the geological features that would consume this land in a few hundred years—far too soon for the accepted course of evolutionary time frames. With every thought that came to his mind, the elements of nature seemed to mock him and challenge his very reason for being.

Why is there sedimentary rock before the Flood? he wondered as he closed the lid on the cargo container. *If there is a God, then why did God create the world to look old? Is this some kind of sick joke, some sort of divine IQ test, or is it something more?*

It was the beginning of a great number of things that would bother Dr. James Spruce.

14

Breach

Dustin Tamilyn double-checked the readings on his computer monitor and looked around the ops center. He peered nervously at the digital clock mounted above the thick window of the Platform bay.

"The team's been away for an hour and fifteen minutes. Dr. Locke, do you mind if I go to the break room for a smoke?"

Cameron smiled at him. "Thanks, Dustin, go right ahead. Great job this morning—really great—no glitches." Alicia winked at him from across the room, silently echoing Cameron's praise of the young man.

Cameron had recruited Dustin to work with him at TRC. He was a mathematician of tremendous skill and natural ability. Dustin had been doing work in complex systems at Santa Fe Institute when Cameron came across him. Cameron had never really gotten to know Dustin beyond the academic shell that all people in the research field seemed to possess, but he liked his youthful and spontaneous approach to math.

Dustin grabbed his pack of cigarettes and left the ops center, walking through the bay from which the team had transferred less than two hours before.

Dustin was a classic nerd, but he made it a priority to tweak the nerd image by growing his curly, wiry hair long and wearing jeans with rips and holes in them under his white lab coat. He would have looked more at home on stage with Nirvana than at a scientific research center.

He entered the elevator, but instead of pressing the button labeled

"Living Quarters," he pressed the button for the lobby.

The ring of the elevator bell tone startled Sally, the receptionist. She hadn't been expecting anyone for many hours. Dr. Locke had said that an expedition would be going back in time, which generally meant a lock-down.

"Oh, Dustin, I didn't expect you," said Sally, seeing the rock star mathematician step out of the elevator.

"I'm just going up top for a smoke," Dustin said with a charming smile.

Sally gave Dustin a confused look. "I thought no one could exit the building when an expedition is away," she said.

"Don't worry about it," said Dustin, pulling a pistol with a long black silencer from the inside of his lab coat.

He pointed it at Sally and pulled the trigger. Her eyes widened in surprise.

A sudden bright flash reflected from the granite walls of the lobby, and Sally fell backward behind the steel divider. A pool of dark red blood began to creep across the dark stone floor, staining the marble under her lifeless form.

Dustin stepped back from the crimson pool, leaving Sally's body. He had long ago steeled himself for this day, and he felt no regret for his action. He had been recruited during his senior year at Stanford by a software firm for a lead software-architect position with stock options worth a reported $25 million, but Cameron Locke's charisma and his siren call of work that would change the world had altered his plans. Now, with the complex mathematics and state-of-the-art software design for controlling the wormhole behind him professionally—not to mention his inability to share top-secret and confidential methods with a company that would reward him with large sums of money—Dustin felt desperate to make his fortune. Salah al-Din's promise of $100 million and passage to a non-extradition country kept him on a singular mission with no distractions.

Dustin stepped up to the glass doors, and they slid away. His footsteps echoed in the parking garage as he headed up the ramp toward the guardhouse.

15

Trek to the Fence

A s the sun rose higher, the grove came to life with the sound of birds, and the honking of the brachiosaur startled other animals across the plain. The revelation of dinosaurs and man coexisting in a young-earth setting weighed on Jim Spruce, and he was visibly agitated.

Captain Loren had landed AARON ten minutes ago, and they pulled the small helicopter to the grove and concealed it under camouflage netting next to the cargo bins.

The team was spread out in a line over one hundred yards, and Lieutenant Calmont was again on point, with Commander Chris Belkins at the rear of the group. The team members agreed to stay near the vegetation and away from the wide-open plains as they wound their way toward the coordinates that AARON had sent back from the fence.

The shafts of morning sunlight were breaking through the thick canopy of atmosphere overhead, dappling the ground. Spruce looked up at the sun. "Has anyone else noticed that the sky is much hazier in this time?"

"I noticed that this morning, just after sunrise. It's like we're looking through a plate of frosted glass," Fernanda said.

"Those measurements this morning showed that there is more water vapor in the air than we are used to—do you think that accounts for the hazy look?" asked Pam.

"I don't know," Spruce answered, shedding his camouflage shirt and tying it around his waist. "I mean, that's a lot of water vapor. It's like a greenhouse here—more intense than the Amazon."

"And zero wind, and that's quite odd," said Pam. "I'm starting to think this place has a uniform temperature."

A shriek pierced the morning air, and the team ducked instinctively as four large shadows passed over the exposed plain to their right.

Jim looked up to see four huge flying creatures. "Pteranodons!" he yelled, hardly able to control himself. The sound the creatures made was eaglelike—a shrill shriek—instead of the gargling sound that Saturday morning cartoons portrayed them as having.

The team watched the four giant winged creatures fly in a V formation; the sun glanced off their translucent skin and gave them a bronze appearance.

As the awe of the pteranodons' flight slowly crept into the background, Fernanda ran up the line so that she could walk next to Neil Stevens. "Neil, you've been awfully even-keeled on this trip so far—how much did you know beforehand?"

Neil smiled. "It's not so much that I knew more than you did, it's just that I've had about a six-month head start on everyone else here to begin to acclimatize myself to what this all means."

"You mean the Garden of Eden?" asked Fernanda.

"Well, that's certainly part of it. But listen, everything we've ever been taught about the world, history, and science almost all of it is wrong. I'm not talking about scientific or historical facts, but the context around the facts is wrong. This expedition, if it ever comes to light, will be the equivalent of a hydrogen bomb to accepted scientific and historical theories. It'll annihilate the careers and theories of thousands of scientists. Science will be on its derrière for a hundred years trying to sift through all of this."

Jim strained over the buzz of insects to overhear and quickly interrupted the conversation. "As a member of the scientific establishment that you are referring to, I can tell you there will still be plenty of people who won't believe this find—" Jim remembered his non-disclosure agreement and wiped his brow—"if it ever comes to light."

"Forget the scientific establishment. How are you feeling about your own beliefs now?" asked Fernanda, waving her hand to shoo away the swarming insects.

Jim looked at Neil as he answered. "I'll admit I'm a proud man, but what I've seen for myself in the past two hours has confronted everything I've ever believed in and destroyed it. I think this device of yours has incredible potential, but consider what it will do to religion and belief systems. Almost anything that anyone has a strong opinion or belief about can now be investigated and confirmed or denied."

Jim adjusted his backpack strap and smoothed out the sweat-soaked fabric of his field shirt. "There are people who will literally kill to keep the truth that your machine could expose from the greater public."

Neil nodded. He had thought through many of the things that Jim was stating.

"You talk about the death of science and history, but I wonder if our discoveries will also mean the death of faith? What if this device actually kills off the faith you are trying to enable?" Jim asked.

Neil slowed his pace as if Jim's statement was an obstacle to physically elude or overcome. "I've never thought of it in that regard, Jim."

⌐⌐⌐ ⌐⌐⌐ ⌐⌐⌐

In the deeply shadowed rain forest, only a hundred yards from the team, a large animal was roused from slumber by a distinct scent. The creature raised its enormous head and inhaled deeply. An out-of-place smell invaded its overly sensitive olfactory cells.

The creature turned and looked at its mate, which was bent over a large nest situated on a cleared patch of the forest floor. The nest held several young versions of its parents. Birdlike peeps emanated from their large heads, and they jumped and climbed on top of each other, competing for the strips of bloody flesh their mother had brought them. Sensing more of the unknown smell and hearing strange sounds coming from outside the shady glade, the male was compelled to take action to defend his mate and their offspring. He began padding toward the edge of the glade.

Lieutenant Calmont, on the front of the line, visually scanned the area to the left and right. His briefing had not prepared him for what he was seeing. While he seemed cool and collected on the outside, he was becoming increasingly uncomfortable in these surroundings.

The sun was baking everyone on the team. The heavy water vapor in the atmosphere made it feel as though they were in a perpetual sauna. Calmont stopped and opened his canteen for a quick swig. The jungle foliage to his left seemed to vibrate, the broad-leafed plants beginning to sway and bounce. Calmont lowered the canteen slowly and flicked the safety of his automatic weapon to the off position.

Whatever this is, it's big, he thought.

The ground was beginning to shake with micro-tremors, and the rest of the team was starting to notice the same phenomenon that Calmont was experiencing farther up the trail. Calmont could see some of the spiked tops of the fence ahead, just over the crest of one more hill.

At that moment, the tempo of the tremors increased. Whatever was causing them was heading their way.

"Commander Belkins," Calmont said nervously into his flexible microphone boom.

"Lieutenant, what's up?"

"Sir, we're about to have serious company, and it's headed this way fast!"

"We can feel it too what is it?"

"Sir, I think it's an animal of some sort—can I suggest we get the group moving, double time? We're sitting ducks all spread out like this."

"Roger that! I'll get them moving back here. Stay alert!" Chris Belkins yelled out the order as though the team was at boot camp. "Everyone, get moving—double time—and keep your eyes open."

Calmont moved behind a massive fallen tree and widened his stance, placing his feet at shoulder width beneath him while pulling his automatic weapon close. The jungle in front of him seemed to vibrate with life. The palm fronds and leafy undergrowth shook from the tremors that seemed to come from deeper in the dark, verdant rain forest ahead of him, but as the tempo of the micro-tremors increased, he was unsure of the direction of the sound. Calmont slowly scanned his weapon left and right, trying to be ready for anything. Sweat poured from his forehead, and he swallowed hard.

With a roar, a giant allosaurus leapt out of the foliage directly behind Calmont. The surprised lieutenant spun around and shot off a dozen automatic rounds into the enormous beast. The allosaurus was agile and tall, at least thirty feet from his head to the tip of his tail. On his head were two small horns, one above each eye. He had two large forelimbs that ended in eagle-sharp claws. The bullet wounds didn't stop the beast, and the allosaurus opened his enormous jaws and let out a roar. The SEAL felt the heat of the predator's breath on his face.

Calmont began a retreat and fired some more rounds over his shoulder as he sprinted away from the allosaurus. He swung his weapon over his shoulder and ran flat out for the repeating spike pattern that crowned the hill.

⌐⌐⌐ ⌐⌐⌐ ⌐⌐⌐

Belkins heard Calmont firing shots, and his ear bud crackled with the lieutenant's frightened and unintelligible words.

Belkins sprinted up the trail, tagging Loren on the back. "Take the rear! Watch our six!"

Chris Belkins came over a small hill and spotted the pursuit. Calmont was sprinting for the fence, with the crimson-colored allosaurus hot on his trail. Belkins raised his gun to his shoulder and held it tightly. He fired in short bursts as he ran toward the creature, hoping to distract it from the lieutenant, who was scrambling to get away.

Lieutenant Calmont ran up to a fence segment. Each barrier was at least thirty-five feet high, with the bottom portion of the fence high enough for a man to walk under without bumping his head. Calmont glanced back to see the allosaurus bearing down on him. He fired off a number of rounds, and the allosaurus screeched in pain. Bullets had ripped open the carnivore's chest wall. Bone and the inner dermis of the hide were now plainly visible, but the allosaurus kept coming. The distance between Calmont and the charging meat-eater was closing fast. Calmont ran for the bottom of the fence segments, desperate to reach the clearing between the man-made barrier and the vegetation line of the Garden. Belkins charged after them, thirty feet behind the allosaurus, pouring lead into the beast's back and legs.

As Calmont ran under the barrier, a blast of fiery heat flashed in his face. A figure of pure flame materialized before him, brandishing an enormous, broad-bladed flaming sword. Before Calmont could say a word, the figure brought the sword down onto his head. The fiery blade passed entirely through Calmont's body, cleaving him in two vertically. The instantly cauterized halves of the lieutenant's body fell away from each other in opposite directions.

The allosaurus cocked his head and looked in confusion at the divided, smoldering remains of his prey lying in the buffer zone between the fence and the Garden.

Belkins screamed at the sight of his comrade being slaughtered before his very eyes. He fired a hail of lead into the blazing figure, the bullets passing harmlessly through the fiery form and slamming into the ancient trees behind the barrier. The figure gazed directly into Belkins' eyes for a moment and then vanished in a flash of amber light.

The allosaurus turned and focused his attention on the attacker running up on him from behind. Belkins squeezed down on the trigger and sprayed bullets into the creature's braincase. The allosaurus let out a short screech as it lost its brain functions. The dinosaur's muscles locked up, and the creature fell to earth with a deafening thud.

The rest of the team came over the final hill and gasped at the sight in front of them.

A massive dinosaur with rips and holes blown through its flesh lay sprawled on the ground. The allosaurus was a deep crimson along the entire top of its body, but its underside was a contrasting grayish-purple. The creature's head was about six feet long from the base of its neck to the end of its snout. Huge, razor-sharp teeth lined its mouth, top and bottom.

Troy Scott ignored the dead dinosaur and jogged right over to the fence, joining Belkins, who was looking through the bottom portion of the huge barrier at his massacred comrade. Chris stood silently, staring at the body of Lieutenant Calmont, which lay about ten feet away.

The buffered area between the fence and the Garden had zero vegetation not even a blade of grass, just dirt and a few rocks. It looked like the burn control lines Troy had seen firefighters use to consume forest-fire fuel and contain a fire. The total buffer area was probably twenty feet wide and appeared to continue along the length of the fence in both directions.

Troy put his hand on the commander's shoulder. "I'm sorry for your loss, Commander—he was a brave man."

Pam and Fernanda were crying and holding one another, trying to provide solace after the violent loss of a team member.

"I have to take him home with us," said Belkins, pulling a rubber body bag from his backpack.

"You can't go in there, Commander. If you step into that buffer zone you'll be killed just like Lieutenant Calmont," Troy said.

Chris glared at Troy and said with disdain, "I won't leave a man behind."

"There's more to this," said Troy. He saw that a debate with the SEAL would be fruitless. Troy picked up the machete that was lying by the commander's pack and headed back to the allosaurus. He walked over to the giant carcass and lifted his machete high in the air, bringing it down swiftly onto one of the slain dinosaur's forelimbs. He continued hacking until a two-foot section of the arm was cut free. He picked up the piece of forelimb and walked back toward Belkins, who was now staring at Troy in disbelief.

"Hey! Are you out of your mind? We haven't had a second to examine this animal and all you can do is chop it up for lunch!" exclaimed Jim.

Troy glanced back at the rest of the team members, who were watching with rapt attention.

"Listen," said Troy, "no one wants to go into the Garden more than I do. We *should* try to retrieve the lieutenant's body and take it home with us. I understand the creed, Commander, and I respect it—I really do. But no one can cross or even enter this barrier, and no one has done so for almost sixteen hundred years during this time period and survived."

With that, the expedition leader slow-pitched the severed dino-limb over the giant barrier and into the buffer area. Before the chunk of meat and bone could touch the barren ground, a fiery flash of white and orange light appeared and chopped the dismembered appendage into two parts. The smell of seared meat instantly filled the air. As quickly as the flash of light had appeared, it was gone.

"When Adam and Eve were driven from the Garden of Eden, God placed an angel with a flaming sword at the entrance of the Garden to guard it," Troy said. "The Bible makes direct mention of the entrance being guarded, but apparently the entire perimeter is defended. No one goes back in."

Everyone on the team nodded in agreement the dinosaur-limb object lesson was still sinking in. Neil Stevens came up to the commander to give his condolences, and Troy walked back down to the allosaurus, where Jim Spruce was taking pictures of the great beast.

Fernanda and Pam examined the fence and marveled at its construction. Each beam was more or less the same size, and the hardware for holding them together seemed to have been made of cast iron. Each rough-hewn timber was about fifteen inches in diameter, and the top of each beam was shaped into a blunt point.

"It's like a giant stockade meets the Berlin Wall," Fernanda said.

"From an iconographic perspective, it's an amazing find!" Pam said. "The whole thing says 'Stay Out!' without any language or signage. It protects and outlines the buffer zone by staying just outside the area void of vegetation. I worked on something like this for Yucca Mountain when I was in grad school. I was asked to design shapes that could be used to explain to future people and civilizations that the contents of the mountain, which stored toxic nuclear waste, were not to be disturbed. Only shapes or icons were allowed no language could be used in the assignment. We came up with the idea of huge iron spikes sticking up out of the ground about thirty feet trying to communicate that something bad was buried below the mountain."

"Looks like someone beat you to the punch by about four thousand years," Fernanda said, putting her hand on Pam's shoulder.

Jim Spruce was excitedly investigating the slain allosaurus, recording video and measuring the outer skin envelope of the beast. "When we get back, I'll be able to recreate this thing virtually on the computer. All the renderings of dinosaurs are guesses based on skeletal structure along with some fossilized tendons and skin imprints that we've found."

Troy watched Spruce perform his forensic work. "Did you expect the skin colors to be so bright? I've never seen an animal that had such an incredible color scheme—this crimson color spread over the creature's dorsal side is incredible." Jim grunted in agreement while holding a pencil between his teeth and struggling with a tape measure. Circular designs of gray and crimson were spread out in a delicate pattern across the sides and back of the dead dinosaur.

Jim stuck his index finger into one of the bullet wounds and probed around. "The hide is similar to that of a shark or reptile, exceptionally thick and tough. No wonder the SEALs had trouble bringing it down." Jim wiped his bright-red hand in the tall grass, trying to remove the animal's blood from his fingers.

"That's just nasty," said Pam, with a grimace.

Vultures and other carrion-eating birds were beginning to gather overhead. "Um, guys," said Fernanda looking up, "won't most predators and scavengers start to arrive soon?"

Jim surveyed the birds circling overhead. "Yes, they will. We should start to clear out."

The team heard a chirping sound coming from the forest just yards away, and tiny heads bobbed above and below the grass line. The small creatures had long snouts and long conical teeth for ripping and tearing food. They were about the size of small dogs and were almost birdlike in their graceful movements. A long, rigid tail protruded from their backs, serving much like a balancing pole for an acrobat. There were scores of them, and probably a hundred more waiting in the forest, just out of sight. Jim, Neil, and Troy backed away from the carcass.

"Masiakasaurus…scavengers," said Jim in amazement as he watched the small dinosaurs swarm over the carcass of the allosaurus.

As the team members retreated from the dinosaur's remains, the "masies" took the ground they had just occupied.

"Man, they're aggressive," said Belkins, pulling his submachine gun out. He let a brief burst of bullets rip out against the ground, and the tiny dinosaurs scattered like cockroaches, heading back to the safety of the grass along the edge of the forest. Spruce and Belkins ran down the fence line to catch up with the others, who were hunched over an open laptop that Rich Loren was operating. Jim glanced one more time over his shoulder to see hundreds of masies now standing atop the carcass, tugging and ripping the colorful flesh from the mighty dinosaur that had chased Lieutenant Calmont to his death.

"Hey, Neil, Troy—can I show you something?" said Rich Loren. He was typing some commands on a small laptop. A cable snaked from the back of the computer to a three-foot mast with a circular pod mounted to the top.

Neil approached with Troy just behind him. "What do you have, Captain Loren?"

"Rich," Loren said. "Let's dispense with rankings. I'm not sure they mean anything in this environment anyway."

Neil smiled. "OK, Rich, what do you have?"

"I'm not sure, but it's not vegetation. I've been bouncing radar waves off the landscape, trying to see if there's anything but vegetation and this fence. The fence is the most prominent signature, but I got a strange reading over here," he said, pointing to the southeast of the Garden and in the direction of the odd radar return. "It's got a prominent signature, like it's got flat sides—a building maybe?" Rich said.

"A building?" Troy exchanged glances with Neil.

"How far away?" asked Neil.

"Maybe two miles," replied Loren.

"I think we should check it out. This part of the Garden would be underwater in the Persian Gulf in our time. A building could have major significance. Let's get going," Neil said.

Neil led the group in a moment of silence at the fence for Lieutenant Calmont, and then everyone started hiking along the fence line toward the mysterious target that had appeared on Rich Loren's instrument.

16

The Raid

Dustin Tamilyn ran up the ramp to the inside of the enormous lockdown door. He pulled his BlackBerry from the inside pocket of his lab coat and typed a short message:

JUST INSIDE DOOR
LOBBY SECURE
TEAM THINKS THAT FARADAY CAGE IS INTACT
PROCEED TO GUARDHOUSE AND PRESENT CREDENTIALS

A mile down the road, on Highway 178, just before the turnoff for the lab, another BlackBerry chimed. The recipient evaluated an encrypted message. A smile curled across his lips, and he put a large white moving truck into gear and pressed on the accelerator.

The TRC guardhouse had been slow all day, and Bob Jennings, the company's senior security guard, was trying to keep busy in the desert heat. Watching cameras, checking various posts and sensors around the compound—it was always the same. Nothing but snakes and jackrabbits attempting entry at TRC.

A cloud of dust billowed behind a white moving truck that was making its way down the gravel road to the guardhouse. Jennings ran his index finger down a sparse itinerary on his clipboard. *That's strange*, he thought. *There's nothing here about a delivery.*

The large truck pulled up to the guardhouse, belching carbon monoxide into the otherwise pure, but arid air. Jennings squinted to see behind the tinted, dirty glass of the truck's cab and coughed from the emissions the truck was making.

The driver rolled down the window and gestured to the security guard. "Excuse me, sir, I think I'm lost. Can you help me with this map?" The driver handed a crinkled map of the Trona area to Jennings. The driver's accent was not local; it had a strong Middle Eastern sound to it, and Jennings vacillated about phoning his encounter to the other security stations inside the compound. He felt his blood pressure rising and anxiety increasing. It looked like the driver was alone as he peered through the rolled-down window. More than anything else, Jennings wanted this large, white, unscheduled truck out of the area, especially during a lockdown.

"OK, I shouldn't be doing this, but there's nothing else going on here today. Where are you trying to get to?"

As Jennings reached for the map to help the driver, he heard a muffled bleep from a silencer followed by a clinking sound behind him. A stabbing pain bloomed in his lower abdomen. He instinctively reached for the painful area, and as he did, he noticed a bullet hole in the side of the truck that was perfectly lined up with the area of his pain. He pulled his hands away and saw dark blood dripping from them. Another bleeping sound came from the direction of the truck, and Jennings fell back, hitting the concrete pad in front of the guardhouse with a thud.

The driver quickly opened his door and placed a large canvas bag on the ground next to Jennings. He put Jennings' feet into the bottom of the sack and unrolled it around the security guard's body until the remains were completely contained in the canvas wrap. He leaned down and picked up Jennings's lifeless form, struggling with the weight as he lifted the body into the cab of the truck. He pushed and slid the canvas sack across the seat until it crumpled and folded on the floor of the passenger's side.

Behind the thick vault wall protecting the parking garage, just thirty feet from the guardhouse, Dustin watched the video feed from a surveillance camera that was pointed just outside the door. He shivered as he watched the cold and calculating terrorist dispose of the man who had smiled and greeted him when he arrived at TRC that very morning. For a brief second the guilt of betraying the people around him began to take hold of him. Dustin closed his eyes and balled his shaky, sweaty fingers into fists.

Stay focused.

After watching Jennings' demise from the inside monitor, Dustin pressed an illuminated button inside the garage next to the giant vault door and swiped his credentials across an access panel.

ACCESS APPROVED: DUSTIN TAMILYN – OPERATIONS

The huge steel door leading to the underground parking garage began to pivot open slowly. Dustin waited inside for the truck and its occupants to pull into the complex.

The driver pulled in and continued down the ramp. The back of the truck opened up, and a man jumped out wearing a security outfit—a perfect match to the uniform that Jennings wore. The man ran back up the ramp, took residence in the guardhouse, and clicked on a digital walkie-talkie.

As the truck cleared the entrance, Dustin again pressed the actuator button and swiped his card. The giant door closed.

No evidence of blood, no explosions, no noise, no fuss. *These guys are professionals*, thought Dustin as he jogged down the ramp toward the truck.

The truck stopped at the lobby doors, and just as the brake lights came on, the back of the truck opened and three men jumped out with military precision. Each man was wearing a hijab with a red-and-white checked pattern and carrying a scorpion machine gun. Two of the terrorists also had canvas messenger bags full of additional magazines and explosives slung over their shoulders.

An olive-complexioned man stepped from the driver's side and unzipped his blue overalls. As the outer garment came off, it revealed a uniform identical to that of the men whom Dustin had just seen jump out of the back of the truck.

The leader was a thin man with a jet-black beard. Dustin recognized him and approached. "Salah, very well done," he said. The three other men were embracing and encouraging each another in Arabic.

Salah al-Din was wanted on every terrorist watch list in the known world. The smuggling of al-Din and his terrorist cell over the porous Mexi-Californian border had been planned for more than a year. The planning and training for the mission took place in Germany, where Salah had hand-picked his team from a small group of Afghani-Taliban refugee fighters. His lieutenants, Raheem al-Azzi and Fatin al-Azzi, were brothers with deep convictions and the willingness to die for the cause. Dalal al-Kader was the youngest and newest member of the team and had been wounded in Tora Bora, barely escaping with his life.

Salah's countenance was deadly serious and focused. "You have done well, Dustin. Allah will reward you for your alliance with us. Is everything set?"

"Yes, but when will I get an acknowledgment of the transfer of my money?" insisted Dustin. He glanced at the imposing men who surrounded him and realized he had very little leverage over these people who felt compelled to kill for religion's sake. Dustin ran his fingers through his wiry hair and realized that he was sweating profusely. He wondered if his comrades noticed his fear. The only thing he had as a bargaining chip was his knowledge of the facility and his biometric signature, needed to get the terrorists to the operations center deep in the mountain.

"In a few minutes, once we have taken the control room," said Salah.

The four men walked over to the elevator and watched as Dustin slid his card through the access slot and pressed the button for the operations center. The button illuminated green, and the metal doors of the elevator slid closed.

17

The Mausoleum

T he expedition walked for about a mile, and from the crest of a hill they could see the glint of sunlight reflecting from a large surface. The fence continued on their left and curved slightly to the east away from them in the distance.

"Man! They built that fence to last, didn't they?" Jim said.

As they got closer, the team could see a building that looked strangely reminiscent of the Lincoln Memorial.

As the straight edges and perpendicular surfaces of the man-made structure broke free of the gnarled forest floor, Fernanda gasped. "You've gotta be kidding me!"

"Columns and roofs designed on the concept of distributed weight shouldn't be around until the Greeks start figuring it out," Pam said.

"Apparently someone forgot to tell these guys!" exclaimed Jim.

As they got closer, the details of the huge structure became apparent. The giant building was made from granite blocks. Massive stairs rose out of the lush vegetation surrounding the building, which looked like the Parthenon from a distance. It wasn't as ornate as the famous Greek structure—no carvings or words, just plain grayish granite—but the columns and the ceiling clearly made the same statement.

There were five massive steps, each over four feet high, that led to the columned peak.

"I think these steps were designed to keep animals out. Most animals would stay away from such high sides—this would be hard for them to scale," Fernanda said.

The team reached the foot of the edifice. The vegetation came right up to it; there was no clear walkway or passage approaching the building—at least not from the vantage point of team.

"Well," said Neil, "does anyone feel like climbing?" Before the words were out of his mouth, Fernanda, Pam, and Jim had already made it to the second step, eager to investigate the amazing and unexpected structure.

It took the team a good ten minutes of grunting, lifting, and assisting one another to get to the top. The granite was not as polished as stonework in the twentieth century, but given the timeline they found themselves in, the craftsmanship was remarkable.

As they reached the top, everyone gazed at the massive opening—a simple, giant doorway where three columns were omitted from the design.

Troy Scott could barely conceal his excitement. "This has to be a monument of some kind."

As they walked inside the building, the team members saw three giant granite chests, about nine feet long, six feet high, and three feet wide. They were spaced evenly across the floor. Behind the chests, engraved in the wall, were strange pictograph characters arranged in a grid-like shape. The characters were miniature boxes, arrows, slashes, and lines.

Pam approached the middle chest, studying the etchings on the front of each. "These are similar to Sumerian characters, but they have their own distinction," she said.

"Can you decipher any of it at all?" asked Fernanda.

"Each of the inscriptions has the symbol for 'first' in it; the second word is different for each chest."

Fernanda examined the third chest. "Look, this last one has some of the inscription from the first and second chests."

"Oh my word!" Troy's exclamation echoed in the cavernous chamber.

Everyone turned to see Troy Scott standing back, taking in Fernanda's and Pam's forensic investigation.

"This is a tomb!" Troy said.

"I would agree with that assessment," said Fernanda. "These chests definitely have the characteristics of a sarcophagus or a coffin."

"It's the tomb of the first family!" said Neil.

Troy pointed to the first, second, and third chests sequentially. "Adam, Eve, and…Abel!"

Pam pulled out a notepad and began to scribble down the names and match them up with the symbols on the front of the coffins. Jim sniffed dismissively at her and started taking digital pictures.

"They must have built this as a monument so that future generations could visit and remember," Troy said.

Neil Stevens was away from the group, examining the interior of the wall closest to what they supposed was Adam's sarcophagus. "Pam, I think I have something for you here."

The wall had a step-staircase design to it, with blocks that jutted out at irregular intervals. On the very top of the sculpture was a line that ran horizontally across the entire wall. The stones that jutted out against this line had symbols like the ones on the sarcophagi.

Pam examined the first stone at the top of the line; the symbols on it were an exact match with the symbols on the first sarcophagus.

"It's a genealogy!" Troy said, unzipping his backpack and reaching into it for a well-worn Bible.

"The first line should extend for nine-hundred-some units along the overall timeline that's the lifetime of Adam. The one below that will be Eve, and we should see two blocks below that from Adam and Eve's union— Cain and Abel. Abel's lifeline should end very soon after that block appears."

Everyone looked at the line that represented the second-born son. Indeed, it ended very shortly after it began, followed soon after by a block representing the third-born son of Adam and Eve, Seth.

Troy pointed at each etched line on the wall successively. "Seth, Enos, Cainan, Mahalale-el, Jared, Enoch…"

"Pam, I think this might even be better than a timeline," said Fernanda. "It could be a kind of Rosetta Stone. By matching the symbols and units of measure from these etchings to the English translation of Troy's Bible, we should be able to piece together a rudimentary understanding of this language system."

Pam nodded enthusiastically as she wrote down the cryptic symbols from the wall and began checking them for commonalities with Troy's Bible. Jim continued snapping digital pictures of the wall.

Pam examined the etched timeline on the wall and made an interesting discovery: all the lines were horizontal except for one. "Why is there a vertical notch over Enoch that continues all the way to the ceiling? It's the only lifeline that doesn't end horizontally."

"The Bible says that Enoch walked with God and was so righteous that God translated him off the earth. God simply took him to heaven," Troy explained.

Jim Spruce ran his hands slowly over the entire length of the sarcophagus of Adam.

It can't be true, he thought. He watched the rest of the team scamper around the tomb like it was a playground, giddy with excitement.

Tomb is the right word, he thought. *Everything I've ever taught or learned about history and science has just died.*

"Guys! Over here! Check this out!" yelled Rich Loren from a corner of the room on the right side of the building. The group ran over to see a hole cut through the roof and a series of stones that jutted out in a pattern similar to a ladder.

"This should be an awesome view!" said Troy. One by one the team members climbed up to the roof.

As they reached the top of the stone ladder and looked out, they could see the fence surrounding the Garden of Eden and even look deeply into the Garden. A huge variety of trees appeared in the canopy inside. Glimpses of the four rivers could be seen. The rivers seemed to converge in the center of the Garden, but it was hard to tell if they actually bubbled out of the ground together as one river.

The trees in the Garden looked ancient; they had huge trunks, and gnarled branches that wound through and around one another were covered in a thick, greenish-brown moss. Lush ferns and beautiful flowering plants dotted the interior of the Garden.

Troy looked longingly at the beautiful site—truly a paradise on Earth. "So close, and yet we can't go over there and look around."

Pam echoed the sentiment. "I'm starting to understand what it must have been like to live in this time with the constant reminder of how good it used to be."

Fernanda pointed at some distant hills beyond the glade that contained the team's equipment. "You can see regular patterns in the landscape over there. It has to be farms and crops." Irregular polygons of green, yellow, and brown appeared quite out of place against the seemingly endless forest canopy.

Beyond the farms and plains of yellow and green alternating patches, the group could see wispy columns of smoke rising from hundreds of small fires.

"Finally!" said Neil. "Civilization."

18

Black Swan

T he group continued surveying the mausoleum of the first family, taking hundreds of digital pictures and extensive video footage. Neil looked at his watch. "We should probably head back to the glade. It'll take us a few hours to get back there."

"I'm starving," said Pam.

"Maybe we can have barbecued dino ribs for dinner," snorted Jim. Pam glared at him while she munched on a granola bar to stave off her hunger pangs.

Commander Belkins took the lead and flicked off the safety of his sniper rifle. As he passed the insensitive geologist, he said coolly, "I'd recommend we keep the chit-chat to a minimum. We don't want to attract something that could ruin our whole week—or our lives." He cocked his machine gun as if to punctuate the sentence with a warning.

Pam smiled and then caught herself. She liked this guy's style.

As Belkins moved toward the front of the pack and out of earshot, Jim muttered, "Settle down there, Commander. We're adults here."

Neil placed a hand on Jim's shoulder. "Hey, let's try to cut him some slack. He's lost a man, and it's weighing on him."

Jim blushed, ashamed of his insensitivity. So much had happened in the discovery of the tomb that the loss of Calmont had been swept to the background.

The team hiked for four hours to get back to the glade, and by then the afternoon sun was starting to cast lengthening shadows across the plain. Small flocks of chicken-sized dinosaurs ran alongside them for much of the way, stopping periodically to look over the long grass, bobbing their heads in a bird-like manner.

Jim's attention was on the sky. He was determined to make this trip back to the glade useful for science; plus, sky-gazing helped him keep his mind off what had happened at the fence. The sun was beginning to set in the west, but the visibility of the yellow-orange disc had not changed all day. To Jim it seemed as though he had been looking through a fogged-up glass shower door for the entire day. There was so much water vapor—and yet there were no cloud formations. Everything was mist and vapor mixing with light and refracting in the upper atmosphere.

Troy noticed Jim staring at the sun and examining the sky beyond, checking for the sun's position.

"A penny for your thoughts, Jim."

"Well, it'll cost you more, but here goes. Those crazy Intelligent Design people have been talking about how the early earth may have had a canopy of water, something about how God created a layer of water above the atmosphere and below the atmosphere—apparently a reference to the ocean bodies. I've been looking up at the sun periodically all day long. The clarity with which we see the sun in the 20th century is vastly different from the view in this time period. It's like a distortion layer is fogging, or masking, what we see as clear in our time."

"Could it be a vapor canopy?" asked Troy.

"Well, I don't think it's very thick if it is there. Some of the Intelligent Design proponents say that the water in the atmosphere was miles thick, but I'd say it's much, much thinner— maybe just a few meters—if it even exists all." Jim caught himself and angrily cursed for vocalizing his latest observation.

Troy had just assumed it was the typical tropical heat, but judging from the condition of everyone's clothes—completely soaked through with perspiration as if they had walked in a sauna all day—he had to agree. "There does seem to be a huge amount of water in the air—like it's coming up out of the ground or something."

"Yeah, almost like the water cycle is reversed," Jim said. "It comes up from the ground, as opposed to coming down as rain, and then evaporates back into the sky."

The team members continued their march through the haze, watching the birds returning to their nests. Jim jogged ahead to catch up with Neil Stevens.

"Do you mind if I ask you something, Neil?"

"Go ahead," said Neil, opening his bottled water and taking a swig.

"Do you believe this creation stuff? I mean, with all the scientists and mathematicians working for you at TRC, you have to have deliberated on the topic more than once."

Neil examined Jim's facial expressions, as if to determine whether Jim was baiting him for a joke at his expense or whether he was serious about this question. Jim's expression betrayed a sincere curiosity, and Neil was sure it was an unguarded moment. Jim had a lot to lose from a credibility perspective in the academic world if the findings from this expedition ever made it to the light of day.

"OK, Jim, I'll tell you my story." Pam and Fernanda overheard Neil and picked up their hiking paces a bit so they could hear the story of a billionaire's conversion to what was considered by many a heretical scientific position, while simultaneously running a scientific think tank that attracted the best scientists and mathematicians in the United States.

"I was once like you," Neil said, "a staunch supporter of evolution—perhaps more by default than by deduction. I was trained by men and women who believed in Darwin's theory, and they felt, as I did, that God and creation were negated concepts. Honestly, until about seven years ago, I hadn't given it a moment's thought. While at TRC I saw a lot of things, worked on a lot of projects that prompted me to reconsider my belief system."

Jim interrupted. "Evolution is not a matter of belief, Neil. It's a matter of scientific fact that's irrefutable."

Neil shook his head slowly and flashed an empathetic smile. "Your world viewpoint is what establishes your belief system, regardless of whether it is evolution or something else. My viewpoint used to be like yours. Now it's changed."

Jim began to get his debate face on, and Pam reached over and touched him on the arm. "Please, let him finish," she said.

"It's really important to understand what the debate is about here, Jim," Neil continued.

"There's hardly any debate about it," snipped Jim. Pam sighed. He was impossible.

Neil tried to turn the conversation to a more civil tone. "Let's define some terms here. Let's talk about the difference between microevolution and macroevolution."

Jim grinned; this was his territory. "Yeah, let's do that."

Neil smiled at Jim's willingness to engage in a debate that had been continuing for decades. "Okay, *micro*evolution is indisputable."

Jim stopped walking, and Pam nearly plowed into his back. "Do you want to debate or not?" he asked.

"Not really," Neil answered, "but yes, let's get to the crux of it. Microevolution deals with cyclical variations within a type—dog breeding, colors of people's eyes, the various races of human beings coming from a common genetic pool, and finch beak variations. These are all concepts of microevolution. It's the genetic lottery within a species, at work to create a variety of characteristics, skin colors, skin pigmentations, eye shapes, and so on—but, and *this* is important, it only works within the *confines* of a species. Most Christians would agree with this. I certainly do. But a tadpole does not turn into a turkey which turns into a chimp which later turns into a human. There is no evidence of microevolutionary processes jumping the species barrier—even when the definition of 'species' is flexible. Even bacteria don't do it."

Jim harrumphed. "Thanks for the elementary lesson, Neil. But you're forgetting the scale of time. Macroevolution is just microevolution continuing on for millions or billions of years."

Fernanda couldn't contain herself. "Jim, we just stood in Adam and Eve's mausoleum. What huge amount of time are you talking about? Sixteen hundred years? Let's say there are gaps in the biblical genealogy, and it's more like five thousand years. Even with adding that time, it's not enough for the theory to work."

Jim didn't look back at Fernanda, but kept marching across the grassy plain.

Pam touched Neil on the shoulder while keeping pace with him. "I'm confused, Neil. What's the debate about? I mean, if you believe that variations occur within species, and that happens over time, and those variations lead to small changes, doesn't that mean you believe that evolution is true?"

"Pam, just because microevolution is the observed way that organisms provide diversity within their species doesn't mean that some meaningless, purposeless mechanism led to it. That is the debate—the mechanism. In the end, regardless of whether you think that evolution led from a single-celled organism to more complex forms of life over hundreds of millions of years or that an omnipotent, loving God created various species and mankind for a specific reason, it comes down to one thing."

Jim scowled. "And what exactly would that be?"

Neil uttered a single word. "Faith."

"Faith is for old women and people with terminal illnesses," said Jim. "Science and faith have nothing to do with each other."

Neil raised an eyebrow. "You're so sure? Jim, creation and macroevolution have something very much in common. They both fill in their missing parts with a basic element. For creationism, the fill-in-the-blank is God, impeccable design, and miraculous events. For evolution, well, it's anything *but* God. There it is in a nutshell." Neil raised his arms to emphasize the point.

"At the end of the day, I guess you could say that each of those fill-in-the-blanks really is faith," said Pam.

"Thanks for that insight, Dictionary Girl!" growled Jim. Pam rolled her eyes.

"So, what pushed you to the creationist viewpoint?" asked Fernanda.

"Well, two things really worked together. I was working on two projects, not seemingly related, involving cosmology and computational biology. There was something in them interrelated and yet not addressed by evolutionary theory."

"Cosmology. Big Bang stuff, right?" Jim said.

Neil nodded. "Yep, it's the Genesis record according to macroevolution, and it's very important if evolution is to work without a master designer. There's a lot of research going into cosmology—a lot of reputations and a lot of science concepts are built on that foundation. String theory, theories of the early universe, how the moon formed—cosmology says it's all related."

"What's computational biology?" asked Jim and Pam in unison.

"I'm not too surprised you haven't heard of it—it's pretty new. The basic idea is to model biological entities in software code—simulating a single cell or the interaction of multiple cells programmatically."

Three pteranodons flew in a V-formation over the group, but the three scientists following Neil's personal journey from evolution to creation had their attention riveted on the owner of TRC.

"What connected both fields for you?" asked Jim.

"Both fields literally gloss over the remarkable evidence of design—the evidence that space, the cosmos, planets, stars, orbits, oceans, animals, molecules, and simple cells are so amazingly complex that they cannot happen just with random events." Jim started to interrupt, but Neil kept going. "And I'm not talking about microevolution, like a wolf becoming a dog over hundreds of years, or all of the kinds of dogs coming from just a few at the top of the genetic tree. I believe that variations *within* species did and do occur with random mutations, and most Christians do too—even if they've never thought about it—but I don't believe in mutations that caused, say, a crystal with a hitchhiking amino acid to become a tadpole."

"So you're a believer in Intelligent Design and not an evolutionist?" asked Pam.

"No, I'm not. I'm a creationist—though I do believe in many of the tenets that Intelligence Design espouses," said Neil emphatically. "ID led me to the conclusion that a designer took so much care and interest to design everything from galaxies to human cells that I had to know why. The *why* was the main question for me, but I have many colleagues who are scientists, and are also secretly Intelligent Design proponents. They would never admit to it, of course, because they are risking everything by admitting that Darwin's theory is inadequate to explain the complexities around us. Many IDers believe and accept the old age of the earth, and by old I mean billions with a capital B. They don't take the Genesis account literally; 'days' to them can translate to millions or even billions of years. ID says that the complex patterns and intricate mechanisms of living things is beyond what unguided, evolutionary processes themselves could achieve. This opens the door for other things to intervene in the process of evolution. The idea of a celestial, omnipotent designer is only one possibility."

Neil laughed. "You know, it's kinda funny. You guys think I'm a lunatic for believing in God, but many scientists espouse things like panspermia as a way that complex molecules arrived on Earth, and they don't get laughed off the stage when they mention it at a conference. Talk about desperation!"

"Panspermia?" Fernanda jumped in. "You mean *aliens*?"

"Yeah, aliens—E.T.—little green men. If science starts to embrace aliens as a possible source of life, then why is a loving God such a laughable concept?"

Jim swallowed hard. He'd been at some of those conferences. Far too many of them were hosted at his alma mater. He cleared his throat. "Neil, panspermia doesn't necessarily mean aliens. It means that macromolecules may have come to Earth from another place by means of comets or asteroids colliding with the earth. Still, I'll acknowledge that panspermia is a stretch." He shifted his feet. "So what's the connective tissue between cosmology and computational biology?" he asked, feeling like he was going around in intellectual circles.

"For me, creation and even the Flood are the ultimate Black Swans," said Neil.

"What's a Black Swan?" asked Jim.

"Hey, I know that one," said Pam, beaming with mathematical pride. Jim nodded, encouraging her to share her definition.

"A Black Swan is a term that refers to an event in probability theory. Everyone assumed that swans were always white in color until black swans were found to exist in Australia in the 17th century. They did exist, but they had not been observed yet, so the Western thought of the day was that swans could only be white. The idea was applied to probability as a description of an event that shatters previously held conclusions based on previous observations."

"Exactly!" said Neil. "And these Black Swans are typically huge in their impact."

"Why do you call creation a Black Swan?" asked Jim. "Everyone knows the story of Adam and Eve."

"But the evolutionists can't accept it, just as Christianity can't accept evolution. Both sides would lose the base of their belief systems—and yes, each one is a belief system. Both require faith. For example, cosmology says that a single point of energy exploded to bring the universe into existence; nobody knows what made that point of energy happen, and no one knows why it did so, but that doesn't matter—it can be anything but God. Do you both agree with that statement?"

Jim nodded, and Pam agreed.

"So let's go with that. Boom! Here comes the universe. Let's add billions of years and lots of randomness to the equation. Everything about cosmology basically states that planets like Earth exist everywhere in the universe—billions of them. We are not unique. Ever heard of the Drake Equation?"

Jim nodded, but Pam replied with a blank look.

"The Drake Equation predicts that Earth-like planets are a function of a number of terms, such as the fraction of stars that have planets and the average number of planets that can potentially support life among the stars that have planets. Then we weight those terms with the probability that some of the planets eventually develop life, and of course, some of those life forms develop intelligence, and so on. So the universe should literally be teeming with life of all sorts."

Pam interjected, "But Earth is rare, as far as we know."

Neil beamed. "It's more than rare, it's unique. It's a planet in the right place at the right time. Everything about Earth—its location in space, its structure for generating a magnetic field, its composition, atmosphere, temperature—is essential for life to exist. Is that just sheer luck?"

"It could be," said Jim sheepishly.

"You might buy it, Jim, but I couldn't take it anymore," Neil continued. "The chance for all of those life-preserving variables to be tuned just right is more than astronomical; it's impossible. Nowadays we hear all this noise about how delicate the environment is and how we're destroying it, and that may be so, and yet evolution says it was enormously robust to keep life from disappearing off of its early precipice—so which is it? We *should* take care of the environment, but not because it could end humanity—because it's our responsibility to a Creator-Designer who expects us to be good stewards of the planet we live on. It's not our most important responsibility, but it is one of them. My conclusion about cosmology is this: Earth was created by God as a special, beautiful place where His creation could choose to serve Him and fellowship with Him in a freewill manner, not as robots or slaves but as friends by choice and loyalty, and as family by position."

The glade was now in sight, and the entire team practically jogged the rest of the way, in a hurry to relax and get some rest—it had been a long day.

Captain Loren disabled the booby traps protecting the cargo bins in the glade, and everyone started pulling out pup tents and erecting them on the damp grass. Little domes of yellow, white, and black nylon began popping up every few feet. Troy and Neil got a stove going and started some dinner.

Jim erected his tent and wrote a few notes in a ragged leather-bound notebook. The geologist then wandered over to the campfire and the small stove that Troy and Neil were attempting to master. "So, what's the biochemical evidence that worked with cosmology to move you to religion?" Jim asked Neil.

"Not religion, Christianity," replied Neil.

"Whatever," Jim said, with a dismissive wave of this hand.

"Not whatever! It makes a big difference. Do you realize that Jesus Christ condemned cold, dead, blind, ritual-following religion in most of His sermons to His followers?" said Neil.

Fernanda, overhearing a continuation of the earlier intriguing conversation, almost killed herself getting out of the yellow nylon tent. "Hey, wait for me! I want to hear this story, too."

"OK," Neil said, stirring some thick soup. "TRC does a bunch of work in both computational chemistry and computational bio-modeling. It was the bio-modeling side that got my attention. We were trying to simulate a bacterial flagellum—ever heard of them?"

Jim and Fernanda shook their heads.

"It's a machine—a biological machine that's every bit as complicated as that cool little helicopter sitting over there." Neil gestured with his head toward the miniature craft that had helped the team discover the Garden of Eden and the mausoleum.

"The flagellum is used to propel cells—kind of like an outboard motor. But the propeller, a whip-like structure, is made out of protein. Now, everyone has seen pictures of proteins and molecules; they grace the covers of most high school chemistry and college biology books. But a flagellum is a collection of macromolecules and proteins working together to achieve a purpose."

Neil filled a number of bowls to the brim with the meat-and-pasta-heavy soup, and Troy handed them to the rest of the crew along with pieces of bread.

"So," said Jim, with his mouth half full of bread. "This motor, this flagellum: how's it work?"

Neil smiled and took a sip of his steaming soup. "Scientists like to call it the world's most efficient engine. The whip-like structure is actually connected to a driveshaft made out of more proteins. It attaches to the driveshaft like a universal joint. The tiny motor also has the analogs of bushings and other items that we've developed in our motors and rotors in the mechanical world. The motor of the flagellum is powered by the flow of acid, which enables the motor to spin at over ten thousand revolutions per minute."

The team grew quiet as they contemplated something so small and so biological moving so mechanically—with such apparent intention.

"Yeah, that's what I thought," said Neil, playing off the silence. "But the part that really slam-dunked the whole design side of it for me was that this miniature motor, that can outperform anything we've built, can suddenly stop within a quarter of a turn and reverse direction at maximum speed—ten thousand RPMs."

"What makes it know how to do that?" asked Pam. "It can't just be the parts themselves."

"That's the very question that pushed me over the edge," said Neil. "Matter, molecules, proteins, and such are separate from the information that makes their complex mechanisms work. While matter can be reduced to very reducible parts, it would be impossible to reduce the information that makes these things work."

"Information—you mean like a computer program?" asked Pam.

"Yeah, that's a good way to think of it. Can a person's mind be reduced to just tissue in the brain, or even down to neurons? Is there more there? Is there a program that tells cells how to operate, divide, multiply, link together? It's this information that seems to be beyond Darwin's particular mechanism of natural selection and mutation. Randomly generated strings of text do not create *War and Peace* or *Huckleberry Finn,* and 747s do not rise out of junkyards. Cells are much more complex than these items, and they were designed from the outset. Getting back to biology for a moment, genes are a package of information, but DNA molecules are the medium— not the message."

Silence followed. Only the crackling of the fire could be heard for a few long moments before Jim spoke.

"OK, so let's just say for a moment that you're right about God creating the universe and designing everything from atoms to cells to supernovas. What's that got to do with your accepting Christianity? You can believe in God without being a Christian, right?"

"The real question is *why*," said Neil.

"What do you mean, why?" asked Pam.

"Why did God do it? I mean, why create Earth in a small spiral arm of an average galaxy? Why create millions of stars and galaxies as far as we can see?"

"Hey! You're the Christian. You tell us," said Jim.

Neil smiled. "Because He loves us and wants a relationship with us. Not a robotic or slave relationship—a relationship of love and fellowship. There's really only one conclusion you can come to after seeing all this design around us and in the universe. God built the whole thing to bring glory to Himself, and to be a sign pointing humans to Him."

Jim threw his empty aluminum bowl to the ground and raised both of his hands. "So what? What's the magical ingredient here? Native Americans and all kinds of cultures have worshiped nature and the gods they believed created it. What makes Christianity special?"

"Well," Troy spoke up, "the evidence of an omnipotent designer is plainly seen by creation, but that's not enough. Another element is needed to complete the picture. The Bible is the story that explains *why*

God created Earth, and it clearly expresses His love for His creation—specifically for mankind." He stirred the remainder of his soup.

Fernanda stopped eating for a moment, contemplating what Troy had explained. She rubbed her wrists as a flood of memories of Catholic girls' school came to her mind. Nuns with no humor, yardsticks, and sore hands were a large portion of the memories. Years and years of catechism now flew through her mind as she heard Neil's terminology. "So the Easter story is connected to the creation?" she asked.

"Absolutely," Troy answered. "You can look at creation to see that God wanted a relationship with mankind so much that He created this world, the Garden, the animals—everything around us. But mankind broke the rules and destroyed the relationship with the Creator. The Creator, again wanting to restore friendship, came up with a plan. A plan to die for mankind, pay the penalty for the broken rules, and take each person's place of judgment. Humans must accept this substitution and ask for forgiveness to be restored to the right relationship with God."

Neil nodded in agreement.

Fernanda's mind again reeled with Sunday school stories. Stories she had long since dispatched to the world of myth now seemed to be more relevant. "So God's Son, Jesus, takes mankind's place by dying on the cross and rises from the dead to restore the relationship with mankind again?" she asked.

"That's right, Fernanda," said Neil.

Jim stood up and held his temples like he was having a migraine. "Wait! Stop for just a moment. You're trying to tell me that the canyon you rappelled down just a few days ago to recruit me onto this team was not only created by God, but that He created that canyon to reveal Himself to humanity?"

"Jim, I'll do you one better," said Neil. "Maybe He created that whole canyon complex to reveal Himself to *you*. Perhaps a better way to think about it, Jim, is this: what if you were the only person in the world? Would that canyon still exist? Would God have sent His Son to die only for you?"

There was an awkward silence for a few moments as the three scientists tried to connect the different parts of the conversation, struggling to fuse their scientific experience and training with their inner compulsions to believe the conversion story of Neil Stevens.

Jim looked away, avoiding Neil's eyes and standing up from his chair. "Right…OK, well, thanks for your opinion."

"Hey, you asked. Remember?" said Neil.

"You're right," said Jim, mumbling to himself. He quickly headed to the nearby creek to clean up his soup bowl and spoon and be alone with his thoughts. As Jim moved out of earshot, Fernanda and Pam politely thanked Neil and Troy for sharing their beliefs with such candor. After dinner, the group cleaned up, changed clothes, and helped Troy and Neil stow the cooking equipment. Jim returned from the stream a few minutes later and stood by the fire with the rest of the team, staring into the embers and glowing coals, contemplating the discoveries of the day.

"Well, I think we'd all like to take a look at the civilization in this time period, and I know that Troy is probably thinking there's an ark getting built around here somewhere. Do we have consensus on going toward the city that we saw from the top of the mausoleum?" asked Neil.

Pam and Fernanda nodded enthusiastically, and Jim and Captain Loren agreed.

"Is this just observation from a distance, or are we going to go among the people of this time?" asked Pam.

"Just getting close to the city will likely require us to change into garb that's more appropriate," Neil said. "We don't want to stand out like Captain Kirk and Doctor McCoy beaming into the Wild West."

"Hey, I saw that episode—the Fight at the OK Corral," said Jim. An awkward silence followed. Nobody had expected the nerdy *Star Trek* reference from an academic geologist.

"How are we going to get some gear into the city?" asked Pam, looking at the bulky cargo bins. Fernanda jumped to her feet and clapped her hands together. "How about a pulled cart or a stretcher?" she proposed. "This is an extremely agricultural society. I imagine everyone has something like that for moving harvested crops and getting rocks out of fields. But we need some intelligence on what people are wearing and how these cart things are constructed in this time period. We don't want our disguise to be the subject of hubbub in the city. Who's up for a little walk to check out the outskirts of those farms we saw?"

"Neil, I'll go with Fernanda and keep in contact with you over the radio," said Chris.

"I'd like to join as well," said Pam.

"OK, kids, bring the car back with a full tank, or you're grounded for a week," said Jim in his best parental voice.

The small team groaned collectively at Jim's attempt at humor and headed out of the glade toward the plain they had transferred to earlier that same morning.

Jim Spruce plopped down on his cot in the quiet confines of his shelter and stared through the mesh net into the sky above the canopy of trees. Some faint stars began to twinkle above, their light mostly blocked by trees that climbed a hundred feet into the evening sky.

Can it be true? he wondered.

Would God create all of this—the universe, Earth, everything—out of His love for mankind? Could God really love me, even though I have denied His existence and mocked those who do believe?

19

Spying on the Farm

(T) he sun was going down, casting huge shadows across the plain, and birds of all kinds were returning to their nests. The cacophony of chirping, squawking, and shrieks from the birds melded into a rich melody.

Chris, Fernanda, and Pam walked about five miles from the glade before they began to see evidence of civilization. Tree stumps with obvious marks of ax heads began to dot the largely overgrown plains. At the top of a rolling hill, the three found a large collection of rocks that was stacked to form a small fence. As Fernanda observed the fence, she noted that concentrated piles of stone began to bisect the landscape into irregular shapes—areas for plowing and planting.

"This is a pretty classic sign of farming—getting the rocks out of the field. It's still done this way in many parts of the world. You can see fences like this from ancient farmers in Ireland to the Amish in Lancaster, Pennsylvania," said Fernanda.

The team continued along the stone fence line and came over the top of a small hill. The sound of bleating sheep greeted them. Chris, Fernanda, and Pam quickly dropped to the ground and crawled slowly to the top of the hill, not sure what they would see beyond the mounds of grass ahead of them.

Chris pulled binoculars from his rucksack and crawled up the embankment slowly.

Over the top of the hill, he saw a small house with walls made from rock, reeds, and a mud-stucco substance. The roof was green with lichens and moss. The house was half underground, half above ground. It reminded him of houses he had seen on TV documentaries, places where Irish farmers had lived.

A cluster of sheep, like a cloud rolling along the ground, ran in a drunken formation across a small field heading for a wooden trough. Chris guessed there were about three hundred sheep all jockeying for position behind the six to eight animals that were lucky enough to be at the front of the feed trough. Beyond the noisy animals, he spied a number of fields with growing crops. He gestured to Pam and Fernanda to join him, and they crawled up to his position. Fernanda smiled as Pam scrambled to take the position nearest the SEAL. Pam's attraction to the young soldier was obvious to Fernanda, but she doubted if Chris had noticed it. Men could be kind of clueless at times, and she didn't need a PhD in anthropology to make that observation.

A farmer and a young boy were completely surrounded by the sheep. The farmer poured a basket of grain into a roughly hewn tree trunk that served as a feeding trough, and the young boy used a long stick to nudge the sheep and organize them into small clusters.

They wore clothing much like that seen in Sunday-school pictures of people in Bible times. Their skirt-like robes ended around the knee and were cinched at the waist with thick leather belts. The top portions of the robes were V-necked and had short sleeves. The man wore a scraggly beard, and he and the boy both had jet-black long hair.

"I'm glad we stopped shaving a few days ago, but it's going to take me a while to catch up with that guy," said Chris under his breath. The door to the small building opened, and a woman carried a large pottery jug down to a stream that ran between the small house and the fields of crops. She wore similar apparel, but her robe seemed to be longer than the man's. The farmer's and boy's ensembles were earth-toned and dirty from wear; the woman's clothing seemed alive with color. The hues were dark, rich royal blue and deep crimson.

The woman returned a few minutes later and spoke a few words to her husband. Pam strained over the farm animals to hear the words.

"Can you make out any of that?" asked Chris.

Pam shook her head, frustrated that she couldn't answer Chris' question any better.

"Stupid sheep," she muttered.

The farmer barked some orders to the boy, and within a few moments they all went inside the small dwelling. The sheep continued their annoying cries and munched their grain as the faint glow from a fire within illuminated the outline of the door of the small house.

The scene was at once familiar and distant. "Imagine a world without TV, phones, computers, the rat race, education, or the American dream— and here it is," Fernanda said.

"I still like TV," said Pam. Chris raised an eyebrow, deliberating on making some good-natured fun of Pam as he processed her statement and matched her up with a list of soap-opera themed shows. Pam preempted his mental list before Chris could open his mouth. "I mean I like the Discovery Channel and PBS and the Food Network . . ."

Chris cut Pam's fictitious TV listing short. "Mmm-hmm" he said with a smile, putting the binoculars back in the rucksack. "We'd better get back to the glade."

As Chris stepped ahead of the two girls, Fernanda bumped Pam on the arm and winked.

"What?" asked Pam, batting her eyes innocently at the other woman.

"Oh, nothing."

During the return trip, the three gazed up at the same constellations and stars they knew from their time. The starlight was hazy and diffused, like the sunlight had been during the day. Within a few hours, the group reached the glade and crashed on their cots for a sound sleep.

20

The Colony

T he sun came up and broke through the glade canopy in distinct shafts, dappling the tents and equipment in a camouflage of light and shadow. Fernanda unzipped her tent and stepped out into the light, stretching.

"Good morning," said Neil, sitting by a small gas camping stove over which he was brewing some coffee.

"We had a great trip down to the farm last night," Fernanda said.

"That's what Chris was telling me this morning," said Neil, gesturing toward the pile of cargo bins.

Captain Loren and Chris were going through the bins and pulling out clothing that looked like it had come from a costume shop or theater that was putting on a Greek play. The styles were biblical, very similar to what Fernanda had seen the night before. She accepted a cup of coffee from Neil and headed over to assist Rich with the clothing.

The rest of the team awoke as the sunlight increased in intensity, and after a quick breakfast, found clothing that would fit them and conceal some weapons. Loren and Chris Belkins each took a P-90 snub-nosed submachine gun that fit holsters on their backs, along with a large commando knife each. Jim built a cart without wheels that resembled a small ladder that could be dragged behind someone. Fernanda noticed his work. "Building a travois?" she asked.

"Yes," he replied. "The Native Americans came up with this design, and I'm sure it's time-tested for long distance. I hope it won't look out of place in this time period."

Fernanda pulled on a leather strap that held the top part of the rig together. "Based on what Chris, Pam, and I witnessed last night, it should blend right in."

Loren loaded the travois with the remote control unit for AARON, a few scientific instruments, some climbing gear, and extra ammunition. Jim covered the sophisticated equipment with a worn leather covering and lashed it tightly to the travois with some long, flexible branches from saplings growing nearby.

After everyone had changed into period clothing, Loren set some last-minute proximity alarms around the camp and pulled AARON to a clearing in the canopy that was still concealed by broad-leafed vegetation.

"If needed, I can get AARON over to us remotely, as long as we're not more than a four-hour flight away. With the craft running full out, that gives us a three-hundred-mile radius from here," Loren said.

"If you think I plan on walking three hundred miles today, you're nuts!" said Jim.

"No problem, Jim. Based on what we saw last night, within a few hours we'll be smack in the middle of civilization," Pam said.

Jim shook his head at Pam's analytical response. "No sense of humor," he mumbled.

The team started just an hour after the sun came up, before the heat of the day made travel miserable. As they made their way toward the farm, evidence of civilization began to spring up all around them. Small grassy pathways gave way to worn dirt paths, which turned into twenty-foot-wide roads. Small farms began to line either side. Their plentiful crops ran right to the edge of the dirt road.

Sometimes passersby gave the team a strange look, and other times they went their way with no concern at all.

The farms became more and more complex as the team journeyed farther into the settled territory. The fields of crops began to look more indus-trialized. Evidence of animal husbandry was everywhere.

"I can't believe how much we underestimated this culture," Fernanda said. "Some of these technologies won't appear on the other side of the Flood for hundreds of years."

A noticeable change slowly came across the landscape. Farms that were once productive and full of activity were in various stages of disrepair, and weeds and saplings outnumbered any crops that had seeded themselves.

A horrific smell permeated the air and overwhelmed the team with a feeling of nausea. It was the odor of rotting flesh. A cluster of people clothed in rags sat by a dilapidated single-room farmhouse. Their appearance reminded Fernanda of people she had seen in shanty towns in India and Africa—victims of extreme poverty and disease. Instead of standing erect, the people were hunchbacked. Their skin was a pasty, pale white, punctuated occasionally with bloody scabs.

As Fernanda examined the group from afar, one of the people noticed her and screamed out.

"Nu-asgab! Nu-asgab!"

The people pulled their scarf-like coverings over their faces with their bloody hands.

Pam recognized some of the syntax. "They're saying that they're 'unclean.' Get back— these people are lepers!"

Indeed, as the group continued walking down the road, the smell became unbearable. Bodies of poor souls that had succumbed to the horrific disease lay strewn in the fields, and small scavenger dinosaurs and rodents were taking their time tugging at and tearing the rotting flesh. The remains of the bodies looked like something out of a nightmare. Facial features were eaten away to leave only featureless heads. Ears, noses, and cheeks had all rotted away in grotesque ways.

As the team members reached the end of the leper colony, they saw a small girl, no more than ten years old, by the side of the road. She held a broken shard of pottery in the shape of a small box. She was beautiful, but her long, dark hair was matted and her clothes were merely rags. Her skinny legs were folded up underneath her, partially concealed beneath a dirty red robe. As the team passed, her big brown eyes looked up and locked with Neil's. The billionaire from another time crouched before this little girl who had nothing. Guilt pricked Neil as he looked at the girl's small spindly arms, covered in white lesions with a few bloody scabs on her petite hands. He knew that in a few months her fate would be the same as that of the disease victims lying in the fields behind them. Neil took a quick glance around. No one but the girl was in the area, and the road was clear up ahead.

"What can we do for her?" Neil asked Fernanda.

"I don't know," said Fernanda. "We don't have the medicine on us here, but if we took her with us—maybe we could treat her in our time."

"Even in our time, the treatments of leprosy are not a hundred percent," said Jim.

"Well, we can, at the very least, leave her some food," said Neil.

Fernanda kneeled before the small girl and brushed her matted hair out of her face. The girl responded as if she had not felt human touch in years. Her small face returned a smile and a trembling lower lip.

Jim stooped down and placed a small bag of food next to the girl. "We should get going," he said.

"God bless you," Fernanda whispered to the girl. She searched for the words in her soul that had long been dormant and tried to utter a prayer for the girl.

While the child could not understand Fernanda's strange dialect, her kindness and pity would have translated across any time period and any language. The girl's eyes widened at the odd food this stranger had provided, and she picked through the bag, pulling out a bit of bread and starting to eat it. Her brown eyes seemed to speak out to the team. Perhaps they spoke of gratitude or relief, or a simple "Thank you," but the team left the leper colony with a newfound appreciation for modern medicine.

As the team pulled the travois behind them and disappeared down the road, a small figure wearing a red cloak and holding a small bag followed them slowly and quietly.

21

Forest Encounter

With the leper colony behind them, the team made its way up the road toward the increasing bustle of pedestrians now lining the road. Evidence for advanced civilization was increasing by the mile. Farms, suburbs and, most of all, specialization of tasks. Armories, granaries, smiths, and markets began to spring up at increasing rates. The tools these people were using and the methods they had invented made one thing clear to Fernanda: everything that modern historians thought they knew about ancient man was wrong.

The road ahead branched into two smaller roadways. Troy paused at the fork in the road and studied each path. "Looks like they both head into the city," he said, pointing to the smoke from hundreds of fires curling over the dense forest ahead.

Jim wiped his face with a handkerchief. "Hey, it's hot here in the sun. Let's go through the forest and see if we can find some shade."

Troy looked at Neil, who returned an ambiguous shrug. "OK, forest trail it is," said Troy, picking up the travois and leading the team into the dense rain forest.

The forest was ancient and almost sacred in its solitary atmosphere. Massive tree trunks with thirty-foot girths lined the pathway, standing like guardians reaching high into the sky. Moss and algae grew like thin hairs on their branches and trunks. Some of the trees were so gnarled and bulbous that they resembled strange animals or even people. The pathway grew narrower as the team traveled deeper into the forest, and the dense, lush vegetation closed in around the path, concealing its entrance. The shafts of milky sunlight that had originally helped to announce the trail ahead were now cut off and trapped in the top of the thick rain forest canopy.

"Oooh, s-spooky!" cracked Jim.

Everyone smiled and laughed nervously. Jim was only verbalizing what the others felt.

While the atmosphere of the deep forest felt haunted, there was more to it than that, and a strong sense of foreboding and oppression fell across Troy. Neil felt it too, and he had the sinking feeling that the reason for his deep discomfort was right around the corner.

The ever-narrowing trail curved through thick underbrush and into a clearing in the middle of the forest. An odor gave away the presence of the clearing before it came into view. The sickening smell of rotting flesh overpowered the heavy musk scents of the forest. The entire team gasped as the leafy fronds bent out of the way to reveal a frightening scene.

There in front of the team were hundreds of decaying carcasses, some animal and some human forms. The stench was overpowering, and Fernanda and Pam pulled their tunics up from their necks to cover their noses in a vain attempt to avoid the offensive odor.

The maze of mangled bodies was shocking to behold, but strange sounds to the group's right caused the entire team to collectively cock their heads and focus on what was taking place in a shadowy valley beside the mounds of rotting flesh. Troy peered through the haze at a small group of…humans, were they? Could they really be human? The forms were crouched over the carcass of a freshly killed animal. Their backs and haunches jerked from the muscular moves of their arms as they pulled the flesh from the bones of this fresh kill. As Troy's eyes dilated and became accustomed to the dimmer light, the true appearance of these forms became clear.

They were naked, mostly; any scrap of clothing resembling a tunic or even undergarments had been worn away to leave a type of loincloth. They were human, but they were more than that—in some indescribable way. Their bodies were deathly thin; the bones of their skeletons were clearly visible under tightly pulled skin stretched across stringy muscles.

They were hissing at each other and chomping the flesh loudly, apparently completely unaware of the spectacle they were making before the small group of scientists who watched in rapt silence. Their guttural sounds were unlike anything Pam had ever heard from any linguistic perspective—if it was language at all. She had never heard the human larynx make the sounds she was hearing emanate from these beings.

The sense of impending doom and oppression flared high in Neil and Troy, more than the others on the team. Their discernment was running on high alert, shocking their inner spirits. Something was very wrong with the group of humans before them. It was not just the desperation and animalistic nature of these poor, wretched people. What they felt was way beyond natural—it was supernatural.

Troy closed his eyes for a moment and silently uttered a prayer to his Savior for protection for the group. When he opened them again he saw one of the creatures looking directly at him, staring straight into his soul. The being threw the remnants of the flesh back into the cavity of the slain creature it was eating and wiped its face briskly with its forearm. The creature jumped from his perch on the decaying carcass and scampered up another rotting hill, cocking and ducking his head, trying to get a better look at the impostors. He—it seemed like a male, with mannerisms that were distinctly masculine—barked an unrecognizable order. The others gathered around him, turned quickly, and took a defensive posture.

"Uh-oh," muttered Jim. Fernanda and Pam moved to the center of the team and grabbed each other's hands.

The shadowy tribe moved away from the carcass and began screaming at the team in a threatening, guttural, primal manner. The sounds they made were horrific and frightening, and they made the hair on the back of the team's necks stand on end. The beings stepped in a fidgety way over the maze of decaying bodies lying between them and the team as if their brains and their spirits were at odds with one another.

Chris Belkins, a seasoned Navy SEAL for over fifteen years, was visibly alarmed. He flipped his weapon off of safety and carefully drew it from the inside of his tunic. "Everyone, be extra careful not to make any sudden moves," he said, studying the creatures that were now approaching them.

Suddenly a banshee-like scream pierced the air as one of the creatures dove onto Belkins from a tree limb high in the canopy. Chris tried to maneuver out of its way, but it moved with otherworldly speed. It was smaller and lighter than the commander, and it writhed on him like a serpent might, wrapping its arms and legs tightly around Chris Belkins' body and scratching him with its overgrown, chipped fingernails. Belkins released the stock of his gun and tried to bar the disgusting creature from crushing his windpipe. His hands and arms slipped across the creature's cold and slimy flesh. Thwarting Chris's grip, the creature slithered around him, scratching and biting. The SEAL almost wretched from the smell it emitted, a noxious combination of open sewer stench and vomit.

Quickly the creature wound its skinny, wraith-like body around the commander's midsection and bit down on his left forearm. Belkins yelped in pain, but finally got the upper hand by bringing his right fist straight into his attacker's face. The creature released its grip on him and bounded backward, in almost a pirouette, holding its face with its hands and screaming in pain. The commander spun around and pulled the trigger on his P-90 submachine gun while aiming at the creature's chest.

What happened next stunned the team.

The creature's body, like a husk, fell amid the rain of bullets and hit the ground, trembling involuntarily. Then a sharp ripping sound filled the air, and a flood of ghostly vapors escaped from the fallen body. It seemed that as physical life ebbed from the human form, the invisible inhabitants that had controlled the body were forced to exit.

Belkins looked down at the person he had just killed. He was only a man, a middle-aged man—much like himself. In death he appeared human and almost peaceful, but moments before, under the control of something else, the man had been like a demonic marionette.

"Demons..." said Troy, hardly believing the word passing his lips. Dark angels: the former inhabitants of heaven and God the Father's servants, until a rebellion resulted in their expulsion.

The other creatures, seeing their leader dead, now rushed the group in a single action. Chris Belkins and Captain Loren prepared to spray lead into the creatures when Neil's voice rang out above the piercing squeals of the charging mob: "Lord Jesus, protect us!" It wasn't meant as a command, but as a prayer. The demonic beings stopped in their tracks, scratching their ears and foreheads with their fingernails and arching their backs in agony. They screamed and hissed at the team and then broke into a full-fledged retreat toward the edge of the clearing, cursing the team in a language known only to them.

Troy had only a moment to grasp what had just happened. In the Old Testament, people were saved by looking forward to the promise of the Redeemer. During this period, the Holy Spirit did not dwell inside of believers as He did in Troy's and Neil's souls. Invoking that balance of power was all that was needed to tip the scales in favor of the small team of scientists.

Pam was shaking, overcome by the scene of mangled carcasses, the smell of decaying flesh, and the violent attack on Chris. Jim and Fernanda crouched near her and attempted to provide her comfort, yet each of them was disturbed.

"What just happened here?" Fernanda asked Jim quietly. Jim just shook his head. He had no words. They were scientists, but what they had seen moments before was not reproducible by experiment and could not be explained by science. They had been outnumbered, and without the help of advanced weaponry from thousands of years in the future, they all should have been dead. But a single phrase from Neil, a Christian, had sent these creatures running for their very lives, or at least for the lives of the poor human beings whose bodies they dominated and inhabited.

Could it be true? Jim thought. *Could there be much more to this than just the debate about the age of the earth and how man came to be?*

The questions echoed in his mind as the team made its way back to the road that wound through the forest.

22

The Suburbs

A head of the team, a foul-smelling grayish smoke seemed to pour from the landscape. Chris pulled his tunic up and covered his mouth. The smoke stung his eyes. He looked behind him at the rest of the team; they were taking the same precautions. The smoke rolled lazily across the ground before finally lifting into the azure sky. He noticed the sound of his footsteps change as he walked cautiously forward through the billowing smoke. Between the shades of gray plumes a man-made structure revealed itself, taking the place of the dirt road. A robust wooden bridge allowed the team to move over an enormous trench that was carved below them.

The smoke had an acrid smell to it—not from burning wood or oil. As the team members crossed the bridge and looked down into the trench, they could see hundreds of slaves with iron axes and shovels cleaving large grayish-white rocks from the sides of the trench.

"It's some sort of mine," said Fernanda.

Jim had a puzzled look on his face. The smell was familiar to him, but he couldn't quite place it. The people in the trench were covered with a white, ash-like substance that made them visually blend into a unified sea of slavery.

Fernanda noticed that many of the workers were shaking uncontrollably as they labored with sharp tools, cutting gray minerals out of the side of the rock face. Some even sat by the rocks in a complete state of palsy, unable to help their comrades with the task of mining. Many of the people were bleeding from their noses, and the bright red color against their all-white faces was striking.

Jim snapped his fingers as he put the puzzle together. "It must be arsenic. They probably mine it for some kind of smelting process, perhaps to form bronze."

Fernanda nodded, remembering a few summer trips to ancient tells in Persia where arsenic mines were excavated during her years as a graduate student. "Arsenic causes muscular atrophy and makes the nasal passages bleed. These poor people are as good as dead; they just don't know it yet."

The huge gray rocks were placed in great piles, and some of the slaves were breaking them into smaller chunks and then, in turn, pulverizing the medium-sized chunks of rock into aggregate. Another group of slaves was shoveling the aggregate into huge ovens and working large wooden poles up and down. The action from the wooden poles worked a leather baffle that stoked the furnaces to high temperatures. The fires raged and the heat increased measurably in the area with every stroke of the baffle.

Just beyond the trench where the miners were working on the arsenic deposits, a choke-inducing smell arose that was worse than the stench of the leper colony. Dense swarms of flies hovered over a greenish-brown canal.

"Ugh! It's a sewage canal!" said Pam, covering her face with part of the scarf she had draped over her head.

The toxic stew of human waste was dotted with carcasses of animals and humans.

"Apparently they use this canal as a giant disposal," said Fernanda. "We must be really close now."

The team plugged their noses and covered their mouths as they fought their way through the thick clouds of flies hovering over the filthy canal.

The smoke from the arsenic mine began to dissipate and clear as the team members moved down the road. Then they all stopped in their tracks to behold the ancient city that lay ahead of them. Even from a distance, the city took their breath away. Parapet-laden walls stretched wide before them—miles across. The walls were a beige color and seemed to follow the rolling hills of the landscape in a terraced manner. Small homes dotted the outskirts of the town, unprotected by the enormous walls that seemed to jut out of the earth itself. Wisps of smoke curled up from the inside of the city and swirled over the sides of the wall like translucent flags.

"So much for cavemen!" said Jim.

23

The City of Unug-Kulaba

A s the team continued their walk into the city, the features of the place became overwhelming. The city was not primitive in any way—far from it. Massive granite walls rose beyond the small homes ahead of them, not just tall but wide as well. The walls encompassing the city were forty feet tall and wide enough for soldiers to walk atop them four abreast. A row of ancient stakes surrounded the more refined wall. Each stake was similar in construction to the ones the team had found barricading the Garden of Eden.

"These stakes must have been an initial defense for the city before the walls were constructed," said Fernanda.

"Yeah, but to protect them from what?" Jim asked. "I'd have to guess, based on the size of those stakes and the angle in which they're positioned, that the city needed protection against large predators—like dinosaurs."

As they passed deeper and deeper into the city limits, the actual development of the city became more obvious. The wooden stakes and thatched mud homes gave way to homes made with sun-dried mud bricks, which in turn revealed rows and rows of stone buildings that began to increase in height and sophistication. Finally the domiciles of farmers and other dwellers outside the city yielded to an enormous moat that made the walls seem even taller than they were.

"It's like a geologic column for the development of the city, except it goes laterally as if the citizens continued to leave their early habitations and move into increasingly more complex dwellings," said Fernanda.

Jim sniped at Fernanda's non-precision. "You mean a geologic *row*?"

Fernanda ignored Jim, a talent she was becoming expert at.

"Look here." Pam pointed to a nearby home that displayed a myriad of the building techniques all swirled together haphazardly. A thatched roof meshed with a combination of mud bricks and roughly cut granite stones. "You can see how the construction techniques continually change over time. They are becoming more advanced as we approach the city wall."

A massive wooden gate patrolled by exceptionally tall soldiers swallowed the road that the team was traveling. The highway was bustling with traders and other people pulling carts and carrying items into the city for sale. The team merged unnoticed into the bustle of merchants, peasants, prostitutes, and city officials that flowed through the gate like a river of humanity.

The inside of the city was a beehive of activity. Merchants and traders on the streets haggled over prices. The poor and maimed begged for food, and clusters of soldiers observed strangers with a critical eye. Prostitutes, both male and female, were in full abundance, offering their services to all those passing through the busy streets. Some of their customers didn't even make it to the privacy of the back rooms.

Chris noticed Troy and Neil looking away from the risqué action, and Pam's face was noticeably red with embarrassment—it was as if the only people shocked by this behavior were those from four thousand years in the future.

Fernanda studied the people that swarmed around her. As in any city, the people's ages and looks were remarkably diverse. Children ran up and down the street, underfoot and colliding with the older people milling in the streets. As adolescence gave way to adulthood, the characteristics of age became more difficult to pinpoint. Fernanda noticed that hair was a good metric to determine some sort of measure of how old these people were— and most of them had hair the color of silvery white. Fernanda saw that most of the white-haired people had protruding foreheads, yet they were still mobile and very strong. There were no signs of osteoporosis or other types of degenerative bone diseases. She scanned the overall population and noted this same feature in many of the mature individuals passing her in the street.

These people are hundreds of years old, she thought.

Water seemed to be a magical part of what made this ancient city tick. Flumes carried water from tall aqueducts all over the city, and in a somewhat haphazard way, crisscrossed each other much like the highways in Los Angeles do. Some of the aqueducts were stone, but many appeared to be made of some sort of dark wood. The flumes glistened in the sun as if they had a resin or fiberglass shell.

Fernanda noticed an aqueduct that was ten times larger than the other flumes. It ran to the top of an enormous angled roof that tilted down toward the plaza. The roof had the same dark, shiny, resin look of the wooden flumes careening overhead. It was at a perpendicular angle to the sun, and Fernanda immediately knew what she was looking at.

"They're using solar energy to heat the water!" she exclaimed.

A desperate scream behind the team caused the merchants to stop their bartering. Even the children stopped their games and spun around toward the cry for help. The crowd parted, revealing a near perfect circle of street pavers. An old man was sprawled on his back with blood gushing from a large cut on his thick, prominent brow. The crimson stream intermixed with his long, white, matted hair.

Pam's hand came to her mouth as she strained to see between the gawking citizens that stood between her and the old man. A trio of soldiers was beating him to death. Two of the soldiers were taking turns holding the man down while the others punched him in the face. His cries were difficult to hear over the cheering of the crowd and the sounds of the soldiers' punches landing against the bones in his face. The garbled words that did reach the ears of the crowd were as universal a cry for help as any distress call Chris Belkins had ever heard. He pulled his pistol from his holster and began to pull his arm free from his tunic.

A hand clamped onto his upper arm. Chris looked back, and Jim locked eyes with him. The geologist nodded behind them, and Chris saw a squad of twelve soldiers, apparently the attacking soldiers' friends, standing against a wall laughing and cheering their comrades on. Chris replaced the pistol and nodded grimly at Jim. This was not the time or place.

As the old man gasped for breath, the third soldier of the group picked up the man's walking stick and a dirty bag containing his belongings and began to walk away. The soldier holding the old man down leaped to his feet to follow the spoils into the crowd. The remaining soldier stood up. Chris was amazed at the height of this man, over seven feet tall and massively built in his upper body—a wrestler's build. The soldier raised his sandaled foot and brought it down onto the man's delicate neck, crushing his windpipe. The soldier sniffed dismissively at his victim and slid his foot across the pavement of the street, smearing the blood as if the sin of murdering this man was as easily removed as mud from his sandal. The crowd slowly dispersed as the soldiers walked away, laughing darkly as the lifeless body of the old man lay in a bloody mess on the cobbled street.

Belkins had never witnessed such blatant disregard for life, especially from soldiers toward a civilian. Under his cloak he double-checked the safety switch on his automatic weapon, flipping it from "safe" to "fire." While he understood why Jim Spruce had stopped him, he knew that he had the firepower to even the score in almost any uneven fight. If it had been only himself, he would have had no qualms in wasting the entire population of people in the street that cheered on the soldiers, but Pam…and Fernanda, too. The women on the team made him weigh the cost of vengeance more carefully.

Neil touched Chris on the arm as if he understood the mental self-torture that he was performing. "Come on. We couldn't have helped him without ending the mission. They probably would've killed us without thinking much about it." Chris' face was somber, and he nodded silently as he turned away from the body of the old man he could have saved.

As the team continued down the street, Fernanda's eyes darted from place to place, aching to know the story behind every item and every person she saw. How the walls were made. How the intricate ironwork on the torch holder mounted to the wall had been crafted—the intimate life of the artisan who forged it. Did he or she have a family? What were his ancestors like? She wanted to know it all. The city was a treasure trove of ancient knowledge waiting to be discovered.

The cobbled street began to open up into a circular courtyard where a huge obelisk rose out of a smoothly cut stone floor. The twenty-foot-tall object had a myriad of runes and strange symbols carved on its four stone faces. Pam and Fernanda approached the large, sculpted stone to investigate the symbolic language. A group of women were seated around the base of the obelisk, rocking back and forth and occasionally reaching out to touch the scribing on the stone. Their lips uttered strange words, and their eyes rolled into the tops of their heads. A wisp of smoke rose from a dish in which some unknown substance was burning that obviously contributed to the women's zombie-like trance.

The obelisk was covered in small, eight-sided rosettes that were etched on the sides of the monument. The symbols were immediately recognized by Fernanda. "These are markings of Inanna," she said.

"Who's Inanna?" asked Pam.

"She was an ancient goddess that was worshiped in Ur, but there's plenty of evidence she was worshiped even before then," Fernanda said. "This could be one of the earlier cities that Ur was eventually built upon—perhaps Kulab, Kulaba, or Unug-Kulaba."

Suddenly the air was filled with the rhythmic pounding of drums. The people surrounding the square and worshiping the obelisk snapped out of their trance and ran into a larger plaza, deeper in the city. The team watched in astonishment as the entire population, attracted by the drums, abandoned all duties to meet together in the center of the city. Traders left their stations, soldiers abandoned their posts, and even the lame and blind forsook their highly valued begging spots and attempted to reach the crowded plaza.

The drums continued to increase in volume and tempo, drowning out the team's ability to talk among themselves. Fernanda and Pam looked to Neil for guidance. He shrugged and pointed toward the crowd, and the team made its way to the plaza to see what could possibly capture the attention of an entire city.

The granite structures of the city were massive, much larger and more sophisticated than Fernanda had expected, with abundant evidence of a clear understanding of engineering and architecture. A central pyramidal temple complex filled the heart of the city and seemed to unify the various sectors of commerce, religion, and residential areas.

A row of full-size statues stood in line before the team. The statues were all depicted as royalty, perfect in their proportions with one exception: their heads were barrel-shaped. Perfectly proportioned faces merged into elongated skulls. Pam shivered at the otherworldly look of these men.

"Who in the world are these guys?" asked Jim, looking at the lifelike statues.

"I have no idea," replied Fernanda.

Fernanda pointed to the sloped temple with steep steps leading to its apex and tried to speak to Pam over the beating drums. "That temple has characteristics of both Egyptian and Aztec architecture." Pam returned a nod in agreement.

As the team members passed through a crowded inner gate, they entered a perfectly square plaza. Smoke from giant copper bowls filled with incense roiled across the expanse of the plaza. As the smoke dissipated a bit, through the hazy translucence the team could see that the full citizenry of the city was assembled. Thousands, perhaps even tens of thousands, of people were crammed into the plaza. In the center of the swarm of humanity, a massive statue of a nude woman posed in a seductive stance stood in the middle of an enormous fire pit. The flames licked to the top of the stone goddess's knees.

"Inanna," said Fernanda, breathlessly.

The heat emanating from the fire pit was intense, and the team tried to protect their faces and exposed skin from the blast. An intertwined stone sculpture of lions in various aggressive poses encircled the fire pit and kept the fuel for the fiery ceremony from spilling out into the crowd.

The drums were reaching a fever pitch, hammering the crowd's eardrums with a syncopated beat that bordered on the painful. The people in the plaza whipped into a frenzy, writhing suggestively with the rhythm and swinging their arms back and forth through the air in unison. Sweat glistened on the crowd from the heat of the fire and the press of human flesh.

A giant man appeared on a platform, shoulder-level with the female statue. He wore a kilt-like garment overlaid with small metal panels of gold and copper. On his face was a metal mask of beautiful copper and gold fragments, welded and fashioned into the striking resemblance of a lion's head.

The man raised his hands, and the drums stopped.

The crowd erupted, screaming in unison. "Ana ila bansur!"

"The man on the platform must be a priest," said Fernanda.

The priest raised an ornate staff into the air and spoke to the crowd. "Sakirna Inanna bansur ka zu gisgal ila!"

Neil looked over at Pam, who was concentrating on the words being spoken. "Pam, can you pick out what they're saying?" he asked.

"The language is similar to ancient Sumerian, but it's different." She strained to hear the words, the tone, everything. "He's telling the crowd to sacrifice their most important or precious possession to Inanna...and something about the prosperity of the...crops?"

The drums resumed; this time the beat was faster than before. A line of women appeared on the platform next to the priest.

"Oh..." Pam's eyes widened in horror. "They...they're going to sacrifice babies!" she said, her eyes welling with tears.

Fernanda's hands came up to her mouth in shock at what she was witnessing.

Troy Scott's face was crimson as his anger flared. His description of this culture's violence back in the conference room of TRC had been ridiculed by Jim, and until now, the ancient people's amazing technological achievements had blinded the group to the main reason that God had annihilated this entire race of humans, save eight. Troy was beginning to understand why God had chosen such a severe and final action. Here, within a day's journey of the Garden of Eden, where God had walked with man, was a wicked city that had forgotten God, whose citizens were sacrificing their offspring to a stone goddess that could not hear or react to their worship.

As the drumbeats again reached a fever pitch, the women, one by one, kissed their infants on the forehead and lofted them into the air over the fire pit. The babies' screams could not be heard over the chanting of the frenzied crowd and the pounding of the drums; the horrific ceremony seemed to be happening in slow motion. Each helpless infant, with its eyes closed tightly and its mouth open in a silent scream, arced through the air and then disappeared into the violent conflagration at the base of Inanna's sculpted form.

Again and again the cruel ritual was performed, until the line of women offering their innocent children was exhausted.

The drums returned to a slower rhythm and then stopped. The throng cheered, and the priest bowed to the people and to Inanna's likeness before he disappeared behind a stone wall covered with cryptic symbols. The drums slowed and quieted, as if to compel an orderly exit from the worship plaza. The crowd began to disperse and resume the activities that had engaged them before the mandatory call to worship.

Pam and Fernanda had tears running down their faces, mixing with the dust from the long walk to the city. They brushed them away, leaving alternating lines of clean and dirty skin. The two women were ashamed and appalled by the spectacle they had just observed. While neither Pam nor Fernanda had children of their own, they wondered how a mother—any mother—could abandon maternal instinct and kill her child in such a spectacle.

Rich picked up the cart, and the team continued through the city, passing markets, open-air eateries, and expansive parks where children played tag and other timeless games.

Fernanda's early wonderment was now tempered; she silently interrogated each person she passed in the streets.

Why are you part of something so heinous? What possible value or solace can an activity like the sacrificing of your offspring bring you?

They had nearly reached the farthermost perimeter of the city after about an hour of walking. The fortified wall of the city stood before them, and they saw a giant stairway leading to the top.

"That should be quite a view," said Neil.

As the team members journeyed toward the wall, past merchants, animals, and children playing in the streets, they gasped collectively at a sight no one had anticipated. They beheld another colossal plaza that seemingly appeared out of nowhere, a plaza of flat stone tiles three hundred feet square, dotted with iron sculptures that were eerily familiar. The plaza was virtually absent of people: just a few men in robes, gathered in small clusters a hundred yards away from the team, were visible.

"This is a huge use of valuable city space," said Fernanda. "Whatever this is…it's special."

A ring of concentric circles spread across the floor of the plaza as if the ripple from a stone tossed into a pond had been frozen in time. Jim dropped down on one knee and examined one of the rings etched into the stone tiles beneath his feet. It included perfectly drilled holes in a near-perfect arc, each hole separated from the next by only a few inches. He looked to the left and right, noting that the perforations formed a perfect curve away from his position. Perhaps it indicated a map, or maybe an orbit. Jim rubbed the top of the stone with his hand and touched some residue around the top of the drilled hole. Dark orange rust appeared on his dirty palm. "Some sort of metal posts were most likely placed into the holes during certain points in time."

"Time and space," said Neil, pointing to the holes and their positions in the overall ring.

"Each hole represents a single moment in time. It's visual calculus!"

The discovery was so unexpected and so novel, it literally made the group forget about the wall ahead of them. They simply stopped and watched the unusual robed men as they made measurements with golden sticks of various sizes. Each of the men was unusually tall, perhaps eight to ten feet—giants when compared to even the tallest of the expedition team. Their heads were deformed, but not facially; their skulls grew taller than normal—almost barrel-like and sloped backward, like the statues in Inanna's temple plaza. Their faces were full of wisdom and wickedness in equal measure.

The tall robed men seemed to be clustering around three iron spheres in the midst of the plaza. The center sphere was enormous, and although it was rusting from exposure to the moist air, it had clearly been fashioned by an artisan with incredible metalworking skill. This sphere was much larger than the others roughly twenty feet in diameter. About fifty feet away was another iron sphere, but this one was much smaller, just a few inches in diameter, and mounted on a metal pole that had been placed into one of the holes on an etched ring. The priests—who also appeared to be scientists—were examining the third sphere, which was further out. The robed men adjusted a structure that revolved around the metal pole, holding up the middle sphere. For a brief second, the men shifted to one side as they examined the structure, and a small, marble-sized object could be seen on the end of a thin metal arm that was bent into an "L" shape next to the larger sphere.

Jim didn't need an explanation; he knew instantly what it was. "It's a model of the solar system! There's the sun, Venus," he pointed to the lonely planet on a pole to their right, "and...Earth!" He pointed to the cluster of priest-scientists surrounding the strange sphere with the protruding arm.

Neil laid his rucksack on the smooth granite floor that stretched out before him. "It looks like the men are trying to determine how the moon orbits the earth. Observation and modeling are a very advanced marriage of concepts for a time period like this."

Just then, the chief priest who had ordered the sacrifice of the babies to the stone image of Inanna strode across the plaza toward the robed men. The mere presence of this man brought the feeling of impending danger, as if evil flowed from him like electricity.

"Um, I think we should get out of Dodge," said Jim.

"I agree with Jim for once," said Pam.

The team members walked back to the travois to continue their journey to the wall. As they exited the plaza, they saw that the outermost orbit of strange bored holes in the floor was zodiac-like, with etchings of Inanna that circumnavigated the entire plaza. The perimeter was patrolled by the giant guards, like the kind that had killed the old man near the entrance to the city. The close association of the city's religion, its scientists, and its military made Jim uncomfortable.

As the expedition members viewed the outer circular ring of the plaza, they noticed smaller etchings that were not depictions of the goddess of the city in the stone face of the curving wall. As they got closer, they saw that one of the curved rock panels had a familiar etching. Fernanda gasped as she beheld an artifact that would make her case for the connections between the cultures of ancient times. In front of her, a small collection of large dots was connected in an almost childlike dot-to-dot fashion.

As Fernanda ran up to the wall, Jim looked over his shoulder, scanning the stone expanse for anyone that might take undue interest in Fernanda's wall gawking. She pressed her fingers into the deeply drilled holes, then looked down at a digital watch on her wrist, pressing a button to bring up the compass feature on the device.

"Come on, Fernanda, let's get going!" said Jim gruffly.

The compass confirmed Fernanda's assumption:

...E...SE...S...SW...

"These drilled holes are star constellations!" she announced to the group with a smile on her face. "This one is Orion." She pointed to the three stars that formed the belt. Indeed, the shape was bounded by the familiar upper star of Betelgeuse and the lower boundary star of Rigel.

Other constellations were etched alongside Orion, but it was the shape and connection of the smaller stars that made the group marvel. The prominent profile of a seated lion was outlined on the stone.

"Is this the beginnings of the Sphinx?" wondered Pam aloud, almost embarrassed to ask a question that bordered on the insane.

"Oh, come on now, that's impossible!" said Jim.

"I don't know," replied Fernanda, rubbing her hands across the etchings and admiring the stonework. "I could spend the rest of my career at this wall."

"I don't think you're going to get that opportunity," said Rich, pointing to the cluster of robed scientists who had noticed this strange group's interest in their oversized experiment. A squad of soldiers began to cross the wide expanse of the plaza toward the small team.

"Come on, let's get out of here," said Troy, picking up the back of the cart and helping Rich lift the hidden equipment mounted on the wood bars that formed the top of the travois. The team wound its way up the forty-foot stairway, and as they approached the top of the wall, a mélange of noises greeted them. The sounds of sheep, lions, elephants, horses, birds—all the makings of a zoo melded into one.

As the team members peered over the top of the wall into the rain forest below them, they gasped in awe.

Troy's eyes welled with tears as his vision was filled with the object he had sought after his entire adult life. Neil slapped him on the back gently, knowing how important the moment was—happy he was there to share it with his friend. Troy smiled at him and wiped a few of the tears from his cheeks. But as he stared out at the massive vessel before him, he muttered something that no one in the group expected.

"We are in so much trouble."

24

The Ark

As the team looked over the top of the parapets on the city wall, in a field a thousand yards away stood the results of a construction project that bordered on the impossible.

"The Ark!" said Neil breathlessly.

"It's done! They've finished the construction," said Troy.

The vessel was enormous, and even at a distance of a thousand yards, the sheer size of the craft was jaw-dropping. The Ark was situated in the middle of a plain, which looked as if it had once been part of the rain forest that carpeted the rest of the landscape. A hundred years of cutting down trees for lumber had resulted in the entire plain being dotted with tree stumps. Young saplings were breaking through the rich soil and attempting to take the place of the enormous trees that had obviously supplied the Ark with its hull support and planking.

The Ark was not brown, as many paintings of the ancient barge had suggested. It was a dark amber color and had an unusual shine, reflecting the environment around it on its massive hull. The pitch resin made the boat glow in the sun as though it had been dipped in honey.

The craft looked to be about 550 feet long and 90 feet wide. It was taller than everyone had assumed—as tall as a three-story building, some sixty feet from the keel to the top deck. If the Ark had stood beside the fortified walls of Unug-Kulaba, the team would have needed a ladder to climb from the wall to the top deck.

The Ark was much more nautical in its shape than the huge, clumsy wooden boxes seen in most artists' renditions. The bow had a spine that rose from the bottom of the boat to the top, ending in a massive stem projection that rose high above the top deck and was almost sail-like in appearance. At the stern, the opposite end of the Ark, a wooden structure projected in the same manner as the bow's spine, but it was on the bottom of the hull. Clearly, it was designed in the shape of a rudder for stabilization, but not for navigation. No movable parts or hinges for adjusting a course were visible. The Ark tapered up at each end, mimicking the form of a huge canoe.

"What in the world are those huge shapes on each end?" asked Pam.

Troy was still lost in his examination of the enormous vessel, but he replied to Pam while analytically evaluating the structure. "It's much more boat-like than I ever expected it to be. It's clear from the design that it's built to withstand waves—really big waves. My best guess is that the projections on each end are related to the ship's steering. Or maybe it would be better to say that they're for orientation. Perhaps the sail part is for catching the wind and orienting the boat perpendicularly to the direction of the wind." He pointed to the wooden shape looming over the bow. "The shape on the stern is clearly rudder-oriented, and perhaps it's designed to work in conjunction with the sail on the bow."

The roof of the Ark had a slight taper as well, and it ended in a central cabin that ran along the entire dorsal side of the boat. The cabin had open windows on either side for ventilation. Alongside the long cabin were ingenious gutters that seemed to disappear inside the boat instead of leading away to the outside.

About halfway between the city wall and the Ark was a barricade of stakes positioned like a fence. "Check out this fence," said Fernanda. "It seems like it's being used as a security device. Are they keeping people out or animals in?"

Each fence element was arranged like a giant jack. The fence posts all passed through a central hub of metal brackets similar to the fence surrounding the Garden of Eden, but perhaps a generation later in design. They rested like giant asterisks in a line across the landscape.

As Troy took in the view, it was clear to him that Noah was a man of some wealth; the average city dweller would not have had the means to achieve a project of this scale. A large dwelling that looked something like a castle was connected to the Ark on its far side, away from the city. A huge wooden bridge extended from the top of the castle wall to the top deck of the wooden vessel. The bridge's huge suspension struts and intricate supports crisscrossed the span, resembling the underpinnings of an old railroad bridge.

On the ground, along the entire length of the Ark's port side, sat a series of large empty kennels. Clearly, the Ark was the source of the menagerie of animal sounds now piercing the air, and apparently the animals were already inside. Beside the Ark, three huge, hollow hemispheres made of metal and lumber rose out of the earth like emerging globes.

"Look, they were using aviaries to keep the various types of birds partitioned," said Fernanda.

Behind the hundreds of now-empty kennels, an enormous stockpile of straw and grain could be seen, as well as crates and jars that presumably held foodstuffs for the eight humans who would attend to the animals for more than a year.

On the opposite side—the starboard side of the Ark—stood three huge cranes built from large, hand-hewn timbers. Each crane was of a different size and different height, no doubt built and used during each phase of the Ark's construction. Next to the crane, two giant mammoths walked side by side, fitted with leather-and-wood harnesses mounted to their backs and cinched across their midsections. The gleaming white tusks of the mammoths were shorn in half, but even at half-length they were impressive and probably deadly. A muscular man stood in front of them, pulling a strap and leading them away from the Ark. In turn, they pulled a rope tight that ran through a network of pulleys on the bottom of one of the cranes. Slowly, a wooden pallet loaded with containers of grain was lifted into the air and placed on the roof of the Ark. A trumpeting sound came from one of the mammoths as it rose up on its hind feet, taking the human leading it by surprise. He quickly dashed to the animal's side and tried to steady it.

Jim Spruce stood on the wall with his mouth open, running his digital camcorder, sweeping it from side to side as he tried to capture the entire scene before them.

In front of the Ark, a fifty-foot-wide pond of burning, bubbling pitch smoked and gurgled. This fiery sea emitted the acrid odor of petroleum that was in a constant battle with the smell of the animals. A variety of cauldrons and iron forges were positioned near the burning pitch pond.

A small, swiftly flowing river passed through the area behind the barrier fence, cutting the land in half. A wooden bridge was built over the river, which seemed to run faster than any of the others the team had seen on their way into the city from the glade. Built next to the bridge was a series of waterwheels that turned at different speeds. A wooden platform extended beyond the wheelhouse, and several horses and donkeys were positioned nearby. A pile of sawed lumber and mounds of sawdust sat adjacent to the wheelhouse. A maze of jigs and templates were just behind the waterwheels, resembling an automotive assembly line.

"Look! It's a lumber mill—powered by water," said Jim.

A massive yawning doorway was open on the port side, with a large ramp leading down to the empty kennels. Scaffolding surrounded the bottom of the boat's hull. The ancient beams of the scaffold had a hundred years' worth of sawdust, moss, and spilled pitch on them, making them a dull black color.

As the team continued to absorb the near-infinite details of the Ark before them, Fernanda turned to Troy. "Why did you say we're in trouble?"

"Because the Ark is done—I mean, it's completely finished! The animals are here and boarded, the food is stocked—technically, there's nothing left to do."

Fernanda glanced at Jim. "What do you think? I mean, there are around twenty thousand different kinds of animals, with twenty-five thousand representing the high end of the estimate. Do you think all those animals can fit in that boat?"

Jim was still taking in the startling scene, but he answered Fernanda in a slow, measured tone. "I don't know. Obviously they're only taking kinds and not species. We know that all the species of a kind seem to have common ancestors, so that seems to jibe. Most of the species of the world are insects, which breathe through their skin and may be able to survive a cataclysmic flood, and fish obviously are not in peril. So we end up with mammals, birds, amphibians, and reptiles that would need the protection of the Ark. Probably around, um, I don't know—seventeen thousand species." Jim scratched his beard-covered chin and drank in the sights before him. "At 550 feet long and, let's say, what, ninety feet wide? And another fifty feet high, we're looking at something like 2.7 million cubic feet."

Jim closed his eyes for a moment and tried to visualize the average pen sizes, factoring in three decks, internal supports, and other nautical characteristics that would govern the internal space available to Noah. "I'd say there's room for probably over 125,000 animals the size of a sheep. So, yeah, I guess that thing should be big enough." He could hardly believe the words coming from his own lips.

Neil looked out across the plain, almost numb with wonder. The boat that lay cradled in its support trusses looked odd and out of place next to the city. The Ark was like an ancient Spruce Goose with nowhere to go and nothing to do but decorate the landscape. He imagined this project had attracted some ridicule at first, but now, after a hundred years, it had simply become a monument to Noah's commitment and belief that what he was doing was correct.

Troy and Neil felt ashamed as they looked at the massive scale of the project that eight people had toiled for more than one hundred years to build, all in faith. This was a boat, but much more than a boat—the thing was as long as a modern nuclear submarine. Both men knew that the faith they exercised in their own lives needed a tune-up. Here was Noah, a man who trusted God implicitly while the entire known world likely ridiculed him.

"How long do you think it would take us to get back to the transmission spot from here?" Troy asked the group, not addressing a specific member.

"Probably at least eight hours. Why do you ask?" wondered Belkins.

"Because I really doubt we'll have that kind of time, and I don't think we'll be here for four more days on this expedition, either," Troy said.

"Why do you say that?" asked Jim.

"They're packing up for the biggest storm of all time," said Troy, pointing to the crane lofting food onto the top deck of the Ark and motioning toward the empty kennels beside the enormous vessel. He turned to Neil and said emphatically, "Neil, when we communicate back to TRC, we must change the destination point to higher ground. If the Flood occurs while we're here, the area we transferred into will be underwater almost immediately."

The team members surveyed the landscape around them, looking for high ground and a new spot from which to transfer. A few hills could be seen behind the Ark, and they rose to a height of about one hundred feet.

"There!" said Troy, pointing to a distant green hillside. "We need to get that point to Cameron."

Fernanda's face filled with concern as the implications of the change became clear. "But I thought that the recalculation process takes a long time. Something like two weeks?"

"You're right, Fernanda, but we need to trust the team at TRC. I would trust Cameron with my life, and Alicia's team is the best in the world." Neil placed his hand on Jim's shoulder. "You may get a front-row seat to see how the geology of this planet was formed, and it might be a little too close for comfort."

Jim gritted his teeth. "I've always loved field work—count me in."

Neil addressed the team. "Gang, we're going to camp on that high point and get the new transfer coordinates back to Cameron tonight."

The sun was beginning to paint the sky with orange and crimson streaks, announcing the commencement of sunset as the team left the city and headed toward the Ark and the high ground beyond it.

As they left, three tall, shadowy figures followed them into the canopy of the rain forest as the sun set on the violent city of Unug-Kulaba.

25

Hike to the Hill

T he team members exited the city and continued their trek south along the Ark construction site toward the high hills they had spotted from the top of the city wall. Walking along the side of the Ark was a surreal experience. The fact that eight people had built this enormous boat over a period of a hundred years was hard to take in—it was an amazing accomplishment.

The team passed a group of citizens making fun of the hardworking family as they took animals into the Ark and loaded foodstuffs onto the roof of the vessel. Even though the team couldn't make out the words, the sarcasm, cursing, and disdain for Noah's family was easily discernible.

The Ark was suspended on an intricate scaffolding system that kept the landlocked vessel level. As Jim studied the techniques that had been used to construct the boat, he marveled at how such an undertaking could be accomplished without the modern-day tools of AutoCAD drawings, load and stress studies using calculus, or even just the benefit of a handheld calculator.

As they continued up the incline toward the hill and began leaving the Ark behind them, the team could see the sun setting and bathing the massive city of Unug-Kulaba in golden-orange light. The drums started up again, and the team members exchanged glances—they knew what the drums meant.

"I've never seen such savagery, such a lack of humanity, and yet for all the paganism, this is an amazingly modern city. Sewers, hot and cold running water, markets, stonework, artisans— they have it all hundreds of years before we would expect it," Fernanda said.

"The Bible says this whole civilization was destroyed by God because of their great wickedness. As civilized as they are...well, I agree with Fernanda. I've never seen anything like what I witnessed there," said Troy.

The team reached the top of the grade and stood on the hill facing the Ark with the city lights burning brightly behind it. A small canopy of trees was a hundred yards away.

"We'll camp in that thicket of trees tonight," said Neil, pointing off to the hillside. "If I can get everyone to sit down for an hour and gather together all the data you have collected today, we'll deliver it to Cameron during the communication back to the ops center. We have about six hours to get the data stored and transferred to the point on the plain where we arrived this morning."

"Well, I'd better get busy getting AARON over here then," said Rich, pulling out his laptop and starting AARON remotely.

Miles and miles away, hidden amid the lush vegetation of the glade that the team had called home that morning, LED lights illuminated on the miniature helicopter's avionics bay. AARON's motor began to power up, and within moments a high-pitched whine filled the air, providing power to the seventy-five pounds of chassis, batteries, and avionics that comprised the smart helicopter's braincase. AARON autonomously scanned the ground and canopy above with its range-finding lasers and determined that it was safe to rise up to an altitude of one hundred feet above the foliage canopy. An instant later, the computer inside AARON gave instructions to the rotor and its collective to move into the night sky. The small mechanical whirlybird continued its rise in altitude and then dipped its nose slightly and sped off toward the team's position.

Loren watched a green blip on his laptop that updated every second with the change in AARON's position. "It's on the way. ETA is about two hours," he said.

Pam and Fernanda worked together to pull data and notes describing their language, dialectic, and anthropological discoveries of the day while Jim downloaded videos and pictures of the allosaurus, the mausoleum, and the Garden perimeter. Neil prepped the USB hard drive that was to hold the treasure trove of the day's findings.

Troy walked over to the top of the hill and sat down, studying the Ark from afar.

It's all true, he thought. Even though he had believed in this magnificent boat since he was a child, it had always been a childlike belief without much scientific evidence. He had spent millions of dollars of his personal fortune and thousands of hours of his adult life researching and looking for the remains of this vessel, and here before him was the evidence he had looked for his entire life.

Neil walked up and sat down next to him, admiring the view. "How would you like to get on that boat and take a look around?"

Troy turned toward him with a surprised look.

"I talked to Captain Loren, who said he'd be happy to help you survey the Ark, and I'd feel a lot better knowing that he was there with you," Neil said.

"Absolutely! It's the chance of a lifetime. Thank you, Neil," said Troy, shaking Neil's hand vigorously.

"Let me get this data transfer underway, and we'll make it happen," said Neil, standing up.

"Neil, this has been the greatest day of my life. Thanks for inviting me along," Troy said.

The two friends gave each other a bear hug and returned to the others to lend a hand with the data transfer.

Jim finished recording the new transfer point based on the top of the hill and handed the coordinates to Neil on a flash drive.

"Let's just hope this whole area isn't underwater when it's time to go," said Jim.

"I agree. OK, gang, tomorrow at 4:30 P.M. we're transferring out of here from this point," said Neil.

"Be there or be square…or dead, whichever comes first," said Jim. Neil tried to ignore him.

After an hour of massaging data and recording messages for Cameron and the team at the ops center, the team heard the distinctive sound of helicopter blades chopping the air. Camouflaged by the night, the autonomous craft flew along the construction site and made a pass over the team's position before turning and landing on the top of the hill.

Rich Loren checked the charge on the batteries to ensure the craft would have enough power to make it back to the plain, while Neil wrapped the hard drive in bubble wrap to protect its precious contents and loaded the device into a drop bucket between the helicopter's skids.

"Rich, when this thing gets to the plain, you need to get close to the ground and drop this USB drive within the coordinates that we transferred into initially," said Neil.

"No problem," replied Rich.

The team backed up and gave the little helicopter space to rev its engine and take off into the night. It was a strange feeling to know that the material on that hard drive would be half a world away and some four thousand years into the future in just three hours.

26

Divide and Conquer

T he night air around the field where the team had transferred hours before was alive with the sounds of birds and other animals engaging in nocturnal activities. AARON whizzed by, scanning ahead and below itself with a laser range finder and adjusting its flight characteristics accordingly. As it neared its destination point, it reduced its forward velocity and began to hover over the preprogrammed spot about fifty feet above the ground. AARON's radar bounced waves off the ground, and the miniature helicopter began to slowly descend. Once it sensed it was on the ground through small pressure sensors on its aluminum skids, it released its payload from a small compartment located under the electronics bay. A small, bubble-wrapped package landed on the wet grass of the field. Sensing a successful drop, the craft began to pick up power. It lifted itself off the ground, wheeled on its axis, and took off into the night to rendezvous with the team again.

At TRC, Cameron was pacing back and forth in the operations center as he waited impatiently for the clock to count down for the transfer. The information included in this payload would be precious. It would provide solid evidence of whether the earth and its lifeforms had evolved from single cells into complex beings over billions of years or whether an omnipotent God had spoken creation into existence. It was a pivotal moment for Cameron, and he knew his life would never be the same after examining the data. He had his suspicions about what the data would look like, suspicions that had begun the day that TRC was unsuccessful in sending objects into the distant past.

"One minute to transfer," said Alicia King, interrupting Cameron's musings. He smiled at her, silently acknowledging her presence. She was a member of Cameron's elite group of mathematicians, handpicked by Cameron himself from the best of the best at Cornell Theory Center. Cameron had plans to groom her into his eventual successor as the lead scientist in charge of all the labs at TRC.

While her professional resume was impeccable, Alicia's childhood had been a mixture of privilege and tragedy. She had been adopted while in grade school into a wealthy Boston family who put her through the best prep schools money could buy. At seventeen, just before graduation from high school and acceptance to Cornell, her adoptive mother and father had been killed in an automobile accident. A huge trust fund had been released to Alicia, but she found no solace in the money and instead threw herself headlong into her studies. She had mastered advanced math, physics, and computer science—a lucrative combination of subjects that made her a constant target of headhunters at search engines and intelligence agencies. Unlike most other experts at TRC, Alicia made time to take care of herself, running three miles a day and continually polishing her professional image. She felt equally at ease talking about integration and differential equations with calculus professors and asking for research grants from stodgy old politicians in Washington.

Secretly, Cameron Locke was in love with Alicia. She was his soul mate, with an intense love for science and an undeniable beauty that matched her insatiable curiosity about the possibilities science and technology could hold for mankind. Many times Cameron had been tempted to ask her out on a date, even though he was ten years her senior and the head of the research division at TRC, but discretion had prevailed. Like Alicia, Cameron threw himself into his job.

"OK, start the sequence," Cameron said.

Since they were not transferring human DNA, the sequence could be much abbreviated. Alicia's slender fingers flashed over the keyboard, and she swiftly sent the command that would begin the transfer.

TRANSFER /T=HERE /F=30.7978N%47.71283E /D=2348 /ERA=BC /DNA=NO

Alicia hit "Enter," and inside the Platform bay strobe lights began to flash intermittently, bathing everyone in an orange glow every other second. The power meters began to peg themselves, and a blue wormhole emerged like a writhing snake from the circular vent in the ceiling. As the swirling cloud of energy reached the Platform floor, the package in a prehistoric rain forest glade disappeared in a flash and reappeared on TRC's blue glass Platform.

"Transfer complete," said Alicia.

Cameron looked at a plasma display that was showing a video feed of the Platform and saw the bubble-wrapped package positioned in its center.

"Alicia, go ahead and disengage the door locks," he ordered.

Again Alicia typed a command into her workstation, and the sound of metal dead bolts pulling away from their cavities echoed in the room. The huge metal door yawned open, and Cameron ran up the ramp to the Platform to grab the precious package. He picked up the USB drive and noticed that the bubble wrap protecting it was still damp with the dew of four thousand years ago. Mesmerized, he caressed the water droplets for a moment and then realized that the real prize lay wrapped inside. He began pulling off the wrap as he headed back into the ops center.

"The first thing we'll do is back this thing up," said Cameron, plugging the USB drive into a port on a dark-gray data server sitting on his desk. A blue progress bar flew across the screen as the contents of the drive were deposited safely in TRC's massive hard drive farm.

"OK, let's see what we can see." Cameron typed a few commands on the keyboard, and a mosaic of images and telemetry files instantly filled the massive plasma display. Cheers erupted in the ops center. Pictures of the mausoleum and the Garden of Eden made the scientists gasp and shout as they ran up to the plasma screens, pointing and commenting on various aspects of the images.

Toward the bottom of the file list was a file named "readmenow.txt." Cameron double-clicked on it and began to read the contents from his friend Neil with a smile on his face, and then his countenance suddenly turned ashen. Alicia noticed his grim expression and pulled herself away from the excited crowd.

"What's wrong?" asked Alicia, placing a hand on Cameron's shoulder.

"We have a big problem. A *really* big problem."

"What is it?"

"Neil changed the transfer point. Apparently the Ark is already built, and they're not going to be staying there for four days."

"What? Well, how long do we have to re-calc?" asked Alicia, her eyes widening as she began thinking through all the work they had to do.

"They want to come back tomorrow afternoon," Cameron said.

"How far away did they move the transfer point?" Alicia asked.

The other engineers and mathematicians had noticed the pair's concerned expressions and stopped examining the screens to listen in on the conversation.

"It's far enough that we have to recompute the entire transfer—the new transfer point is over ten miles away."

At hearing this news, the engineers and mathematicians began complaining and swearing among themselves.

"Gang, settle down," Cameron said to the mass of engineers standing beside the screen covered with high-resolution photographs of the Garden of Eden. "We just got news that the away team needs to change its destination point. We have to bring everyone back sooner than we expected," he explained.

An engineer raised his hand timidly. "Like how soon?"

"Tomorrow evening."

The team of engineers started buzzing again.

Cameron raised his hands to quiet them down. "I know, the calculation takes two weeks on our system. But we don't have two weeks—we have less than twenty hours." Cameron's face took on a deadly serious expression. "This isn't a homework assignment, and it's not for a thesis. These are our friends. We must make this happen. Imagine yourself putting your life in the hands of anyone in this room. You're the best of the best. Let's make it happen."

"We need more computing capacity—a lot more," said Alicia.

"I'll take care of that. In the meantime, get the source code ready to distribute. Break the functions down so that we can give the code to different agencies and get the answers back individually," Cameron said.

Alicia nodded and waved to some engineers and software geeks to join her in a conference room.

Cameron walked over to a small alcove behind the ops center and closed the door behind him. He could look through the glass at a larger room, now full of engineers struggling to break the source code of the program that managed transfers. He could tell that spirited debates were already going on in true prima-donna fashion, but he also could tell that the engineers would get the job done. Cameron had learned early in his career to surround himself with the best, give them an impossible challenge, and get out of their way. Sometimes it got messy, but things always happened.

Anyway, he had a lot of faith in Alicia, who was busy organizing the many tasks to be computed.

He dialed Admiral Turner's number on his cell phone and waited for a connection.

"Admiral Turner's office," the assistant answered.

"Yes, Miriam? This is Cameron Locke at TRC. I need to speak with the admiral immediately, if possible—it's an emergency."

"He gets that a lot. I'll pull him out of the meeting."

"Thanks, Miriam." Cameron almost smiled. Paying special attention to the administrative assistants of important people was a diplomatic technique that Neil had taught him, and it had just paid off.

Shortly, a stern voice was heard from the other end of the line: "Turner."

"Admiral, Cameron Locke here."

The voice turned decidedly kinder. "Cameron, it's great to hear from you. How's the expedition?"

"Well, sir, the expedition is doing great—they've found the Ark and the Garden of Eden, and we have some great data sets—but they're also the reason for my call."

"What can I do for you?" asked the admiral, his voice filling with concern.

"Well, we need to change the destination point, and the team needs to come back sooner than the timeline we agreed to earlier. Do you remember how long it takes for us to recalculate a trip?"

The admiral closed his eyes and pressed his fingers on his eyelids, reliving the tour of the TRC data center. "About two weeks, if I remember correctly. How soon do they need to come back?"

"Tomorrow night," said Cameron sheepishly.

A wave of expletives turned the air blue, and Cameron pulled the cell phone away from his ear while he let the admiral express his feelings.

"How much computing power do you need?" asked Turner.

"About 250 Teraflops; we need about three supercomputers dedicated to this problem," said Cameron.

Again the air turned blue as the admiral used all the curse words he could conjure up.

Cameron finally interjected. "I have the team breaking the source code down into three parts. We can calculate the different terms in three places and do the whole thing in parallel, but we need you to help us get access to some big machines."

"What about TRC's computing resources?" Turner asked.

"They're already at full capacity working on the basic equation."

"I assume you know the machines you need," said the admiral.

"Yes, sir. Here's the list: Red Storm at Sandia Labs has about one Teraflop capacity that we can use for a simple part of the equation. Then we need the Columbia Supercomputer at NASA Ames; it has about fifty-one Teraflops. I know the lead mathematician there—he'll give us what we need. Finally, the Blue Gene system at Lawrence Livermore has about 280 Teraflops of capacity."

"You owe me big time, Cameron."

"I know. Can you help?"

"I'll make it happen. Get the source code to me and we'll get this done."

"Thank you, sir!" said Cameron, hanging up the phone.

Cameron walked along the hallway toward the conference room where he had left Alicia in charge. Loud shouting and passionate debate could be heard coming from the room.

Cameron smiled. *Nerds*, he thought.

Cameron had recruited almost all of them personally, but there was something about computers, software, mathematics…they made people who loved them wear their hearts on their sleeves. Very, very bright engineers, all of them; the kind of people who can change life for millions of others, but they had little to no social skills.

He was grateful for all of them.

He rapped on the window of the conference room and motioned to Alicia, who was standing at a whiteboard assigning responsibilities. Alicia gave the marker to another engineer and made her way out of the room.

"Man, it's a goat rodeo in there," she said, closing the door behind her.

"I know. I know the type. I *am* the type," Cameron said with a smile. "I have some good news."

"I could use it," Alicia said, returning his smile. Her eyes were a bit bloodshot from the stress of managing unmanageable people.

"Thanks to Admiral Turner, I have three of the biggest machines available for you: Red Storm at Sandia, Columbia at Ames, and Blue Gene at Livermore."

"Awesome," said Alicia.

"How's it going getting the source code broken out?" Cameron asked.

Alicia turned back to the window and looked at the whiteboard. A hastily-sketched timeline with unintelligible deliverables was scribbled across it. She sighed as she thought about the overwhelming amount of work it represented. "We're almost there. The only issue is that as the terms come back from these other sites, we'll have to run the final process here for the end result. We won't have a lot of time to assemble the different terms, and we get only one shot at this."

"Well, we'll just have to be careful, won't we?" Cameron said, putting his hand on her shoulder and looking in her eyes without distraction. "I have full confidence in you."

She smiled back at him. He knew she was on top of it, and that was important to her. "Can I share the news with the team? It'll buoy their spirits."

"Sure. Let's try to get that source code to Admiral Turner within the next hour, please," he said as he turned to go.

As Cameron walked back over to the ops center, he heard cheers erupt from the conference room as the engineers got the news about the extra computing power being brought to bear on the problem.

27

A Midnight Trip to the Ark

The night air was filled with muted sounds emanating from the city and the animals in their kennels inside the Ark. As the moon approached its zenith in the ancient sky, all sounds subsided. Beyond the Ark, torches could be seen flickering on the walls of the city, the parapets of the wall strangely silhouetted and outlined in the amber light.

Three figures dressed completely in black with dark stripes painted diagonally across their faces worked their way to the top of a towering ancient tree—one of only a few trees on the ridgeline that hadn't become part of the Ark's structural components over the last hundred years.

Troy watched as Rich Loren unzipped a long, black canvas bag and pulled out a mesh of carbon-fiber slats connected with scissor-like aluminum fittings. Rich and Chris Belkins pulled the mesh tightly and ran lightweight poles behind the walls, performing the action four times until a high hide took shape.

"Most scientists use these hides to observe animals in their natural habitat," said Rich, working with Chris to mount the hide. The tree's stout branches were gnarled and thick as it towered over the rain forest floor like it was holding up the sky. Rich layered a thick camouflage canvas front across the mesh, disguising the hide as part of the tree. He looped a cable around the trunk and coupled it with a bracket to form a lasso.

"OK, the hide's done. Let's get you to the Ark. This should hold our weight pretty well."

"Should?" Troy asked nervously, looking over the edge to the ground fifty feet below.

"Here, you'll need these. We won't be using flashlights for most of this," said Rich, handing Troy a pair of night-vision goggles. "When we get to the inside of the Ark, it may take a second for the sensors to adjust themselves, but when we're wearing these things, it'll be like midday inside the Ark."

Troy placed the goggles over his head, adjusting the straps for a tight fit. The goggles for each eye spun counterclockwise independently, adjusting their focal distance as he looked from the ancient tree to the Ark and back at the two soldiers.

Rich lifted a long crossbow-like device to his shoulder and pressed a small button on the top of the sight aperture. A small red laser dot danced nervously on the stern of the Ark a few hundred yards away.

Rich sucked in his breath, focused the dot on the middle of the central beam that ran the extent of the stern, and pulled the trigger. The grappling arrow whistled through the night air, swiftly unwinding a thin cable behind itself.

Thunk!

The arrow embedded itself deep in the wood of the stern, creating a solid anchor. Loren pulled back hard on the cable to check the anchor point for integrity. He tightened the cable line using a ratchet assembly that had been lassoed around the large tree until he felt the cable become taught. The silver cable gleamed in the moonlight like a giant spider web between the high hide and the Ark. He pulled an aerosol can of silicon out of a small tool bag and sprayed a pulley that had a handlebar chassis welded to it.

"This should make the ride quieter and reduce any resistance on the cable," said Rich.

He pressed his headset talk button. "Commander Belkins?"

"Yes, sir!"

"After we're away, please move the anchor point lower on the tree so that our departure is smooth off the Ark."

"Roger that," replied Chris at the foot of the giant tree.

"This should be a kick in the pants," said Troy with a smile.

"I'll go first," said Rich.

Rich pulled his night-vision goggles down over his eyes and let the sensor adjust to the night illumination. A second later, he jumped off the high hide, holding onto the handlebars of the zip line.

With a faint **zzzzz**, the zip line quickly transferred Loren to the Ark's stern; he squeezed the hand brake so that he wouldn't noisily slam into the back of the boat.

Loren took a quick look around. Seeing no one near the end of the Ark, he swung his muscular leg over the side and stepped onto the top deck.

Again the distinct sound of the zip line could be heard, and in a moment Troy arrived and pulled himself onto the deck.

Commander Belkins began to readjust the anchor point lower on the tree as the duo disappeared into the hull of the Ark, glistening under a full, silvery moon.

The first thing Troy noticed as he walked along the deck was that the joints were beautifully fitted, not at all what he had expected. The two made their way across the deck, carefully placing each step; the dark, honey-colored pitch resin made the entire surface slippery, like wet fiberglass.

Rich Loren walked over to the boxes Noah's son had placed onto the top deck with the crane just hours before. The grain inside them was pulverized into fine flour.

Along the entire top cabin, which spanned the length of the Ark and was perfectly aligned to the spine of the boat, a gutter trench ran on either side, just below the windows. It was not hard to imagine waves greater than forty-five feet crashing onto the side of the Ark during the storm of the ages. The gutters tilted downward toward the stern at a slight angle, so that the water that would land on the front of the Ark would run along these troughs toward the stern.

With the top deck sufficiently examined, the two men crawled through an open window and disappeared inside the Ark. As their night-vision goggles adjusted to the darker interior of the Ark, the men finally saw the inside of a vessel that had baffled historians, scientists, and theologians for millennia.

The interior of the Ark was divided into three decks or floors. Larger rooms occupied the bottom of the boat, and smaller cages were placed on the middle and upper decks. Iron bars ran from the upper deck to the bottom of the boat.

The mystery of the gutters was finally solved once the men were inside the Ark. The gutters fed channels that led down to each floor; each floor had its own channel that ran parallel to the ones on the top deck. The water would be channeled into drinking troughs for the animals. At the top of the Ark, below the top deck, a reservoir would collect water from the massive waves that would crash onto the top deck, providing hydration for the crew and animal passengers.

The moonlight was flooding through the huge, yawning door, where ramps led to each floor. Ladders were positioned after every three cages and provided vertical access from the upper deck to the bottom of the boat.

As the two men walked down ramps to the lowest deck, they noticed that occupied birdcages were hung in the open spaces above every animal cage on each floor. It seemed that every available space inside the Ark was being used for something—either as an animal holding area or for stocking food. Evidence of design and forethought was everywhere they looked.

As Rich and Troy moved into the middle deck, a pair of small jaguars snarled and took turns hiding behind each other. Troy saw numerous pairs of animals, each in its own pen. Each pen was remarkably self-contained. The water trough, which would be fed by the gutters acquiring water from the top deck and other drainage points, would provide the animals a drink at any time desired. The floor of each pen was built with slats that allowed animal waste to drop beneath the pen and be collected without the animals having to leave the pen during the daily cleanings. A circular grain dispenser was mounted on each wall, shared among the plant-eating animals in adjoining pens.

Troy moved to the edge of a medium-sized pen containing a pair of okapis. The shy animals darted away from the men and tried to blend into the wall opposite the strangers. "Young animals," he said with astonishment. "Creationists have speculated for years that Noah took young animals aboard to save room and weight."

"Makes perfect sense," said Loren. "They eat far less, they're easier and safer to move around, and you can pack more of them into a small space. Smart planning, if you ask me."

Rich and Troy continued their journey to the lower deck, trying not to disturb the baby animals, which in fact were remarkably docile. It was almost as if the Ark itself had a calming effect on them. As the explorers reached the bottom of the boat, they noticed a number of carts that ran on wooden tracks for the entire length of the Ark. The carts were eight feet square and about three feet in depth.

"What do you suppose these are for?" asked Rich, placing a hand on the side of one of the carts.

"Maybe it's for food. You know, transferring it to each cage," Troy said.

The single set of tracks had four carts on it. Oddly, only two of the carts were covered in the same resin material used on the outer surface of the Ark.

Troy knelt down and studied the floor next to the tracks. The stalls for the largest animals were slatted and elevated about a foot above the base floor. They were clearly built to allow the animals' waste products to fall below the slatted floor to a rolling cart beneath each stall. A small latch was at the end of each side of the solid floor. Troy pushed and unhitched the latch, and the floor began to roll toward the center of the boat within easy reach of the center track and the strange bins.

"Oh—poop," Troy said, getting out the way of the rolling floor section.

"What?" Rich asked.

"Poop! Waste! This bin is a poop conveyor, and those carts must be for food. The resin- covered ones will be loaded with animal waste and dumped overboard, while the food will come in behind," Troy said with a smile, clearly proud of his discovery. He pushed the floor section back underneath the stall and reset the latch.

"A 'poop conveyor'? You definitely ought to coin that term," said Loren with a chuckle.

Troy followed the track down the length of the Ark, reaching out and running his hands across the inner support beams as he walked. He had dreamed of being inside Noah's Ark since he was a small boy in Sunday school, and now here he was, walking on one of the decks of the vessel that would save mankind.

Troy shined his flashlight against the inside wall of the Ark and gasped in amazement.

"What is it?" asked Rich.

Troy pointed to the hull as he swung his flashlight left and right across the structure. "The planks outside—they ran horizontally, correct?" he asked.

"Yeah, I'm pretty sure," replied Rich.

"So the construction internally has planking that runs vertically, as if the inside is a shell that's used to reinforce the outer hull. It's almost like some sort of laminate. Check out these dowels every few feet," said Troy, running his fingers along the wall.

"Maybe it's designed to deal with sheering forces," said Rich.

"Possibly. The workmanship is truly amazing," replied Troy.

After walking for a few minutes along the inner track, Troy and Rich were surprised to find an unusual structure positioned in the center of the Ark—a large, cylindrical shaft of thick wooden beams that connected to the bottom of the hull and reached to the top of the second deck. The shaft was about twenty feet in diameter—a perfect circle. Rich discovered a wooden ladder that began on the bottom track, and he climbed it to the second deck. Troy quickly followed him on the opposite side of the ladder. When they reached the top of the second deck, the two peered cautiously over the edge to find a hole at the top with a thick coating of resin and reinforcements leading from the shaft to the sides and bottom of the ship.

Troy shined his flashlight inside the dark shaft. The sides were steep and slippery, coated with the resin they had encountered on the top deck. The light from Troy's flashlight barely reached the bottom of the hollow shaft, and they could just make out the beams and shadows of scaffolding outside that held the entire ship off the ground. The reinforcements inside the hull all converged at the cylindrical shape, seeming to indicate a specific design and purpose.

"A moon pool?" asked Rich.

"It must be," said Troy, running his hands across the lip of the massive well. "Noah and his sons must have designed this to reduce stresses that might break the boat in half, like what may have happened to the *Titanic*. This structure allows the water level to rise and fall within this cylinder, and it helps to distribute the loading forces uniformly."

Rich agreed, pointing to the track below them. "I guess that's where they off-load refuse, like the dung that the animals produce, and other trash. The opening's right in the middle of the boat, which would help with balance as well."

"This thing in use probably acts like a giant piston, with rising and falling water pushing and circulating clean air through the entire craft like an air conditioner," added Troy.

"Amazing," said Rich. "They've thought of everything."

"No, I think they had help...divine help," Troy said.

Rich simply nodded silently, which, for him, was a big deal. He had been able to professionally compartmentalize the discoveries of the last twenty-four hours, pushing the implications of the findings to the "policy makers" as he had his entire career. Rich had seen many things in the black operations world that had caused him to question the existence of God, but standing in this amazing vessel, designed to save righteous human life and the objects of creation, Rich Loren thought about God for the first time in a very long while.

"We should head back soon," said Troy, looking at his watch.

As Troy and Rich left the moon pool and headed toward the stern of the Ark, they came to another strange room. A large wooden table was positioned in the center, and angled shelves lined the walls. Troy examined the oddly-shaped shelves. They slanted slightly downward, instead of being flat like modern shelves. Straw was inside each of the shelves, and cylindrical terra-cotta vessels were laid on top of the cushioning material. Each of the vessels had a cork-like stopper covered with a dark, tar-like substance, creating an airtight seal.

"It's gotta be a library!" said Troy, barely able to contain his excitement.

There were dozens of clay vessels, and they seemed to be arranged in a specific order. Some of the bins were filled to overflowing, while others only held a few containers.

"I have to have a look," said Troy, pulling one of the vessels from the shelf.

Rich handed Troy his sharp commando knife, and they carefully extracted the cork from the top of the clay container.

Pop.

Troy placed his hand inside the vessel and grasped a scroll that was made of some sort of parchment. He carefully unrolled the brittle material and placed some small rocks from a nearby basket on each corner of the large paper.

The document contained a map. Modern landmasses were indiscernible, and unrecognizable borders and landmarks filled Rich and Troy's vision. After staring at the map for a few moments in utter confusion, Troy saw something that looked familiar. "Ah, look, here's Eden," he said, running his finger over an undulating river system. The rivers of Eden were clearly identified to the northeast. Small glyphs were positioned every few inches along rivers and coasts.

"These small markings must be cities and perhaps even trade routes," said Rich pointing to a few of the triangular marks.

The realization of multiple cities with the sophistication of Unug-Kulaba was intimidating. Troy, astonished, stepped across the map with his finger, pointing at each marker. "Look how many there are! I guess I always thought there were only a few cities in this time, perhaps only one big one."

Two larger glyphs, rendered in a different color than the others, dominated the lower portion of the map. A large triangular glyph was positioned near the Nile just as it broke into its familiar delta shape, and another glyph was further to the west in the center of the landmass.

"Wait a minute. That large glyph beyond Egypt is way too far to the west. It's where the Atlantic Ocean is today," said Rich.

"Not only that, but it's in the same area as the Azores. The continents haven't separated yet," concluded Troy. "I have to get a picture of this." He reached into his pocket and produced a small digital camera. Rich looked around the rest of the room as Troy snapped pictures of the ancient map.

"You know, I'd love to take this with us, but we both know that history would likely be quite different without all of this knowledge going to its destined place." Troy rolled the parchment up again and placed it inside the clay container.

"Wherever that is," said Rich.

The two explorers left the awe-inspiring library and headed for the stern of the Ark.

28

Discovery in the Ops Center

C ameron walked back into the operations center to check a few parameters for the upcoming transfer and draw up a more precise project plan for getting the team back.

The ops center was quiet except for the sound of fans cooling delicate electronic components in the dark gray data servers. Screen savers danced on the black screens of the high-powered workstations. Something on Dustin's workstation caught his eye.

A minimized window on Dustin's task bar was flashing for attention.

Cameron clicked on the window; it sprang up and showed a line graph of power consumed by the entire facility. The gauge was recording slowly, and the day's activity—the buildup of power, the transfer, and the power consumption of the building before and after the transfer that morning—was being charted, along with the smaller transfer that had occurred a little over an hour earlier.

Well, that's odd.

Cameron sat down in the ergonomic chair in front of the workstation and studied the graph.

Why is the power so low? It's almost like the entire Faraday cage is down.

He looked at a digital dashboard displayed on a massive plasma screen in the front of the room. He scanned the list.

POWER: 80% AVAILABLE
HARD DRIVE FARM: POWERED
FARADAY CAGE: POWERED

The dashboards and gauges say it's up, but the power consumption says otherwise.

Cameron walked back over to his workstation and clicked on an icon that fired up a surveillance camera program. He could observe the entire complex from his workstation; the networked cameras connected to rooms all over TRC returned their images to his desktop. He called up the break room in the living quarters, expecting to see the rebellious mathematician with his feet propped on the back of a chair, smoking away. It was empty; no sign of Dustin.

Strange.

He scanned each of the rooms and found no evidence of Dustin. He clicked to the lobby but didn't see Sally there. Bringing up his Instant Messenger list, he saw Sally's name with her presence depicted as a green light—telling him she was at her workstation and available for conversation. Then he double-clicked her name and spoke into a microphone wand attached to his keyboard.

"Sally, are you there? This is Cameron in the operations center."

No response.

Cameron clicked on the lobby camera icon and sent a command to the camera to move left and right and sweep the room in a wide angle. As the camera swept to the left, Cameron could see that the frosted glass doors leading to the garage had a dark shape concealed behind them—a large, rectangular shape.

Was it a vehicle of some kind? Jennings, the security guard, would not have let a vehicle into the facility—not during a lockdown, unless...

His mind wheeled with a dozen what-if scenarios, and he rapidly evaluated each of them for possibility. He clicked on the camera icon for the parking garage, and a large white truck appeared on the screen.

Cameron clicked back to the gallery of video feeds and clicked on the lobby again, but this time from a camera mounted on the wall above the frosted glass doors and facing the elevator. He moved the camera left and right, panning across the marble floor. There! He saw something behind the brushed stainless steel reception desk. He clicked on the zoom button and brought the image to full screen. A high-heeled shoe filled the screen, with a black pool of liquid reflecting the shoe and the lights in the high ceiling—Sally.

He clicked on the surveillance window and it flew back down to its original spot, flashing continuously. Cameron ran back to the conference room, where everyone was still loudly in debate.

He burst through the door, and the debate ended—all of the engineers and mathematicians in the room stared at him in surprise.

Cameron held his finger to his lips to indicate silence. "Get your stuff and quietly follow me!"

No one questioned him; everyone grabbed his or her things and complied.

Cameron led the group of eight to a doorway that opened to a stairwell. He turned to address the frightened group. "Do what I say, and don't ask any questions." Sweat was pouring from his forehead, and the others could see that he was deadly serious. He turned and began his run up the stairway to the next level. The mass of engineers followed along, with folders, large rolled-up diagrams, and soda cans in tow.

"There's been a security breach. I don't know how bad it is yet, but I'm assuming the worst. Go up one floor to the data center and lock the floor down—no one comes in and no one goes out. Once you have it locked down, notify Power to do the same. Carry out your assignments with the source code. Get it distributed, get it run, and get the results back here. Your only priority is to bring the away team back—period. Nothing else matters. Does everyone understand?"

The team nodded. The gravity of the situation was becoming clear.

One of the engineers timidly raised his hand.

"Yes?" said Cameron, running his hand across his forehead.

"Once we run the equation, how do we get back down here and run the Platform from the ops center?"

"Leave that to me," Cameron said.

The group started up the stairway, and as Alicia passed Cameron, he grabbed her arm. He locked eyes with her as the rest of the team passed them to get to the data center. Alone now in the stairwell.

"I need your help—they can do their job without you." He wished he could leave her out of it, put her behind a door with armed guards in front, but like it or not, he was well aware that she knew more about the complex than he did. "You know how we can use these systems and the environment against these...well, I don't really know who or what we're dealing with." Cameron wiped the sweat accumulating on his eyebrows and forehead.

Alicia put her hand over Cameron's, clearly frightened but resolved.

"Let's do it. They're no match for the both of us," she said forcing a smile. As she turned and went back down the stairwell, Cameron followed.

Man, I love this woman.

29

Ambush

While Rich and Troy explored the Ark, the rest of the team was unwinding and relaxing after a long day. The team was positioned around a small fire, enjoying tea and coffee and exchanging theories about the various sights and sounds they had experienced during the previous thirty-six hours.

"What are your thoughts, Jim?" Fernanda asked.

"Mixed. I'm conflicted inside in a major way."

"What do you mean?" she asked.

"I thought I knew how everything was formed on the earth. Sure, I had questions, but the basics—the way I looked at the world—were always based on evolution. You know, billions and billions of years and the constant progress of evolutionary processes."

Jim took off his hat and scratched his head. "Now, well, now I feel like I don't know anything. I sure can't go back to the university and teach that stuff. This has been a life-changing event from an academic perspective. And yourself? Surely an anthropologist like you has had quite an awakening."

Fernanda thought for a moment. "Jim, I guess I feel the same way. I wasn't prepared to see the architecture we witnessed today, and down the hill about three hundred yards from us is a boat that signals that the Bible was accurate in its recording of the origins of man. The civilization in the city down there is advanced—more advanced than anyone could have guessed—but depraved. The people remind me in many ways of the

Mayan culture, which was super-advanced and then disappeared in a few years' time."

"Well, I don't think you are too far off," Neil put in. "In a few days, this whole world is going to be set back to the Stone Age by the greatest cataclysm this planet has ever seen. All of this will be gone without a trace."

Jim and Fernanda stared into the campfire, thinking about the day's events, while the smoke curled up above them and exited through the top of the rain forest canopy.

"I'm going to find some water and get cleaned up," said Pam.

Chris jumped at the chance to be with Pam. "I'll go with her, sir."

"Thanks, Commander."

"Chris."

"Excuse me?" Neil said.

"Neil, please call me Chris." He grabbed his rifle and slung it over his shoulder.

"OK, Chris," said Neil with a smile.

Pam grabbed a washcloth and a bar of facial soap from her rucksack and motioned to Chris. "We'll be back in a few minutes," she said.

Chris and Pam made their way down a steep slope from the top of the knoll to a small stream about four hundred yards away, on the side of the hill directly opposite the Ark construction site. The broadleaf plants bounced and retracted as the two moved through the dense foliage toward the water source. The moisture falling from the leaves onto the vegetation underfoot made the path slippery, and Pam fell and caught herself several times during the short trip.

Chris was exhausted, and he tried to summon the energy to be alert. He flipped his sniper rifle to safety so that a round would not fire into the air if he lost his traction and fell against his gun on the slippery trail.

The darkness of the evening was settling around them, and birds were returning to their nests high in the forest canopy. A small herd of dog-sized dinosaurs hooted and chirped in the distance across the plain to another group of plant-eaters.

The bugs got thicker as Chris and Pam approached the small stream. Clouds of gnats annoyed Pam, and she slapped the back of her neck and rubbed the tops of her ears to keep them off. The plants began to lose height, and then, in front of the two travelers, a crystal-clear stream of water appeared, burbling and careening around smooth rocks. The water was about a foot deep, but rocks were strewn through the riverbed in such a way that a pathway could be found across the small stream.

Pam spied a perfect rock for crouching on and jumped from the edge of the vegetation to the top of the rock. She rotated her arms a few full revolutions to regain her balance.

"Nice one, Nadia," said Chris with a smile.

Pam smirked and pulled the washcloth and soap out of her pocket. The night air was beginning to cool, and the partially obscured stars reflecting in the dark, clear water created a beautiful sight.

Pam ran her fingers through her hair, drawing it into a ponytail. She ran the bar of soap through the water and worked up a lather, massaging her forehead, neck, and cheeks with the iridescent bubbles. It was a relaxing ritual and one she would have enjoyed in any time period—ancient or modern.

Chris tried to pay attention to the surroundings, but watching Pam wash her face was mesmerizing. He turned away, embarrassed, after he saw that she noticed him looking at her.

After a few minutes of massaging the soap into the pores of her face and neck, Pam dipped the washcloth in the stream and used it to wash the soap off. She shivered from the coolness of the water. "Brrrr. That's much better," she sighed.

As she wrung the cloth out, she felt a twinge on her neck. She instinctively swatted at it, expecting to see the small, mangled body of a mosquito or gnat as the perpetrator of the pain. She was surprised when she pulled her hand back to find a small dart with bright feathers protruding from the tail end. She felt her neck muscles spasm slightly and sensed a rush of heat filling her body. She tried to stand, but her muscles failed her. As she started to lose consciousness, she let out a moan with all her strength.

"Chris! Help!"

The darkness closed in around Pam, and she felt the icy chill of the stream roll over her body as she fell sideways into the water.

Chris turned around, startled. "Pam!" he cried out, jumping into the stream. As he leapt off the embankment, three pinpricks stung his neck on the right side. The poison was fast-acting. By the time he landed in the stream, his muscles had already lost their tension. Chris turned and saw the silhouettes of two huge men dressed like soldiers looming over him and Pam. With every ounce of strength he could muster, he flipped off the safety and fired off a single shot, muffled by the silencer and the sounds of the night around them.

Bright yellow stars shot out to the distance before Chris's eyes as he splashed into the stream next to Pam's paralyzed body. His vision narrowed into a gray tunnel as the two large men huddled over them, and then all was black.

Dustin's Dilemma

A
licia and Cameron ran back to the operations center together. Alicia picked up her laptop, which had a wireless connection to the Internet and access to the local systems at TRC. Cameron pulled his keys out of his pocket and opened a small steel lockbox that was mounted at the back of the room near a fire extinguisher. He pulled a black pistol out of the box, along with two magazines of bullets.

"A gun? What are we going to do?" Alicia asked.

"I'm not sure. I'm working on it," said Cameron. "We need to know what we're dealing with first." Cameron clicked a few times on the surveillance program that was running on one of the workstations in the operations center. The program flickered as various views of the complex appeared on the screen. He saw Dustin and three other men he had never seen before, and he knew they did not belong at TRC. He closed the surveillance program's window to hide his foreknowledge of the raid.

Cameron looked around and saw an air vent about three feet in diameter that was used to vent the heat generated by the electronics into the main ventilation system. The vent was covered with a wide wire mesh that snapped on from the outside. Cameron jumped up on the worktable directly below it and pulled on the mesh. It snapped and gave way, exposing the black circular tube.

"Give me your laptop."

Alicia handed him the computer, and Cameron set it up in the vent.

"OK, let's get you up there." He grabbed Alicia's hand and helped her up to the top of the table. Cameron bent down and interlaced his fingers to make a foot support for the much lighter and more petite Alicia. She placed her running shoe in his hands and pushed up, reaching the vent. She felt around inside, noting that the dark vent curved away from the vertical shaft into a larger, rectangular horizontal vent. She crawled her way up and positioned herself in the rectangular space.

Cameron followed Alicia, positioning himself upside down with his legs jammed against the top of the vent and his arms hanging below the opening. He did a sit-up to pull his upper torso into the vent while his fingers clenched the wire mesh. He positioned the mesh of welded, thick metal wires flush against the circular metal skirt of the vent and pulled. The thick-gauge wire strained and snapped into place, securing the mesh cover. Cameron pushed with his hands to move his body up and lifted himself into the rectangular space with Alicia.

⌐⌐⌐　⌐⌐⌐　⌐⌐⌐

On the other end of the operations center, the elevator doors slid open, and men wearing hijabs and armed with machine guns checked the view and moved into the room, hugging the concrete wall. After checking their immediate area, they motioned to the others waiting in the elevator to follow. Salah walked out confidently, followed by Dustin. The squad of terrorists and the nervous mathematician walked into the operations center just moments after Cameron had pulled the mesh closed.

"Where is everyone?" Dustin asked.

"What do you mean?" Salah said with a serious look.

The young mathematician answered the terrorist cavalierly. "This whole area should be crawling with operations staff," he said, waving his hands at the empty chair and workstations.

"You careless fool—you failed us." Salah slapped Dustin across the face. "They are alerted to our presence."

Dustin brought his hand up to his face, rubbing his cheek. The sting of the slap and the verbal assault rattled his nerves, and he began thinking he had made a big mistake in tying his destiny to this man.

"They can't leave—they still think there's a lockdown," Dustin said, walking over to his workstation. "I'll find them."

Dustin fired up the surveillance program and rapidly found the video image for the various rooms in the complex. "Ah, there they are. They're in the data center. Something must be wrong with the supercomputer."

"Will this stop our mission?" Salah asked.

"Nope, everything is ready to go. I ran the program for your trip over the last few months at low priority. I masked the process ID so it looked like the maintenance for the hard drive farm."

The technical explanation clearly annoyed Salah, who was beginning to fidget with his pistol. "Then let us each take our place in history," he said.

"Yeah, right…history…whatever," said Dustin. "OK, let me get you on the Platform, Salah. But first, there's the small detail of my money." Dustin folded his arms across his chest and tried to use his skinny, wiry body to demand an answer.

Salah said something in Arabic to the man standing directly behind Dustin. The man grabbed Dustin's left arm and pulled it backward. A sickening pop came from his shoulder socket. Dustin screamed out in pain and dropped to his knees on the floor of the operations center.

Salah walked over to Dustin's crumpled form and lifted his face with his finger. "You are going to fulfill your duty to Allah without payment," he said, looking directly into Dustin's eyes. "And in return, I am going to make your last moments less painful. Do I have your understanding?"

Dustin arched his back in an odd alignment to keep his ligaments from ripping further and nodded in anguish.

Alicia and Cameron listened in horror from their perch directly above the operations center. They heard every word clearly as the voices echoed up the vent.

Salah uttered another phrase, and the man released Dustin's arm. Dustin's upper body convulsed in spasms, trying to realign the twisted ligaments and tendons of his shoulder. He rolled his arm laterally across his chest, and his shoulder snapped back into place. He clutched his arm in pain and held it under the elbow while rising to his feet.

The terrorists gathered into a small cluster and held hands, uttering phrases and reassuring one another. Their eyes were closed, and they seemed to be praying.

Dustin walked over to his workstation and typed a few commands with his right hand, slowly pecking out the letters and symbols. The lights around the steel platform began to strobe. Orange and red flashes reflected off the terrorists' resolved countenances.

"I want to confirm my final destination," said Salah, walking confidently over to Dustin's workstation.

Dustin typed a few lines, and the date and position of the transfer appeared on the large plasma screen.

June 3, 1967. 8:16 P.M.
Jerusalem, Israel
Latitude: 31.77090°N
Longitude: 35.22918°E

Salah smiled at the screen and looked back to his friends excitedly. "So, it is. May Allah protect you, my brothers. Tomorrow at this time, this world will be very different indeed."

Salah turned and walked toward the Platform. He hurried up the metal ladder and stood in the center of the Platform beneath the enormous vortex emitter. "You may begin," said Fatin, one of Salah's terrorist brothers.

Dustin nodded hesitantly, knowing that every command he typed would bring him closer to his own demise. He pressed "Enter" to send the command to the system, and the whine of the turbines began to increase. The power meters began their march to 100 percent, and digital indicators went from red to yellow to green. Dustin typed in another command, knowing it might be his very last. The swirling blue vortex appeared above the Platform and rotated slowly above Salah. Salah raised his hands as if he were encouraging this inanimate force to swallow him whole. Within moments the swirling light had enveloped Salah's form and transferred him to his destination point.

The vortex disappeared, and the whine of the turbines began to ebb.

Shouting and laughter came from the two other terrorists as they cheered their leader's journey toward immortality.

Dustin sensed his chance and jumped out of his chair, running to the back of the room. He punched a large red button labeled HALON that was protected behind a thin safety-glass shell on the back wall. Immediately a column of thick fire-suppression gas streamed down out of a nozzle directly above the terrorists. Dustin ran toward the large vault door on the right side of the control room and pushed on the huge door, trying to speed up its motorized opening. The terrorists were screaming in Arabic at each other, blinded and choked by the column of vaporous gas that was filling the air.

Cameron could smell the Halon creeping up the vent and knew that he and Alicia would have to move or be overcome by the gas. Alicia was way ahead of Cameron, typing furiously on her laptop, bringing up a schematic of the environmental system at TRC. She clicked on an emergency vent and activated it. Another air vent just a few feet from Cameron and Alicia went into overdrive and began to clear the air.

Dustin pushed on the large door with all the strength of his right arm. The door slowly yawned open, and Dustin and a cloud of escaping Halon entered the Platform bay. The terrorists were making their way through the fog to the door in hot pursuit. Dustin ran down the concrete floor of the Platform toward the elevator on the other end of the bay.

Fatin pulled out his pistol and fired a shot at the fleeing mathematician.

Dustin felt a sharp pain, like a bee sting, in his right thigh. He kept running, but his leg failed him and he fell to the floor. Reaching down to his right leg, he found a bullet hole and blood and bone fragments mingled in the denim of his jeans.

Cameron slid down the vent like it was a waterslide. His arms were folded across his chest, and he held the pistol in his right hand. He crashed through the wire mesh and landed on top of the workstation table. Much to his surprise, the room was completely empty. The only movement was the rolling vapor of Halon being sucked into the emergency vent. He stepped aside and made room for Alicia on the tabletop. "Come on, Alicia!" He heard her slipping against the metal skin of the vent, and then suddenly she appeared. Cameron did his best to steady her as she landed on the tabletop.

The two terrorists pursuing Dustin had caught up with him and stood over his bleeding form. Dustin was partially lying down and leaning up against the concrete, holding his leg. He looked up to see a black pistol with a long silencer pointed directly at his head. A moment later he saw the motion of Fatin's finger squeezing the trigger.

Dustin's lifeless form crumpled onto the floor of the bay as the empty brass shell casing from Fatin's pistol clattered on the concrete surface.

With Alicia safely out of the vent, Cameron jumped down and ran to the massive steel door through which Dustin had just run. He pressed the "Close" button. The door began to move. The terrorists looked over their shoulders in surprise to see the large vault door closing. They yelled at one another in Arabic as they sprinted toward the thick door.

"Alicia, seal the doors!" screamed Cameron.

Alicia pounded out commands on her keyboard to both massive doors, and the latches responded with the secure *thunking* sound of steel bolts engaging their keeper counterparts and sealing the doors from the outside.

"Done!" Alicia announced.

The terrorists pulled on the massive vault door and banged on the steel with the butts of their weapons, but to no avail.

Fatin ran to the front of the Platform. He held his automatic weapon at waist level and depressed the trigger, firing bullets into the window of the operations center. The bulletproof glass resisted at first, but then began to crack.

"We have to do something!" screamed Alicia. "That glass won't hold forever!"

"Bring up the Object Test program and set it for 100,000 BC!" Cameron commanded.

Alicia typed furiously on the keyboard as Fatin continued to assault the glass with lead. A small opening formed on the window and shattered, showering the equipment with a hail of glass fragments.

Alicia screamed, ducking under the desk, but still typing furiously.

"OK, it's up," she shouted.

"Cook 'em!" yelled Cameron as he returned fire toward the terrorist on the Platform. Fatin ran backward and jumped off the steel platform, standing against the wall out of the range of Cameron's gunfire.

Alicia activated the program, and the turbines began to hum; the power progressed rapidly to 100 percent, and the blue swirling vortex again appeared in the Platform bay. The terrorists tried to escape the swirling torsion energy, but all the exits were locked. The energy vortex swirled down from the ceiling, seeking all the organic objects in the payload bay. The torsion energy from the vortex gripped the terrorists trapped in the bay, and then, as the equation broke down and the destination point failed, all the molecules in their bodies ignited at once, turning the two terrorists and Dustin into burning pyres of ash on the floor.

Tracking

(F)ernanda stood on the ridge of the hill overlooking the ancient city they had visited just hours before and did her best to imagine the lion-outlined stone wall standing in front of her in the plaza. Slowly she aligned her body to face the imaginary etchings. She pushed some function buttons on her sophisticated watch and called up the digital compass feature.

The digital display spun across the various cardinal directions as the device established its internal bearings.

...E...SE...S...SW...

Fernanda looked above the horizon and matched up the three stars that made up the Great Hunter's belt—the constellation Orion. Four thousand years of processional orbit had altered the position of the constellation. The familiar boundary stars on either end confirmed Fernanda's suspicion. Betelgeuse shone with its familiar golden aura, and Rigel beaconed back to her with an eerie blue glow. Fernanda visualized the stone wall again and tried to match up the smaller stars to see how the enigmatic outline of the Sphinx might appear to these ancient astronomers.

A small beeping sound rang out from her watch, jarring her from scientific observation back to reality. Fernanda looked at the time that had triggered the alarm: it had been more than forty-five minutes since Chris Belkins and Pam had left to refresh themselves at the stream.

Fernanda noticed that Neil also was looking at his watch and pacing nervously. Although she didn't know Neil well, she knew enough to recognize when he was worried about something.

Neil held down the microphone talk button on his headset. "Chris, come in, this is Neil."

Static blurted back at them.

"Something's wrong. I can't raise them on com," said Neil. "They should've been back by now."

"I agree," Fernanda said. "Should we go out and look for them?"

"I have a better idea." Neil walked over to the travois and pulled a small black instrument from the hand-fashioned sled.

"The embedded tracker we injected into everyone has a radio beacon installed; if Chris and Pam are anywhere within a few miles of us, we'll see it here." Neil turned on the small machine as he spoke, and it quickly booted up.

AUTHENTICATION REQUIRED

Neil ran his thumb over the reader.

ACCESS GRANTED

A green scope came up on a black background; three clusters of dots appeared on the screen. "That's us there," said Neil, pointing to a small blob of three signatures that represented himself, Fernanda, and Jim on the highlands.

Fernanda studied the display. "This point is directly north of us and close; that's Rich and Troy. So these two over here must be Pam and Chris."

The display showed two dots to the right of the highlands, almost conjoined in their proximity, moving slowly toward the city of Unug-Kulaba.

"Do you think communication is out? Why would they be going back to the city?" asked Fernanda.

"Belkins wouldn't do that. He would've informed us before taking an action like that, especially with Pam along," Neil said. "My suspicion is that they are *not* returning under their own will. The real question is, are they still alive?"

Fernanda paced anxiously and looked out across the valley at the city with its flickering torches. "We have to go after them," she said. "What can I do?"

"Well, we can't do anything until Rich and Troy get back. Let me get them back here so we can figure out a plan." Neil switched his headset to Channel 2 and pressed the talk button.

"Rich, this is Neil, over."

A crackle of static preceded a response from Rich Loren. "Loren here. Neil, this is an amazing boat—much more advanced than..."

Neil cut him off. "Sorry to interrupt you, Rich, but we have big problems up here; can you cut your trip short and get back here ASAP?"

"Roger that. Let me get Troy and take this zip line off the Ark, and we'll be right there."

Within a few minutes, the unmistakable sound of a zip line in use could be heard, and two darkly clad figures walked up to the team's encampment.

Neil ran the situation past Troy and Rich, and they began to consider alternatives.

"We'll have to wait until they stop moving, and then we'll take action," said Neil.

A brachiosaur hooted in the distance as the worried team members began to formulate a plan.

32

Salah's Mission

S alah al-Din's head was spinning. The transfer had disrupted his equilibrium, and he found himself lying on his side in the middle of a small dusty hill, just outside the gates of Jerusalem. As he rose to his feet and focused his eyes, he saw a golden dome gleaming with the orange and red light of a brilliant sunset. Mysterious and wondrous, the Dome of the Rock was the most sacred of all the religious sites in Islam. Salah knelt and kissed the ground and prayed, thanking Allah for getting him there successfully.

This was the neighborhood he had grown up in. But in his childhood, it was occupied territory—Israel's property. Then, he was the alien, not the Israelis.

A subtle flapping noise pulled Salah out of his reminiscing. He turned toward the sound. A nylon flag of Jordan snapped in the evening breeze.

But things felt different now.

The aroma of family dinners being served in a thousand homes filled the air. Fires burned in trash cans, and young people hung out on the street flirting with each other. Flames escaped the tops of the rusted metal barrels, illuminating the ancient walls of Jerusalem.

Even with the territory under Jordanian authority, the place was preparing for certain war. Plywood was being hastily nailed over storefronts, and sandbag machine-gun nests were everywhere, populated with Jordanian army men smoking cigarettes and talking quietly among themselves. Their rifles were always close at hand.

Salah walked up to the soldiers and extended well-wishes to them. They eyed him suspiciously and gripped their guns tightly, ready for anything. After offering some platitudes and small talk, which Salah knew he was not skilled at, he asked for the location of the closest command center. The soldiers pointed toward a walkway and gave him some directions. Salah thanked them and gave a blessing.

Adjusting his hijab, Salah ran up the walkway, indulging his fantasy of what Jerusalem would be like in his children's time based on the mission he was about to accomplish. Salah's foreknowledge of this time played in his mind with the fidelity of a TV documentary. With the Straits of Tiran recently closed to the Israelis, Egypt's President Nasser had galvanized the Arabic world in its thoughts of retaking portions of Jerusalem that had been lost in 1948 during the Jew's fight for independence, a crucible of battles that had produced the fledgling, reborn Jewish nation. Hundreds of thousands of refugees, forced off their land during that time, now dreamed of returning to family homes and farms that were now in Israeli territory.

As Salah walked down the streets of Jerusalem toward the command center, he dreamed of a new future for the Middle East—one without the fighting, without the barriers and soldiers.

A future he had the power to create.

33

The Prisoner

As Pam opened her eyes, slowly the definition of the dimly lit room began to take shape. She was lying face down on a cold stone floor, and her whole body ached with bruising from the rough handling by the soldiers who had carried her from the stream to this cell. As she struggled to stand up, she found herself in a cramped six foot by ten foot jail cell. A foot-tall window fitted with iron bars was on the back wall, and a shaft of moonlight angled through the rectangular opening. On both sides of her were stone walls, and before her stood an array of iron bars flanking the main hallway that allowed access to other cells. A foul-smelling, primitive toilet was in the corner of the room, with sludge and cockroaches adorning the hastily cut rock seat. Pam gagged at the repulsive odor.

She squinted and made out at least two other prisoners in cells across from her. Directly across the hall, she recognized Chris Belkins' form crumpled on the floor. In the cell next to him, a prisoner was on his feet, leaning against the iron bars and watching Pam's every move.

The other prisoner studied her shamelessly. He did not have long hair or a beard like the citizens of the city she had observed the previous day. His clothing was rather modern, beige with what appeared to be black leather boots. His shirt had markings on the cuffs and on the upper parts of the sleeves that she could not make out.

Pam ignored the stares of the prisoner and focused her attention on Belkins. "Chris…Chris," she whispered. Chris's body moved slightly, and

Pam exhaled with some relief. He rolled over on his back and let out a moan. His neck was black and blue from the three darts that had been used to take him out at the stream. He sat up on the cold floor and then pulled to a stand using the iron bars in the doorway for support.

"Are you OK, Pam?" he asked, his voice garbled.

"Yes, just bruised—and I have a five-alarm headache."

"Where are we?" asked Chris.

"I think we're back in the city, if I had to guess—some kind of detention area." Pam walked to the small window in the back of her cell and looked out. The fires burning at the guard stations along the massive city wall illuminated the night. She could hear muffled tones from the people talking in the street below her.

"We're definitely inside the city. It looks like we're near one of the outside walls and probably thirty feet off the ground. There's a street below us," said Pam.

Chris quickly checked himself—the abductors had taken his communication headset, rifle, knife, and belt.

The prisoner in the other cell spotted a small American flag patch on the upper right sleeve of Chris's shirt. His voice pierced the darkness. "Sind sie Amerikaner?"

Pam immediately recognized the language as German and mentally translated it: *Are you Americans?*

"He's German!" said Pam to Chris. "How is that possible?"

The prisoner, frustrated with the delayed response and sensing some recognition from Pam, turned to her and pointed at the flag again, increasing his volume. "Sind sie Amerikaner?"

"Ja, wir sind Amerikaner," replied Pam, confirming to him that she and Chris were Americans.

A stream of German flowed into the night air as the prisoner pointed to his upper arm and the marks on the cuffs of his shirt. Chris moved to the iron gate that separated him from the German prisoner. He could just detect two black lightning bolts in a tight formation against the contrast of the beige fabric.

"He's SS! But that's impossible!" Chris exclaimed. Then he saw the band of red cloth around the man's upper arm and the unmistakable, frightening crisscross of a swastika. Even here, so far from home, the atrocities that the symbol represented caused Pam and Chris to become filled with hatred and disgust.

Pam swallowed. *How had he come here?* "Wie kamen sie hier?" she asked the German.

"Ich bin ein Testpilot mit der Luftwaffe," the man answered.

"He was a test pilot with the Luftwaffe," Pam translated for Chris.

"That makes sense. The Bell Project?" asked Chris.

Pam asked the prisoner, and his eyes shot wide open. He began jumping up and down in his cell with excitement, with German running so freely from his lips that Pam could barely keep up.

"Oops!" she muttered.

"What do you mean 'Oops?'" asked Chris.

Pam took a deep breath and looked at Chris. "He wants to know if Germany has won—he must think that our knowledge of the Bell means they have. Should I tell him?"

Chris shrugged. "It doesn't matter. Why not?"

The prisoner locked eyes with Pam as if he could make her respond exactly how he expected. "Hat Deutschland gewonnen—waren wir siegreich?"

Pam spoke the words in German, translating quickly. "I'm sorry to tell you this; the war has been over for over fifty years. Germany was defeated and is now an ally of the United States."

The prisoner's hand went into his hair as he pulled and scratched his scalp, tortured by the revelation. He slowly slid down the gate of his cell as if all strength had left him. After a few moments he looked back at Pam with tears in his eyes. "Der Führer—was geschah mit dem Führer?"

Pam closed her eyes and gathered her composure. How to answer this question? What had happened to the Führer? It wasn't every day you told a soldier that everything he had sacrificed for was for nothing. She said it plainly, as if reading from a sterile history book in high school. "Adolf Hitler killed himself in an underground bunker in Germany in April 1945."

The man pulled at his hair with his hands and sobbed uncontrollably. Chris was surprised to find empathy in his heart for this man. "I wonder how long he's been in here?"

"Let's find out," said Pam. After a brief pause to let the prisoner compose himself, she asked, "Wie lang sind Sie hier gewesen?" The German answered, pointing to four marks scratched into the wall of his cell.

"He says his aircraft crashed a mile from here in a field near a small farm. He's been here four weeks."

"This time travel stuff really messes with your mind," said Chris. "I'm too tired to think about it right now."

The German queried Pam with tears in his eyes, his anguish and sadness obvious.

"Welches Jahr das ist?" he asked.

Pam replied, "2348 BC."

The airman slumped to his knees and put his face into his hands. "Nein. Nein. Nicht!" he cried.

Salah's Mysterious Destination

(C) ameron unlocked the huge steel door and ran into the Platform bay. He found no bodies—just small piles of white ash, lying eerily in thin, wraith-like shapes. A pile of ash near the concrete wall was all that remained of Dustin. Cameron's eyes welled with tears, and anger flared in him. He had known Dustin since the young man was a sophomore in college. He had watched Dustin's educational progress and mathematical achievements with interest. Dustin had been at the top of Cameron's short list for recruitment to TRC. Why had he felt it necessary to ally himself with terrorists?

Seeing there was nothing he could do, Cameron ran to the elevator and punched the button for the lobby. He knew what to expect. He understood what type of men the terrorists were. They never would have allowed someone to know of their presence during such an operation.

Cameron found Sally in the lobby, sprawled on the marble floor behind the desk. Her eyes were still open, looking straight ahead. Cameron brushed her eyelids shut with his hands and grabbed a sea-foam green sweater that was hanging over Sally's chair. He placed the sweater over her face and straightened her dress and limbs, trying to bring dignity to a tragic situation.

Cameron's anger flared. *Dustin, what have you done?*

Dustin had paid a high price, the ultimate price, for his allegiance to these terrorists. Men who had no allegiance to anyone but their murderous mission.

Cameron locked the front doors and ran some commands from Sally's workstation to seal the complex and lock down the external entrances. He headed back to the elevator and pressed the button for the operations center. Admiral Turner had been right; there had not been enough security in place at Two Roads Corporation.

Cameron returned to the ops center to find Alicia and Sandy Moran, the historian, looking at a number of Web pages displayed on Alicia's workstation. Among the Ivy League elite that staffed the various departments of TRC, Sandy Moran stood out starkly. He didn't hold any academic degrees, which put him on the outside in TRC's highly academic atmosphere. A high-school dropout, Sandy was an insatiable reader of history books—any book, really; he would happily devour anything in print. In fact, Sandy was one of the brightest people Cameron had ever met, which was why he was on the short list of hires when he was tapped by Neil to lead the research division of TRC.

Sandy's appearance didn't really help him garner respect with the post-doctoral nerds who sat around in multicolored beanbag chairs in the labs at TRC. Sandy was a balding forty-something and weighed in around 430 pounds. He had an affinity for unusually bright shirts, khaki pants, and suspenders. He was always reading something, and sometimes he would bump into people in the lab hallways because he was so engrossed in a book.

Cameron valued Sandy's insight and had found him invaluable in the Chrona project and other wormhole projects at TRC. Cameron could ask Sandy almost anything about the past, and the man could not only replay it like a movie with great drama and color, but could also extrapolate where certain changes in history might lead. In a situation such as Cameron found himself in now, he was happy to see his two best people collaborating on a solution.

Alicia leapt out of her chair when Cameron came into the ops center, but she could tell from his facial expression that things were bad.

"Sally's dead. She was shot in the lobby. There was nothing I could do," Cameron said.

"Oh, no. Poor Sally." Alicia leaned against Cameron and slipped her arms around his waist. Tears from her blue eyes fell onto Cameron's black T-shirt.

Cameron gave Alicia a tender hug and tried to comfort her, but he felt that the best approach would be to focus everyone's attention on the terrorist who had traveled back in time.

"What do we know about the time period their leader went back to?" Cameron asked Sandy.

"Almost everything."

"What do you mean?"

Sandy took a deep breath. "It would seem that the terrorist leader went back to June 3, 1967, and the transfer point tells us a lot about his intentions." Sandy clicked a button, and a digital map of eastern Jerusalem filled a plasma monitor.

"What happened in Jerusalem in 1967?"

"The Six-Day War—the war that pretty much defines the next forty years of conflict in the Middle East."

"OK, Sandy, give me the rundown on this. Alicia, did you download everything we have on this topic?"

Alicia nodded and listened intently as Sandy spun up on the Six-Day War.

"In 1967, Egypt, Syria, Jordan—basically every neighbor around Israel—decided to destroy Israel as a nation. They entered into an Arab alliance and began to send signals of war to the world and to the Israelis. They blocked Israel's access to the Straits of Tiran, which is a critical source of fresh water for the state of Israel. The United States, perhaps the best friend of Israel at that time, was embroiled in the Vietnam War and was concerned about overt connections to the conflict. The Soviets had strong connections to Egypt and Syria and had actually provided many weapons systems to their armies."

"So the U.S. was afraid to get involved and get dragged into two wars simultaneously?" asked Cameron.

"Right, but that doesn't mean they were disinterested, just that their hands were tied. The CIA seemed to think that regardless of who attacked first, Israel would win."

Cameron chuckled. "Yeah, 'cause the CIA is always right about everything."

"So why did the Egyptians want to attack—didn't they have the same intelligence that told them they might lose?" Alicia asked.

"Perhaps they acknowledged that at first, but as the citizenry heard the rhetoric and the fires of nationalism were stoked by Gamal Nasser, the Egyptian president, things reached a critical mass that couldn't be stopped," Sandy explained. "It became a matter of pride and, to some extent, the place of the Arab alliance to erase Israel's existence."

"So the Arab alliance started a roller coaster they couldn't stop," said Cameron.

"The race for us here, it seems, will be to get Israel to continue with their plans—or perhaps more to the point, to ensure that they attack first." Sandy paced the floor while rubbing what was left of his blond hair. It stood almost straight out from his balding head. "If a modern-day terrorist succeeds in reaching them, Nasser and King Hussein of Jordan will have intelligence both on their lack of preemptive attack plans and the ramifications of their inaction in the forty years to follow. The foreknowledge this terrorist has taken back in time with him is the threat we face here—not the chronology of the battle we know took place."

"So, if the Arab alliance were to attack first, or if they change their plans radically, how would that change anything?" asked Cameron.

"It's very hard to say. We don't know how this terrorist will inform the Arab block of Israel's defenses and offensive plans, and perhaps most frightening, we don't really know if he took anything back with him."

"You mean like nuclear plans or a device of some sort?" asked Alicia.

Cameron looked at a trace report from the Platform. "There's no evidence of plutonium or uranium traces in the transfer to 1967. He didn't take any fissile material back with him."

"Maybe he just needs plans or evidence of that material in that time frame," said Pam.

Sandy shrugged. "Hey, we could speculate all day long. His foreknowledge of the event is the main thing here. On the flip side, if the terrorist succeeds and Israel is destroyed or profoundly altered, it could impact our future in a massive way. Israel's Mossad and the CIA have always shared intelligence. If that were to go away, who knows what would happen during the weapons buildups in the 70s and 80s during the Cold War?"

Cameron had a worried look on his face. "So everything we know in our time might be extremely different if this terrorist leader succeeds."

"Oh, man!" said Sandy, lifting his bear paw-sized hands and resting them on his balding dome. "I was just thinking. If the US stayed out of the war— It was a regional conflict, but if the terrorist throws the timeline off, then everyone's estimates of Israel's timing for winning will be wrong. Egypt, Syria, and Jordan would make huge progress in the early hours of the war. They could destroy Israel's army and air force and continue killing, even going beyond the military personnel and into the citizenry of Israel. The Jewish communities in all the Western nations would demand reciprocity, and Russia would view this pressure as America's getting involved in the Middle East. The Soviets would build up arms and support Egypt and Syria with weaponry—but what if it were to go further than that?"

"You're talking about World War III," said Cameron.

"Yep. This would be a much bigger deal than just a few missiles in Cuba."

"So someone has to go back to 1967 and beat that terrorist to the punch," Cameron said.

"Who would be crazy enough to do that?" asked Alicia with a bit of a laugh. She looked at Sandy, who immediately looked away. Alicia flicked her eyes to Cameron. His face was like a stone: resolved.

"Not you!" she blurted.

35

Gamal's Gambit

june 1967

Cairo, Egypt

G amal Abdel Nasser looked out the window of his expansive office at the crowds in the plaza below his presidential residence. His head was pounding with a migraine like a knife was being jabbed into the back of his head. He threw some aspirin into his mouth and swallowed the pills without water.

Nasser was the second president of Egypt, and he had taken power with his army during a coup in 1956. The people outside were shouting his name and cheering in fever-pitch synchronicity. Even with the pain, Nasser smiled; his vision for a Pan-Arabic nation was the driving force behind the rally. He hoped for a new, powerful nation of strong, secular Arabs that would stretch across the Middle East, from Egypt all the way to the northern alliance member of Syria. Nasser had spent the past few years building the relationships with the monarchs and leaders of the other Arab nations that were essential for making his vision a reality. Egypt and Syria had mutually linked their futures to one another by vowing to attack Israel if either country was attacked by the fledgling nation. Amar, Nasser's general, had assured him that the Egyptian air and ground forces would be able to take out the Israeli military.

Nasser stared at the signs being hoisted and waved amid the sea of people chanting his name. The streets were filled with black-and-white pictures of him as he had looked in his younger years. He saw other signs—signs with guns held in clenched fists, signs that read "Death to Israel" in Arabic, and white skulls painted on black cloth. These reminded

Nasser that the pride and nationalism on which he had poured fuel had a dark side, and possibly a nature that was uncontrollable.

Only one small barrier stood in the way of his plan—a small nation of 2.5 million people who were celebrating the nineteenth anniversary of their unlikely and, some said, prophetic founding.

The events of the past few weeks had taken an almost singular direction—an impending war with that small but powerful nation. If Nasser's plan held, they would lead to the extermination of the nation of Israel.

Anwar Sadat, Egypt's vice president and one of Nasser's most trusted advisors, had returned with intelligence from Egypt's superpower ally, the Soviet Union, just a few weeks before. The information, which the Soviets said was highly probable and demanded action, stated that Israel would attack Egypt in the next few weeks. This news allowed Nasser to quickly call up the military reserves of his country, and the peasants and middle-class citizens of Egypt had responded unanimously. The poor of Egypt loved and adored Nasser because of his generous support of farmers and the giving of land to the neediest people of the region. Within a few weeks, an army forty thousand strong was parading through the massive plazas of Cairo on its way to the Sinai Desert.

Behind the massive troop formation, an iron fist of three hundred Soviet-built tanks and four hundred and fifty armored personnel carriers guaranteed rapid destruction of any Israeli defense. The military parade was broadcast throughout the Middle East, with a psychological warfare effect on the Israeli people. Rabbis were sanctifying local parks in the city of Tel Aviv and around Israel in preparation for mass burials. The economy was stalled, and city streets were being fortified with sandbags and concrete barriers.

Nasser turned from the window to the general, who was sweating profusely as he sat nervously in a chair across from Nasser. "Are you sure?" Nasser asked the general, staring directly into his eyes, looking for deception.

"Yes sir, Mr. President. The Soviet intelligence is wrong—Israel is not mobilizing for attack."

Nasser swore and slammed his fist onto the ornately carved wooden desk.

"Look out that window. The entire nation—no, the entire world—expects me to order the destruction of that country, and you're sitting here telling me that this military buildup and mobilization is based on nothing factual." Nasser's hands were shaking as he threw the newest intelligence report on his desk and pointed at the nearest door. "Get out of my presence!" His face was crimson with anger, and his finger shook from frayed nerves. The general made a hasty exit, like a beaten dog, and the door slammed behind him.

The Egyptian president stared at the intelligence report sitting on his desk, and slowly a plan began to come clearly into his mind.

He pressed his call button and a secretary came to his door.

"Get me the Secretary of the United Nations," he ordered.

36

Dawn Ritual

The early morning air was disrupted by the sound of drums beating. Pam awakened with a start and saw Chris looking out his window into the interior of the city.

"Strange things are afoot at the 7-Eleven," he said.

"What's going on out there?" Pam asked, rubbing the sleep from her eyes.

"A crowd is starting to form in the plaza again, like yesterday."

"That's not good. Another set of sacrifices?" she asked.

Chris was standing on his toes and straining to look through the small window of his cell onto the plaza below. "Looks that way. This is *some* wakeup call!"

The three prisoners heard footsteps outside their cell doors. Chris quickly moved away from his window as two enormous guards opened a large iron gate and walked over to the German soldier's cell.

The giant guards had the same appearance as those they had seen in the courtyard containing the worshiped obelisk. They were at least ten feet tall, perhaps taller, but their most striking aspect was their heads. They had sloping foreheads and massive, back-reaching cranial structures. The soldiers' appearance reminded Pam of some ancient Egyptian dioramas she had seen of pharaohs and their families. The heads of the ancients always seemed to be oblong. She had just assumed it was an artistic style, or perhaps an early form of perspective. She noticed that one of the guards had six fingers on his hand—a sure sign of giantism. Were the people in this society looking for the trait and breeding soldiers of this size? Was this some sort of genetic engineering without the test tubes?

The other guard emitted a dark and frightening laugh and spoke to the German soldier cowering in the corner.

"Sakirna Inanna ka zu gisgal bansur!"

Pam struggled with the strange accent and the few words she could translate, and then some of the meaning became clear to her: *This coward will make an excellent morning sacrifice to Inanna.*

Pam said nothing, expecting the soldiers to turn and face her and Chris, but they didn't. The gate to the German prisoner's cell swung open, and the guards marched into the small holding cell. The German soldier screamed and twisted and arched his back, trying to make it difficult for the guards to come near him. The guards simply looked at each other and laughed. The larger of the two drew back his arm and punched the German square in the face, knocking him out cold. His limp body fell to the floor, and blood dripped from his obviously broken nose. The guards each took hold of an arm and carried him down the passageway and out of the prison. Gates closed behind them, at least two times that Pam could hear. She stared at the dark patch of blood on the cobbled floor and the trail of spattered blood that headed out of the cell block—the only evidence that remained of the German's existence.

Chris approached the iron gate separating himself from Pam. "Did you catch any of that language? What did they say to him?"

"Well, it wasn't good news. Something about an adequate sacrifice to Inanna," she said.

Chris wiped his hand across his face as he did the math. "We have to find a way out of here, or we're going to be next!"

Pam nodded in agreement. "I'm sure the team is trying to figure out where we are and how to get us back. They won't leave us here."

The drums continued pounding in the background, increasing in tempo now.

Poom poom poom poom poom—each beat resonated against the stone walls of the plaza and echoed through the alleys of the city.

Chris moved over to the window facing the plaza. The entire town, it seemed, was assembled. The people were writhing and swaying in unison like one giant organism. The demonic rave swept over the entire city, spell-binding the thousands of citizens who had assembled for the morning sacrifice to Inanna, the goddess of the city.

The high priest again appeared, but this time he stood high on a massive stepped pyramid that towered over all the buildings in the city. It reminded Chris of the ancient Mayan structures in the Yucatan Peninsula. The clothing he wore was made of thin golden plates arranged in a short skirt and tunic. Dark red fabric reinforced the back and peeked out from between the golden panels. A massive fire burned at the base of the stairs leading to the top of the pyramid, and the now-familiar form of Inanna was visible through the smoke.

The high priest raised his hands into the air just as the sun was breaking over the horizon and driving the shadows of the early morning away. It was a dramatic scene that whipped the crowd into a frenzy.

Chris could see the two guards appear now behind the priest with a solid grip on the German prisoner, who had regained consciousness. The crowd cheered at the sight of the frightened man. His beige Luftwaffe uniform seemed so alien and so out of place, and the victim's appearance only fueled the crowd's hatred.

The drums pounded and the crowd began shouting in unison the name of the goddess: "Inanna!"

The drumbeats increased in tempo and broadcast a complex, syncopated rhythm throughout the city.

"Inanna!" yelled the citizens, awash in the moment and moving trance-like to the beat.

The priest raised his hands, palms facing the crowd, and the drums abruptly stopped. A hush settled over the entire city, but the tension of the moment remained in the air like a giant coiled spring waiting to be released.

The two guards stepped forward and positioned the German on his back atop a small table-like platform. They tied his arms to the table with thick leather straps.

"What's going on out there?" Pam asked desperately. Even though she couldn't see the ceremony, she could feel it—like an evil cloak of darkness settling over the entire city.

"Believe me, Pam, you don't want to know," Chris replied.

The German turned and twisted his head back and forth, trying to see what was coming next. He arched his lower back, and his legs pushed up, trying to take the pressure off his arms and upper back.

The high priest brought out a bronze sword with a broad blade. He raised it into the air, and the crowd cheered. The German airman focused on the blade, and his eyes grew wide in horror. He shrieked, but the cheers of the crowd drowned out his solitary scream. The blade glinted in the early morning sunlight and then disappeared in a blur as the priest swiftly brought the sword down, decapitating the German soldier.

The crowd was electrified by this murderous act and began their droning chant to Inanna once again. The priest grasped the locks of the German's blond hair and lifted the severed head above his own. Blood spurted and spilled everywhere. A cheer went up from the crowd, and the priest lobbed the head into the air. It rolled down the long, steep stairway, bouncing and leaving a slimy bloodstain at each point of impact. The battered head careened down the stairs and landed directly in the fire at the base of Inanna's stone image.

Chris pulled back in horror from the act he had just witnessed from the prison window. As a soldier, he had seen many atrocities of war—he had seen friends and comrades in arms shot dead just inches from him during a firefight with the enemy, burned bodies smoldering in the ruined hulks of exploded tanks—but nothing like this. This was pure brutality, violence for no other reason but the thrill of it. These ancient people were offering sacrifices to a being that could neither hear nor speak nor acknowledge their worship.

Chris shrank down against the wall of his cell. "I'm starting to understand why God drowns this whole place."

He looked blankly through the bars at Pam. "I just hope we're not here when it happens."

37

The Manager of Israel

june 1967

Tel Aviv, Israel

L evi Eshkol sat in the darkened war room. A single fluorescent bulb mounted from the ceiling shone shafts of bluish-white light through swirling streams of cigarette smoke. As the prime minister of Israel, Eshkol was the exact opposite of the man in Egypt who dominated his thoughts. Eshkol was a non-charismatic, managerial leader. Peace-loving in nature and profoundly averse to controversy and antagonism, he found himself swimming with sharks—people who would rather shoot first and then ask questions. Along with him, five generals and their immediate reports sat around the long, rectangular table.

The dull cheering noise of the throngs outside in the streets of Tel Aviv penetrated the normally silent, stoic environment of the Defense Ministry Building. The cheering brought a rare smile to the prime minister's face.

Nineteen years. Was that all it had been?

Israel had only been in existence as a newly established nation-state for nineteen years—its establishment an event that some people called prophetic. The small, fledgling nation was literally surrounded by enemies on all sides, enemies who were dedicated to pushing the 2.5 million Jews that occupied the land God had promised them into the Mediterranean Sea.

The nineteen-year celebration seemed to fade out as Eshkol's attention focused on the intelligence reports and terrain maps that were spread across the oak table. His smile was brief and disappeared behind wrinkles and worry lines of concern.

He asked the question again.

The question that had to be answered.

"Will America, our staunchest supporter, continue to sit idly by, as our enemies in their tanks and aircraft amass at our borders and prepare to obliterate us?"

Yitzhak Rabin, one of Eshkol's generals, stamped out his cigarette and exhaled a gray plume into the stale air of the conference room. "Prime Minister, perhaps it doesn't matter anymore. We must preserve our way of life. Waiting for our only supporter, who is now mired in a war of its own and fears the retaliation of the Soviet Union with nuclear weapons, does not bode well. *You* must make the decision to strike, or it will be too late."

Eshkol pulled his glasses off and rubbed his eyes. *Vietnam.* America's headline-gripping quagmire had no end in sight, and they could not afford another conflict—especially in a place like the Middle East, with its incendiary potential.

Eshkol placed his hands on the table and pulled a military map toward him. The crinkled map was covered in red highlights and marked up with military icons. "President Johnson is not likely to intervene. None of our signals intelligence shows anything more than lip service and empty threats to the Arab alliance."

A block of blue icons on the map represented the three thousand men in the reserves he had activated. The block seemed to come alive in Eshkol's mind. He could see images of young men with their families, their beautiful wives and playful children. The happy images then took a darker turn, filled with the Star of David flag draped over wooden coffins, crying women, and orphaned children.

He slowly wrung his hands in the fluorescent light.

I hate this…this decision. What kind of a decision is it to save ourselves by killing our best young men?

He looked around the table, surrounded by the various branches of the Israeli Defense Ministry, men conditioned to respond without emotion, without a second's thought. It seemed simple to them. Orders—that's all—just orders. Not men, just objectives to be taken, ground to be defended or captured.

He was so unlike the roomful of warriors he found himself in.

"What of Nasser's call to the United Nations that we intercepted?" he asked.

Aharon Yariv, of Israeli Intelligence, opened a manila envelope and scanned the most recent report. "As you all know, Nasser made the request to the United Nations that the peacekeepers leave the border. We expected the UN to be bogged down with bureaucracy and meaningless platitudes as it always is, but they have declared that their forces will evacuate the buffer zone within forty-eight hours."

The shock of this revelation seemed to reverberate anew through the room. Eshkol's voice was shaky. "Perhaps the UN will change their mind. Maybe I can get President Johnson to…"

Aharon Yariv dropped the manila folder containing the report to the table, interrupting the prime minister. "Don't be a fool! They have done what Nasser asked them to do. They are nothing more than a puppet. They didn't even ask for advice or a second opinion from the Security Council."

Eshkol nodded sheepishly, not sure of how to handle the interruption. "This is very out of character for Nasser, and very dangerous."

A red-faced general at the end of the table lost his temper and slammed his fist to the table. "This is unacceptable, Prime Minister. Yes, a single artillery shell in one direction or the other could ignite a conflict that has the potential to carry the entire globe into a world war."

He let the words hang in the air and then pointed his stubby index finger directly at Eshkol. "But, *you*, sir, have a responsibility to the people and the future of this nation to take decisive action. Defend its very survival now with the information you have at this moment. The time for negotiation is done. We must fight!"

The demands of the general faded into the background for a moment as Levi Eshkol thought of the public meeting between Yitzhak Rabin, his army chief of staff, with David Ben-Gurion, Israel's first prime minister, a few days before. Ben-Gurion, who had led his people through the dark days of 1948 to their independence and establishment as a nation, had railed at Rabin for hours, criticizing him for isolating himself and the nation and not giving diplomacy a chance. Rabin, caught in the middle between the military and Eshkol, had suffered a mental breakdown. Eshkol looked across the table at Rabin, who seemed tortured at the obvious decision staring them both in the face. Time was running out, and with the people's confidence in Eshkol at an all-time low, respect from the military was also ebbing.

"Prime Minister," Yariv said. Eshkol, visibly shaken, looked at him.

"We must deny the Egyptian army any more time to organize and prepare for war. The enemy is emboldened. Egypt has seized control of the Straits of Tiran. They now control a good portion of our citizens' source of drinking water, not to mention a strategic shipping port."

Eshkol stood up and sighed heavily, the weight of his thoughts obvious. "You'll have my decision tomorrow morning."

As Levi Eshkol left the conference room, one of the generals muttered under his breath, "If we survive this, it will be in spite of his decision."

38

Breakout

A mile away from the city walls, Captain Rich Loren sat in the high hide he had used to begin their zip line journey to the Ark the previous night. He opened an aluminum case and quickly scanned the parts of his sniper rifle, separated by foam cutouts. With military efficiency, he assembled the gun, screwing the silencer down tightly onto the end, and loaded a thirty-round magazine.

He peered through the rifle's scope and aimed the laser dot between the iron bars of each prison cell's window. After flashing the small red dot into a cell, he waited for one minute and then moved to the next cell.

As the drums and celebration of the sacrifice continued, Pam was sitting on the edge of the wooden frame that was her cot. Something caught her eye. A red laser-beam dot wiggled nervously on the wall.

"Chris, it's the team," said Pam, jumping off her bed and running to the window.

"Quick, signal them and let them know which cell you're in," Chris said.

Pam stuck her hand out the window and gave a thumbs-up, then held up two fingers, trying to convey to the sniper that Chris was also there.

A smile crept across Rich's mouth. He pressed his microphone transmit button. "Neil, I've located Pam and Chris."

"Great work, Rich. Let's try to convey what we're going to do," replied Neil.

"Roger that."

Rich took a deep breath and held the rifle butt tightly to his shoulder. He again put the crosshairs on the window where he had spotted Pam's hand some moments before and pressed the laser.

"There it is again!" said Pam.

The laser point just sat there for a moment and then began to circle slowly. Chris and Pam watched intently, trying to determine what meaning the sniper was attempting to communicate. The red dot continued its orbit uninterrupted. Chris knew talent when he saw it. He squatted down and watched the whirling, focused dot.

Rich was sweating profusely; it required a huge amount of focus to keep the laser-beam in a tight, consistent circle.

"Circles? Continuous circular motion?" guessed Chris.

"Motion! That's it," Pam exclaimed.

Pam and Chris turned toward each other simultaneously: "AARON!"

Pam again stuck her hand out the window. She put one finger up and moved it in a circular motion as if to echo the laser dot. Loren again pinged Neil. "I think they understand."

"OK, let's move forward with the plan. Fernanda, go ahead and start up AARON," Neil said.

Fernanda nodded and clicked a few keys on the laptop that was driving AARON. The miniature UAV's engine hummed, and the ten-foot-long carbon-fiber blade began to turn slowly. Jim and Fernanda had fashioned a long pole that protruded perpendicularly from the miniature helicopter's aluminum skids. The pole stuck out about fifteen feet, only allowing ten feet of clearance from the spinning blade that provided lift for the intelligence vehicle. The long pole had a black canvas bag connected by Velcro straps.

Rich Loren looked through the scope and scanned along the city wall between him and the wall of the prison. From his perch in the high hide, Rich saw two sentries walking along the wall at different points. One was patrolling at a corner point toward the front gate, and the other was directly in front of the prison area. Rich couldn't see between the city wall and the prison wall, and he wondered how many soldiers might be there.

We'll all know soon enough, he thought.

AARON made a pass across the top of the ridge where the team had camped out and headed over toward Rich's position. Fernanda panned the camera mounted under the nose of the helicopter and focused in on Rich. He gave a thumbs-up, and Fernanda clicked on the next waypoint icon that was positioned just outside the city wall.

Jim Spruce waited in a lush glade that stretched from the entrance of the city up the back of the hills toward the team's encampment. His job was to install a kill point that would stop anyone pursuing Pam and Chris after their escape. Jim was struggling to build the twin tripod-based platforms that held the M-134 mini-guns—computer-controlled Gatling guns that were thirty inches long, weighed in at sixty pounds, and fired up to four thousand rounds per minute. Each mini-gun had six barrels inside one spinning cylinder.

Jim positioned the two Gatling gun platforms about fifty feet apart, one at a higher elevation and the other just a bit lower in the glade. The platforms stood about six feet above the forest undergrowth, barely clearing the giant leaves and long grasses that covered the floor of the glade. A power supply and computer were connected to each gun platform by long, thin cables, which Jim pushed into the ground with tent spikes. He placed a number of wireless perimeter sensors on tree trunks and spread them about two hundred feet from the base of the gun platforms. The invisible sensor network would react to anyone coming through the area and train the guns on the intruders in an inescapable crossfire.

After placing the last sensor, Jim went to the computer that controlled the aiming and firing procedure and powered it up. Once authentication took place, the mini-guns came alive, pivoting in unison and then moving separately. The weapons had the capability of analyzing targets and training fire on them together as a unit or separately, thus allowing more targets to be destroyed. Jim clicked on the screen and set the entire system to safety, removing the possibility of harming anyone until the right moment.

Jim stepped back and evaluated the deadly trap he had just constructed. The combination of the sensor net and the mini-guns, with their high cyclical firing rate, guaranteed a slaughter. He thought about how deadly this technology would be in the wrong hands in the wrong time period.

Actually, he thought, *I am* the wrong hands in the wrong time period, *but if it helps to save our lives, so be it.*

Jim pressed the talk button of his headset. "OK, the sensor network is up and the mini-guns are ready."

"Great work, Jim. We'll let you know when Chris and Pam are headed your way," Neil responded.

～～　～～　～～

AARON swept over the long field and passed the Ark on its way to the city wall. The drums in the background masked the noise of the droning electric engine. Rich Loren looked through the sniper scope and evaluated the targets on the wall. He knew he could not let any alarms be sounded about the team's attempted jailbreak. AARON reached the waypoint and went into a hover just twenty feet from the wall and a few feet off the ground.

"AARON's in place," said Loren. "Everybody stay frosty; this will get interesting very quickly."

Neil came on the com line. "OK, Fernanda, you're up."

Fernanda, manning the laptop controlling AARON, clicked on the next waypoint that Rich had preprogrammed for her. AARON rose and reached the top of the city wall, hovering just below the wall's edge on the outside. A guard that had been walking his post noticed the wind and turbulence being generated at the corner of the city wall and strode over to investigate. Loren saw him coming a mile away; he pulled the sniper rifle tight to his shoulder, placed the dancing red laser dot on the soldier's helmet, and slowly squeezed the trigger.

A slight bleep sound came from the silencer, and a small, red, vaporous cloud materialized around the soldier's head as he collapsed in a heap on the top of the wall. Loren scanned up and down the wall; he saw no other soldiers.

"Fernanda, the coast is clear," Rich said.

Fernanda clicked on the next waypoint, and the UAV pulled out of its hover and moved forward over the wall, sinking down behind it. Fernanda grabbed the joystick that swiveled the camera mount on the helicopter's nose. She looked up and down the street beside the prison wall to check for soldiers. Seeing none, she clicked on the waypoint that would put the miniature craft just outside the prison wall. AARON nosed down and moved forward obediently.

Rich was watching a soldier in a parapet on the opposite end of the city wall from the soldier Rich had shot. At the sight of the helicopter, the soldier looked puzzled but unsure of what to do. He grabbed a long spear and ran along the wall toward the center of the city. Loren watched him running and followed him with the scope.

The giant soldier had never seen anything like this shiny bird that flapped its wings in a circle. As he was running, he lifted his right arm into the air and prepared to throw his heavy iron spear with all his might. Just as suddenly as he had begun running, he was lying dead on the top of the wall with a small hole in his temple and a pool of blood forming under his enormous body. A mile away, Loren put a new magazine of ammo into his sniper rifle and continued to scan the city wall.

Fernanda kept her eyes on the camera and also on a small gauge that measured the distance around the helicopter. The narrow street was only about fifteen feet wider than the diameter of the carbon-fiber helicopter blade. The laser range-finder sensors on the sides of the helicopter constantly relayed the distances on the gauge, and Fernanda made some trim adjustments, taking into account the long pole that extended from the side of the helicopter.

Pam watched the helicopter move closer and saw the pole with a bundle attached to it.

"They're using AARON to deliver a package. It's attached to some kind of pole."

AARON reached the cell block and began to elevate to the level of the cell windows. This was the tricky part—keeping the pole from hitting the wall and knocking the precious rescue cargo into the street below while preventing the spinning rotor blades from crashing into the stone walls and taking the helicopter down.

Pam put her arms out through the iron bars as a gauge for Fernanda.

The camera rotated on the front of the helicopter to face the wall and focus on Pam. She could almost reach the bundle, and she pressed her body tightly up against the iron bars. The dust being swept up from the street below billowed everywhere in the cell, and it stung Pam's eyes.

Monitoring the video feed from the camera, Fernanda could see Pam's arms, and she nudged the flight joystick slightly right and forward to position the helicopter so that Pam could reach the rescue pack.

As Pam reached out and released the Velcro straps that secured the pack to the pole, Fernanda put the helicopter in a hover and let out a huge sigh of relief.

Neil was looking through a set of high-powered binoculars. "Awesome job, everyone; it looks like Pam has the goods."

Pam undid the Velcro straps and pulled a small canvas sack between the bars and into the window. Fernanda took note of Pam's success and pulled the helicopter away from the prison wall, then guided it into the air and over the city wall, where it went into a hover out of sight.

As the dust and debris settled in the street, Pam opened the canvas sack to find two headsets, two military pistols with some extra ammunition magazines, and a block of C-4 explosive putty and a small detonator. Pam quickly flung the extra headset through the iron bars into Chris's waiting hands.

"This is Belkins; come in," Chris spoke into the headset.

Neil's voice came on the line. "Chris, it's great to hear from you. I'll let Captain Loren give you the intelligence on the situation and what we have planned."

Pam put on her headset, and she and Chris listened intently to the plan while she loaded a magazine into the pistol and slid it across the stone floor to Chris. Pam broke the C-4 into four pieces. The explosive had the consistency of silly putty. She threw each of the golf-ball-sized blobs through the iron bars to Chris's waiting hands.

Chris quickly broke one of the balls into a smaller piece about the size of a marble. He fitted it into the lock mechanism of the cell and ran two wires from the small detonator into the C-4. Pam turned her cot onto its side and hunkered down behind it while Chris positioned himself in the corner of his cell as far from the door as possible. He twisted the plunger on the detonator, and a bright flash of light filled the prison. Pam lifted her head to see the remains of a small white cloud rising to the top of the prison and Chris working to get her cell gate open.

Pam and Chris slipped out of their cells and into the prison hallway. "This is Belkins. We're out of our cells and working our way out of the building."

Just as Pam and Chris were preparing to move down to the first floor, they heard voices and deep, foreboding laughter—headed their direction. A large wooden door with iron reinforcements separated them from a stair-case leading to the street. Chris placed his ear against the door, listening to the voices on the other side. One…two…possibly three different voices could be extracted from the routine conversation. Chris put up three fin-gers to Pam. She nodded. Chris took one side of the door, and Pam took the other. The sound of someone working the lock of the wooden door broke the silence, and Pam and Chris slunk down against the wall as close to the floor as they could get.

The door swung open, and a giant soldier walked into the hallway. He blinked, letting his eyes get used to the intensity of light in the hall. As his eyes focused, he saw Pam scrunched in a ball on the floor to his left. He lunged at her, and Chris fired his pistol directly into the back of the soldier's cranium. A burst of blood spurted against the wall above Pam. The soldier landed in a bloody heap on top of Pam. Hundreds of pounds of dead weight pressed her to the floor. Chris pushed the hulking soldier off of her.

"Are you OK?"

"I think so."

Chris grabbed her by the hand. "Let's go!"

He pulled the wooden door open and peered into the stairway—no sign of any other soldiers. Pam followed closely behind Chris as they made their way down the stone steps.

When they reached the bottom of the staircase, the low rumble of voices could be heard just beyond a stout wooden door, the last barrier between them and freedom.

Pam and Chris pressed themselves against the stone wall, trying to create as small a profile as possible if the door should swing open and the soldiers discover them.

The headsets came alive with a burst of feedback.

"OK, guys, pay attention—and for Pete's sake, don't shoot me."

It was the voice of Troy Scott. Chris bent his knees and lowered himself into a squatting position with his back pressed hard against the craggy stone wall. He motioned to Pam to take the same position as he tried to visualize what the room would look like once he kicked the door down.

Troy's voice again came over the headset. "On three."

Outside, Troy barged into the prison block wearing clothing that looked like that of any other commoner, stumbling about in front of the guards as if he were drunk. The guards looked at him with disgust.

"Swarak inna tuwalek!" yelled the guard.

"I couldn't agree more," said Troy with a smile, stopping his drunken shuffle. "Hey, guys! Check these out." Troy pulled two flash charges from his tunic and threw them on the wooden bar that separated the street from the innards of the prison.

The metal cylinders rolled down the wooden table and rattled to a stop in front of the guards. "One," said Troy into his headset as he retreated into the street.

A guard picked up the cylindrical metal charge and held it close to his face, examining it curiously. He had never seen anything made out of metal with such a perfect shape.

"Two."

Troy scanned up and down the street. He detected no guards, just citizens going about their daily business.

"Three!" Both the charges went off and lit up the prison entry with a bright flash and smoke. The guards screamed out in fear and held their eyes, momentarily blinded by the phosphorous light.

Chris kicked the wooden door with the heel of his boot, and it swung open on its iron hinges, hitting a guard who was doubled over coughing from the smoke. The impact caught the guard squarely in the side of the head and knocked him out. He fell to the floor, motionless. Pam pulled her hand up to cover her nose and mouth, and she and Chris waded into the sea of writhing bodies and swirling white smoke.

One of the guards who had taken the German soldier to his doom recognized Chris and Pam through the smoke and reached for his sword. The unmistakable sound of a metal blade sliding from its scabbard filled the air. Chris pointed his pistol at the guard's head and pulled the trigger. The silencer made its familiar bleep noise, and the guard fell, not seeing the lightning-fast round that entered his temple and exited the back of his head. The soldier hit the ground still holding his sword.

In the smoke, the room's contents seemed to merge. Tables, chairs, soldiers—everything blurred together into a uniform tone of gray. Suddenly, a form lunged through the thick smoke and grabbed Chris by the neck. Startled by the attack, Chris tried to wheel around and deflect the move, but the monstrous soldier was far too large and too tall to be affected by the tactics Chris had learned in Special Forces.

Pam stormed through the doorway behind Chris and placed the muzzle of her pistol directly against the side of the giant's head. Her finger twitched and trembled against the metal of the trigger.

"Shoot!" gasped Chris, trying to break the soldier's headlock. "Shooot!"

Pam pulled the trigger, and the giant fell to the stone floor with his hands still encircling Chris's neck. Chris pulled himself free of his assailant's death grasp. Gasping for breath and coughing from all the smoke in the tight alcove, Chris managed to stand, and both he and Pam exited the prison into the bright, morning-lit alleyway of the street. Pam's face was full of apology for her hesitation. Chris grimaced from the pain and rubbed his bruised neck.

"It's OK."

Troy rushed through the open door to find Chris and Pam and the dead soldiers. The smoke rolled out of the door and into the busy street behind him. "You guys all right? I guess those charges really did the trick, huh?"

Chris looked out the door and scanned the street for any soldiers. "What made Captain Loren pick you for this?" asked Chris.

"I drew the short straw," Troy said with a smile. "Come on, let's get out of here!"

The trio hustled down the alleyway in search of the massive city gates.

39

Computation

cross America, the greatest supercomputers and computing clusters in the country's weapons labs and intelligence agencies were grinding away on the massively complex algorithms that Cameron had divined from the German Chrona project. Each machine plowed through billions of calculations per second, performing delicate differential equations, integration across many dimensions, and topological calculations of space-time. Each of the expensive supercomputers computed only a few of the terms needed for TRC to get the team back. As each processor finished its workload, the results were automatically fired back to the TRC mathematicians via a secure Internet connection.

The TRC engineers and mathematicians watched the terms come back from the machines that Admiral Turner had promised Cameron. They squinted at the terms and double-checked them for rationality while eating crunchy snacks and drinking ultra-caffeine-laden beverages, fueling the late-night computing binge. Small piles of empty, crumpled soda cans adorned the tables. Each computer scientist tapped on his own workstation, making the keyboard glisten with the grease from the chips he was consuming for quick-energy brain food.

Alicia watched a massive plasma screen that was displaying the progress of the entire equation. She estimated they had about forty minutes left before all the terms would be crunched. Then, all the individual terms would have to be entered and run as a single final process to bring the team home successfully. She looked at the big digital clock flashing red LEDs to the team and displaying the countdown to the transfer.

45:00
44:59
44:58

This would be a close call. Alicia pulled up a chair, brushed her blond bangs out of her eyes with her hand, and helped a stressed-out mathematician double-check the terms that had just returned from the Red Storm supercomputer at NASA Ames.

40

Cameron's Choice

ameron took a yellow legal pad into the conference room and began to form a list of things he knew he would need for the trip back to Israel.

Trip? Cameron smiled wryly as he thought of the word. This was no trip—it was a one-way ticket. TRC had never sent more than one team back in time, and soon there would be three away teams, one of which did not wish to return. Cameron knew there was little chance he could come back.

Too many variables, he thought.

Why him? There were other, younger people who would make this trip, perhaps even make this sacrifice, to remain in the 1960s. Cameron could even help get them back, because he knew the inner workings of the machine and the mathematical and procedural shortcuts that could be used to bring someone back faster.

No, he thought. He would make this journey. He had made the breakthrough with the temporal equations that had started in Nazi Germany. He had discovered how to handle questionable elevations in the destination coordinates. He had basically conceived of how this machine would work in a safe and reliable manner. It really was *his* responsibility. If anything were to go wrong with the timeline, if anyone were to use it as a weapon, then blood would be on his hands. He already felt guilty about the scientists who had been incinerated during the ancient history tests. He had been irresponsible and reckless, assuming that he knew how old the world was.

Cameron punched the speakerphone button on the Polycom conference system and entered Admiral Turner's number into the phone. The secretary's voice again came across, and Cameron asked for the admiral in a courteous tone. Moments later, the admiral's gravelly voice came on.

Cameron explained in detail about the breach, the terrorists, what they knew about the timeline, and what al-Din's likely intentions were. Turner took it in quietly and solemnly on the other end.

"So someone has to go back there and stop him," said Turner.

"It's going to be me," said Cameron. "I'm responsible for it, for everything—the machine, the capability. I'm going in less than an hour."

"What about the other team? Can you get them back and yourself in such a short period of time?" asked Turner.

"Maybe," came the reply from Cameron.

To Turner, that sounded an awful lot like "No."

"Can I send you help? Can I send a Special Ops person with you? Cameron, what can I do to help you?" the admiral pleaded.

"No. Don't send anyone. You can help me by supporting Alicia and the rest of the engineers and helping Neil keep this facility going after I'm gone. Keep TRC funded and moving forward. I've sacrificed my whole life to make TRC a special, unique place. Sure, Neil had the money, but I did the recruiting. Leaving this place is like leaving my family."

Truer words were never spoken. Cameron had never married, never had children. TRC was his family; the college recruits were like his children. He had sacrificed everything for Two Roads Corporation. And now, at the end of it, he would need to leave it to protect everyone he loved from an uncertain future.

"Cameron, the last thing you need to worry about is TRC. I will make sure its technologies and people are well protected," vowed Admiral Turner. "Listen, if for whatever reason you can't get back to the present and you get stuck back there, look me up—you'll have special knowledge that could sure save lives and keep America from making stupid mistakes."

Cameron laughed nervously. "That might very well be the strangest job offer I've ever had."

"I mean it—every word. Take care."

"Thank you, sir. I guess no matter what, I'll see you later. Goodbye." Cameron punched the phone icon on the Polycom unit and terminated the call. He leaned over in his chair and held his head in his hands; he knew he needed to get going, and the stress of what lay ahead of him pounded in his mind.

A knock on the door startled Cameron, and in walked Alicia and Sandy with a small pile of equipment. "OK, Cameron, the machine is powered up, and Sandy and I have a number of things to give you."

"OK" Cameron replied, resigned.

Sandy jumped in and started pointing out what each item was. "Cameron, here's a USB flash drive that contains all of the history of the world, at least as recorded by historians from 1966 to the present. There are also files of contact names at the American Embassy in Tel Aviv. These people can talk to you and get you to the Israeli Defense Ministry. Remember, if the Russians find out that we know how this ends, it could ignite a world war. America won't want to be involved explicitly because of Vietnam."

"The drive also contains the battle plans for both the Israeli and the Egyptian armies," added Alicia. "All of this equipment will obviously have no peer in that time period. The largest computers back then are all using vacuum tubes, and integrated circuits are still a few years away. We're sending you back with two laptops, two flash drives, and five rechargeable batteries, as well as two power supplies and a number of AC/DC converters. My guess is this might make the technology last as long as ten years."

Sandy glared at Alicia for saying it that way—assuming that Cameron would not make it back. She put her hands on her hips and stared at the floor for a moment, trying to collect her thoughts. When her head did come up, her lips were trembling and her beautiful eyes were glossy from tears. She tried to speak, but her voice cracked. "Why you? There are other people...in the military, in the intelligence community...others...that can make this trip."

Cameron pulled her close, not sure of what to say for a moment. "I'm not sure we could trust the military to do the right thing here."

"I'm sorry, Cameron." Alicia hugged him. "I don't want you to go."

Cameron lingered in the embrace. He stroked her blond hair and kissed her on the forehead. "I'm so sorry, Alicia, but I have to—it's my responsibility. TRC will need you—both of you."

Cameron looked at Sandy with tears in his eyes. "Please don't let the dream of TRC end."

The embrace of the three colleagues was interrupted by an engineer who barged into the conference room and stated that the equation calculation to bring the 2348 BC expedition home was almost complete. It was time to send Cameron to 1967.

As Sandy walked away, Cameron was stopped in his tracks by Alicia's warm hand as she reached out to grasp his.

"Cameron, I have to tell you something," she said quietly, gazing up at him.

He turned and looked into her eyes, communicating the same message back to her.

"I know…me too," said Cameron, embracing her.

On the far wall of the room, the digital clock in the conference room continued its relentless march forward. Only ten minutes remained before transfer.

Cameron and Alicia walked down the hallway to enter the operations center and were met with a line of engineers, mathematicians, and computer scientists, most of whom had been recruited personally by Cameron. Tears welled in his eyes as he hugged and shook hands with them rapidly on the way to the Platform entrance. After five minutes of farewells and appreciative words, it was time to go. Cameron gave Alicia a kiss on the cheek and closed the steel door behind him. He quickly ascended the ladder to the Platform and stood in the center of the grid of stainless steel and opaque blue glass pads. After unzipping his backpack and rechecking the inventory of equipment, he gave the operations room a thumbs up. Alicia nodded sadly.

"Power up the system bus," Alicia said to an operator, her voice trembling.

A hum filled the room and slowly built to a deafening roar. The tornado of light appeared above Cameron, swirling and pulsing as if possessing its own intelligence. Cameron closed his eyes as the drone reached a fever pitch. Alicia watched the red digital clock count down:

3, 2, 1…

The swirl of energy engulfed Cameron, concealing him from view, and then a burst of light erupted from the center of the Platform and Cameron was gone.

"Reset the system for the expedition," said Alicia, wiping tears from her face and concentrating on the task at hand with a determined expression. There was a lot of work to be done in the next few minutes to ensure the successful return of Neil Stevens and company.

41

Pursuit

hris, Troy, and Pam ran down the street looking for the main city gate. Troy had gotten turned around in the tight city streets and was now using dead reckoning to find his way out. As they turned the corner, they ran into an entire platoon of soldiers marching in a line. As they slowed their pace and tried to look inconspicuous among the other citizens in the street, a horn sounded, disturbing the calm morning air. Someone had discovered their escape!

The giant captain leading the band of soldiers screamed out and pointed his huge spear at the escapees. Pam, Chris, and Troy couldn't make out the language, but the intent was clear. The small team reversed course and ran away from the squad, which was now in hot pursuit.

Troy pressed the intercom button and tried to control his voice as he gasped for breath while running at an all-out sprint.

"Neil, we're being chased back toward the prison by a **krzzz**…"

"Troy, this is Neil. I didn't copy your transmission. Say again!"

Troy repeated the message, but the reply from Neil was the same. No copy.

"My headset is down!" Troy shouted.

Rich looked through the scope and saw the flurry of activity as guards ran along the top of the city wall. He depressed his intercom. "Fernanda, can you fly AARON back over the top of the wall and create a diversion?"

"I'll see what I can do," said Fernanda, gripping the small joystick and watching the instrumentation and camera for clues as to how far the wall was from the hovering craft.

Pam's lungs burned as she tore through the small city streets, avoiding pedestrians, beggars, and merchants. The giant soldiers pursuing them did not take any such care and trampled anyone in their way.

Fernanda directed the UAV to fly over the wall and panned the camera along the busy street. She saw Pam, Chris, and Troy running up the street toward the helicopter, and the squad of soldiers following close behind them.

Chris saw the small chopper glinting in the late-morning sunlight and yelled out. "AARON! Come on you guys, it looks like Neil is trying a diversion!"

A small dust devil formed beneath the helicopter, and as the three team members ran underneath AARON, the swirling dust helped to conceal their exit from the soldiers as they continued up the street.

The soldiers were taken aback by the strange carbon-fiber-and-aluminum bird with a single spinning wing. Their jaws dropped open, and they took a defensive posture against the robotic helicopter. Fernanda smiled as she positioned the helicopter closer and closer to the street. The sonar tucked between the aluminum skids pinged on the laptop speakers, informing Fernanda that the road was only six feet below the craft.

Pam, Chris, and Troy found their way to a giant stone gallery that led them to the court containing the obelisk they had seen the previous day. Soldiers atop the walls examined everyone passing through the massive iron gate beneath them. Pam and Chris tucked their pistols under their clothing and tried to walk in a casual manner. Troy looked up at the wall and saw a guard peer over the edge. Even as Troy looked away, a look of recognition appeared on the soldier's face, and he shouted to another soldier in a nearby armored tower. A horn blast sounded, and soldiers from around the wall began running to the gate.

"Will this never end?" Pam said, out of breath.

"Watch out!" screamed Troy, taking Pam by the hand and yanking her out of the way. A spear slammed into the wooden post where Pam had been leaning only moments before.

The horn blast brought resolve to the squad of soldiers being held at bay by AARON. The leader pushed forward and extended his spear toward the translucent spinning rotor disc. Impact! The metal tip of the spear sparked, and the helicopter began to buckle and undulate as the effects of an imbalanced rotor shuddered through the inner mechanics of the engine.

"Um, this is Fernanda. I think we're going to lose AARON here in just a second," Fernanda radioed to Rich.

Rich squinted through the scope, watching the confrontation. "So be it. Just don't waste the opportunity to take some of the soldiers with it."

Fernanda pressed a key on the laptop, and the vehicle responded by moving forward toward the squad in a heads-down attitude. Again, a soldier jumped forward and stabbed at the transparent wings of this strange mechanical bird. The imbalance of the damaged rotor blade was reaching a critical point, and red alarms and indicators were lighting up all over the laptop's display as Fernanda monitored AARON's flight.

Fernanda clicked on the tail rotor and shut it down. Immediately, the small helicopter, unable to compensate for the torque of the main rotor, began to spin on its axis, the tail boom spinning clockwise around the entire body and narrowly missing a soldier's head. The tail boom continued revolving, and Fernanda gave the command for AARON to head into the wall behind the soldiers. The armed men scattered as the craft lunged. AARON exploded as it crashed into the stone wall. Shrapnel of aluminum, fiberglass, and carbon fiber shot everywhere, hitting walls, stone floors, and human flesh. A small, dark cloud of smoke curled upward over the wall, and Rich Loren looked through his scope to view the damage.

"Good job, Fernanda. I'd say you pretty much disoriented that group of soldiers."

"Hey, it's not every day you can destroy a million-dollar piece of equipment and get accolades for it," responded Fernanda while running down the back ridge to meet her friends, who were making their way out of the city.

Troy, Chris, and Pam were running flat-out, dodging the spears that thumped into the soil all around them. Chris turned back to see soldiers rappelling off the walls and towers in an effort to pursue the three escapees on the ground.

"This way," said Troy, running down a narrow street parallel to the fortified wall. The small road had narrow intersecting alleys that branched off of the main passage.

Which one to take? thought Troy, his mind racing.

From the shadows of an alleyway the fleeing group heard a raspy voice. "Nin-urta. Nin-urta."

Pam peered through the shadows to see a small, spindly form in a red cloak. Small hands appeared and pulled back the hood to reveal the small leper girl.

"It's the girl from the colony," she gasped.

"She must have been following us all the while," said Chris.

Troy pointed to the wall, attempting to communicate with the small girl. "How do we get outside the city?" he asked. Pam tried to translate as best as she could.

The little girl ran down a small alley and motioned for the group to follow along. Chris heard the shouts of soldiers behind him. "I don't think we have a choice. Let's follow her," he said.

The team ran down the alley, following their small guide. Her bare feet splashed through the dirty water as she ran, her red cloak flowing behind her. They turned a corner, and the alley seemed to dead-end in a thick, ancient wall segment.

"A dead end! We're cooked!" shouted Chris, pulling his pistol out and pressing himself against the stone wall.

The girl pointed to a series of old hand-hewn boards that were covering an opening. "Nin-urta makim kalag-ga."

Pam quickly grasped a few of the words their young rescuer was speaking. "It's a tunnel!"

Troy looked down the alley. A small stream of sewage was running through the boarded-up section, and he could hear the sounds of a small waterfall inside the drainage system beyond them.

"It's a sewer. It will lead us out of the city. Come on!" he said, straining to rip the boards from the small tunnel. The remainder of the boards came free easily, and the team faced a small forty-five-degree tunnel that headed down away from them. The smell of raw sewage met their nostrils.

"We have no choice," said Chris. "I'll go first, then Pam; and Troy, you help the girl down."

Chris climbed into the opening and slid down the slimy waterslide that emptied twenty feet down into a pool of sludge that was knee-deep. Pam disappeared into the opening, and Chris helped her with the landing. Troy turned to the girl. "OK, sweetheart, you're next." Shouts from the pursuing soldiers echoed down the alleyway. The girl hugged Troy and ran away from him, toward the shouting.

"Wait! Come back!" screamed Troy.

"Troy, we can't wait—come on!" Chris shouted.

Troy watched the leper girl run away from him, her small feet splashing and pattering on the few dry cobbles, her red cloak a swirl of motion. The soldiers turned the corner to see a blur as Troy dropped into the slimy sewer inlet.

Pam looked around as Troy splashed into the filthy water. "Where's the girl?"

"She ran off," said Troy, coughing at the stench rising into his nose and throat.

Noises above the team announced that the soldiers had found their escape route. Chris stuck the nose of his gun up through the sewer pipe and pressed the trigger. A rain of bullets headed upward through the ancient passage, pulverizing rock and mortar. There was a yelp at the top and then silence, as if the soldiers were trying to figure out what to do next.

"Let's go," said Chris, slinging his weapon over his shoulder and heading away from the drain. The small group made their way through the sludge and waste of the city. Rats and cockroaches ran across their paths and swam across the top of the greenish-yellow film covering the top of the water. The dark passageway narrowed and turned left.

"We have to be outside the wall by now. Look for an opening," said Troy.

Just then a chunk of stone broke off the ceiling, and a long wooden shaft with an iron spearhead fell across the water.

"Troy, you and Pam run ahead. I'll hold them off as long as I can!" shouted Chris.

Troy and Pam scurried past, and Chris leaned up against the side of the tunnel and fired shots through the darkness. He heard a scream and a splash.

Troy and Pam ran down the passageway. It was narrowing fast. Ahead, a burst of sunlight reflected from the sewage and lit up the inside of the sewer.

"There it is!" cried Pam.

Behind them, they heard more gunshots as Chris ran toward them.

Troy and Pam made it to the gate first. Iron bars barricaded their exit in a thick wooden frame fitted into the wall. Troy rattled the bars with his hands. They were solid, unyielding.

"We're trapped!" yelled Pam over her shoulder as Chris headed their way.

"Get down!" screamed Chris as he took aim at the bars and their wooden support structure. Pam and Troy ducked to the side and covered their faces as the hail of bullets chiseled the wall and splintered the wood frame in a thousand pieces.

As Chris approached Troy, he tossed the submachine gun to him.

"Keep firing until you're out of ammunition!" he yelled as he passed Troy and continued to the shattered remains of the wooden support. Chris put his shoulder down and ran headlong into the gated exit. The bars held at first, then exploded outward as the splintered wood and weakened metal gave way under Chris's muscular assault.

Troy fired into the dark. He could see soldiers gathering in the darkness. Their eyes glinted in the gunfire.

Pam and Chris pulled the remaining barrier from its hinges and dropped it into the water below them, revealing a sewer pipe that headed upward into the bright sunlight. A spear flew through the darkness, clipping Chris's shoulder and ricocheting off the stone blocks. Troy saw the soldier and put his sight on him. He pressed the trigger and watched the soldier's body fall into the water. His fellow soldiers shrank back, deeper in the sewer, away from the invisible weapon that had killed their comrade.

Troy pulled the trigger once more to keep them at bay.

Nothing. He tried again.

"Let's go! The gun is out of ammo!" screamed Troy.

Pam had made it up through the sewer and was helping Chris out. Troy jumped up through the outlet and pulled himself up to the lip, struggling to get through the length of the pipe. An arm grabbed at Troy's leg, trying to pull him back. Chris pulled out his commando knife and stabbed down. Troy's body jerked upward and out of the pipe as the soldier released his grip.

The trio found themselves on the outside of the city between the fortified wall and the long spikes surrounding the city. "Let's go!" shouted Chris. They ran down the embankment of the sewer canal toward the canopy of trees a thousand yards away.

Pam's radio crackled to life. It was Jim Spruce.

"Lead the soldiers to the glade; we have a little surprise for them," he told her.

Pam located the tall tree canopy that formed the glade and spotted the ridge that the team had climbed just yesterday evening. She followed the glade with her eyes to the top of the hill where the team had pitched their camp. "Guys, follow me. I know where we're going!"

As the team members ran toward the jungle canopy, they entered a cemetery that contained the city's dead. Tombstones and rock markers of thousands and thousands of people who had inhabited Unug-Kulaba during the past millennium dotted the landscape. Everything from polished stones to miniature mausoleums to wooden markers created an obstacle course between the fleeing trio and the soldiers behind them. The ground gave way beneath their feet as the ancient graves caved in, slowing the fleeing team members' progress. Pam looked over her shoulder; the pursuing soldiers were struggling, too. Their thick legs and sandaled feet punched through the dirt, breaking into the crypts of the long-dead.

Pam burst through the low foliage surrounding the glade and saw Jim waving his hands as he stood atop the ridge. As she ran toward him, she saw the mini-guns in place on the raised platforms. Chris and Troy followed right after her, and they all met up with Jim. Seeing that the entire team was out of the way of the guns, Jim pushed a button on a remote control, armed the sensor net, and dove beneath a fallen log. He held his breath.

As the soldiers followed the team into the glade, the sensors mounted on the tree trunks around them picked up the disturbances in the air and triangulated them in a microsecond. The computer sent the gun platforms the angle coordinates to which they needed to pivot, and within moments a short burst of gunfire from the Gatling guns filled the air.

The guns pivoted on their motorized mounts, aligning their lethal barrels to the concentrated blobs of the soldiers in their memory, and with the cold precision of a computer sent a hail of lead into the flesh of the confused pursuers. The flying bullets cut the soldiers down like so much grass. The soldiers that were bringing up the rear tried to move around the edge of the glade, unaware that any movement was enough to give the guns their location and rain bullets on their position. There was no way to escape.

After a minute of bursting gunfire, Pam raised her head from her covered position to see a mass of dead soldiers piled up in the glade and smoke curling from the muzzles of the multi-barreled Gatling guns.

42

The Road from Jerusalem to Tel Aviv

ameron blinked as his eyes adjusted to the moonlight overhead and the spotlights outside of Jerusalem. He reached out to get his bearings. The transfer had put him in a momentary state of disorientation. Pulling his backpack snug against his shoulders, he tightened the nylon straps. Up ahead he spied a road crossing in front of the old part of the city. For a brief moment he gazed at the golden Dome of the Rock glistening in the moonlight.

He had to get to Tel Aviv, and fast, but first he needed to make his way out of this part of Jerusalem. He ran down an unpaved road that passed by several ancient olive trees and soon approached a road that headed north and out of the old city.

It wasn't long before a beat-up taxicab made an appearance. Cameron hoped he was finding the driver in the middle of his shift and not on his way home after a long day. He flagged him down and held out a wad of money. The cab screeched to a halt. "I have U.S. dollars—I need to get to Tel Aviv." The scruffy-looking driver took one look at the wad of dollars in Cameron's hand and quickly waved for him to get in the cab. Apparently the cab driver was anxious for a currency that might still have value the next week. With all the uncertainty of a war in the next few days, the dollar held a lot of attraction.

Cameron stepped into the yellow-and-white cab and kicked some trash from his side of the seat and floor to the other side. The interior smelled of strong cigarette and cigar smoke, bad body odor, and another odor that Cameron couldn't place at the moment and wasn't sure he wanted to. The ashtray on the back of the front seat was nearly overflowing with cigarette butts. The floor was covered in empty soda cans and crinkled food wrappers.

As the driver wound through the narrow streets of Jerusalem, Cameron could see that the citizens were bracing for the worst. Sandbags were piled everywhere, windows were being boarded up, and the normally jammed thoroughfares were vacant. The economy was stalling as merchants contemplated their own mortality. Teams of high-school boys dug trenches in the glare of floodlights illuminating the darkness.

Cameron got comfortable in the vinyl seat and lifted the lid of his laptop while turning the intensity of the screen to low. The cab driver cocked his head to look over the seat, obviously very curious about the mysterious blue glow emanating from Cameron's backpack. A folder sitting on the laptop's desktop background was labeled "Cameron–1967." He moved his mouse to it and double-clicked. A window popped up and displayed an organized list of reading materials for him by date. As he read through the items that Alicia and Sandy had prepared for him, he closed his eyes to suppress the feelings of isolation. In this time period, most of his friends and colleagues had not even been born yet, or were just small children.

The dilemma plaguing Cameron's mind was whether or not to contact the U.S. embassy and the CIA operatives stationed in Tel Aviv. He knew they would have access to the Israeli generals and the Jewish intelligence network, perhaps more completely than anyone else, but could he trust them? The laptop he held had details of the next forty years of world history—the Vietnam War, world elections and coups, the Arab Oil Embargo of 1973, the invasion of Afghanistan by the Soviet Union, and, perhaps most valuable, the demise of the Soviet empire into a bankrupt pile of ideological rubble. The information he carried in his head and in the computer on his lap was the most valuable asset on the planet. If he were to make contact with a young, overly ambitious intelligence officer, it could change everything—maybe in the wrong directions.

Abruptly, he decided that he would not involve the Americans—he'd go it alone. The value of the information could be used to bargain his way home to America or into the meeting room with the generals on the eve of war breaking out. He wondered what was more dangerous: bargaining with the Israelis during a war for their survival or working with the CIA covertly.

As he continued to read about the major players in the Six-Day War and the tactics used by both sides, Cameron noticed a spreadsheet named "make TRC happen.xls" tucked in between the historical text files. He double-clicked to bring it up. The spreadsheet was thousands of rows tall, with columns containing dates, stock symbols, and market-close values—the U.S. stock market from 1970 to 2009. As Cameron scrolled through the seemingly endless sea of numbers, he realized that Alicia and Sandy had almost guaranteed TRC's existence by providing this file to him. He closed the lid of the laptop, sending the electronics into a deep hibernation, and zippered his backpack.

"Driver, please take me to the Israeli Ministry of Defense." The driver studied Cameron in his rearview mirror with a clearly worried look on his face, but he nodded in understanding.

"American?" asked the driver with a thick Israeli accent.

Cameron smiled and nodded. "Does it show?"

"Yes, you look like a rich American," replied the taxi driver.

Cameron slouched a bit in the vinyl seat.

Not exactly tactful is he? Let's change the subject.

"What do you think about the prime minister?" asked Cameron.

The cab's speed seemed to increase, and Cameron gripped the slippery vinyl.

"Eshkol? He's a coward!" The cabbie waved his arms around. The taxi swerved through the streets, barely missing pedestrians and stacked-up sandbags.

Maybe this guy's really Italian, Cameron thought. *Watch where you're going, will you?*

"Give me a general to run this country. All this waiting, all this diplomacy. It gets us nowhere. Nowhere!" The cab rattled as they drove through a pothole.

A car passing from the opposite direction honked its horn, and the driver cursed as he drove by. The taxi driver doubled the curse back and gestured out the window, but he didn't lose his train of thought. "The man will get us all killed. He acts as though he's never had to fight for anything. Always concessions with him…anything but a fight."

I'll be killed if I stay in this cab much longer, thought Cameron.

Finally the pothole-covered cobbles became smooth asphalt, and the conversation and the ride more comfortable. After a while the driver fell silent.

Cameron gazed out the window at the Israeli countryside lit up by the full moon and began to wonder what this world looked like to the expedition only five hundred miles to the east, but four thousand years in the past. His lack of sleep and the rhythmic rocking of the car lulled Cameron into a well-deserved nap.

43

Cameron and Dayan

june 4, 1967

Tel Aviv, Israel

C ameron was jolted out of his slumber by a wicked pothole. He rubbed his eyes and looked through the smeared, dirty window of the taxicab. It was still dark, but the eastern sky was beginning to have a yellow tint as the sun rose. The driver pulled up to a robust cement building, standing five stories tall with narrow windows.

About a thousand people stood around the front entrance, shouting and screaming. Some held signs that read "Give us Dayan" and "Eshkol, defend Israel." Some of the protesters simply waved Israeli flags in support of the fledgling nation.

"Ministry of Defense," announced the driver in his thick accent as he pulled the cab over near the building.

Cameron gave the cabbie his fare, including a generous tip, and asked him for a few Israeli coins in exchange for an American dollar. A local bus station with a long covered plaza containing coin-operated lockers was next door, and Cameron decided to use a safeguard.

Cameron found an empty locker on the lowest level and placed his backpack into its grimy interior. He dropped an Israeli coin into the slot and pulled the locker key out, hearing the lock mechanism click into place. A stone wall stretched across the front of the bus depot, and several concrete benches were placed in regular intervals along the sidewalk leading toward the government buildings. Cameron sat down on a bench and pretended to tie his shoes while placing the locker key under a large, flat rock in the mulch beneath the bench. He felt ridiculous performing this action—like he was in a really bad spy movie—but he knew he would likely be searched, and the markings and number etched into the key's metal bow would not require Sherlock Holmes to figure out where the key had come from.

Cameron stood up, noting the bench's position and the distinct flat rock that hid the means of access to all of his earthly belongings. Taking a deep breath, he walked back over to the Ministry of Defense building. He wound his way through the crowd, passing people who were frightened yet at the same time angry at the Israeli officials. The crowd was growing more restless by the minute. A woman behind Cameron shouted, "Give us Dayan! Give us a leader! Give our children a future!"

It was obvious to Cameron and virtually everyone in Israel that Levi Eshkol's cool head and diplomatic approach were losing to the charisma of the famous general who had defeated the Egyptians once before and could very likely repeat his success.

Cameron stood out in the crowd. His black T-shirt and Levis looked out of place—too refined and too clean. Finally he made it to the front of the throng, where he found three Israeli army men holding the crowd at bay with automatic weapons and nasty dispositions. Just as Cameron reached the front of the pack, a large steel door opened and a highly decorated officer stepped out with two more soldiers flanking him. Cameron saw an opportunity and pushed to the very front of the line. After a moment of jostling and thrown elbows, he found himself face to face with the officer and the two nasty Israeli soldiers, who were not in the mood for any unruly behavior.

Cameron took the small square of paper he had scribbled on at the bus depot and said a single word, "American," while reaching out and handing it to the heavily guarded officer. The military official took the scrap of paper and unfolded it to read two short words: "Red Sheet."

The officer's lit cigarette tilted forward from his tightly pursed lips, hanging precariously for a moment before falling to the cement floor. He motioned to the soldier directly in front of Cameron and uttered some unintelligible order. Cameron glanced away from the high-ranking officer just as the blur of a rifle butt came down on his head, and then everything went dark.

The two soldiers guarding the officer picked up the unconscious body of the strange American, placing his arms across their shoulders. As they dragged the unconscious scientist across the hard cement floor of the Ministry building, the officer placed his shiny black boot on the still-smoldering cigarette and extinguished it with a quick motion of his ankle. He turned and followed this very interesting American into the building, leaving the screaming Israeli people behind.

⸻ ⸻ ⸻

The sound of a wax-coated paper container being popped was followed by the repulsive odor of smelling salts, and Cameron awakened to find himself in a dark room with a single overly bright light above him. The lamp's intensity nearly blinded him, blocking out all details of the room. He wanted to touch his head where the soldier had sent him into unconsciousness with the butt of his gun, but he found himself restrained, seated in a wooden chair with his arms bound behind him. Cameron squinted and was able to distinguish a small wooden desk and a very bored-looking Israeli soldier guarding the only way out of the room.

The man who had opened the smelling-salt packet came around to Cameron's left side and sat on the opposite side of the desk, examining him with a quizzical look.

"Who are you?" asked the Israeli, pulling a pack of cigarettes from his shirt pocket.

"Cameron Locke. I'm an American," replied Cameron, shaking his head as he tried to become fully alert.

The response caused the inquisitor to hesitate, squinting at Cameron as he struck a match, lit his cigarette, and took a long drag.

"An American?" echoed the intelligence officer sarcastically, exhaling a stream of smoke that began to swirl through the bluish-white light. "Are you with the CIA, the NSA, who?"

"I'm with no agency, per se. I have important information for Prime Minister Eshkol and General Dayan that is time-sensitive and crucial to your future survival as a nation," said Cameron. He wasn't sure if that response would get him hit on the head again or help to move the conversation in a more constructive direction.

Skepticism riddled the officer's face. "I see." The officer looked intently into Cameron's eyes and evaluated him for deception. "Why would an American citizen, who is *not* connected with the U.S. Intelligence Community, be willing to help us, when the nation itself won't lift a finger to come to our aid?"

"I agree this is odd—and you're right," Cameron said. "America will not come to your rescue; you are alone here. If my country becomes involved, it will draw the Soviets into the conflict, and very soon we will all be looking at another world war. How you respond to this challenge in the next twenty-four hours will define everything about your country for the next forty years."

The Israeli intelligence officer coughed and laughed. "Are you a prophet?"

"No, sir, but if you don't attack the Egyptian airfields preemptively tomorrow morning at 7:55 A.M., then the information I have for your generals, which could save your country, might not have as much value. Time means everything."

"How do you come to know this…this…information?" asked the intelligence officer. He placed his head in his hand as he studied this strange man with interest. This was not just about interrogation. The prisoner was passionate in his belief that Israel should attack an enemy that wanted to destroy it, yet he was speaking in an almost past-tense manner about a timeline the generals had yet to arrive at in the room next door.

Cameron smiled; he could see he was breaking through. "I know a whole lot more. Let me work with you. Let me speak with Prime Minister Eshkol or General Dayan."

The officer left the room for a few minutes and returned with a tall, balding man who wore a black patch over his left eye. Medals and awards due a general adorned his uniform. The man had an intimidating presence, but Cameron, recognizing him from the photos on the laptop, breathed a sigh of relief and smiled. "General," he said, nodding as respectfully as he could while being bound to a chair.

Moshe Dayan, the legendary maverick Israeli general, stood quietly before him. Charisma and confidence seemed to flow from Dayan like electricity. The intelligence officer who had questioned Cameron earlier nervously struck a match, lit another cigarette, and again polluted the room.

Dayan stared at Cameron intently through the cigarette smoke curling in gray tendrils through the stale air of the interrogation room. "Are you an agent?" he asked.

"No, sir," said Cameron. "My nation cannot be seen to be helping you directly. The Soviets and the United States are standing back waiting for this conflict to begin, one way or another."

"Your government does not know you are here?" Dayan asked. The surprise in his voice was obvious.

"No one on Earth knows I'm here."

"Why would you help us? What information do you have that we don't already know?"

"Well, that's kind of the problem. Everything I know is also known by another man like me, who, right now, is trying to convince the enemy…your enemies…to listen to him. If they do, then in simple terms, it's likely that the nation of Israel will cease to exist. General, Israel must act now. The problem is not the Straits of Tiran or the armored forces amassing in the Sinai. It is the existence of Israel. Nasser's challenge must be answered. This war cannot be fought on your soil. If it is, you will be shifting the advantage of the war to the enemy."

"Our estimates say we'll win no matter what," said Dayan dismissively, turning his back to Cameron.

"You mean, if you attack at 7:55 A.M. on June 5th with aircraft, destroy their airfields and air force, and then send a three-pronged armored attack against the Egyptian army in the Sinai Desert?"

The rapid revelation of the secret conflict that was to take place within the next few days seemed to crash over the general like a mighty wave, and he froze in mid-step. The general looked at Cameron with his mouth half open. "These plans are not even finalized yet—how can you know such things?"

"Remember, everything that I know, the enemy will know—sooner or later."

Dayan turned and sat on the edge of the wooden table. "There's a debate raging right now between the politicians and the military. The decision of whether to attack now, preemptively, or wait for diplomacy is tearing the nation apart. You seem to know much about our plans and, more importantly, the outcomes. Will diplomacy work?"

"No, it won't," Cameron replied. "You must attack, and you must strike before the enemy attacks you. If the enemy destroys your air force, you will not have a way to protect your armor—and that will be the end. Please let me help you, General. It's not just your future. It's mine too."

Dayan ran his hand across his face and brought his fingers down to a point on his chin as he evaluated his options and weighed his trust in this strange but well-informed American.

"What more can you offer us?" he asked.

Cameron shifted uneasily; his arms ached. *What else can I offer this guy? It has to be something valuable—something that helps everyone.*

Suddenly, he had it.

"Okay. Here's a big one for you," said Cameron. "In three days, toward the end of the conflict, the Israeli Air Force will accidentally attack an American signals intelligence ship in the Mediterranean. Thirty-eight sailors will die. You'll chalk it up to a military mistake, and the Americans will, of course, try to conceal the accident as much as possible. It will damage your relationship with the U.S. Intelligence Community for decades, not to mention the lives of the families that have to live with the cover-up. Let me help you, and you save that ship in return."

That was enough for Dayan. "Loose him," said the general to the intelligence officer.

"Just one thing, General," said Cameron.

Dayan raised his eyebrows suspiciously.

"No one can know I was here, or what I told you and your commanders—ever."

Dayan stepped back a moment and crossed his arms across his chest. The selfless statement was not what he was used to dealing with. Requests for money, more power, and influence—that was how this game was played. His stock in Locke jumped a notch.

He nodded and led Cameron to the heavily fortified war room.

Cameron hoped that at this moment, Salah was having as difficult a time as he had just had in trying to get the Egyptian command structure's attention.

44

Rupture

T he sun was eclipsed for a moment as a massive asteroid passed in front of it before igniting into a fiery ball. The icy visitor had been captured by Earth's gravity, and its demise was now certain. The asteroid had originated in the outer reaches of space, but it wasn't perturbed from its lazy orbit by anything material or calculable. Rather, an omnipotent, invisible force had literally grabbed it from space and flung it toward the earth. A massive mega-continent lay before it as it blazed toward its target.

Jim Spruce looked skyward as a meteor the size of Mount Rushmore came into view on the horizon and curved through the atmosphere, trailing a massive plume of orange-and-black smoke. Fragments breaking off from the main body of the asteroid created showers of streaking meteoroids that burned themselves out in the thick layer of atmosphere. The silence of the moment was shattered by a massive sonic boom that crackled across the landscape. The team watched the plume of fire and smoke curve across the hazy blue canopy of sky to their south.

Ten miles below the earth's crust, a four-thousand-foot-deep subterranean ocean waited, encased in a shell of granite above a layer of basaltic rock that made up its floor—the great fountains of the deep. The tremendous pressure of the earth's crust was supported by massive limestone pillars that had shouldered the weight since the planet was created two thousand years before. Each day, Earth's rotation and the gravitational pull of the moon caused the subterranean chambers of water to oscillate and chisel these pillars thinner and thinner.

The massive pressure of the earth's crust floating ten miles above this hidden ocean served to seal the water beneath it, prohibiting its escape to the surface. The superheated underground ocean water had pushed on its rocky prison rhythmically twice a day since the beginning of time. The thick brine, containing vast amounts of dissolved limestone, salt, and quartz, continued to increase in pressure, aching to be released from the stone titan keeping it captive.

The asteroid arced over what would become the continent of Africa and slammed into the ground above the land that would one day be called Madagascar, instantly vaporizing the rock and water beneath it on impact and transferring its energy into the earth's crust. An invisible blanket of iridium, part of the asteroid's makeup, evaporated and ejected itself upward into the atmosphere. The force of the comet's impact ripped a small hole in the thick granite shell, the ceiling of an enormous cavern of the underground ocean. The granite seal atop the subterranean chambers groaned as the massive pressure pushing from below and the decreasing pressure from above reached the critical point. A small crack appeared on the floor of the seabed and shot north and south at a rate of three hundred miles an hour.

The team members watched the sky turn a deep shade of indigo, and an ominous silence settled over the landscape.

The silence was interrupted by the birds all around them launching into the air.

Suddenly an intense burst of light flashed on the horizon, and a curtain of black literally moved the horizon line up, continuing upward at an incredible pace and blotting out the blue of the sky. A massive shock wave expanded outward from the black curtain, and the clouds literally dissolved to get out of its way.

Troy didn't have much time to put it all together, but his mind worked fast enough to form one thought. *It has started.*

The shock wave hit Rich Loren's position first, blasting him out of the high hide and knocking him to the ground. The equipment that had been organized in a neat pile on top of the ridge shattered into hundreds of pieces; the delicate electronics stripped from their circuit boards and scattered across the grassy hilltop.

A fraction of a second later, the shock wave reached Troy and the team, picking them up and hurling them into the glade as if they weighed nothing. The shock wave continued over the landscape, flattening trees and launching small animals into the air.

The giant stone blocks in the city's walls buckled and vibrated as the wave blasted against the man-made barrier. A continuous cracking sound accompanied the wave of pressure as trees broke in half like matchsticks in the wake of its incredibly powerful assault.

The tear in the earth caused by the asteroid's impact increased in length, running for about a thousand miles along the future African border. The tear continued northward at the same time, passing between Greenland and Iceland on its way to the top of the planet. As the depth of the tear grew, the crust split further. The tear ripped open the underground chamber, where the trapped water was exerting millions of pounds of force per square inch on the granite covering, ready to burst forth and finally be released.

The underground ocean, now freed from its rocky prison, blasted upward out of the newly formed trench. The massive and sudden acceleration of the water molecules caused huge volumes of the subterranean liquid to flash-evaporate. The cooling effect of this action fueled the increasing expansion of the rift, and the vapor began to reach supersonic speeds on its way to the surface.

As the water spewed from each chamber and shot upward into the atmosphere, the limestone pillars that had separated neighboring chambers lost integrity and collapsed, allowing the water to pound over the limestone as it exited toward the surface.

The air filled with deafening sonic booms as the rock, salt, and water from the fountains of the deep burst into the sky and accelerated into the upper atmosphere. Some of the water failed to break free of the force of Earth's gravity and plummeted downward, impacting the landscape and smashing organic material in its wake. The water and rock that did break free of gravity continued traveling into the upper atmosphere, freezing and solidifying nearly instantaneously.

Troy landed on the ground flat on his stomach after having been pitched through the air. He was lying about forty feet from where he had been standing just moments before. The raging sound in Troy's ears had not lessened. He lifted his head out of the tall blades of grass that had nearly been flattened by the twenty-mile-an-hour winds howling across the hilltop.

Troy saw that the sky had turned a dark gray-brown. Millions of tons of earth and clay had been vaporized and carried upward by the water jets now coursing into the sky. The horizon was almost completely black, but it retained an eerie transparency that was refracting light.

Just then a rugged stone formation the size of a two-story house came crashing out of the sky and hit a city tower. The sound of the collision was deafening—bodies, stone, and mortar from the wall erupted into the air, as if a bomb had just gone off.

⌐⌐⌐ ⌐⌐⌐ ⌐⌐⌐

The echo of the crash brought Jim Spruce to his feet. He quickly checked himself for injuries, and finding only cuts and bruises, ran toward the place where he and his colleagues had been standing only moments before. The wind, like a jet turbine, began to increase. Bits of vegetation, dirt, and miniature pieces of bark flew in all directions, stinging Jim's eyes and skin. Along the way he found Pam, who was literally wrapped around a large tree. He ran up to her and cupped her face in his hands, rubbing mud and dirt from her skin. She moaned and opened her eyes.

"What happened?" she asked groggily.

"I don't know, but I'm pretty sure it's not good," said Jim with a rasp. The air was full of dirt. The sky behind Jim became a noticeable shade darker, and lightning forked across the sky.

Pam tried to move, but her arm would not cooperate. A stream of fiery pain stabbed up its length. "Oh, my arm," moaned Pam, holding her left elbow.

Jim helped her to sit upright under the tree and slowly lifted her sleeve to find two bones with jagged break points jutting out of her skin.

"Oh, boy! OK, well, you have a big-time fracture here." Jim grabbed a nearby branch that had been ripped from a tree by the shock wave and used some thin, strong vines to lash it to Pam's left arm, creating a makeshift splint.

"Sorry, Pam. It's the best I can do right now." Jim found himself shouting as the wind grew to a howl. He helped Pam to her feet. "We have to get to the top of the hill and find the others."

The meteor impact had knocked Chris head over heels into a shallow stream, an inlet of the larger creek where he and Pam had been ambushed the night before. He scrambled to his feet and ran full-out against the wind to find Jim, Pam, and Troy staring at the horizon. Boulder-sized rocks were falling from heaven, smashing into the landscape and the city of Unug-Kulaba.

"This is it! It's the Flood! It's started!" screamed Troy, pointing at the massive water jet sending vaporized water high into the air.

A mixture of glowing red volcanic lava and water vapor shot upward into the sky, mixing with one another. The rock partially solidified as the water vapor flashed to steam, creating instantaneous rocky columns a hundred feet high that stood for a few moments like a mirage of sandcastles before being eroded by the water and steam flashing around them. Heat from the steam and lava rolled across the landscape in an invisible wave. The already humid air was increasing in density as the spewing vapor entered the atmosphere. Jagged bolts of lightning began to strike across the sky in front of the iridescent curtain of water that continued blasting upward along the horizon.

"Where can we go?" shouted Pam over the wind and the explosions of lava.

"We have to stay on the highest point possible for as long as we can. Come on!" Troy led the group up the hillside, leaning into the howling wind and dodging loose branches that were flying like machetes through the air.

The tear in the earth's crust continued around the southern reach of Africa and headed toward the city of Unug-Kulaba. Every few miles the split traveled, subterranean caverns below released their massive payloads of water. The shock waves created when the underwater caverns gave way caused multiple tsunamis to form and beat the shoreline with forty-foot waves that crashed into the landscape and pulled lush plant life, dinosaurs and other animals, and people off the shoreline and into the ocean.

"We have to get up there *now!*" screamed Troy, pointing to the top of a knoll. The team scrambled up the side of the steep, slippery hill toward Fernanda, Rich, and Neil, who were waving at them from a hundred yards away.

As the three made their way up the hill, the air around them became heavy with moisture, as if a dense fog had just rolled in. The water vapor being propelled into the atmosphere from the fountains of the deep was reaching a critical mass and causing large water droplets to form. As the weight of the droplets increased and the force of gravity halted their acceleration, rain began to fall for the first time ever. Raindrops in super-dense formations fell from the sky in sheets and torrents. Some of the water droplets had been propelled so high into the upper atmosphere that they had frozen and formed golf-ball-sized pellets of salty, dirty ice.

The city nearby was a scene of horror and chaos. The comet-like rocks cartwheeling out of the sky had turned the streets into a war zone. Each time a massive boulder hit a wall, tower, or other edifice, it released a shower of razor-sharp rock fragments into the air that sliced through human flesh and stonework alike as if they were nothing. At the same time, the water pouring from the fountains that had burst open around the planet began to make its way up and over the low hills of the Mesopotamian plain. Torrents of water and muddy sludge full of drowned animals and flotsam from the rain forest came rushing up against the city walls in ever-increasing depth. As the atmosphere's temperature rapidly alternated between warm and cold air masses, lightning strikes began to fork and crisscross against the darkening sky, and the wind speed picked up to hurricane-force levels.

Neil could see the Ark bucking from its scaffolding supports as the torrents of waves dashed against the wooden hull. The Ark slowly but surely began to slide down the slight grade of the valley floor that had served as its construction site and move toward the city where the people lived who had cursed and laughed at Noah and his sons for more than a hundred years. Wooden cranes, scaffolding, and empty animal pens were swept aside by the sheer mass of the Ark's weight as it slowly slid in the direction of the city walls. Small saplings that had sprung up where their botanical parents had once stood bent and snapped under the enormous weight of the giant wooden vessel.

As the team made it to the top of the knoll, they looked back through the mist at the Ark slowly heading toward the doomed city.

45

Air War!

june 5, 1967

ot water coursed over Cameron's weary body as he let the pulsating spray from the showerhead massage his tense neck and shoulders. He had been up all night with the Israeli generals, discussing plans for the upcoming attack and timetables for command decisions. His insights and suggestions to the top brass had at first been scoffed at and ridiculed, but then as more and more detail was given and further clarity arose within the group, attitudes emerged that Cameron had not expected—appreciation and respect.

Dayan had allowed Cameron to get a quick shower in his personal washroom before the attack, which was set to begin in a little over an hour. The exhaustion of being awake all night, undergoing scrutiny by incredibly bright men, and enduring the complex politics that hamstrung the men making decisions had taken its toll on Cameron. Slowly, he slid to the floor of the tiled shower, letting the steam and hot water lull him into a brief slumber.

*　*　*

The silver Dassault Mirage attack aircraft mirrored the sandy desert floor in its shiny aluminum skin as it left the black runway, retracted its landing gear, and ripped through the arid atmosphere of the Middle East. It was a brilliant sunny morning on June 5, 1967. The pilot, Elan Friedman, a thirty-year-old Israeli airman, pushed down on the yoke and kept the sleek fighter low, only one hundred feet above the Mediterranean. The blue-green water of the sea below reflected the Mirage's delta wing shape like a shadowy shark.

Elan was excited, nervous, and fixated on a single goal: the destruction of the Egyptian Air Force—a mission he had planned for and rehearsed with his fellow airmen for more than eight years. Elan had a wife and two small boys, but he swept thoughts of them from his mind. Instead, he chose to focus on the landscape that he and his small squadron were approaching at over six hundred miles an hour.

The concentration required to keep the aircraft low and evade radar detection stations along the Egyptian border taxed Elan to his breaking point. The shirt under his olive flight suit was drenched with sweat. Every fiber of his being was wound tight like a spring.

Almost every plane in the Israeli Air Force was being used for this pre-emptive attack. Only twelve planes remained for defense. This would be either a successful attack or a crushing defeat—there was no middle ground. He knew that if Israel failed—if he failed— everything he loved and cared about would be wiped off the face of the earth.

The five Mirage fighters in his squadron burst into view above the sprawling suburban area of Cairo and continued their course to the west side of the city. Elan could see citizens in the streets and on the rooftops enjoying breakfast and meeting in the marketplace, completely unaware that a conflict had begun.

Elan broke radio silence as the airport became visible in the distance. Short chatter between the pilots allowed the small fighter team to prioritize the targets and choose approaches. Even though the squadron members had planned and rehearsed this attack for years, the permutations that took place at the last minute had to be worked out during the final moments before the strike.

Three of the fighters pulled to the left and formed a small V-shaped wedge while lining up with the runways. Their job was to disable the concrete runways while the other two fighters took out the Egyptian MiG-17 and MiG-21 fighters sitting on the ramp awaiting their pilots.

Elan watched as the three fighters headed toward the middle of the main airport runway and dropped their five-hundred-pound bombs with great precision. The olive cylinders rolled end over end and ignited a massive fireball that hurled concrete, rebar, and shattered navigational lights all over the airport. The three fighters made a quick turn, and before the debris from the strike had finished falling from the sky, they bombed the shorter and less-used peripheral runway.

The aircraft sitting on the ramp were now trapped; there was no way for them to take off, and there would be no air support for the Egyptian armored forces that were arrayed in the Sinai Desert 120 miles to the east.

Now it was Elan and his wing mate's turn. They banked their aircraft to face the MiGs that were parked in perfect rows on the concrete ramp. Elan pulled back on the trigger and let a burst of thirty millimeter rounds from the Mirage's cannon blaze through the thin aluminum skin of the MiGs neatly arranged on the ramp. The rounds sliced through the planes and hit electrical and fuel systems on the Soviet-built fighters, which immediately ignited and exploded.

Behind the MiGs, a number of Tupolev Tu-95 "Bear" bombers were being refueled—no doubt awaiting the order to bomb Tel Aviv and other major Israeli cities. Each massive bomber was the size of a Boeing 707 jet, and the silver fuselage and four turboprop engines mounted on each plane's wings glistened in the clear, bright morning sunshine.

Elan made a tight, high-G turn and felt the pressure suit squeeze his thighs and keep him from passing out. His heart was pounding like a hammer. As he came out of the turn, he lined up the parked enemy bombers in his bomb sight and waited for the perfect moment.

Now! He released the bombs and headed to a spot directly between two of the bombers that were being refueled. A massive shock wave preceded an orange-red fireball that ignited and destroyed the two bombers sitting helplessly on the tarmac.

Elan banked the fighter and looked over his left shoulder to survey the damage. All of the aircraft had been destroyed; the runways were disabled—there was nothing left to bomb. The five silver jets regrouped north of the airfield and headed back toward Israel. A pillar of black, oily smoke filled the sky behind them, joining scores of other smoke clouds that were appearing all over Egypt.

The plan had worked! Elan looked at his watch; it was 7:55 A.M. Elan undid the latches on his oxygen mask and pulled it away from his face, then pulled at a braided gold chain around his neck. A small Star of David emerged from the neck of his flight suit and glinted in the sun. He kissed the precious metal and looked at the picture of his wife and son wedged between the instruments before him. He looked out the window at the landscape sliding below him and said a prayer—a prayer he hadn't uttered since he was a teenager. This was no longer a secular war.

Short radio broadcasts from the pilots were coming into the military command room in Tel Aviv. The cigarette smoke in the room was thick; it seemed as though everyone in the room was smoking a cigarette, and the hazy air burned Cameron's eyes. He could tell that the weight of the state of Israel was gradually being lifted from General Moshe Dayan's shoulders as the status reports came in. In the space of just three hours, the entire Egyptian air force had been destroyed. The air war had been wildly successful—more than 280 bombers and jet fighters were history.

The war would now shift to the Israeli and Egyptian tanks that were cooking in the Sinai Desert.

46

Solving the Equation

(A) licia and the rest of the engineers chewed on any fingernails that still remained and engaged in other nervous habits as they watched the plasma screen in front of them. Only five minutes remained before the team would be transferred back to this time period. Two terms were left to solve in the overall equation—terms that governed the balance of the swirling energy field and the depth of the destination point. These had been some of Cameron's greatest breakthroughs—to discover how to derive the destination depth of an object and how to sweep it through the vortex intact.

Three hundred miles away, the massive supercomputer at NASA Ames completed its final differential equations for the balance term and dumped the floating point number to a Web service that returned the result a second later to the waiting systems at TRC.

"Only one more left!" Sandy exclaimed, watching the screen nervously.

"What's the time count?" asked Alicia.

"Two minutes," came the answer in unison from a number of mathematicians double-checking the results that had been coming in all morning from around the country.

The landline on Alicia's desk rang. Alicia nervously picked up the receiver and held it to her ear.

"Alicia King."

"This is Alex Phong at the Red Storm Complex at Sandia Labs. The computer cluster that was working on the depth term has just overheated, and we have to restart the calculation…"

Alicia dropped the receiver and ran up to the front of the room.

A confused voice could be heard emanating from the abandoned receiver as it bobbed up and down like a miniature bungee jumper from the side of Alicia's desk: "Hello? Hello?"

Alicia ran to the row of engineers who were working on the last term—the variable for elevation. The lead engineer scratched his head, confused about what to do next as he stared at the equations on the screen and the matrix of choices the others near him were giving.

"Move!" Alicia said to the lead. The overweight programmer shifted to a nearby chair and hunched like a whipped dog.

Alicia apologized without looking at the young man as she typed a hundred miles an hour. "Sorry, Charles; we don't have much margin for error on this. We don't have any satellite information about this terrain, so this will be a huge guess."

"Can't we just run the job again on Red Storm?" asked another programmer.

Alicia glanced at the clock. "There's no time for that. We have to plug this in and go."

Alicia's fingertips raced over the keyboard as she entered equations she knew by heart into the differential equation editor of Mathematica. No matter what she simulated, she could see that the term would include an area of between ten and fifteen feet below the team. She tried to imagine what kind of load that would put on the energy systems and the Platform itself during a transfer; she had no educated guesses. Alicia asked the team of mathematicians for a quick vote. Fifteen was the answer—they would err toward the opportunity of the largest amount of space to be returned.

47

Red Sheet!

Cameron stood against the back wall of the war room and watched intently as the generals studied the map of the Middle East and positioned small colored blocks that represented battalions and divisions of Israeli forces. With the aircraft of the Syrian and Jordanian air forces burning in heaps of molten metal on cratered runways, it was time for the Israeli Defense Force to crush the armored threat of the Egyptian army in the Sinai. General Yeshayahu Gavish, the commander of the Southern Front, gave the order to commence the tank attack. The radio operator at the far end of the room clicked a button and passed the order down the chain of command. The code word for attack began to cascade through the communication network—"Red Sheet!"

Many miles away under a net of brown camouflage, the command came over the encrypted communication circuit. Inside a tank turret, a driver pushed a square illuminated button on a complicated control panel. A whirring sound met his ears as the communication antenna rose to its full height.

The deafening sound of diesel engines from hundreds of Israeli tanks assaulted the air as the vehicles' iron treads began clinking and squeaking, propelling the defenders to battle. It was time to crush the threat that was sitting in the desert sand, waiting to strike like a coiled cobra.

In the middle of Sinai, more than nine hundred Soviet tanks, hundreds of howitzers, and the artillery of the Egyptian army stood ready, waiting for the command to attack.

Across the Sinai Desert, an electronic warble was received across the communications equipment of the Egyptian forces. A worried Egyptian communications specialist dialed back and forth across the frequency band, desperately trying to find a good signal—something that would allow the generals to guide them.

The warble modulated and whistled as the needle moved across the spectrum of the radio band. Israel was jamming them!

Cameron watched as Gavish moved three small red blocks on the map to locations that represented his three-pronged attack against the Egyptians. The map beneath the blocks showed the three major roads that allowed passage across the Sinai Desert into Israeli territory.

He's blocking them and setting a trap, thought Cameron.

"Contact the generals and order them to execute their orders," commanded Gavish. The radio operator acknowledged him. He turned back to his knobs and dials, sending the radio message to the far-flung troops.

Cameron's gaze moved to the northernmost block on the map. It represented General Tal, who had 250 tanks and a paratrooper brigade under his command. Hopelessly outnumbered by four divisions of Egyptian armor, Tal's responsibility was to secure the northern passage of the Sinai. Forty miles south of the Rafah Gap, Ariel Sharon's order was to pit his armor against the fortified Umm Qatef region, relying on a battalion of tank destroyers and a regiment of sixty M-48 Patton tanks that Israel had purchased from Germany in 1965.

Away from the cool confines of the war room, the Israeli army charged at full speed across the Sinai Desert. Tanks and heavy trucks with support equipment drove at breakneck speed across the sand dunes. The dust from the tank treads and truck tires was choking the infantry, who tried desperately to protect their faces and lungs from the agitating clouds of dust particles.

An Israeli commander, Shmuel Gonen, came to the top of a sand dune and spied a column of Egyptian tanks in the distance to his right. A bright white reflection of glass sparkled on the silhouette of a distant Egyptian tank.

They see us! The Israeli tank turret rotated rapidly, and the gunner pressed his face against the rubber gun sight, lining up the tank and gauging for wind and humidity.

"Fire!" he shouted.

The tank recoiled in the sand as the round left the barrel of the gun, covering the mile between the two adversaries in a moment. The round slammed into the turret of a Soviet-made Egyptian tank, piercing the armor and exploding inside the turret. The unfortunate soldiers inside never even had time to think before the tank became an inferno.

⌐ ⌐ ⌐

Across the expanse of the Sinai Desert, the same story was playing out. With no air cover, the Egyptians were in full retreat. Israel's jamming of radio frequencies prevented the commanders in Cairo from communicating vital information to their troops.

Gavish mashed a stubby cigarette into a glass ashtray and exhaled while studying the map. "Order the southern command to attack in a pincer movement and destroy the remaining Egyptian units."

"Where shall we do this, sir?" asked an intelligence officer.

Gavish pointed on the map west of the Sinai. Cameron squinted through the swirling smoke to see the mountainous passes where the remaining Egyptian armored forces would be defeated. Cameron watched in fascinated silence as the actions of a few men created history and impacted directions and lives for millions of people in the Middle East.

Another officer piped up. "We are getting reports that news agencies are reporting a decisive Israeli victory." Gavish's hard facial features melted for an instant as he smiled.

Hundreds of billowing pillars of black smoke rose into the air over the Sinai Desert, marking burning and abandoned vehicles of the Egyptian army.

Three main roads into the Sinai Desert had become a killing field, and Israel, beyond all predictions, had decimated the largest and most heavily equipped Arab army. The rest of the world was beginning to realize that this Israeli routing of the Arab alliance was redrawing territory lines across the Middle East.

48

Holy City in the Balance

june 7, 1967
Eastern Jerusalem

Y ou must act! Every minute you waste here brings us closer to defeat!" screamed Salah al-Din at the Jordanian commander. A radio operator in the command center stopped his constant scanning of the radio band for a moment, waiting for the commander to lose his patience with this insolent stranger.

The exhausted commander picked up the maps and pages of material that the strange man had revealed to him less than an hour before. "Even if these maps and plans are correct, which I doubt, it would take us days—perhaps weeks—to plan an attack like this."

Seething, Salah paced. He glanced at the clock on the wall. The attack on the city of Jerusalem would occur soon. His eyes darted across the room, evaluating the men, the arrangement of the furniture, the space between himself and the commander.

I must take action.

The silence was broken by an explosion in the distance. The room rattled as the shock wave dispersed across the buildings. The commander, standing perfectly straight with arms crossed across his chest, pursed his lips and exhaled deeply. "I have given you well over an hour of my time. Your story is, quite frankly, unbelievable. You are asking us to change our attack at the spur of the moment and coordinate this across the Egyptian and Palestinian forces. It is the Egyptian military command who is giving orders here, not us. Our forces are greater than those of Israel. The whole world acknowledges this. Even the Jews' greatest ally, the United States, is frightened to help. Allah is with us."

The commander walked over to the radio operator's gray console and flipped a switch. Two aging speakers crackled to life with news of the war. Glowing reports of Egyptian forces entering Israel filled the air, along with boasts from the military establishment of outrageous success and massive Jewish retreats. The commander smiled at Salah. "Brother, listen to the news. The Israelis are in disarray. We are winning. You have nothing to worry about. You'll see."

"Don't be a fool!" screamed Salah. "This rubbish that you call a news report is our own propaganda. The truth is that the Egyptian air force is already a smoldering ruin, and this ground that we stand on will soon be under Israeli control unless you act now!"

The door behind the commander opened, and another officer quickly walked in to hand the commander a status report. The commander quickly scanned the report, and without looking at Salah, turned and headed toward the door. "I'm done with this conversation. Escort this man to the street, and don't let him back in." The guard at the door clicked his heels and nodded. He was tired of this stranger's behavior and disrespect. He brought his rifle off of his shoulder and began to approach Salah.

Salah turned to grab his satchel from the chair next to him, as if preparing to follow the soldier. He pulled out the pistol with the silencer— the very gun that only hours before had dispatched Dustin into oblivion. Salah pointed it at the commander and radio operator, and both stopped what they were doing and raised their hands. Moving the gun rapidly between the three men, he quickly and nervously passed the sight of the gun over the three targets. The guard at the door dropped his rifle to the ground and placed his hands in the air.

Salah glanced at the clock, and his face flared crimson.

"It's too late to make a victory possible!" he screamed. Spittle flew from his mouth. "Your lack of faith your failure to embrace me and the news I have. You will give account of yourselves to God!"

More bombardment from the Israeli commandos on the city limits could be heard reverberating against the ancient walls of the city. The trio of prisoners glanced at one another.

Salah, sensing the effort to communicate and coordinate, fired a round into the cement ceiling of the command center. The hostages ducked instinctively. He pointed the pistol at the commander. "This is your last chance, brother; order the shelling of the Israeli quarter." Salah's voice trembled with rage. The commander and the radio operator looked in shock at Salah, not sure what action to take.

An explosion again filled the air—close this time, much closer. The room seemed to move in slow motion as a whoosh filled the room, and Salah's clothes fluttered for a moment as a pressure wave moved through the air of the bunker. The light in the room flickered between bright and dark as the wave passed. Cement particles and dust flew into the air as the walls surrounding the men trembled under the blast. Salah blinked and shook his head; a high-pitched whine filled his ears. He licked his dry lips, tasting pulverized cement particles. He put his hands to his ears and brought them back down. Dark red stained his white, powder-coated hands. The concussion from the incoming Israeli shell had damaged his hearing. The overhead light swung on its short cable back and forth like a pendulum. Within a second, the shock from the explosion had passed, and time seemed to return to its normal pace.

The Israeli commandos have entered the city! I have failed!

Salah saw the guard at the door reach for his rifle, and he pointed his pistol at the young man and squeezed the trigger. No sound came from the gun, but the soldier's body recoiled as the round pierced his chest, killing him instantly.

The nervous radio operator to Salah's left lunged for the pistol, grabbing Salah's upper arm. Defensively, Salah spun around, placing his back to the soldier, and brought the full force of his elbow into his assailant's gut. The radio operator gasped and released Salah as he fell to his knees, clutching his stomach.

Salah kicked the radio operator in the face and brought the pistol down on his head, knocking him unconscious. The commander had moved from behind his desk and was running for the door to alert the soldiers who manned the anti-aircraft battery just twenty feet away. Salah pivoted and aimed his pistol at the man's back. He pulled the trigger. The wall in front of the commander flooded with red as he fell to the floor. Salah looked out the door at the soldiers twenty yards away. They laughed and smoked cigarettes as they stood near the fifty-caliber machine gun surrounded by an oval of sand bags. Salah quietly closed the door and dragged the commander's body behind the desk.

Malice wrapped its arms around Salah, and hatred bloomed in his being. Hatred for this war, for his enemy, for his failure to convince his brothers, and most of all, for his own failure to act sooner. He stared at the radio console's myriad of buttons, gauges, switches, and cables.

I can't stop this war, but I can make these Israelis pay with their lives. I can change the destiny of this part of the war.

Trembling, Salah stood in front of the microphone and pressed the transmit button. He felt the power of commanding thousands of men pulse through his veins; he could feel his heart pounding in his chest as adrenaline raced through him.

"This is a message from headquarters to every soldier within sight of the Holy City of Jerusalem. All artillery batteries are to begin the immediate shelling of the Jewish quarter, and all soldiers are to take as much ground in the old city as possible. Allah is with you."

Salah released the button and sat down in the radio operator's chair. His lips curled with a smile of murderous hate as he listened to the confirmations flowing back across the communication circuits, exulting as the military chain of command passed the order his order down the line.

The Israeli air-raid sirens began to blare across the ancient city, and announcers on loudspeakers pleaded with the citizens of Jerusalem to head to bomb shelters. Then a pounding filled the air with a slow but constant tempo as artillery shells began their rain of destruction into the city. He closed his eyes as he listened to the whistling of shells passing overhead on their way into the Holy City, drawing power from his brothers as they cooperated in his personal jihad.

Salah was so enraptured in the moment that he failed to notice a blinking green light on the communication panel labeled "Clear Text." He had transmitted the order to bomb the city in the open, with no encryption, and the Israelis were listening.

~~~ ~~~ ~~~

The Israeli command post bunker buzzed with activity as status reports were shared with General Dayan. Cameron tried to stay out of the way. He pressed himself against the back wall near a radio operator who was working a dial and listening for the enemy's transmissions. Cameron slowly drank a coffee that was mostly grounds while the radio operator turned the dial in minute increments across the band, trying to capture any stray radio traffic that might give the Israeli army an advantage.

Methodically, the radio operator worked the dial with closed eyes, concentrating on the blurps, bleeps, and voices cascading across the airwaves in a cacophony of noise. Suddenly, he held up his hands to stop the noise in the room. He had discovered something important in the sea of signals beaming through the airwaves. A commander went over to him and plugged the large pair of headphones resting around his neck into a receptacle on the front of an instrument panel. He said something in Hebrew to the young surveillance officer, who pressed a button and reversed the reel-to-reel tape for a few seconds before pressing "Play."

"General Dayan?" said the superior officer. The general looked up at him from the war planning table, and the room became very quiet.

The officer continued, "I think I have something here. It's a strange command that is coming from the Jordanian quarter of Jerusalem."

Dayan nodded and glanced at Cameron as the young surveillance officer clicked a switch. The room was filled with the radio chatter of military units communicating back and forth with bleeps and warbles that indicated some sort of encryption.

Suddenly Salah's voice broke through. Cameron nearly dropped his cup of coffee when he heard it—the same voice he had listened to when he was hiding in the vent with Alicia; the same voice that had threatened Dustin in the operations center.

"That's him," said Cameron, slamming his fist on the table, "and if you don't get him off the airwaves, you're going to lose hundreds of men. They'll be slaughtered like cattle, because he knows what you'll do and where you'll go in the city."

As those words tumbled out of Cameron's mouth, the surveillance officer again raised his hand and increased the volume of the speaker so that the room full of generals and the prime minister could hear the radio signals.

Salah's voice was clear and strong, full of conviction. "Brothers, focus your ground attack and artillery on the Lion's Gate and the road leading to the city from the Kidron Valley. Many of the attackers will be paratroopers; they should be arriving within the hour. Attack without mercy, or you will lose much land to Israel. It is your children who will suffer."

The generals and Eshkol were shocked as they looked at the battle plan in front of them, illuminated in the fluorescent lights of the bunker. Small blue blocks, representing the commandos targeted in Salah's murderous order, sat atop the campaign map. The legend below the blocks read "Kidron Valley" in a small arc of text. It was as if Salah could see the map and was describing it to Israel's enemies in perfect detail.

Dayan stood up from the war planning table and responded, but not to Cameron. "Can you triangulate the signal?"

"Yes, General," responded the superior officer hovering over the surveillance man. Dayan looked at the board and ran his right hand over the top of his head, thinking of a solution.

"Send a defensive fighter to the location and take out that radio installation," he ordered.

〜〜〜 〜〜〜 〜〜〜

The shells continued to rain down on Jerusalem, and ambulances and makeshift fire brigades hurried to the areas that had been bombed, where dead and disfigured victims awaited them. Israeli hospitals and clinics began to fill with the innocent victims of Salah's hatred.

Salah al-Din found that the Jordanian command bunker, situated high on a wall and looking down into the ancient city of Jerusalem, was a perfect place from which to watch the destruction of the Israeli army. He raised a pair of binoculars to his eyes and focused his gaze on the Kidron Valley and the road that entered the Lion's Gate. Olive-drab buses escorted by three half-tracks adorned with painted Israeli flags were making their way up the road. A shell exploded on the road and over-turned a bus full of Israeli infantry. Salah was elated—his brothers were responding!

⌒ ⌒ ⌒

On the south side of the city, an old F-86 Saber jet, purchased from the U.S. but bearing Israeli markings, banked steeply and headed northeast. The plane was the least potent of the Israeli air force, with just a fraction of the capabilities possessed by the more modern Mirage fighters that had destroyed the Egyptian aircraft. The pilot had received a flash message directly from the top of the command chain, and he made ready to perform his duty. He activated a switch on the instrument panel directly in front of him, and a green lamp illuminated, indicating that a five-hundred-pound bomb under the right wing of the aircraft was now armed.

The soldiers outside the Jordanian command bunker, just a hundred feet from Salah, who continued to bark orders at the Jordanian army, looked up and saw a silver flash glinting in the afternoon sun. The dark trail of burning jet fuel and the screeching jet engine gave away the Israeli plane's position.

The soldiers jumped behind the anti-aircraft gun, attempting to fire a curtain of bullets in front of the plane and bring down the aircraft that was heading for them at over three hundred miles an hour.

The Israeli pilot concentrated and peered through the front of his canopy, lining up the plane with the target ahead of him. A few rounds from the anti-aircraft battery tore through the thin aluminum of his left wing, but he stayed on target. The crosshairs of the canopy lined up on the small brick command building, and the pilot released the steel-encased bomb and banked left, rolling the aircraft to make his exit more difficult for the Jordanian soldiers to track.

The olive-green bomb dropped at a shallow angle. It whistled through the arid atmosphere and glanced off the hard stone surface of the roadway beside the command center, skimming and clattering across the plaza in front of the building. The two Jordanian soldiers ducked behind their sand-bag semicircle as the bomb passed them and slammed into the walls of the command center, knocking over a supporting wall and sending debris and dust into the air.

The two soldiers slowly raised their heads out of their shielded position as the noise dissipated and the dust and debris settled. They looked at the caved-in wall of the command center and the slight damage that had occurred around them—miraculously they were untouched. They turned to face each other and started laughing.

A dud, they thought.

A moment later, they were engulfed by a brilliant flash of orange-white light, and the temperature soared to a thousand degrees as the two soldiers, Salah, and the command center were vaporized in the bomb's explosion

⌐ ⌐ ⌐

The Israeli paratroopers and commandos poured through the Lion's Gate, covering each other as they flanked the Jordanian army. Half-tracks and trucks brought reinforcements as the ground that had been occupied by Jordanian troops for seventeen years came under the blue-and-white flag of the state of Israel.

The Israeli soldiers fanned out across the temple mount, dodging bullets and mortars that were launched into the city from the hillsides, where a dug-in Jordanian unit still fought. Some of the commandos moved through a small gate and alley near the remains of the Second Temple. Huge white blocks, still scarred from the fire that had claimed Solomon's house of worship, stood silently by as the troops filed past.

The small alley led to a large plaza, and the soldiers collectively gasped as the sacred white blocks of the Wailing Wall stood before them. Small, tenacious plants growing in the cracks between the stone blocks seemed to reach out and ask each soldier to send a prayer heavenward. The stoic paratroopers and commandos fell on their knees and uttered prayers, some of them for the first time in their lives.

The war was transforming the secular nation that had survived the Holocaust, and the Middle East would never be the same.

The ancient city of Jerusalem was now entirely under Israeli control.

49

The Last Moment of the Antediluvians

T he Ark careened into the side of the city wall, sending rock and wooden platforms lined with handrails flying with a loud cracking sound. The high waves were now eroding the walls, and the simple mortar that had been made hundreds of years before gave way under the merciless beating of water mixed with branches, sludge, drowned animals, and human corpses.

The citizens of Unug-Kulaba climbed on top of the walls and evacuated the streets that were filling up with rushing water. The pressure of the water pushing on the massive iron gates of the city ensured that there could not be a mass exodus through a large thoroughfare.

An enormous rock the size of a four-story building blasted into view and slammed into the city, striking the peak of the plaza where the German officer had met his fate just hours before. Shards of rock and metal sliced though the humid air, decapitating people and animals in their path before becoming embedded in the interior of the rock wall surrounding the city. For the first time in a hundred years, the fires of the sacrificial edifice used to worship Inanna were extinguished.

The Ark slowly settled against the side of the city wall, its hull looming tall over the slowly disintegrating city structures. Rain was pouring down now in a massive torrent, making the smooth stone of the wall slippery as an ice rink. Priests, guards, and everyday people scrambled up the landing and stairs of the inner wall to reach the top and escape the deadly river filling the streets. Seeing the water rising below them and more massive waves coming from the coastal areas miles away, many people began diving off the wall and grabbing onto the sides of the Ark in any way they could. The smooth, resin-covered surface denied their grasp, and they slid down the sides of the boat, leaving behind broken fingernails and bloody finger paint.

A desperate giant soldier on the wall, seeing the results of jumping onto the Ark's slippery outer surface, raised his spear to pierce the resin and sink the spearhead into the wood below. He imagined that he could make his way up the side of the Ark using swords and spears to form stepping surfaces. He lifted the long, heavy spear with his strong arm, and just as he prepared to thrust it into the side of the wooden boat, a bolt of lightning forked through the sky and struck him. The voltage coursed through his massive frame, frying tendons and muscles and exploding the cells of his body on its way to a grounded place. The soldier fell backward onto the stone wall, spear still in hand. The smoke emanating from his charred form was quickly extinguished by the torrent of rain now cascading over the top of the wall like a waterfall to the street below. The city was quickly filling with floating corpses, market carts, food, and furniture from the flooded houses.

The citizens continued throwing themselves against the slippery resin on the side of the boat that denied their grip, and they slid down and slammed into the mash of humanity that was trapped between the massive vessel and the wall of the city.

The people cried and screamed while banging their bloody hands on the sides of the smooth wooden hull, but their voices could not be heard by Noah and his family, who were huddled together inside the Ark three decks up, holding and consoling one another as the world they had known began to disappear around them.

Again the earth buckled as an earthquake shuddered through the crust of the young planet. Each time a series of the fountain chambers emptied, the weight above the cavern bore down and the chambers collapsed, sending seismic waves across the landscape. The water above these collapses rendered the seismic waves in liquid, and a huge tsunami coursed toward the city of Unug-Kulaba.

The waves struck the city from the east, breaking down the main iron gate. The slime and sewage of the waste canal had been picked up by the waves, and it coursed through the city, bringing with it an overwhelming stench. The white arsenic dust from the mines nearby floated on the surface of the water and entered the air passages of the few people still alive who were bobbing atop the ever-increasing depth.

The floodwaters swept around the walls of the city, heading westward. Once the force of the water hit the massive Ark, it torqued the huge boat clockwise, rotating the hull away from the wall and down the valley floor away from the city. The water was now fifteen feet high and growing deeper by the minute. The displaced weight of the Ark was beginning to buoy the boat, and it slowly moved down the valley toward the deeper water that had lain restlessly below the earth's crust since the creation.

Through the fog rolling across the valley, Troy could see the water quickly eroding the foundations of the city walls. He saw the massive iron gates moving away from the mighty city they had once guarded. The walls crumbled in slow motion into the interior of the city, crushing people and animals who struggled to stay above the surge of water that was slowly but surely drowning the city.

Comets of rock the size of skyscrapers began to fall across the landscape with increasing frequency. In the distance, Jim Spruce could see massive fountains of water mixed with erupting lava shooting high into the atmosphere.

And then, just when the team figured it couldn't get much worse—it did.

The rupture that had freed the subterranean ocean from its underground prison had made its way around the horn of Africa and begun traveling up the eastern coastline, skirting Madagascar on the east and continuing northward at a rapid pace. A supersonic jet of water shot into the air as the pressure beneath overwhelmed the pressure above the tectonic plates. The rupture continued, following the path of least resistance, and headed toward the peninsula that would become the Persian Gulf, just miles southeast of the city. The rift broke perpendicularly across the bottom of the landmass and ground to a halt, but not before compressing the rock layers momentarily in an elastic, bow-like action that sprang back, sending a massive seismic wave through the rock.

The team felt a low rumble course beneath their feet, gaining intensity by the second. And then a terrible, deafening sound filled the air as the fountains of the deep began to rocket their briny contents into the sky. The initial rift had occurred thousands of miles away from them, but this one was just six hundred miles away, and the effect was mass devastation like nothing these scientists had ever seen.

As this new rift fired its trapped subterranean water into the atmosphere, the ground around it crumbled into the massive upward water stream, which pulverized the rock and vaporized sludge into fine particles that mixed into the water blast. Rock and debris jettisoned by the blast began to freeze high in the atmosphere, losing velocity and succumbing to the earth's gravity. The icy balls of rock, mud, and frozen water dropped back into the thicker atmosphere, raining down a lethal soup of water vapor, mud, and hailstones on the ancient world below.

Jim picked himself up from the ground after having been blown off his feet by the last earthquake. He was amazed and terrified as he watched a mixture of muddy vapor and massive torrents of rain pouring from the sky. For a moment he mused at how scientists for hundreds of years had joked about how much rain it would take for a global flood to cover the highest mountains. Seeing it up close was nothing like anyone in the scientific community had ever imagined. He was witnessing the most cataclysmic event in Earth's history. Lava flowed out of the earth as the barriers between molten rock and solid rock were stripped away. The lava shot up into the sky and solidified into bizarre, otherworldly pillars when it hit the water blasting from the rift.

Miles from the team, a massive wall of water rose from the surface of the Persian Gulf and pushed its way northward. With the volume of Lake Michigan and Lake Superior combined, the wave rushed toward the ill-fated city of Unug-Kulaba at more than two hundred miles an hour.

Jim Spruce was numb as he watched and listened to the deafening roar of earthbound comets of rock pounding the landscape like small tactical nuclear bombs. A thick sludge of muddy water was now cascading over the lower valley near the city wall, slowly adding flotsam, vegetation, and the carcasses of animals to its deadly mixture. Jim watched in amazement and fear as he witnessed the beginnings of the fossil records that would be discovered thousands of years later.

The team struggled against the howling wind and nearly horizontal rain that was stinging their faces. They watched as thousands and thousands of the citizens of Unug-Kulaba abandoned their city and ran, scratching and crawling up the grassy slope toward the team's position. Children and elderly men and women who had fallen were trampled as others pushed their broken, crumpled bodies into the mud and slime that was now coursing down the hill.

Jim squinted through the wind and muddy rain to get one last glimpse of the Ark. Its dark outline was obscured by the haze and water vapor rolling across the valley floor between the frightened expedition team and the remaining structures of the city of Unug-Kulaba. A moment later the Ark left his line of sight and headed toward its special, divine destiny.

A lightning bolt forked out of the dark sky and struck an ancient tree behind Jim, illuminating the dark with an eerie indigo glow. His attention was jerked from the Ark back to the storm. The wind howled and whistled around him. He felt helpless. Doomed. There was no escape. He squinted through the stinging rain to look back at the Ark.

It's gone.

Only mist remained where he had last seen the boat, and Jim looked back toward the crumbling city. *Everyone else in that city is going to die.*

Jim looked at the rest of his teammates, who were struggling against the storm.

We're all going to die, too.

Shivering from the dropping temperature and sheer terror, Jim huddled next to Pam and Fernanda. They were holding each other, covered with mud and bits of shredded vegetation. Jim looked over and saw Pam praying, her lips trembling. With the world ending all around him, he turned his heart and thoughts toward God. Not sure of where to start or how to turn his mix of emotions into a ritualistic prayer, he did the best he could. He was surprised by the sincere but primal urgency of his own prayer.

God, I see it now; I believe—You exist! I believe! Save me! Jim opened his eyes and looked over his shoulder, hearing a roar louder than a thousand freight trains bearing down on him. The tidal wave that had begun miles away was now nearly on top of the team. The crest of the massive wave foamed with trees that had been uprooted miles before and now punctuated its face like spinning and twirling bayonets in the water. Jim saw the dark green of the rain forest and the gray of the sky momentarily reflected in the face of the gargantuan liquid wall as it flew forward, swallowing the landscape.

"This is it!" screamed Loren, preparing to pull the trigger on his submachine gun and fire into the hysterical mob that was clambering up the slippery slope.

The mob had nearly reached the team when a brilliant flash of white light illuminated the landscape, and a spherical area measuring thirty feet in diameter was suddenly scooped out of the ground atop the hill. The mob reached the crater and kept going, piling into the muddy hole and filling it to the brim with desperate but doomed human beings.

A moment later, the giant tidal wave approaching from the opposite side of the hill crashed over the top and swept all of the people into a watery mudslide of death.

Alicia's finger released the "Enter" key that had initiated the transfer. The blue-green tornado of energy swirled and undulated over the empty steel Platform, and the TRC team of mathematicians and engineers watched as the energy level began to peak.

Alicia's attention turned from the energy-measurement panel to the load-bearing meters tracking the weight being returned on the Platform. A small sphere of white light began to appear in the center of the Platform and expand outward, causing muddy soil, grass, plant life, and parts of the destroyed cargo bins to materialize. The muddy globe of slime, team members, and vegetation began to lose its shape, and it slowly spread out to cover the entire surface of the stainless-steel-and-blue-glass floor.

The Platform strained under the tremendous weight of mud. Steel brackets began to stress, and steel bolts sheared in half. Finally, after a loud cracking sound, the steel framework gave way. The TRC personnel in the operations center could hear a series of popping noises coming from the bottom of the Platform as the bolts sheared off from the stress of the weight on the steel trusses that held the structure off the concrete floor. The Platform collapsed with an enormous crashing sound.

As the mud and slime gave way under their feet, the returned team perched atop the muddy ball of earth began to slip and slide down the steep sides and onto the hard concrete floor of the bay.

Troy and Neil blinked and shielded their eyes from the bright halogen lights shining down on them from the operations center. The vines that had hung in the rain forest canopy above them slowly became thick, silver cables, and the overhead tree trunks became the cavernous, concrete ceiling of the Platform.

Both men let out a cheer and hugged one another before helping Fernanda, Pam, Rich, and Jim step off the slimy, muddy heap that continued to spread out across the concrete bay.

Pam scanned the group, and her eyes darted across the mud and vegetation. Tree trunks, vines, plants, and rocks all swirled together. "Where's Chris?"

She ran around the back of the Platform, looking through the twisted and knurled trees for any sign of him. Finally she found him, struggling beneath the spidery roots of a fallen mangrove tree. He was engulfed in mud, pinned beneath the trunk, and fighting to breathe. She pulled twigs and branches away from his face and pushed the slimy mud away from his mouth so he could gasp for air.

"Is everyone OK?" he rasped with concern.

Pam smiled and touched his face. "Yes, everyone made it."

Chris looked at the makeshift splint and the dried blood from Pam's compound fracture. "Are you OK?"

Pam smiled and nodded. "Yes, I'm fine...now."

Chris closed his eyes and sighed with relief. He opened his eyes again to find Pam kissing him. The rest of the team cheered in the background for a moment before Fernanda stepped between the gawking spectators and the couple. "Come on, kids, this is an adult moment."

Alicia opened the sealed steel door and rushed to help, followed by other engineers and mathematicians who had worked through the night to make the safe return of the stranded expedition a reality.

On the opposite side of the bay, the elevator bell sounded, and a squad of marines armed to the teeth poured into the operations center. Behind them, Admiral Nathan Turner strode in confidently. Neil immediately noticed something different about the admiral's stride: he wasn't limping anymore.

The mud-covered expedition members hugged, cried, and laughed as they celebrated their safe return with the TRC personnel, standing in front of the only remains of the antediluvian civilization from which they had barely escaped.

They were back.

50

Liberty

june 8, 1967

Tel Aviv, Israel

Brilliant shafts of sunlight burst over the horizon in the Middle East, highlighting the lingering, thinning columns of black and gray smoke that were rising lazily into the air—the temporary markers of battles fought and won.

The victories had been decisive for Israel. The tiny nation now controlled the area from the bank of the Suez Canal to the eastern side of Jerusalem. While the conflict had begun with a well-crafted plan, toward the end of the ground effort it had become a free-for-all. The Israeli generals had continued to push into more land as victories became almost serendipitous. Now almost three and a half times as much land was under the Israeli flag than had been just a few days before.

As the Israeli commandos continued to take land and redraw the borders of the Jewish state, the superpowers began a political chess game to contain the conflict. The Soviet Union was rushing MiG fighters to Armenia, and its diplomats were beginning to employ rhetoric in assisting Arab allies as they attempted to contain the Jewish advance.

Egypt had ordered a massive retreat and recalled any remaining troops that had not been destroyed in the Sinai Desert. Tangled masses of burnt bodies and the molten metal remains of trucks and tanks were now the grave markers of what had been one of the mightiest armies on the planet. Those who had not perished in the armor battle were captured by the Israeli army—thousands and thousands of Egyptian soldiers were now prisoners of war.

The battle for Jerusalem had done something that neither Eshkol nor the generals ever could have anticipated. The nation of Israel had been galvanized by the conflict and transformed from a largely stoic and secular citizenry into a nation embarking on a religious war. The very secular nature of war had now become sacred.

On the Arab side, the seeds for extremism had been sown, and Jordan's King Hussein, a descendant of Muhammad, had failed. The king had failed to protect one of the Muslim world's holiest places, the Dome of the Rock.

In the Israeli war room, reports of victories continued to stream in over the communication circuits. General Dayan and General Sharon decided to go out and view the victory for themselves, determined to make a triumphant entry through the gates of Jerusalem.

Cameron Locke approached the generals as Moshe Dayan and Ariel Sharon began to collect the personal effects that had been spread over the planning table, intermixed with maps, notepads, and intelligence reports.

"General Dayan, I think it's time for me to make a discreet exit," Cameron said quietly.

Dayan grabbed a helmet from a nearby table and tucked it under his arm. "That's probably for the best. From this point on, we'll be hounded by the press of every nation on Earth—which can have its own benefits." The media-savvy general smiled and extended his hand. "Cameron, the State of Israel deeply appreciates your efforts and your help. We will keep your secret, which you'll find is an important measure of friendship."

Cameron smiled appreciatively and returned the general's firm handshake.

"I'll have the sergeant here give you a ride to the dock, where I believe you can arrange transport home to the States," said Dayan.

"Yes, sir. I believe I can manage that," said Cameron, turning to leave.

"Oh, one more thing, Dr. Locke," said the general, with a slight tease in his voice.

"What's that?"

"You wouldn't happen to know who wins the next five World Cups, would you?" asked Dayan, raising one eyebrow.

Cameron smiled. "That would be valuable, wouldn't it? Goodbye, General."

After a short trip to the bus station to retrieve the backpack he had stashed earlier, Cameron returned to the Ministry of Defense building to find a tan jeep waiting with an impatient Israeli sergeant staring intently at his watch.

During the brief ride through the streets of Tel Aviv, Cameron could see the blue-green water of the Mediterranean Sea and a number of military ships patrolling the coast. He thanked the Israeli sergeant for the ride; the man seemed a bit put out at having to provide taxi service to this strange American during a time of national emergency. The jeep's tires squealed as the officer sped away.

Throwing his backpack over his shoulder, Cameron walked down the gravel pathway that led to the dock. A small, unmarked powerboat was waiting up ahead to take him to the USS *Liberty*, now anchored just off the coast of Egypt. The sun was setting, and a golden tint washed over the landscape. Cameron paused to watch the sparkling crests of waves on the Mediterranean lapping against the shore, and he began thinking about Neil and the expedition, wondering if they had made it back safely.

Ahead on the dock, Cameron could see a figure silhouetted against the golden setting sun. It was hard to make out the face, but when Cameron squinted he saw a familiar blue duffel bag with a white logo in the form of a Y with a small, stylized forest in the branch of the letter. A line of text encircled the figure: "Two Roads Corporation." A slender woman with beautiful blond hair, wearing khaki shorts and a white T-shirt, filled his vision.

It was Alicia King.

Cameron ran down the ramp to the dock and scooped her into his arms, hugging her tightly.

"Alicia…what…why are you here? How did you know where to find me?" he asked, stammering.

She smiled and looked into his eyes. "I waited for five months after the expedition returned. I watched all the changes to the timeline since you went back. When I saw that the *Liberty* did not get attacked, I knew exactly how you got home."

Alicia held out a paper that had a thirty-year timeline diagrammed on it. "You know, I know everything that you do over the next thirty years…everything." She shook her head and smiled at him. "You make the same mistake again, Cameron."

"What mistake is that?" he asked.

"You don't marry; in fact, you never even date. Your whole life is consumed with technology and TRC and science—again."

"You're judging me on things I haven't even had a second to think about since getting here?" he asked with a chuckle.

Alicia ignored him and continued reading the paper in her hands. "No kids, either."

"Not only can history change," said Cameron, pulling her close and grabbing the paper from her hand, "but so can a man."

Alicia smiled. "Bet on it. That's why I'm here, Dr. Locke. Do you think you could you use some company for the next thirty years?" she asked.

It was an engagement, and neither of them had to say anything. The answer was obvious as the powerboat headed out to sea. Cameron held out the paper with the timeline and released it into the salty ocean wind, watching it glide and twirl and finally land and float away in the undulating waves.

The powerboat pulled alongside the freedom ship and continued aft to the place where some sailors lowered a small ramp. The turquoise waves slapped against the gray reinforced-steel hull and sent spray up into the air as Cameron thanked the powerboat captain and helped Alicia reach the ramp. Checking to ensure that he had all of his belongings—the only things he and Alicia owned in the world—he pulled himself onto the ramp as the small craft sped away.

Cameron walked up the steps of the ramp and was assisted by a young officer who had just helped Alicia aboard. Cameron took his hand firmly as he set foot on the deck of the super-secret spy ship. The young officer looked vaguely familiar. Cameron extended his hand with a kind smile and introduced himself: "My name is Cameron Locke."

"Welcome aboard, Dr. Locke; we've been expecting you. Captain McGonagle would like to see you in his cabin," said the sailor. "I'm Ensign First Class Nathan Turner; please let me know if I can do anything to help you."

Alicia and Cameron smiled at each other as the young future admiral with a dazzling naval career ahead of him stood before them. Holding hands, the two made their way to meet the captain of the spy ship.

Four thousand years in the past, across the turbulent waves and the swirling flotsam and debris from two millennia of human advances, a huge wooden vessel carrying a family with nothing but faith in their hearts floated on the golden crests as the sun hung low in the sky. The Ark sailed toward the horizon, containing the bloodline for the Savior to come and hope for a new world that would join in spiritual fellowship with the Creator of the universe.

Acknowledgments

Like many things in life, this book has brought me people to thank. Bringing a book to market is an interesting journey. It begins with the spark of an idea, winds through plotting and casting of characters, and slowly turns into a manuscript with rough edges, half-baked plots, underdeveloped characters, and abuses of the English language. This page is dedicated to the people who saw beyond the rough edges and breathed life into my initial idea.

Many hours of researching the theories of Dr. Walter Brown proved useful, as did enlightening conversations with Mr. Bert Arrowood regarding date ranges and the overall structure of the Ark. Tim Lovett and his technical evaluation of the design and structure of the Ark were indispensable as well. Carol A. Hill of the American Scientific Affiliation has also done great work on the possible location of the Garden of Eden.

A huge thank-you to the people at Answers in Genesis, who gave the permission to use the diagram of the Ark's hull design that was developed by Tim Lovett—thank you for all you do in defending the Genesis account.

Any errors in the theories expressed in this novel are solely mine; they are not those of the scientists and engineers who put their reputations, careers, and livelihoods on the line to advance theories and data that contradict the theory and purposeless mechanism of macroevolution.

I am so grateful to my friends who reviewed my early work on this book and provided valuable feedback and support: Chris and Beth Caldwell, Dave Caldwell, Tim and Carla Meell, Pastor Scott Wendal, Pastor Lamar Eifert, Dawn Pleasants, Matt Manney, Ben Coulton, Jenalee Good, Paige Martin, Phil Martin, Lydia Martin, Avy Whittle, Dave Davis, Pastor Ernest Grooney, Nathan Gifford, Matt Wendal, Nathan Villanova, Chris Lovett, Pastor Randy David, Robin Maples, Dan Bressler, Dan Wooster, Lois Rall, Joe Hicks, Rory and Troy Bond, Jeff Rapp, Jamie Aylestock, Carol Cobb, Kelly Unruh, Rebecca Levis, Jan Wilkenson, Pastor David Jones, Jodi Kappel, Andrew Harrod, Joe Poley, Pat Reeves, Jeff Hamm, Charles Cobourn, John and Mary Bergstrom, Nathan Gray, Beth Cappelletti, Henry and Thea Miller, Joy Caldwell, Phil Spence, Dinah and Rebecca Misiura—I can't thank you enough for your time poring over the worst of my early drafts.

A huge amount of thanks goes to Cindy Ley for her command of the English language and her help in editing early parts of the manuscript.

Thanks to the great people at VMI Publishing for taking a chance on me, especially Bill Carmichael, Lacey Hanes Ogle, and her outstanding team. I'm proud to be published and associated with your fine organization.

Very special thanks to Rachel Starr Thomson, my editor, who pushed me and challenged me to create the very best manuscript I could make. Thank you for all the attention to detail and polish the final draft received.

Thanks also to my sister-in-law, Bonnie, for sharing articles and ideas that she has come across as a teacher and for her honest feedback. My mother-in-law, Donna, for her support and help with grammar in the early stages of the book. My sister, Marnie, who from the very beginning has been my greatest cheerleader and supporter in my efforts as a writer.

My parents, whose sacrifices have translated success to me in so many ways—words are not enough. Finally, my wife, Susan, who was surprised to find that I wanted to be an author and supported me throughout the entire project. I love you, honey.

Bibliography

What follows is a list of books, periodicals, journal articles, and other sources that were helpful to me in the preparation of *Wayback*. This book is fiction; the reader should not assume that any author listed below agrees with ideas or viewpoints I express in this novel.

Adam, William Henry and Davenport. *Egypt Past and Present: Described and Illustrated.* T. Nelson and Sons, 1885.

Agoston, Tom. *Blunder! How the U.S. gave away Nazi Super secrets to Russia.* New York: Dodd Mead, 1985.

Alt, David. *Glacial Lake Missoula and Its Humongous Floods.* Mountain Press Publishing Co, 2001.

Ancient Greek Computer's Inner Workings Deciphered. http://news.nationalgeographic.com/news/2006/11/061129-ancient-greece.html .

Austin, Steve. *Grand Canyon: Monument to Catastrophe (Field Study Tour Guidebook).* Santee, Calif.: Institute for Creation Research, 1992.

Bamford, James. *Body of Secrets.* Doubleday, 2001.

—. *The Puzzle Palace.* Penguin Books, 1983.

Behe, Michael J. *Darwin's Black Box: The Biochemical Challenge to Evolution.* New York: Touchstone, 1996.

Benton, Michael J., Crispin T. S. Little. "Impact in the Caribbean and death of the dinosaurs." *Geology Today*, November-December 1994: pp. 222–227.

Bower, Tom. *The Paperclip Conspiracy.* London: Michael Joseph, 1987.

Brown, Walter T. "The Fountains of the Deep." *Proceedings of the First International Conference on Creationism* . Pittsburgh: Creation Science Fellowship, 1986.

Cook, Nick. *The Hunt for Zero Point.* New York: Random House, 2001.

Dendera Egypt & Astrology. http://www.geocities.com/astrologysources/classicalegypt/dendera/index.htm.

Diagram of the Israeli Tank Attack for the Six-Day War. http://www.zionism-israel.com/maps/Sinai_1967_I.htm.

Enheduanna. "The Exaltation of Inanna (Inanna B): Translation." In *The Electronic Text Corpus of Sumerian Literature.* Oxford: University of Oxford Library, 2004.

Filkin, David. *Stephen Hawking's Universe: The Cosmos Explained.* Basic Books, 1997.

Mystery of the Megaflood: Examining the World's Most Catastrophic Flood. Directed by Ben Fox. 2005.

Fulco, William J., S.J. "Inanna." In *The Encyclopedia of Religion*, by William J., S.J. Fulco. New York: Macmillan Group, 1987.

George, Andrew (Translator). *The Epic of Gilgamesh.* Penguin Books, 1999.

Good, Timothy. *Above Top Secret.* London: Grafton Books, 1989.

Green, W.H. *Primeval Chronology.* Bibliotheca Sacra, 1890.

Hagstrum, Jonathan T. "Antipodal hotspots and bipolar catastrophes: Were oceanic large-body impacts the cause?" *Earth and Planetary Science Letters*, 2005: pp. 13–27.

Harkabi, Yehoshafat. *Arab Attitudes To Israel*. Jerusalem: Keter Publishing House, 1972.

Herodotus. *The Histories (Reprint)*. Baltimore: Penguin Classics, 1965.

Hill, Cindy A. *The Garden of Eden: A Modern Landscape*. American Science Affiliation.

J. E. Allen, Marjorie Burns, and S. C. Sargent. *Cataclysms on the Columbia*. Timber Press, 1986.

Jacobsen, Thorkild. *The Treasures of Darkness: a History of Mesopotamian religion*. New Haven and London: Yale University Press, 1976.

Johnson, Lyndon B. *The Vantage Point: Perspectives of the Presidency 1963-1969*. New York: Holt, Rinehart and Winston, 1971.

Katz, Samuel. *Battleground-Fact and Fantasy in Palestine*. New York: Bantam Books, 1985.

Keller, Gerta, et.al. "More evidence that the Chicxulub impact predates the K/T mass extinction." *Meteorites & Planetary Science*, 2004: pp. 1127–1144.

Libby, W.F. *Radiocarbon Dating*. Chicago: Phoenix Books, 1965.

Lorch, Netanel. *One Long War*. Jerusalem: Keter, 1976.

Lucas, James. *Last Days of the Reich*. London: Grafton Books, 1987.

Lusar, Rudolf. *German Secret Weapons of World War II*. London: Neville Spearman Ltd., 1959.

Marlow, Michael S., Alan K. Cooper, Shawn V. Dadisman, Eric L. Geist, Paul R. Carlson. "Bowers Swell: Evidence for a zone of compressive deformation concentric with Bowers Ridge, Bering Sea." *Marine and Petroleum Geology*, November, 1990: pp. 398–408.

Melosh, H.J. "Can impacts induce volcanic eruptions?" *International Conference on Catastrophic Events and Mass Extinctions: Impacts and Beyond, Lunar and Planetary Science Institute Contribution*, 2000.

Mitchell, Stephen. *Gilgamesh:A New English Translation*. New York: Free Press (Div. Simon & Schuster), 2004.

Molnar, P., Lyon-Caen, H. "Some Simple Physical Aspects of the Support, Structure, and Evolution of Mountain Belts." *Geological Society of America*, 1988: pp. 179–207.

Myth of Inanna and the Underworld. http://www-etcsl.orient.ox.ac.uk/section1/tr141.htm.

Neprochnov, Yu.P., V.V. Sedov, L.R. Merklin, V.P. Zinkevich, O.V. Levchenko, B.V. Baranov, G.B. Rudnik. "Tectonics of the Shirshov Ridge, Bering Sea." *Geotectonics*, 1985: pp. 194–206.

Ollier, C., Pain, C. *The Origin of Mountains*. London: Routledge, 2000.

Orth, C. J., et.al. "Iridium abundance patterns across bio-event horizons in the fossil record." *Geological Society of America*, 1990: pp. 45–59.

Parker, R.A. "Ancient Egyptian Astronomy - The Place of Astronomy in the Ancient World." *Philosophical Transactions of the Royal Society of London Series A, Mathematical and Physical Sciences*, May 2, 1974.

Peretz, Don. "Israel's New Dilemma." *Middle East Journal*, Winter 1968: 45–46.

Pierazzo, E., H.J. Melosh. "Understanding Oblique Impacts from Experiments, Observations, and Modeling." *Annual Review of Earth and Planetary Science*, 2000: pp. 141–167.

Poupinet, Georges, Nicholas Arndt, Pierre Vacher. "Seismic tomography beneath stable tectonic regions and the origin and composition of the continental lithospheric mantle." *Earth and Planetary Science Letters*, 2003: pp. 89–101.

Pritchard, J. *Ancient Near Eastern Texts Related to the Old Testament, 2nd Ed.* Princeton: University Press, 1955.

Purcell, Edward M. "The Efficiency of Propulsion by a Rotating Flagellum." *Proceedings of the Natural Academy of Sciences USA*, October 1997.

Ranney, Wayne. *Carving Grand Canyon.* Grand Canyon Association, 2005.

Roux. *Ancient Iraq.* Suffolk, England: Penguin Books, 1966.

Sachar, Howard. *A History of Israel: From the Rise of Zionism to Our Time.* New York: Alfred A. Knopf, 1979.

Sagan, Carl. *The Demon-Haunted World: Science as a Candle in the Dark.* Ballantine Books, 1997.

Saggs, W. F. *The Greatness That Was Babylon.* New York: Mentor Books, 1962.

Schultz, Peter H., Raymond R. Anderson. "Asymmetry of the Manson impact structure: Evidence for impact angle and direction." *GSA Special Paper 302*, 1996: pp. 397–417.

Shipilov, E.V., A.Yu. Yunov, Yu.I. Svistunov. "Marine Geology - A Model of the Structure and Formation of Aseismic Elevations on the Ocean Floors." *Oceanology*, 1990: pp. 193–196.

Stroebel, Lee. *The Case for a Creator.* Grand Rapids, Michigan: Zondervan, 2004.

The Electronic Text Corpus of Sumerian Literature. http://www.etcsl.orient.ox.ac.uk/section4/tr4072.htm.

The Geological Society of London. "Paleontologists in dire straits name dinosaur for the Sultan of Swing." January 25, 2001.

van der Hilst, Robert D. "Changing Views on Earth's Deep Mantle." *Science*, October 29, 2004: pp. 817–818.

Woit, Peter. *Not Even Wrong.* New York: Basic Books, 2007.

Wolkstein, Diana & Kramer, Samuel Noah. *Inanna: Queen of Heaven and Earth.* Harper Perennial, 1983.

Worldwide Flood and Diagrams of the Ark's Hull and overall structure. http://www.worldwideflood.com/ark/ark_images/ark_images.htm.

Six Days in June: the War that Redefined the Middle East. Directed by Ilan Zi. 2007.